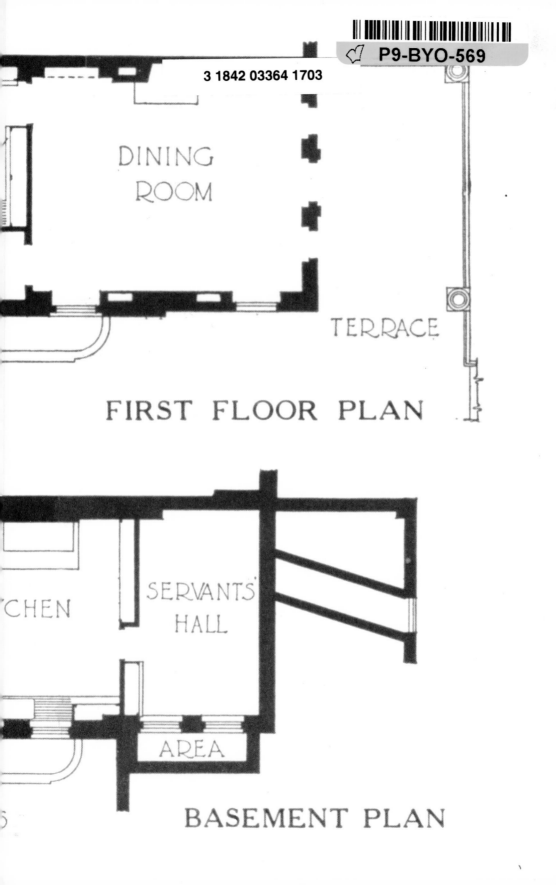

FIRST FLOOR PLAN

BASEMENT PLAN

ALSO BY CAROLYN FERRELL

Don't Erase Me: Stories

DEAR MISS METROPOLITAN

DEAR MISS METROPOLITAN

Carolyn Ferrell

HENRY HOLT AND COMPANY

New York

Henry Holt and Company
Publishers since 1866
120 Broadway
New York, New York 10271
www.henryholt.com

Henry Holt® and Ⓗ® are registered trademarks of
Macmillan Publishing Group, LLC.

Library of Congress Cataloging-in-Publication Data

Names: Ferrell, Carolyn, author.
Title: Dear Miss Metropolitan / Carolyn Ferrell.
Description: First edition. | New York : Henry Holt and Company, 2021.
Identifiers: LCCN 2020034260 (print) | LCCN 2020034261 (ebook) | ISBN
    9781250793614 (hardcover) | ISBN 9781250793621 (ebook)
Subjects: LCSH: Kidnapping—Fiction. | Kidnapping victims—Fiction.
Classification: LCC PS3556.E72572 D43 2021 (print) | LCC PS3556.E72572
    (ebook) | DDC 813/.54—dc23
LC record available at https://lccn.loc.gov/2020034260
LC ebook record available at https://lccn.loc.gov/2020034261

Our books may be purchased in bulk for promotional, educational, or business
use. Please contact your local bookseller or the Macmillan Corporate and
Premium Sales Department at (800) 221-7945, extension 5442, or by e-mail at
MacmillanSpecialMarkets@macmillan.com.

First Edition 2021

Designed by Steven Seighman

Printed in the United States of America

1 3 5 7 9 10 8 6 4 2

For Linwood,
and for Ben and Karina

DEAR MISS
METROPOLITAN

When at last we knew how little
Would survive us—how little we had mended
Or built that was not now lost—something
Large and old awoke.

—TRACY K. SMITH, "AN OLD STORY"

(Preliminary Draft: Special Weekend Feature: "They Would Not Let Go")

~~Read this story~~ Open these pages and you may feel sickened by the cruelties mentioned herein: three girls are kidnapped and held hostage in a dilapidated house in the New York City borough of Queens. They become known as the victim-girls.[1] Their captor, a man described in vague terms by all the prominent news outlets,[2] locks the girls away in chains, ropes, and other ~~cruel~~ devices, including thumbtacks and carpet nails; in his world, a paper clip can be as unholy as an iron maiden. ~~Kidnap victims can abound in a city like ours~~ Though each girl is abducted at different points, the aggregate period of confinement is ten years, during which time crimes[3] such as rape, asphyxiation, verbal degradation, and general torture occur with frequency. A number of pregnancies are said to have resulted from the sexual assaults, though to the best knowledge of the forensic detectives assigned the case,[4] only one pregnancy is carried to term. At the time of the rescue, one of the girls is not accounted for, leading investigators to

---

1. Credit for this description goes to Mathilda Marron, former advice columnist of the *QM*.
2. He has been described at once as a school bus driver, a Cineplex usher, a Target employee, a plumber, and a fraudulent beneficiary of SSI.
3. Crimes perhaps unimaginable to the outer-borough mind.
4. Those brave men and women included Sergeants Raymond Fiore and Lewis Quincy; Detectives Harold Amor and Lucy Sutherland; and scores of others too numerous to print.

suspect the worst.[5] Currently this veritable house of horrors has been left to its own volition; local politicians continually ask to have the place razed or repurposed; thus far, no one city agency has stepped up to meet this challenge. When asked, the residents of this leafy ~~somewhat cigarette-strewn~~ neighborhood—hovering between Sutphin Boulevard to the west and ~~Linden Boulevard~~ Rockaway Boulevard to the south—have no real idea how to move forward. It appears they are still in some state of shock ~~and culpability~~. None claims to have suspected a thing; several weeks after the fact, the people of Amity Lane remain at a loss as to how such a criminal mastermind could have lived right under their noses all that time.

Research: Amina Whitehead-Mensah, *Queens Metropolitan* **staff intern**

---

5. Subject still has not been recovered as of this date.

FERN

She lay down in the first bed but it was too hard. She lay down in the second bed but it was too soft. Finally she lay in the third bed and it was just right. She drifted.

"Goldilocks and the Three Bears"

ONCE UPON A TIME

The mother worked the night shift, meaning we only heard her footsteps when dawn was about to crack. Sometimes she crept into our room and pulled the sweaty hair from our faces and kiss-kissed us. Sometimes she straightened the covers, the colonial bedspread, the tiger print throw from Dollar Haven. *Slaap, kindje, slaap, daar buiten loopt een schaap.* The night sky changed from a purple bruise to a rust-sweet surprise, and we often awoke singing along with her. *Een schaap met witte voetjes, die drinkt zijn melk zo zoetjes.* We rose, dressed without concern, ignored our bellies, opened the front door. *Slaap, kindje, slaap.* On a good day people would come up to us on the street and say, Lady, you got yourself some gorgeous kids! We loved that. Yogurt, eggs, fresh Wonder bread from CTown, a pair of Almond Joys—but only if we promised to always listen! *I don't want to tell you kids again!* In another life, the mother had been a little Dutch girl—her father wore wooden shoes, just like in a fairy tale—and because she subsequently was disowned by him for falling in love with *Zwarte Piet*, we became her burden, her impossible dreams. *To fight the impossible foe. Sleep, children, sleep.* The three of us were colored three different shades of dark (think: coconut, fig, and raisin), but people on the street understood we belonged to one another: the mother's nose was our nose, her crow's feet ours, too. People would gush: Lady, can I steal one of these kids from you, the pair of them look so daggone cute!

We loved that.

When she came into our room after the night shift (or the double night shift or the double-double night shift), our hands rose to smooth her wrinkles, rub her forehead so that good memories could swim back in. Jones Beach on superb summer days, Rockaway Beach when the Long Island Rail Road was too expensive. We bought ice cream sandwiches for our mouths and smeared Coppertone lotion on our skin and counted the rays of sun that tickled us happy; we'd stay all day, and sometimes we'd be able to get back home on our own, but others we'd have to call someone—a man of some sort—to pick us up, seeing as how the money budgeted for the return trip was gone. *What in the hell?* Hopefully the man of some sort wouldn't be mad. Cotton candy, a Solo cup full of boardwalk sangria, a kiss on an unshaved cheek—these could soothe him. Then: back through the front door, a whole lot of grumbling. Sometimes the mother adjusted the blinds on the window so that the moon could pour over us; sometimes she pushed our twin beds together as one and told us not to breathe. *He might get mad,* she said, and then: *Well, why the hell should I care if he gets mad? I'm not his slave,* and then: *Sleep, children, sleep.*

We were her little babies. The mother said we were her little babies. She shooed the cat named Lasagna off the foot of the bed and turned low the sailboat lamp, the one painted in rainbows and soft waves, making the room look like a planet. Sometimes we fell to sleep instantly. Sometimes we smiled in our nightmares, so strong and courageous we fancied ourselves. Sometimes a cool wind blew in after she left, and we knew in our bones we had to remain motion-less, dream or no dream. He might get mad. *To bear, with unbearable sorrow, to run, where the brave dare not go. Sleep, children, sleep.*

What was that smell in the caverns of her neck? Was it Jean Naté or 4711 or White Shoulders? Was it the fragrance of Hostess blueberry pie, snatched from the ICU canteen? Or Band-Aids and rubber gloves slipped into her pocketbook from an unlocked ER cabinet? The mother's bouquet could've come from a bottle of bright red pills that, when you touched them by accident, left your fingertips looking as yummy as red SweeTarts.

We inhaled; then watched the sun rise on the other side of the blinds once the moon was emptied out; garbage trucks grunting their way up and down Linden Boulevard and farther down, airplanes swiping across rooftops and hairdos and men's voices, which shivered under the skin of everything. Sidewalks grew long; streets fattened. Were there actual farmers on Farmers Boulevard? Was the mother still with us? Kiss-kiss, kiss-kiss. Hush now, babies! I'm here. And he says he's not mad. Mother's made it all right!

HELPMEET

She was a licensed practical nurse (LPN) at Jamaica Hospital, a few bus rides away; after the original father disappeared, she worked full-time on a bunch of different floors, different units. It was a long dry spell, but she did love us because she had us. And then somewhere along the line she met the first boyfriend—a dude from Custodial/Laundry—and he was not at all mean. In fact, the first boyfriend told her she was the most lovable person he'd ever met, and that Bud and me were as sweet-faced as the rescue dogs they had up at the shelter in Rego Park.

The mother's good ICU and ER and OR patients were always happy to see her, always smiled when she approached their beds, clear-eyed or not; they loved the way she took their blood pressure, soothed their fever foreheads, whipped away their soiled sheets with a tender hand. Don't look, she'd tell them. Don't look and it won't hurt. Don't look and it won't be there. They learned not to complain, and it made the mother feel good.

That was key: the mother feeling good. We loved sunsets and moonsets but nothing more than the feeling of the mother feeling good. Nothing like it on earth.

When she was feeling *less than good*, however—when she was down, when her lovability was in question; like for example when the mother's *mean* patients complained about her: the mother's slatted eyes, how hungry and nauseous they were, the better to eat them with; when she neared their IV stands and a cold wind blew off her skin, an iodine haze clogged their nostrils—the patients got antsy. We're afraid of that nurse, they said. She's cold, really cold. And it was not only the patients. The LPNs gossiped about the cabinets she ransacked when she thought they weren't looking. The registered nurses (RNs) mumbled about her fucked-up charts, unshined Easy Spirits, and stone-cold bad breath. The doctors complained about her dozing in corners and waking up an entirely different person, a veritable Nurse Anna/Mrs. Hyde—*God knows we don't need any more of them about!*—because at these times the mother was feeling *far from good*; and it was at these times that she did her criminalizing: stealing pills from other, unsuspecting cabinets (CCU PHARM, PED ONC) and crawling into newly made beds and closing her eyes while the ward clerks tottered about, cursing her in the foulest Polish and Spanish and Creole. The mother went into every cabinet in Jamaica Hospital, praying that one of them would change her for the better. She walked past the cafeteria and the gift shop and the volunteer station, listening for the footsteps of happiness to echo down the corridors of her life. She named her pills after our favorite Genovese Drug Store candies but told us never to touch them, that they were only for grown-ups: SweeTarts, Milk Duds, Skittles. The World thinks it's gonna get me down, she'd say. Bit-O-Honeys, Mary Janes. Well, the World's got another thing coming, let me tell you. Mounds, M&M's, Almond Joys. One time the mother came back after a long shift and instead of opening the blinds, threw a book against our bedroom wall: *Test Success for RNs Third Edition.* I know I'm an idiot, she sobbed. So why even try? Nobody likes me. The people in the hospital, they don't want for me to touch them.

How can you say that? we asked. Here, have some SweeTarts. You aren't an idiot. And we've been dying for you to touch us since forever.

I'm trying the best I can, the mother cried. Why do the patients in the beds get all the attention? Don't I count, too?

Never you mind, we said, rising from our squashed bed and pulling open the blinds to see the purple morning bloom begin to oxidize. The mother shrugged off our hands. What the hell you talking about, kids? I'm nothing but a goddamn idiot! Don't you want to be proud of your mother? Get this book out my face. Anyway, it would probably take me ten years to pass this RN test!

How could we never be proud? We love you just the way you are. Touch us as much as you'd like.

Tears abated. Bud and me made the mother a breakfast of powder eggs and Mrs. Butterworth, and afterward we rubbed her ankles with lanolin. Tears blazing. Didn't the doctors know how much she knew? That book knowledge was only a small part of her power? *Shit, goddamn, fuck. There's no way I'll pass, why even try? I'm as smart as all them put together!*

We scrubbed the three-week dishes clean, brought the cat Lasagna into her lap. All the time ignoring the first boyfriend sitting asleep on the sofa in the hallway, head propped against the wall. We told the mother she was beautiful, picked up the test book, and opened it to the middle.

TEST QUESTION #38

A nurse is caring for a client in the mental health clinic. Which of the following responses by the nurse would be MOST appropriate?

1. Were you always like this?
2. Focus on the fact that you have a happy, healthy family somewhere.

3. Tell me what happened.
4. Losing one's mind is often the only alternative.

TEST QUESTION #39
Define the following acronyms:

a. EKG
b. RCA
c. WTF
d. LSD

We know you have it in you! Please hold *Test Success for RNs Third Edition* in your hands and look at it! Don't you want to be a winner? We know you have it in you!

I'll just fail.

We're here to make sure you don't. When we grow up, we want to be as smart as you. We want to win like you. Win at every test like you!

The mother's face when finally holding the book and looking at the pages: priceless. The mother's face smiling in our direction: priceless. The mother's face as the hidden SweeTarts from her uniform pocket began slinking into her eyes, taking every wrinkle and crow's foot with them: priceless. Let me try later, kids. I gotta sleep. Please keep it quiet out here. Don't bother me. Malcolm, wake the hell up! This isn't a hotel! Kids, don't let me see or hear you for the next couple hours, you hear me? Don't touch me, whatever you do. Now sleep.

Alone, we fed the cat Lasagna the rest of the eggs and sat at the living room window. We watched the birds hop from one branch to the other on needlepoint feet. What were the words of that lullaby again?

Bud began to cry because he thought we'd forgotten them. Poor Bud. So quick to not believe.

Before heading into the mother's bedroom, the first boyfriend glared at us, tossing *Test Success for RNs Third Edition* at the hallway wall. Don't you know she hates it when fingers are pointed, he growled. We did; we knew everything. Still, we apologized, and then he slammed the door. Her feelings had nothing to do with the fact that she kept circling the wrong answer. *Shut the hell up, first boyfriend, you don't know gobbledygook! She's more ours than yours, motherfucker!* (Hush, Bud cried. He might can hear us, Fern!) *Why don't you come out, first boyfriend, and listen to the truth? It might make you turn and run with your goddamn tail in your legs!* (He can't hear our thoughts, Bud!) (But our thoughts might could accidentally come from our mouths, Fern!)

Crying like crazy. To soothe my brother, I started to tell the story about why the mother really acted the way she did.

(Oh, I hate this story, Bud said.)

Once upon a time, the mother was delivered into the World on wings. She had an okay father. She had, however, a mother who was no more than a fuzzy Polaroid. The World wasn't paying attention when it doled out these two parents. Well. Time went on. I'm gonna be different than these two, the mother told herself. And then she turned around again and here was the World once more, giving her two funny-looking kids! *Come on, World, what games you playing with me?*

The mother—being a native Dutchwoman by way of Aruba and !Xhosa country (a *real* Nubian Queen, she said)—was *just this side* of pleasantly pink. As a child and then burgeoning young woman, she'd run the gamut of colors from pure white to paper-bag brown, and God knows there were people on the streets of her beloved Alkmaar who looked at her and thought her utterly lovely, despite any perceived dermatological disadvantages. One day an American GI at a small bar called the mother utterly lovely. He praised her long legs and fur on the back of her neck. He admired the pebbles of her teeth. The mother fell in love.

(I wish it could be another ending, but then it wouldn't be us, Bud observed.)

So. She came to this country and lollygagged and had two precious babies and all the while studied for her LPN and won. First to Maimonides, then to Brooklyn Methodist, and finally to Jamaica Hospital— the mother learned the ropes in all the right places. She learned that hospital people favored white faces most of all, in second place Chinese, third place Puerto Rican. She learned that janitors would yak your ear off about the way Indian doctors talked, like it was pretend English. The Dominican cashier in the gift shop bragged that her family had come from Spain, the conquistadors, just look at the shape of her own noble face. The Trinidadian phlebotomists said Spain was nothing but a dumping ground compared to the West Indies. The mother listened and learned. Secrets being that every nurse dreamt of houses, though the Jamaican ones usually got no further than Laurelton or else redeployed toward Valley Stream. The Chinese nurses made a beeline to Huntington Station on Long Island. The Catholic nurses headed even farther out, to Babylon, where the breezes of the Great South Bay dampened their uniforms. Where was someone like her to go? The Black/white/Black LPN whose eyes had once been compared by the original father to stones in a river?

(I like that, Bud said. Stones in the river.) (Me, too, Bud. Amen.)

Now. She emerged from the bedroom and, leaning over the stove, used a scorched oven mitt to wipe her cheeks. Her mouth was traced in red.

You're disrespectful, the mother said to me. I only want you to be the best at getting better, I said. Bud picked up the test book. He rubbed the mother's back as she leaned on the stove, mistaking a ballpoint pen for a Virginia Slim. He and I had both scoured *Test Success for RNs Third Edition*. Big words, not enough pictures. Sort of like fairy tales. The mother wheeled around. *Didn't I say don't touch? I'm only flesh and bones.*

TEST QUESTION #51

You are caring for a patient in the ER. The patient has been drinking alcohol and is asking for medication. When you instruct the patient that they have to wait to be seen by a doctor, the patient becomes verbally abusive. You then obtain restraints and instruct the patient that if they do not calm down, you will chain their ass down. What can you be charged with?

a.   Assault
b.   Battery
c.   Negligence
d.   Good Samaritan
e.   Knowing fucking more than any cop does in his little pinky

TEST QUESTION #68

You have been assigned to triage patients today. Which patient would get the highest priority?

a.   A patient who ate spicy pizza and who is now complaining of chest pain
b.   A patient who complains of ankle pain when ambulating
c.   A patient who thinks the nurse should actually be tested for stress
d.   A patient who has had children

Regardless: the mother would forever be a fountain. Bud and I lifted her from the stove, placed her like a doll baby into one of the waxed kitchen chairs. When she felt better, we would tell her she was beautiful and that as a kid she must have had lots of friends. We would tell her that the World loved her, always had, from the time she was a twinkle in her father's eye. We would say, Please take the test. You're going to ace this thing.

And we'd kiss her right back into the next night shift.

The first boyfriend came into the kitchen and rearranged the mother on his lap. You and me could go far, Anna, he said. We could go far, if you just stopped feeling so damn sorry for yourself.

He lifted his hand as if to convince her.

(I'm skipping ahead here—the mother's first boyfriend is a tart reminder of so much raggedyness—but is it too much of a cliché to say I had suffered my own share of evil menfolk way before Boss Man ever entered the picture? That I myself was a victim's victim? A character from an episode of *Law & Order*? A lurid headline from the *Queens Metropolitan*? Did I lie down and take as much as I did because that was all I'd ever known? A predetermined victim of all of evil mankind? Truth is, I've been asking those questions for ages. But no doctor has ever helped me come closer to *practically* answering them, not even TV's Dr. Ezra and his "expert" "staff." Truth hurts. But I shouldn't skip too far ahead.)

The first boyfriend eventually disappeared, to prison or to the rehab center in Springfield Gardens. Maybe under a corrugated cardboard roof at Jamaica Station. Could have seen that coming a mile away.

We are enough, we whispered to the mother as she breached our nightly dreams—catching midnight dragonflies and baking 4 a.m.

cookies—but in the rust-sheen of daybreak, there she was at the kitchen table, shouting that she didn't need any raggedy-ass man. She was a damn good mother with two damn good kids and so what if she kept circling the wrong answer? Who needs a crap Significant Other? Plenty of fucking women before me . . . it is what it is, she trailed off. It is what it is, Bud and me repeated.

And lo and behold: just me and Bud and the mother in our own little nighttime/daytime universe containing flickers of hopeful colors and lampshades and bedspreads and planets. Was that as close to heaven as we ever got? The answer is still TBD.

What follows came as a shock to Bud and me but only because we lived, as the mother's first boyfriend told us, with blinders on. After some desert-dry time with her fig-and-raisin kids, the mother started feeling lonely. The World was not taking pity on her. The World was not understanding how hard she had it and failing that fucking RN test for the third time and people on the street complimenting her less and less, looking away from her hair all a mess and two kids who didn't (when you looked closely) resemble her AT ALL. Her own mother was pure pitch-African, leading her father—a man so white he was clear—to try to abandon them at Schiphol, 1962. He wasn't fast enough; the mother's mother was already on a plane back to safety. She eventually morphed into that fuzzy Polaroid. The mother's father dropped his child at the Municipal Orphanage, but six years later came to get her, the baby, the girl, the mother-wit-in-training; and she suddenly found herself alone in a land of liquor-edged language, oblivious Formica-faces, and enough *Zwarte Piets* for everyone to enjoy. It was said she was her father's spit and image. Most everyone in Alkmaar agreed. *I'm only flesh and blood!*

We're stalwart, we murmured. We're steadfast. We ARE the OG Significant Others.

The mother smiled. How cute! You know I love you. Let me kiss-kiss you good night!

That notwithstanding—she went out and got herself the second boy-friend.

SYMBOL

He had a name we couldn't pronounce even though it was only one syllable. The mother showed us a picture they took in one of those photo booths where you could sense a carnival at the edges, merriment and gaiety and popcorn and funnel cakes—a carnival to which we hadn't been invited. Bud and I felt afraid. What if the first boyfriend decides to come back? we asked. Or what if the *original father* shows up?

That deadbeat? she said, making perfect towers out of long white pills, gauze pads, single-use minis of codeine cough syrup. Forget him. I told you never to ask about the original father. Don't look at me like that. And please don't touch.

(Because the mother had always refused to mention the original father's name [INSERT HERE], we would have to, on school forms, write [UNKNOWN] or [UNSPECIFIED AT THIS TIME]. We never knew the shape of his eyes; if there was any old clothes belonging to him in the apartment—a necktie, a pair of gym socks—we never found it. Every now and then, the mother liked to sit in the kitchen and burn whole piles of Polaroids from boxes entitled WEDDING and MORE WEDDING. The second boyfriend egged her on. That man wasn't any good for you, Anna. Him and his middle-class mentality. Fucking asshole deserves to go up in smoke.)

No questions, just answers.

We prayed to her. And she prayed back. The mother's arms brushed against our sleeping heads—we felt the swaying meat of those arms graze our pimples and warts. She was more than a fountain. She was a waterfall, an ocean. Her breath smelled of peppermint tea and ash; as time went on with the second boyfriend, she would stumble into our room smelling of Welch's grape juice and pickles. Stuffy closets and vacuum cleaner bags. She'd say things like, How would you two kids like a new baby brother or sister?

We paused.

Then there were those days when we would find her laughing over a plate of real scrambled eggs and *I Love Lucy* on the small kitchen television. *Test Success for RNs Third Edition* spread-eagled on the counter next to the sink. No sign of the second boyfriend but Jean Naté for miles. The mother was a tsunami.

TEST QUESTION #47

The home care nurse is visiting a client with a diagnosis of hepatitis of unknown etiology. The nurse knows that teaching has been successful if the patient says which of the following statements?

1. "I am so sad I can't hold my baby!"
2. "I will eat only after my husband eats."
3. "I will punish my children if they try and use my eating utensils because clearly there is something wrong with me, and why the hell are they eating my food?"
4. "I will make sure I clean everything I touch. I will not take my anger out on others."

We made sure to say the right things. We tried not to ask the wrong things. But what was better than those two squashed-together beds at night, where cotton sheep jumped over rainbows and fingers tasted like the rusty rings of Saturn?

SPONTANEOUS COMBUSTION

Did you know that there are thousands of streets in Queens? They all sound like flowers or royalty: Astoria Boulevard, Springfield Boulevard, Kissena Boulevard, Francis Lewis Boulevard, Queens Boulevard, Hollis Court Boulevard, Long Island Expressway, Cross Island Parkway, Grand Central Parkway, Hillside Avenue, Union Turnpike, Steinway Street.

There are beautiful anomalies. Gas station ruins in a part called Briarwood, which runs below a part called Fresh Meadows, which runs below a part called Oakland Gardens—who could ask for more lovely names? $300 CASH FOR YOUR CAR posted on an aluminum fence on Tuskegee Airmen Way. The intersection of Farmers and Linden Boulevards, where a jolly AME church proclaims "Everybody Is Somebody"—how could these places not move the most stubborn heart? Don't even get me started on Utopia. I've always dreamed of living in Utopia. The imagination can go a long way.

The imagination could (but didn't) lead you down a street called Amity Lane. To the naked ear, that absolutely might sound like the definition of nice.

FAST FORWARD

In 2007 I was lauded. Lauded in the newspapers as one of the so-called victim-girls or victim-females. Praised, respected, lauded, stuffed and admired like Edgar Allan Poe's raven on Dr. Watson's perch. People said I was a role model, a girl to look up to. A heroine, a phoenix risen out of the ash, a young valiant who'd overcome all obstacles to be free. People said: Think of the horrors that those *victim-girls* endured—ten years in a prison, and before that, thirteen years in various crazy-nutcase households—it's a wonder any of them are still human! People learned my particular Boss Man story: sexually abused, impregnated and aborted, beaten senseless, degraded in every way possible. A victim's victim, in other words. A victim-female to be lauded. No longer a question, but an answer. After the rescue, the World looked at me and found the praise/horror-names it needed in every one of my angles, like a kaleidoscope with permanent designs.

Problem being: I was not your average everyday survivor. I was nobody's stereotype. REAMS, in fact, could have been written on my originality.

My name—totally unique. Fern Daisy Delores, supposedly given to me by the original father, though of course, I wouldn't know. You won't find another Fern Daisy Delores in all of Queens, not even in the botanical garden over in Flushing. That's a joke; please laugh.

My skin color—stirred brown like the *te con leche* from El Nilo, the Dominican restaurant on Sutphin Boulevard. Or maybe you could describe me like the auburn tilapia from Seafood Heaven on Farmers Boulevard, or the medium black-eyed peas from Harkey's Soul Heaven on Foch. Comparisons abound. The mother once told me my skin came from the original father—mud puddle in the morning, caramel brat in the afternoon, crybaby brown at night—because the original father was nothing more than plain old American Negro from somewhere unimaginative like the Bronx or Staten Island. Don't ask her which.

I'm unique. I'm special. Always have been. Back in the day, my dancing was one of a kind. Bud thought I could move my arms and legs like no one else on the planet. Had the original father boogied like that?

I was not him, though. I was no one but myself. Even my nighttime dreams were exceptional, not your usual black-and-white real-life regurgitations. As a child, my dreams used to be long affairs, furnished with lovable animals and street fairs and hot chicken wings; children yelling in odd languages; pogo sticks hopping through the desert. Please don't laugh. Sometimes my dreams left me wanting more. During those times—in Boss Man's abode, natch—I'd close my eyes in exhaustion and dream up chocolate women with laps as large as lasagna pans, all beckoning to me. *Come on, Fern. Don't be afraid.*

Each individual suffers their own individual pain. That much we know. Add to that the fact that each individual can live his or her trauma way before it actually happens. Please take me seriously. A person can be hit before they're hit. Hurt before they're hurt. They can be stolen without physically leaving the room, they can be locked away for years before they're even born. It's a proven fact. The problem being: how to get the World to believe this?

Look at me. Been there, done that.

They once did an episode of *Law & Order* on this very phenomenon. There was this kid who knew he was going to be abused well before the abuse happened—a preordained sufferer, Ms. Refuge called him before dozing. I watched this episode with Gwinnie in our picnic-chair hospital apartment—and damned if I didn't close my eyes and start shaking. Ms. Refuge fast asleep with her knitting. Nurse Happiness rushed in and thought I was having a brain attack. *Doan yuh nuh die on me, gal.* Pressing me to her bosom though hospital rules were: no pressing; but no one questioned Nurse Happiness's methods, ever. My shaking fit passed; the doctors couldn't figure it out. Just one of those things, Dr. Badbreath joked. Maybe you're just acting sick to get more ice cream, ha ha. Go to hell, Gwinnie said under her breath.

Ms. Refuge, though. When she awoke she tried to make sense. That was what we were there to do in the first place: living in that picnic-chair hospital and trying to understand a world we'd never imagined and yet had recovered from. *You're soaking in it, girls!* You didn't really have a panic attack, Ms. Refuge explained once the doctors and nurses left. What you are doing is *reliving and identifying and healing.* A trigger of some sort took you back, she said. Back where, I wanted to know. Ms. Refuge frowned and put her knitting on the floor. That's enough for now, she said. Don't ask too many questions. She showed us her York College catalog and let us gaze upon the course names—words in a fairy tale: Child Abuse and Neglect 101. Abnormal Psychology 101. The Exceptional Child 102. She believed her online psychology courses would really take her places. One day I'll have my own office near Central Park in the City, she said, taking up the knit two, purl two. Movie stars will come to me for help, the most important people on the planet.

She could identify dreams, nightmares, the smallest shake of the skin. The tiniest tremble of the eye. I want to know the truth, I cried. Where did I go back to?

Gwinnie put her arms around me. Please don't be afraid, Fern, she said reassuringly. You know as good as me that their truth is overrated.

How I loved Gwinnie for that.

You can experience pain and suffering in all sorts of ways before they manifest in real life, Ms. Refuge explained another time—pain involving hands, silver chains, butts, plastic knives. You can fight back before anyone has laid a finger on you. You can be a ghost before you actually die.

But who would believe a girl becoming a victim before her time? A stereotype that's not a stereotype? Attracting punches, scratches, licks, and wounds before actually earning them? It's a test from up high, Father Flaplips concluded, on one of his frequent trips from the picnic-chair hospital chapel; you, my girl, and your companions were destined to have your faith tested.

I pretended that that last comment didn't bother me in the least.

When Father Flaplips said, What doesn't kill us makes us stronger, we laughed both behind his back and to his face, then begged Ms. Refuge to save us.

You can be hit before you're hit. You can be stowed away for years before you're even afloat. It's been both scientifically and television-ally proven.

Of course, I wasn't thinking this when I was back at home with Bud and the mother and the mother's second boyfriend. I had no interest in *Law & Order* to begin with—that was the mother's jam. She claimed she could figure out the bad guy in the first five minutes; after that, the show was boring as stink. Don't be spoiling my figuring things out, the second boyfriend said from his chair propped up against the living room wall. I love me some *Law & Order*, Anna. I love it like it's no tomorrow.

Oh hush, [Unpronounceable Syllable]. Who the hell watches *Law & Order* anyway?

I thought she might know. I thought she might know that my actual jam was *Soul Train*. Maybe it was the original father's, too. He could be watching. He could be proud of his crybaby. Don't laugh. I was actually happy when I thought about my life like that.

HOW TO TELL IF YOU WERE BLACK AND PROUD

Back in the day. Bud and me watched it every Saturday morning at 11. Not the new version, with that weird light-skinned dude trying to be a super-freak Don Cornelius when in reality he was nothing but smoke and mirrors and a grade-school haircut—and to make matters worse, in the background, all that shit for dancing he called *moves*. Hell no. Bud and I watched the real classic *Soul Train*. Don Cornelius's Afro trumping over everything like the World Trade Center. The dancers moving like desserts in a hot lunch cafeteria. When it wasn't Saturday morning—when it was just me and Bud alone on a weeknight after making a mess of the Hamburger Helper the mother had claimed was so easy to prepare—we loaded VHS tapes into the creaky player and let loose. Who cared about eating?

These were the mother's second boyfriend's old VHS tapes that he kept in the closet my mother had given him after their third date. Just after she started the double-double shifts and returned home only to devour the pill skyscrapers built on the kitchen table. We listened for her with our eyes closed tight. *Sleep, children, sleep.*

He had a million of those tapes, it seemed—all the way from the Love Unlimited Orchestra and the Ohio Players to Ashford & Simpson singing "Somebody Told a Lie" to the Temptations' best lip-synched version of "Papa Was a Rollin' Stone." (*You can have the hall closet as well,* the mother told the second boyfriend. *You can have whatever you want, [Unpronounceable Syllable]. Please stay.*) Me and Bud *Soul Train*–lined up in front of the TV in the back bedroom and grooved—meaning we bumped, we grinded, we thumped, we winded—to Earth, Wind & Fire, the Gap Band, Labelle, the Emotions. We boogied down the small hallway into the living room and further up the hallway to the small kitchen TV, where another tape played—Chaka Khan singing on the *Soul Train* stage wearing a fur bikini, chaps, and head feathers.

What luxuries. Two TVs playing at once plus the songs that also played in our heads. A bounty of riches.

Why can't we look like her? Bud wondered out loud. Back then I didn't think it was weird for a boy to want to wear a fur bikini and chaps and I still don't. Bud applied the mother's lipstick (*Coral Beach*) to his face, and I got out her oldest-time wigs (*Helge I* and *Helge II*). The mother's hair had been ice yellow at Schiphol Airport; brick-road yellow when she went to the Municipal Orphanage; and then corn yellow when she was a young woman madly in love with the original father. After we came along, she took to wearing brown wigs (the *Julia,* the *Cecily III*)—or braided wigs meant for browner women, buns meant for truly dark women, chignons that could hide any trace of the Old Country, anything—the mother claimed she had a million looks. If the original father didn't find her beautiful, well, he was missing out, fuck him and fuck all the boroughs he'd dragged her through, just to leave her here, alone in the heart, that fucking test book staring her in the face day after day! *Don't ask me about him ever again, you hear? I've had it with your questions! He didn't think you were his! Let's just leave it at that! Motherfucking motherfucker.*

We loved her wigs. We debated between the *Cornrowed Cleopatra* or the *Lena Horne Loop* but eventually settled on wearing the mother's unused hair of the future: I chose her *Afro,* Bud her *Room 222 Flip-do.*

They were still in the wig-store bags. She'd never notice. There was hope in our moves.

Dancing to the TV. *Hey, Don Cornelius, look at me and my brother!* We created a rhythm that had its roots in the Precambrian era: a dance that had endured slavery, colored bathrooms, and the bullies at the hot lunch lines at PS 187 in Jamaica (where I was in the eighth grade, Bud in the third). Donna Summer's lips spoon-fed us seasons of love. Barry White, big as a coffin, made our stomachs flutter. If you could've seen the scene—us moving up the hallway to the kitchen and then back down to the back bedroom, repeat, repeat; a gangly girl and a stubby boy, flailing like a backward liberation movement, as if we'd been chained to the music, irreverent, two-faced, no other choice but to beg forgiveness from God the Father for making us move our hips the way we did. Any sort of escape from the glory of *Soul Train* being impossible, that is.

(We didn't know much about God the Father but figured it was never too late to learn.)

We weren't supposed to take the mother's second boyfriend's tapes without asking. But how could we resist?

Jamming. It was an intoxication I have not found since. I am telling this all from the perch of life lived, escaped, and lived all over again.

December 2039, and I am currently sitting on a bench in Central Park near Columbus Circle, right next to Gwinnie, who is nonchalant as a tumbleweed. We've never danced together because Gwinnie was sadly born with two left feet. Despite her obsession with Prince, she couldn't bop even if you shot a cowboy's pistol at her toes. The city buses pass us, the M104 (which I have come to admire) and the M101 (which takes us straight back to the picnic-chair hospital), and from some car somewhere music blasts that is unmistakably the O'Jays singing "I Love Music." I feel my lap quake and my legs quake with the memory of the old *Soul Train* grooves. I wish to hell I could share that with Gwinnie, the feeling in the veins of my veins.

Back then, Bud and I blasted the TVs until the sound on each was as fuzzy as the screen; we laughed at each other and wished our Saturday morning would just repeat itself on some time-travel loop. Our arms were not our arms. Our legs—in fantastical twists, in near-perfect splits, kickbox certainty—nearly broke the furniture of the back bedroom, the sofa bed where I had started sleeping most nights, the dresser that wouldn't fit into the room I officially shared with Bud. The secretary desk, rescued by the mother's second boyfriend from the dump *brand-new.* (*Thank you, my darling. I so love it when you look out for the kids and me.*) When Don Cornelius came on at the end of the program to raise his fist goodbye, we could feel our hearts breaking. Love, Peace, and Soul. We fell backward and wouldn't let go. Total drama, crybabies, spoiled-brat potential, but we didn't care.

You KNOW you look like a bunch of fucking idiots.

Premature summer, possibly the end of April, lilacs busting the air. The mother's second boyfriend leaned against the door, chugging his Hawaiian Punch. We lay spread-eagle on the floor, trying to catch our breath. The mother's second boyfriend lit a cigarette even though the mother was a nurse and hated that kind of unhealthiness. *Who in the hell told you jerk-offs you could dance? I think whoever told you that must be brain-dead.*

Bud up and said, Whoever told you *you* could think?

I gurgled. In a braver world, that sound would have come out as a laugh.

The second boyfriend slapped me in the face. Nothing big, in the scheme of things. An imaginary indentation of five fingers across a blue sea of girl. Bud looked at me and burst himself into tears.

Questions were deadly.

The mother returned home from her shifts at Jamaica Hospital (the 11–7 and 7–1) and looked at my face in the leftover rust of the room—*What in the hell happened to you?* Her fingers felt the streaks of tears on my unwashed face. It doesn't have to be like this, she whispered. Like what, I asked. Like this, and this, and this, she answered.

Minutes later, she stomped into the living room and yelled her head off at the second boyfriend (not mentioning the secret phone call where I begged her to come home before her shift was done and her dismayed answer: *I can't, baby. Plus you fighting with him is not exactly a life-threatening emergency*): YOU GODDAMN CHILD ABUSER WHAT GIVES YOU THE GODDAMN RIGHT TO LIFT A FINGER AND MY CHILDREN ARE LIKE YOUR REAL SON AND DAUGHTER AND LOOK AT HER FACE AND IS THIS HOW YOU GONNA DO ME? I'M FROM EUROPE BY WAY OF NUBIA, IN CASE YOU DIDN'T KNOW. I GOT MORE BRAINS IN MY LITTLE PINKY THAN . . .

The second boyfriend was all flopped on the couch next to Bud, examining the slipcovers with his fingertips. *Please be quiet, my love. Me and my quote unquote son are trying to enjoy the Ice Capades.*

Bud had stopped crying. His face was a varsity blue. The old college try.

The mother switched off the TV and stood in front of it, folding her arms across her chest like a warpath. What the hell was she working her butt off for? To come home to this nonsense? So what if the kids started it? They were *kids,* dammit. And didn't he say just the other day that they were as good as his? Didn't he?

Please turn it back on, Anna. They say Olga Korbut is going to make a comeback. A miracle of modern nature.

Couldn't he stop lazing long enough to wash the dishes, for fuck's sake? Stop taking money out her rainy-day underwear drawer? She was better than the entire borough of Queens combined, being that her father's mother's mother had come from royalty, why didn't he remember her telling him that? A princess of Imaginary Egypt—and look how he was treating her ascendants' descendants? How could she trust him if he did these things when she wasn't looking? Plus—did he *really* need more than the two closets? What the fuck was up with all those tapes—VHS was on its way out; didn't he get the memo? Shit almighty! Get with the program, man! All the hours I work only to come home to a black-and-blue face on my little chocolate crybaby? Would it make it easier if I put them in some sort of program for when they're out of school? Listen, man. I work and I slave. Don't have it easy like the royalty from times before—I'm a strong modern woman yet I like to think of them as yours and mine together. Just the other day you said you did, too.

Bud had crawled to the back bedroom and slipped himself like a knife under my blanket. We were quiet. Maybe the second boyfriend would smack her and go. We'd experienced that sort of farewell from men before.

To the second boyfriend, the mother said, Shit. I'm doing my best.

And later, to Bud and me: You have to show grown-ups respect. You don't know what all they have had in their past. You must always be the bigger person.

By the light of the next moon she drifted into our bedroom and flushed the air with the fragrance of cherries and eucalyptus. Cough drops, we could have a bag each. A jar of VapoRub, good for coughing fits of tears. The mother touched my face and said, I expected better from you, Fern. You don't call a grown man an asshole, not even behind his back. Especially one who is trying his best to be the father you never knew.

I sat up. I threw the cough drop bag at the wall.

You've never given me any trouble before this, Fern.

I threw Bud's VapoRub at the wall.

Stop that now, the mother whispered. Wake yourself. It's just a bad dream. Wake yourself. She brushed my hair from my face. You are perfect, but I don't want you to be a pain anymore, Fern. Not to the new father standing right in front of your nose.

I didn't tell her about the night before, when the second boyfriend tucked me into bed. Not like a father at all.

Because in the scheme of things, that tucking in was, of course, the most unsurprising, unoriginal phenomenon of all. Such a cliché: evil stepfather seeks bad romance with unwitting girl while mother is out making a living. *Baby, where you been all my life? This is different, I swear. Not what you thinking, honey. Your mom don't get me like you. And my feelings, they're as real as they come. Can't you see?*

Puh-leeze! A cliché, yes. But then, such a singular plight.

WAITING FOR PRINCE

I was a prisoner for so, so long. Years. How was that humanly possible? Why didn't anyone find me? Why had my page been torn out the book for so long?

I was stashed in a haunted house. I heard sounds. Mice. Dead babies. Loads of them. Talking, singing, baffling, fighting. I think I could live to be three hundred and never forget the sound of those sounds. They're not merely a part of the BEHIND WORLD. They're PRESENT WORLD and FUTURE WORLD coming at me like a boulder down Baisley Boulevard.

Boss Man was cruel. That first day when he captured me, he hung me upside down like a sack of Yukon Gold. Not a dog to be seen. It was instead these two clotheslines in (what I supposed was) the attic. Or maybe it was the former dining room or maybe the kids' bedroom from the Precambrian time when this was a human abode. I was too afraid to find out. My wrists were roasting under rope fire; I felt as if they would break away like doll hands. Boss Man came in and did his business with me and said if I screamed it would make things worse. What could be worse? My mind fell into a heap, where I heard the mice in the baseboards, pitying my fate, singing their little cheddar hearts out for me: *This is what it sounds like when doves cry.* Disappearing into the further depths of I know not what. Should that have made me feel better, knowing the mice were witnesses and could possibly tell BEHIND WORLD where I was? I was not losing my mind; this really *was* a question. I waited. I hung and sank. I existed. Upside-down nosebleeds and brain meat trickling from the ears. I blamed the mice completely. I was not losing my mind.

KEEP YOUR OPINIONS
TO YOURSELF

I once peeped Prince on *Soul Train*. The mother's second boyfriend was drinking the last bit of the Eight O'Clock and saw me standing there. He called Prince a fag. Said there was no way a red-blooded American female would be into him, those lady legs and eye makeup. The mother's second boyfriend looked at me out the corner of his eyes. Was I a fag hag? Did I like men with pussies? He laughed before I could answer. All the while Bud standing behind him with the biggest Dutch oven lid you could ever hope to behold.

RODENTIA

When we were actual victim-girls.

They were there. Friends, Romans, and countrymen. They were in the walls, the floors, the pretend windows and pretend doors, their voices chattering on an even keel as though nothing was new under our sun. Boss Man did his thing to me, cut me down off the clotheslines. Didn't bother taking off the blindfold and now, years later, I thank him for that. Boss Man did not want me to die. He fed me some magic beans (Goya, black), tossed me on a bed of straw, chained my foot to a pipe that leaked faux Taster's Choice (brown-as-shit water that could be easily imagined into morning joe), and left me for hours. Days. A constant pecking and pulling and pushing, but it also felt like I was the only person in the world.

I was placed somewhere, but where?

Boss Man's voice roared like an echo chamber. The ground was soft and hard, wet and dry; there was high altitude and low lowitude, longitude and shortitude (think being crammed into a massive silver thimble). Soon I learned that if I felt around the place long enough, if my hands were free, I could discover things. One day the ground was concrete. Another day shag carpet. Another day I discovered a drain in the shape of a human face. My hand discovered it, I should say, no blindfold but eyes too blacked out to distinguish countenances. I felt around some more: a length of thread, a dust bunny, and a safety pin.

A safety pin.

I hid it in my stomach folds (which in those early days were not as saggy flat as they would become) and begged the mice not to tell on me. I said I was going to do something big with this safety pin, that I'd make myself free and come back and save them, too. The safety pin was a solid shine. A glimmer. But days went by and: guilt. How could I use this weapon on anyone—that was not playing fair, I was not being good, I was not respecting grown folk, I was revolving too many evil questions and answers in my mind, I was not being good. I removed the safety pin from my folds and begged God's forgiveness for thinking I could take someone else's life. Murder was the worst thing, wasn't it? Please God. Why do you put such thoughts into my little head?

God said back, The only way you can make this right is to confess.

Boss Man laughed. You think you coulda taken me out with this shit? Even blindfolded, you couldn't hurt a fly. Remember I am the hand that feeds you. He tossed the safety pin into the nothingness of the stairs, where the mice eagerly made a grab for it.

Then he slung me back up on the ropes. Blindfold tight as a mummy, hands taped to my sides. He said, I'm the guy with your best interests at heart, bitch. Don't you forget it.

The mice shook their heads. What was you thinking, they asked, their little mouths about to go all Limburger-crazy on me. Those were the early days. I had much to learn.

DEVILMENT

When it was just me in the house with Boss Man. When it was just me as his first and only MODEL EMPLOYEE (Ms. Refuge later confirmed that my kidnapping took place circa October 1997)—when the idea of leaving that house was so original, as unripe as a banana still in its bunch—I had to make a lot of promises.

My lips chafed with the wallpaper paste of promises.

After the safety pin: I had to promise not to take and hide any other dangerous weapons I might come across in the workplace. Yes, he called our home THE WORKPLACE. I had to promise to refer to myself as his MODEL EMPLOYEE. It wasn't because I worked so well. Boss Man said that when he first glimpsed me, I looked like a model, and that was why he had to have me.

I had to promise not to scream out of worker frustration, or from the hot fluids on my body, or from the cold of being naked most of the time because of (what I imagined was) snow in the air. How long had I been gone? How long, Boss Man? I had to promise not to cry due to the lack of birthday parties, which I knew for a fact came around at least once a year. I had to promise to be gay, not in the fag way—Boss Man said he chose the straightest girls he could measure—but in the old-fashioned sense of the word, as in "Gay Paree." If I worked hard enough, there would be rewards. BEST MODEL EMPLOYEE OF

THE MONTH. But I could not cry. I could not holler. I could not think of police or original fathers or superhero mice. No, this was a new chapter. This was not the time for old happinesses. I had to promise to forget old things. Old things were BEHIND WORLD. Useless. Nonutilitarian. A nagging mother or a nosy schoolteacher. BEHIND WORLD was nothing but poison. Your brother, the one you say likes to dance with you and wear your mother's old wigs? Are you sure he's not a fag? Because thinking of fags can mess up THE WORKPLACE big-time. You are a woman. You are red-blooded. THE WORKPLACE is you.

(That's what Boss Man said in the beginning. Later he added: *Beware of nosy street urchins and busybody cops and old ladies with nothing better to do than snoop around scribbling things to themselves on old-fashioned steno pads.*)

I had to promise to say nothing to nobody, or to even think about saying nothing to nobody, or to even remember a time when I was not a MODEL EMPLOYEE. As such I needed to keep my trap shut. If I knew what was good for me.

But who would I see? I asked. You took my eyes, ears, nose, and lips away.

Women in the workplace, Boss Man grunted. It's always something.

Day after day after day. What was time? The mice couldn't answer me if they tried.

Let me explain, Boss Man said elsewhere. Windows boarded every-where because what did I need to see outside? Everything I needed was here. Let me explain. You're nothing but a little fresh mouth—you don't think I heard you call me a monster the other night? You were sleeping when you said it, but a name is a name. I won't get mad this time, but watch yourself. This ain't the home you used to know.

Elsewhere: From now on you need to concentrate on your work. You are forever mine. I am your Original Boss Man. "Never duplicated or overestimated—trademark TM." Try and remember that. Let me tell you everything I expect of you. Obey, if you ever want your feet to touch the floor again.

(I wanted to say, I'll do what you ask; but then I fell asleep, passed out, over-comatized myself, dead to rights, all of the above. When I came to, he was gone. I heard motors in the distance, couldn't tell which one was his. Felt snow in the air—how long had I been passed out? Couldn't feel my extremities. Even though every part of me hanging on those clotheslines was *totally* extreme.)

Not all men are the same. Not all girls get caught up in evil fairy tales. Still. Your mind can make thousands of connections. Even if you are nothing more than a runaway passel attached to a clothesline rope.

The smooth surface unbroken by the tiniest of dust motes traveling the air.

Boss Man had left me alone now for a long time and then. I was like a gull feather traveling up and down over the crest of the whitecaps in the Whitestone bay. The pole rope burnt my skin. Sleep came in up and down waves like a lie detector. I struggled with my shoulders, my elbows, the remnants of my hips. Yes, I promise to be a good MODEL EMPLOYEE. It's what I always wanted! Yes, I'm telling the truth! Now please take me down from here.

Blackness. Fists. No oxygen. Night. I awoke to Boss Man frowning. Will you state that from here on in, you are solely the property of my business, he asked.

Yes, I state.

The ropes were cut, my back hit the floor like a Posturepedic mattress ("Leave off the last 'S' for savings!").

You know what you gotta do, the mice whispered from the various holes all around. I opened my eyes and saw those beady little things take me in. A draft of tails scurrying nowhere. It really was snow outside, that much for sure, because it was snow inside, too. The aroma of dead trees. Otherwise, I had no clue.

MISSING: ONE THANKLESS DAUGHTER! WAS TROUBLE ONCE BUT ME AND MY SIGNIFICANT SOUL MATE AND HER INNOCENT LITTLE BROTHER DO BELIEVE IN THE POWER THAT EVERYONE CAN CHANGE. HEY IF YOU'RE READING THIS: SLAAP, KINDJE, SLAAP.

CAN YOU?

How? How to hear the footsteps of happiness down the corridors of your life when you've lost all auditory sense?

How to envision sunny days when your eyes are swollen shut?

How to know that an escape hatch is nigh—when your lips are sealed like Krazy Glue, your insides stripped like tree bark, your hands fastened to a piece of bloodthirsty wire resembling nothing as much as outstretched paper clips? How?

I hear you over there. Who are you?

I hear you, too.

What are you?

No idea. I thought I was a girl. Now that's all bullshit.

I like the way you sound.

I hear you, too.

Can you help me?

I was about to ask can you help me?

Birds of a feather. My mama says that. She's probably on her way.

How many days is it?

No fucking idea.

Maybe I'm a ghost. No one can see ghosts. My mother's a ghost.

You sound like a girl. Tell me what's your name?

Fern.

Gwin.

Are you crying?

Are you crying?

(Quiet.)

(Quiet.)

(Quiet.)

(Quiet.)

You still there?

When was I never?

GWIN

*She fell into a deep, deep sleep and could only be awak-
ened by love's true kiss. She did not want to wake up like
that. She wanted to wake up just the way she was.*

"SLEEPING BEAUTY"

TUNNELVISION

Okay, listen up. Prince, he was my life from day one in my mama's utero, wish I could call it 1999 but then I'd be lying; 1999 was another sort of year. I was born, I grew up. Cambria Heights, Elmhurst, Far Rockaway, here. One family, two family, three family, two. I never knew my father, but I did know a man named Mr. P, and he graciously volunteered to take on the job despite the fact that my mama was my mama and between us it was only so much love to go round. Would he be able to love us both—would *she* be able to love us both—would I? Because in those days I wasn't really into people, my plan being: live happily ever after while playing Prince on the boombox. Mr. P changed that. He was nice, he was friendly. He didn't talk about an old country and he didn't call the upstairs neighbors *American trash*. Mr. P was limestone brick, through and through. I mean, really: look at him and you'll see the shorelines of underground rivers. You see it in his face, the sturdiness of sandstone in the creases of his countenance, around which flows the hidden Sunswick Creek, its prehistoric landscape buried deep within Queens, the sunken sea monsters and marble and minerals. I saw Mama as the wide mouth of a river and me as the estuary—and if Ecology 8 teacher Mr. Giordano ever thought I was sleeping while he was talking, he's clearly got another thing coming.

What I'm saying is that I always thought me and Mama and Mr. P could all be part of something together, why the hell not? The Earth's elements have accommodated more souls than our three at any given moment.

I could trust him, Mr. P, to bring home my favorite King Vitamin cereal from CTown, which I right away downed in about a quart of vitamin D milk; asking the upstairs Brown family if they could please turn their Stevie Wonder records down as I was trying hard to study for my math test and didn't they know I was a *straight A student?*; taking my temperature and writing a note to the attendance office that did say I was sick but didn't say I would be watching stories with him all afternoon. *All My Children, One Life to Live.* We started to really like each other, me and Mr. P, with Mama off to the side, like coleslaw or pickles. I didn't care that she might be feeling jealous—I would take his care over hers any damn day. He drove me to Girl Scouts and then back out again when I told him I hated badges—I can do everything already, I said, and he replied, Of course, why didn't I think of that? Mr. P drove me for ice cream over at the skeleton of the world at Flushing Meadows Park and he didn't stop at just one: can you imagine getting a strawberry shortcake AND a toasted almond AND a soft serve cone, all at the same time? His care.

My favorite song is "I Would Die 4 U," Mr. P told me one time. I hadn't mentioned a damn thing about my abiding love for Prince. But it was just like Mr. P to understand what was in my damn soul.

Summer, fall, winter, back to summer again. Dead of winter.

Then it came to pass that another love moved in. Church. Church and all its discontents.

Mr. P liked to say under his breath, Religion is just between a man and his God, and that's as it should be. (I didn't understand, but

I went with it anyway because of the way his face looked when he said that.)

But nevertheless Mama sat us down and said it was a new chapter about to begin for us. But why does it have to be *that* book? I asked. Hush, child, Mr. P warned. Don't be disrespectful.

Mama continued: My new chapter begin last Thursday. I'm a new woman and yuh coming long fuh de trip.

I answered, All I remember you doing was going to CTown for some cube steak, but you took longer than cube steak should take so I thought maybe you were stopping in Dollar Haven for some secret shopping seeing as it's almost my birthday in a couple months but I had no idea you were messing with some church, Mama—

Respect, child, Mr. P said, a little louder.

Mama looked me up and down at that kitchen table. She said, My life come alive dat late afternoon when de Witnesses invite me to join dem. Right in front of de CTown.

Ah, I said.

My life come alive again dat next afternoon when dem knock upon me door.

Oh, was that the one time you didn't slam it shut in their faces?

Dat de beginning, light and life, amen.

Mama!

Girl, yuh nuh play wit me now. Yuh listen and comprehend.

Mr. P looked at me and I looked at him. Understanding that from that moment on, it was going to be a Witness's journey for her, take it or leave it. We innocent bystanders knew for a fact that being a Witness meant no dancing, no laughing, no birthdays, no secret Santa, no getting out of control. (As in Matthew 5:37: Let your yes mean yes and your no sure as hell mean no.)

(Mama made the full-on conversion. But what to do when Mama secretly waggled her meat to my Prince boombox? She didn't think I saw her. But lo and behold! She waggled, she danced. She was a coveter, just like me, just a smidge.)

Mr. P told me he saw Prince on *American Bandstand*, but I told him he must've mistook that show for *Soul Train*, and he simply winked at me and said, I was just testing you, girl.

The day after the Witness Revelation, Mr. P helped me do my homework while Mama was out standing on the frosty corner of Merrick Boulevard and 170th, smack in front of GLITZY HAIR, smiling her heart out. What was she looking for? And tell me why—*why* was there so little love to go round for us but then so much for those anti-birthday-partiers? Why did two-timing smiles seem to grow on trees? All that summer and fall, Mr. P was there, often with no expression at all. His head was elsewhere, forget the fakeness. He taught me to use the basement washing machine. He showed me that there was nothing wrong in actually reading the directions on a box of Duncan Hines cake mix instead of guessing what goes where—he taught me how to *really* read. He showed me the right way to lock the bars on our doors, windows, escape hatches—no one would bother us, ever. He showed me how to calligraphy my name, Japanese demon–style. I felt shivers when he showed me how to ride a bike in the driveway of our crumbly two-family, right under the eyes of those Brown family kids in the upstairs apartment window. Mr. P touched the groove of my back as he pushed me off, and the shivers left me. There ain't a whole lot of people in this world to trust, he said to me. But I do indeed am one of them.

Sounds like the ideal life, no? Food, bicycles? Maybe there was even talk of us moving to the Charles Memorial Houses in Howard Beach. Mr. P was feeling hopeful and he wanted to take Mama with him. Me as well, but then, that was never a question. I would follow Mr. P to the ends of the earth.

And in my happiness—things were going to be different; things were going to continue to flow with love—in my ignorance, I just kept turning that boombox a little louder every day. "Raspberry Beret," "Baby I'm a Star." Life was good as it got—I swore I heard Mama tapping her foot in the anteroom right before putting on her Witness smile and heading toward Junction Boulevard and Ninety-Ninth, to stand smack in front of ORGANIC DRY CLEAN, her stash of *Awake!*s diligently pressed in her hands. (As in Proverbs 13:20: The one dancing with the wise will become wise.)

She left. I turned up the volume. It actually *was* the ideal life. A few lies never hurt anybody.

You and me are on the same page, Mr. P said to me one day in the not too distant future.

That was never a lie.

PLOT THICKENER

So somewhere along the line Mama's Witness foot stopped tapping. *Dead* dead of winter, inside and out.

She never had gone in for those Kingdom Hall songs. White people music, she said. Plus how much salvation could you hope for from white people? Yes, Mama, I said. IMHO, Kingdom Hall music sounds like it only belongs in elevators and such, dentist offices. Sure enough one day Mama put her *Awake!* magazines on the shelf and took out the record player from underneath the hallway sofa. Something she'd carried over on a TWA jet from the Old Country. One record in and she ignored the Lord's voice shouting, QUIT TOUCHING THE UNCLEAN THING! and began moving her body in a way struck down her blood. She moved in a different, unmotherly way. She moved her body in something not prayer. She danced until the bolts of sweat pouring from her arms, legs, and head onto the floor made her fall on the couch and catch her breath. A pause, a drink of fresh crumbly two-family-house water. Then back to the dance, with only the shortest pause to the closet, to remove the hallowed boxes of family Polaroids, pictures of ladies she'd known in her life—Auntie Esme from Kingston, Auntie Bluebell from Gun Hill, Auntie Beverly from Laurelton—countless more, all the same brown, all-weather face. Where were the men? Who the hell cared? *Dem ladies make whole life*, she kept saying to herself, laying on the next round of records, moving. *How I miss mi Aunties so!* Turning up the gospel as loud as it could go, ignoring the stamping broom of Mrs. Harriet Brown from the upstairs apartment—Mama called me from where I was standing behind the door and asked that I be the lookout at the front window, to make sure no Witnesses were passing by. I pretended as I was told and went right back behind the door. Other than their stainless steel smiles, what made those Witnesses look any different from normal people? Meanwhile the records were laid upon like hands: Claudelle Clarke clear-singing "My God Is Real." Evangelist Higgins plain-singing "I've Made a Vow."

Jamaica was in the glacial air of our Queens. So was the *American trash*, who—according to Mama—could be forgiven in these moments. Sister Rosetta jaunt-singing "Up Above My Head." Inez Andrews moan-singing "Mary Don't You Weep."

She see but she blind, Mama shouted, her hips and shoulders, slow and fast, moving like an entirely new faith.

Days and days of this, a ritual. She never knew I was watching her. She mopped the sweat from the floor with the dress she'd just removed. Girdle, bra, bloomers. A few days before Christmas, she banged her ankle against the door behind which I was standing; my head crumpled like a cardboard box of ornaments. She collected herself, turned the music even louder. Would the Brown family go deaf? But, oh—the Polaroids of those women in her hands. They loved Aretha Franklin freak-singing "Amazing Grace." Gloria Bailey strong-singing "Jesus Be a Fence All Around Me Everyday." Those Polaroid women neither leaving nor staying.

Mr. P hummed that shit as well. On the sly I said to him, I know you be digging Prince just like me. To which he replied, It's a whole lot of crosses we have to bear, Gwin. Try and be a good girl.

Next day Mama looked me up and down at the dinner table. I'm only a woman, she sighed. I continued eating. I didn't want to shrug cause I was only a woman, too.

Next day Mama went into my room while I was struggling at the kitchen table with long division problems from Mrs. Kiluk of Special Ed Math 8. She gathered all my CDs and cassette tapes in her bare arms and wheeled them past me and opened the barred door and dumped them in the trash cans out front.

My posters—torn off the walls, crumpled into paper fists.

My magazines, pilfered from the darkest recesses of my twin mattress.

I imagined those Brown kids looting through my treasures in the trash cans, *early Christmas, come on down!*, wondering who in their right mind would get rid of this bounty? Prince, the King of Kings! What lunatic would toss . . . and then they would see Mama come out the door with her hands on her hips and her snow boots on the wrong feet. Her expression announcing they best not be digging through our things. Even though she was the originator of all this mis-happenstance. The Brown kids would scramble like rats back up to their apartment. The entire crumbly two-family would shiver.

Dat dere is the stuff of heathens. I nuh raise you for dat, Gwindolyn.

(But why is it a bad thing to be a heathen? If you remove the *TH* and replace it with a *V*, you get a much more realistic word, just saying.)

Change, change, change. Change of Fools. All that gospel music took effect, dug its claws in deep, never let go. Mr. P changed. He started talking the same mess as Mama. He was not one for *Awake!* or *Watch-tower*; nevertheless, he started strutting around with a little green New Testament and rubbing his thumb along its edges. He asked me what did I think tomorrow would bring? Did I fancy myself immune to the calamities of the world? If I did, then I was sadly mistaken. Mr. P claimed that a good church background could perhaps get me far in life, ensure me a better future than the one I was currently ensuring myself. Look at him, what a mess his life had turned out?

What do you mean? I asked.

He said, Perhaps living in the Lord will heal all your wounds, Gwindolyn. Heal the wounds between you and your mama. What wounds? I asked. Mr. P furrowed and unfurrowed his large black brow. You should forgive your mama ninety-nine times, she's only trying to save you, he said. Ninety-nine times? I asked. That's too much, even for a Jehovah's Witness! Mr. P said, Your mama loves you. I for one have never known such a love. I've been selfish with you. We cannot stop her. We can only go along and see if what she's doing is truth. I for one am not entitled to question.

But I thought you and me knew the truth all the time! *Diamonds and Pearls*, Mr. P! *Diamonds and pearls!*

I've been selfish with you, he repeated. All that Prince music might have you running the streets, Gwin, and what a waste of life that would be. You know what I'm saying, girl. Just look upstairs. Tamika Brown. Planning a baby shower in the ninth grade.

When I was quiet, he said, Be kind to your mama. She's the only one you got.

To which I shouted, When have I never?

To which Mr. P shouted, Do I have to spell it out for you? F-A-M-I-L-Y-W-A-Y. What a hurting that would cause you. The song ain't the problem. You get me?

To which I *had to* laugh—right in his damn face. Yeah, I got him—but did he *get me*? *I* was in the eighth grade. *I* had no intention of becoming a wife and mother in the ninth grade—*I* was no Patty Hawkins or Kensie Jenkins or Fannie Winters—or even Tamika Brown. Besides: if I became a wife and mother, then what would Mrs. Kiluk of Special Ed Math 8 say?

Mr. P had already closed his eyes. There is nothing more precious on earth than a mother's love, Gwin. Don't forget. You only get one. Shame I never had the experience.

What in the SAM HILL has that got to do with me?

From then on, Mr. P generally went his own way. He asked me how my day at school was and told me when he thought the sky looked like rain. Once, he mistakenly broke free from his new mind and wanted to know if I needed a new winter coat; would I like to go with him to the Salvation Army? They had good things over at the one near Jamaica Hospital.

But I was done. DONE. I wanted him to stop speaking in tongues. Who the hell did he think he was? Acting weirder and weirder each and every day. What if I acted weirder and weirder each and every day? Since there was no real way I *could* do it, I *faked* it. I would show Mr. P, I would show Mama how *wrong* they were by pretending how *right* they were. So.

I faked hanging out late, faked conversating with the eighth and ninth grade wives and mothers (though they STILL were not an attraction,

I have to admit); faked started failing my classes, faked started avoiding the look on Mrs. Kiluk's face when she saw me in the hall. (God, I hated that word: *potential*.) Faked doing the chore of cleaning the bathroom, faked saying good morning to Mrs. Brown on the way out the front door of our crumbly two-family, faked answering her when she asked if we were doing another spring cleaning soon? Not that she really cared, but were we? Were we wanting to get rid of any size 14 women's dresses? Size 12 kiddie shoes?

I faked grace over food, faked bedside prayers. *Now I lay me down to sleep, God, you just one big-head creep.*

Girl, what got into yuh?

Accordingly, things got worser than worse on Mama's end. Church music in the shower. Church music during *Judge Judy*, church music in the middle of the night. Church music with all its supplications, prevarications, libations, and gyrations. Church music before dinner. Church music after dinner (when all I really needed was help with my Special Ed Math 8 but was faking it too much to ask); church music seeping into my brain when I wasn't looking. Church music taking over unused corners and making itself at home. Prince lurked in my mouth, but then the music spilling forth from my loins was Dorothy Norwood's "Somehow I Made It." Church music affecting my Prince—how I hated that. Mr. P played gospel on WWRL and sometimes driving along toward the McDonald's near the airport, he would look at me and I would look at him and we knew—*we knew.* But it is so damn hard when you are a lie, when you are faking just about everything. Literally moments later he'd say, *I'm no ice cream father, Gwindolyn. Can't you just do this one thing?*

I'll never eat ice cream for as long as I live, I remember thinking.

Out the car, up the steps to school where I'd take my seat and begin to fake fail the math test. Mrs. Kiluk waited a good fifteen minutes to finally say to me: *Gwindolyn Parsons, will you please cease and desist? The other members of this class want to do well on their exam, not listen to your old-time church songs. No offense to your mama but sheesh.*

That's what she called them, old-time. And her being a white lady, I wondered how she knew this? There was no way in Hades Mrs. Kiluk had ever heard of Sister Rosetta or Gloria Bailey—or had she? Was it possible she (being as whitewashed as a chicken leg) had heard Alicia Myers singing "I Want to Thank You"? Or M.C. Hammer rapping "Goin' Up Yonder"? Mrs. Kiluk was all of four feet and deaf as a doornail. She wore a white lady's mustachio; most humans at PS 176 hated her. Most save for me. She said she was switching me into Regular Math 8 even though I'd been purposely screwing up my tests. She told me I really belonged in Honors Math 8, but one step at a time. Mrs. Kiluk told me Mrs. Foster would be my new teacher next year, and could I get my *act* together and just go back to being who I used to be, i.e., not a faker? Mrs. Foster only dealt with genius children such as myself. I switched to whistling Prince, though I knew Mrs. Kiluk didn't care for Prince either.

(Later Mrs. Kiluk would take me aside. *Gwindolyn, where is all your potential? I know this is not you.*)

It was, though. Meanwhile, back at the ranch, Mr. P continued to be as much of a lie as Mama. He got mad and made me go to bed without supper. He got madder and made me write I LOVE JESUS LIKE JESUS LOVES ME a hundred times in my composition book. He came into my room one night and kissed me on the forehead. I couldn't hate you if I tried, he said. But you only get one mother in life. Remember that.

What happened to yours? I asked.

I was not a good son, was all he answered.

Let's see. One day—a whole year of me loving and not loving Mr. P and remaining lukewarm on Mama—she went and got annoyed with the world (for no reason I could discern) and all but moved into Kingdom Hall over by Francis Lewis Boulevard. A building with no windows, unless you count the grates on the basement egress. She tried to get me to join the Witnesses and then called me a godless tramp for running away at the door each time. But tell me: who in their *right mind* would go into a church with no windows? And add insult to injury: why would I allow some suck-ass Elder tell me that Halloween was off-limits? Hell yes, I ran away . . . away from the doors of Kingdom Hall, all the while hoping Mama would come to her senses. Follow me, take me into her arms. It was not hopeless to have hope. Did she really love this place? All they talked about was end days, and no presents under the tree, and no looking back. (According to James, somewhere in the Bible: You do not know what your life will be like tomorrow.) Tell me honestly, Witnesses: Who *really* likes to stand with all the other Witnesses on street corners and try to make friends with complete and smelly strangers? Who *really* likes to knock on doors and pretend you don't see the episode of *Judge Judy* in the background *you* yourself wanted to be watching? Who really liked to think about the end of the world? Be honest, Witnesses!

Certain devastation was on their horizon, and *they seemed to like that fact a whole lot.*

One day Mr. P up and said he was going to visit a relative by the name of Miss Claudette over in the Pomonok Houses on Parsons Boulevard, and he packed his overnighter, which looked more like

Mama's suitcase from the Old Country. I'll be back in no time, he said, cupping my chin. That was the last I saw of him.

When, after a week of begging my mama to tell me what in Jehovah's name had happened to Mr. P, she wiped away a genuine tear and bade me listen. We were sitting at Regular Math 8 homework in the kitchen, her hand on mine. *Dat man's gone six feet under,* she admitted, kissing my eyelids, my cheeks, nothing but flashes of the Sunswick Creek, now wasted to watery memories of the Pleistocene.

Gwindolyn. My angel.

That was how I learned of his death.

EXCUSE ME BUT I NEED A MOUTH LIKE YOURS

I've said this before: my mama hated my Prince. *What sorta name—funny man dat—do he even like ladies???* (Believe me, her question did indeed have three question marks behind it.) Mama told me that Mr. P would be turning over in his grave if he heard me singing that filth. *"Little Red Corvette"?* Code word for: Intercourse. *"Diamonds and Pearls"?* Code word for: Reckless Abandon. *You get me? Mistah P died knowing yuh good girl. What he now be saying up in heaven?*

I couldn't imagine my world without Mr. P. I wished my mama dead instead. No regrets. Simple as pie.

Why listen dem nasty song name "1999"? Code word for: Armageddon. But wasn't her end of days supposed to have happened long ago?

We were standing in front of the shutterless Kingdom Hall over by Francis Lewis Boulevard—and once more she tried to make me a part of them. Nice clothes, hair brushed and straightened. My teeth brushed so many times they felt like stones in a river. Or smooth rocks at the bottom of the ocean. We no longer mentioned Mr. P's name. Even though it had only been a week.

Mama walked proud into Kingdom Hall and introduced me as her treasure, but I cut out of that place like a bat out of you-know-what. Didn't listen to the yelling in the wind. Locked the apartment door behind me. Sat in the bathtub. *I'm just a crazy fool, lost in the world of love* . . . Got out, dried myself, walked around our downstairs home smelling like lavender. Opened cabinets and stamped roaches. Ran a second bath, got right back in. Did not bother to look at a single sheet of the Regular Math 8 homework or *Julius Caesar* from English 8 or the Pre-Chemistry 8 review; just dropped my fat naked ass under heaps of pink bubbles thanks to Love's Baby Soft (I dumped the actual perfume into the tub!!!) (Yes, three exclamations!!!) and legs that danced in the air, bubbles flying, the floor a miserable lake— just days before, as it so happens, Mrs. Brown screeching at Mama asking how did she expect their darling Tamika to learn her Special Ed Math 9 when there was so much ruckus involved?

What ruckus? Mama had asked.

I'm just a crazy fool . . . I heard Mama's footsteps. You have NOT heard footsteps until you have heard Mama's footsteps.

Yuh possessed nuh question, she stated, slamming open the bathroom door and pulling me out by my ears. She told me to get myself dressed. To come see her in the kitchen when I was halfway decent. She looked at my naked body, my hands dragging along my thighs. Those used to be her thighs, once, too.

I arrived in the kitchen, tee shirt, GreatGirl jeans, socks. Mama was calm, Christian music playing on the kitchen radio, a man singing, James Cleveland, her secret sacred crush. Mama thought of the Old Country and ground her teeth—it wasn't fair! Girl was an enemy yet was not one. Why come here to this unholy place of red bricks and aluminum siding and half-dead sidewalks and sanitized beef patties and flat skies and sickly trees and ungrateful white people and lazy Black people? Sinners by the dozens abounded—was that a test of the Lord? Add to that an ungrateful daughter—pure stake in the heart. (Love covers a multitude of sins: Peter, Chapter Something or Other.)

Eventually the smell of lavender on my body turned to rust. The early-evening sun was as dimpled as the early-evening moon. Had both those planets been laughing at us? Mama would not look me in the face. She told me to go buy a loaf of bread. Wonder.

Out of thin air she produced two dollars and gave them to me without so much as a smack upside my head when I asked, *What bread only costs two dollars?* Rose from her chair as if in a trance. Mouthing the words JESUS JESUS JESUS. Gently shoved me toward the door, threw my winter hat behind. It wasn't actually that cold that day. But I grabbed up the hat (which went well with Mama's gloves, which I stole straight out her pocketbook, along with twenty-one more dollars, as she headed to the bedroom). Bye, I shouted. Her last words in my direction: *I want you to be in truf.* Goodbye, I said. As I closed the door, I could feel her fading into the hallway carpet. I heard the locks behind me. Radio silence.

I walked all the way to Genovese Drugs. The hell with the bread, I was thinking. *How can you just leave me standing, alone in a world that's so cold?* I wanted candy bars. Baby Ruth, Butterfinger, 3 Musketeers. I was her kid, she was my mom, God made us that way. I could only afford twenty bars so I went back home to get more money. I was her kid, she was my mom. Found the locks glued shut. Or maybe changed. I ran outside and looked, but the bars on the windows simply glared. I buzzed myself back into the vestibule (thank you, Tamika Brown)—kicked the metal fire door numerous times, screamed out Mama's first name over and over. It was a name from the Old Country, her home. All doors leading to nowhere.

Hell yeah. I knew that what Mama was doing was against the law. But at the moment, I also kind of liked it.

I wondered if Mr. P was looking over me. I pretended the night wind was his arm around my shoulder. Family Brown turned down their lights. It was all good—I had the arm of the wind on me, blowing hard. Bitter, confused-hearted chill. I moved to the sidewalk, hoping to be seen. And as if by Jehovah's command, an arm *did actually* appear and drag me by the scruff.

Will miracles never cease, I remember thinking, my last laugh for a long time.

(Had Mrs. Kiluk ever known the majesty of Prince Rogers Nelson crooning "Mary Don't You Weep"? Many years later, sitting on a park bench in Central Park next to my savior, Fern, I felt that yes. Yes. She quite possibly could have.)

MARY DON'T YOU WEEP

My mama's gonna be so mad. She's watching me out the window. Take your fucking hands off me.

She's gonna come get me.

Fuck off me, pervert!

(No, this isn't really happening.)

Don't, don't, don't.

I'm a church girl, I swear!

(Please don't!)

Yeah, I said some things I wish I could take back. Mama hated Prince, do you hate Prince?

Please, please, please.

Yeah, I shouldna left those hallowed doors but.

(No, this isn't happening.)

God help me.

What did I do to deserve this? I can kill you, too. Take this rope off me and see what I can do.

God.

Where am I?

Jesus! Hear me for once!

MISSING: ONE PRETTY-NUFF GIRL WHO IN REALITY BE
WICKED BRAT SHOULD BE HOME DOING CHORES OR AT
LEAST BRUSHING UP ON HER *SOUL*! PLEASE RETURN.
EVEN IF SHE SINGING GODLESSNESS.

FERN

God Helps Those Who Help Themselves.

Benjamin Franklin

THE OLD COLLEGE TRY

So you all know what's about to happen.

But before you get to those waterworks, another interruption: *Dig if you will the picture*: two girls smiling. No, they are not on the boardwalk at Coney Island or Rockaway Beach . . . but their faces are about to break open. In other words, they're smiling the biggest watermelons God has ever seen. God, in fact, had to step back and admire his handiwork: *Damn, did I do that?* The girls' faces are bruised, their hands grimy gray. Chains, maybe barbed wire, snake into their silhouette. From the one side they look like angels (even if they're on the cusp of their most gruesome decade ever)—because no amount of house dirt can hide those cherubic cheeks. From the other side they look like the Devil. No, they are not possessed, nor have they been drugged into altered states. These girls are cheery; one could even go so far as to say they are *buoyant*, and though they are moments away from being slung farther apart by big huge meaty man-hands, the girls are positively upbeat.

They have discovered each other. One time, two time, three. It's a secret, but they feel like shouting it to the world: I AM NOT ALONE!

In the flash of a microscopic eye, they see each other's outlines and forget all doom and gloom. Forget that just moments ago, they believed they would die here, all by themselves, forgotten, left behind like so much dust bunny dirt. The truth is, the girls have found a way to one another. They've found that if they claw against the sheetrock/floors/ceilings and find a gash or a slash in the fortifications, they can actually see one another. Gaze upon a *new countenance*.

You.

YOU!

YOU!!!

These girls are (as per the poem that Mr. Canton made us read *even though we were in Western Civ I*) SURPRISED BY JOY (*impatient as the Wind, we turned to share the transport— Oh! with whom?* Each other, natch!)—these girls are relieved. It was if they'd suddenly been blanked into normal girls in a normal world, a normal Queens, flip phones on faces and Game Boys in pockets. Gwin and me recognize eyes and noses and, in general, the full flavor of our faces, and we try to reach our cheeks with our hands—but damn those chains! Never mind. Never mind. At least we can *see*.

You!

YOU!

YOU!

YOU!

Our imaginations revved back up. Gwin and I saw ourselves almost as if we were two characters in a book of fairy tales. Two fun-loving females *flaneuring* around Flushing Meadows Park or else strolling the ever-enticing Queens Center mall or dipping into an empty church, about to take it over the way church should be taken over. Our fingers (worn to nubs in only fourteen days or fourteen months) felt like piano keys. *I can hear your breath! No, I can hear yours! Can you sing something, just so I know you're real?*

We didn't dare say Boss Man's name. But we thought it many times, the air around us souring if we were quiet in our minds. But who could be quiet? Miracles were taking place! The hole in the dividing wall (concrete? muslin? cardboard?) grew larger, right before our eyes. There was no house wind, no toppling—I was a real shadow and so was she; even if all we could do was ask, over and over: *Are you there?* and answer: *I am.* And widen our eyes in astonishment: Does this mean—?

DOES THIS MEAN—?

DOES THIS MEAN—???

And soften our faces with each iteration: How can it not?

(I won't tell you everything that came immediately after *that*. It's so, so much. I'll leave that to your own fruitful imaginations.)

What I will share instead are the following fairy tales. They *did* happen to Gwin and me. Our voices ran like boulevards to and from each other. *Do you remember what pizza tastes like! Hell, I can't even remember what pizza is!*

To hear a voice is to beg for a story. Our bones soon understood that we weren't each other's rescues, not in the freedom sense we'd begged for. Her profile and mine were all we had: Boss Man's victims, his dolls, his fatalities, his targets, his babushkas, his casualties, his *don't-call-us-victims-cause-we're-so-much-more-than-that*. We eventually stopped crying. We told each other our nicknames. We asked the obligatory mother questions. We told each other stories. We promised one another we'd remain strong. We rejoiced a handful of minutes in human time.

I'm Gwin and maybe can I help you?

I'm Fern. I mean the same thing.

ONCE UPON A TIME, IN A LAND FAR AWAY

a. I have this great little brother, Bud. You would SO love Bud. Even though once he told he'd make me a Christmas Club account but I would need to give him my allowance of thirty dollars because that's how much it cost to start one, and he didn't blink an eye. I found the money, stuck it in his pocket. He was only a little kid. What the hell did he know about money? Bud busted out crying. Talking about *I'm so mean, I'm such a mean brother.* (Turns out a Christmas Club account didn't cost anything.) Innerly, Bud had discovered he could not be a criminal, not even for the least division of an hour. Let's go and make up, he cried; and then us sneaking out, to the deli at the end of the block, where we found bikes (carelessly) leaning against a telephone pole. We took off. One of the best days in my life. Our lives. We whirred for miles, the street asphalt, the dogshit elms, and toward the Hall of Science—right up to its fat belly, the forever-closed glass doors. Nothing. Many a school trip had been undergone here, and in our various school lives, we'd spent much time laughing the place off (*This museum is so damn lame!*) to secretly admiring the two space rockets in the yard (*God, I love science. Me the hell too!*)—just Bud and me flying by, screeching like we invented screeching. At one point, Bud threw his bike to the ground and commenced climbing

an old sycamore that sat blottoed right in front of those rockets. *Fern, come look!*—my brother, climbing where no man had
ever climbed before, sliding out to the farthest branch like a
nightingale—oh Bud, my heart's *best treasure*! I watched him;
I couldn't stop. He told me to go search at the front doors for
fallen change, but then I reminded him of the thirty dollars in
my pocket—better to spend them now, he called out, than to
let anyone else find them. Like who? Bud peered down like a
hawk. Was he about to jump? Minutes later and there we were
at the mysterious ice cream truck mysteriously looping around
the mysterious Avenue of Science. *We'll take two*, I said—and
then the strange looks from the mysterious man in the mysterious ice cream truck—who, when I got back to Math 8,
I learned was Winona Johnson's uncle, somewhat tickled in
the head from grenades that had gone off too soon in his own
hands. (*Don't you be making fun of my uncle! Thank him for his service,
goddamnit!* Now, now, Winona, I was just saying that he looked
lonely, that was all, lonely as a cloud, and me and Bud wanted
to make him feel not lonely, so we gave him our money and he
gave us his best Strawberry Shortcake. Is that okay, Winona?
*Girl, you best leave me alone. Ain't nobody asked you to buy anything
from that cretin!* I hear you, Winona, girl. I got me a cretin at
home, too.) And so it went.

We get the bikes, ride around the front of the art museum,
detour to the Grand Central Parkway, laugh at crows trying to
pick up dead cat meat there, spin back round to the giant skeleton of the world, and lie down in the grass. Bud didn't laugh
when I said I wanted to grow up to be anything *but* a nurse.
A lion tamer, maybe. An authoress. A famous cook on TV
where I jumped over chairs, drank grape juice pretending to
be red wine, and deep-fried butter for breakfast. Bud laughed.
He told me about wanting to have ten or more kids on a farm

upstate with his "spouse," and when he said "spouse," he looked at me but I didn't laugh. No words necessary—did I mention that the air was warm and the fuzz on our arms felt like bruised peaches? Why can't moments like that last forever? Did it really happen? I think so. We eventually return to the telephone pole, count the remaining money—*hey, did Winona's uncle cheat us?* Ideas swirling: Let's do this again tomorrow, okay? Sure thing. Then, back inside where we lived: dinner at the hands of someone, bedtime, no books, plenty of dreams. The Creamsicle sunrise, the Dutch singing. *Sleep, children, sleep.* Next day Bud and I snuck out as soon as the mother left for her extra shift at the hospital and we ran to the telephone pole, but by then the bikes we'd so thoughtfully and respectfully replaced were gone.

b. I was alone. Someone left the damn door to the damn Assembly of Faith open, and who in their damn mind would choose to ignore such a thing? Damn if it wasn't me. In exactly one hour it was gonna be the Caribbean Queen tryouts—Pastor Williams had said the week before that Billy Ocean himself was coming to be a guest judge, but when I said who the hell is that, Pastor Williams told me any more opening my mouth and my chance would be ruined. I wanted to point out that Mama promised me I would win. Yes, she said she would return to this church but ONLY FOR THE CONTEST; the Witnesses were her life now. She said all I had to do was apply myself. I was no looker but neither was she, and back in the Old Country, she had won Miss Banana Leaf, so miracles *can do* come true!

I wanted to say all that.

I was alone in the Assembly of Faith. No other girls for miles around. Mama was outside in the parking lot talking to someone who could've been a deaconess or a Dime Savings Bank teller. I twirled around the pulpit and then I went up on the stage and twirled some more. I could twirl. I could twirl like nobody's business. Then Assistant Pastor Todd came in. *What you doing here so early, Miss Gwindolyn, don't you have homework like a good girls?* and I wanted to scream, LIKE A GOOD GIRL! but I didn't. Assistant Pastor Todd stood at this same pulpit alongside Pastor Williams every Sunday and Wednesday and Friday and Saturday and argued us into being good. When they spoke, people nodded their heads like robots, agreeing and agreeing and taking their medicine right up till they walked back into the parking lot, where it was all: *Who died and made them preachers God? Flabbergasting fake-ass Philistines.*

I was all by myself. The walls of the Assembly of Faith were covered in gold. The cross behind the pulpit looked down in the dumps. I felt around in my pocket for my application for the Caribbean Queen contest; Mama had signed my name for me. GINDOLYN. How the hell can you forget how to spell your own progeny's moniker? I waited for Assistant Pastor Todd to use the men's room, went and locked the door behind him, retook the pulpit, opened the first page of the Bible, and gave a damn good speech. Friends, Romans, and countrymen. Lend me your ear. What the World needs Now is LOVE, SWEET LOVE. Not PUNISHMENT for trying to live your best life. And YES, IT IS POSSIBLE IN THE EIGHTH GRADE TO KNOW WHAT YOUR BEST LIFE IS. Amen. I walked up and down the aisles, imagining those with sin in their heart—boys who wouldn't get any Kentucky Fried Chicken for a week just because of some damn C- on a math test, girls who thought about ways to cast spells to make those chicken boys love them—and I began to sing. *Glory, Glory, Hallelujah! Teacher Hit You with a Ruler! Glory, Glory, Hallelujah! His*

Troops Keep Marching On! If you asked me, I sounded like an angel. Beauty pageant winners need to be on their A game! Wit, intelligence, creativity! Back up at the pulpit, watching the girls slowly file in and laugh. *I'm Coming Out! I Want the World to Know, Got to Let It Show!* Mama being nowhere near my action and thus not knowing the depths of my corruption. In time, the last of the wannabes trickled in. Hot curlers. Wicked weaves. Flat irons flatter than Alley Pond. The mothers asked, Where's Assistant Pastor Todd? Ain't he supposed to be judging this tryout?

Ooh, I heard it was Billy Ocean!
Girl, stop lying!
As God is my witness! (No pun intended.)
What?

I was already anticipating a whipping from my mama because she didn't like things that in Queens and overall America were known as *a sense of humor.* But I couldn't stop singing. I could not remove myself from the pulpit and I could not allow the hands of a newly freed Assistant Pastor Todd to pull me down, into the pit of unworthy girls. At least they had their looks. No brains, but who cared. Certainly no sense of humor. No way in hell was I the prettiest Caribbean Queen. *Now we're sharing the same dream. And our hearts they beat as one.* But here's what I could win for: daringness, kindness, a good heart. And let's not forget: *a sense of humor.* (How my mother regretted letting me watch all those Bugs Bunny cartoons.) When we got home, she said this was another instance of my confounding devilment. Said that if *this* church didn't make me a good girl, she would keep searching until she found one that did.

Wouldn't you like to come to Kingdom Hall with me?

Is that a serious question?

(We all want to be the good girls we want to be. Why didn't my mama get that?)

Because *this day.* Up and down the church. I preached, I sang, and from the stained glass windows surrounding, I felt Jesus. I went and put the Bible back on the pulpit. I tore up my application to become the next Caribbean Queen and let the pieces flutter to the ground like doves. I felt Jesus. Assistant Pastor Todd as red in the neck as any Trinidadian man can get. I felt Jesus; but at one point I had to tell that sucker to stop laughing or he'd get us both in more trouble.

WESTERN CIV I

Surprised by joy—impatient as the Wind
I turned to share the transport—Oh! with whom
But Thee, long buried in the silent Tomb,
That spot which no vicissitude can find?
Love, faithful love, recalled thee to my mind—

Etc. etc.

LINNAEUS

We found each other. We took stock of the rules quickly.

When you are lost, the first thing is: *cry*. The second thing is: *cry*. The next thing is: *scream, cry, beg, rant, cry, forget, kick, dig, holler, beg, regret, cry*.

Remember is not on the list of things to do when you are lost.

It's not part of the system that has been worked out by you and whatever God or Jesus is looking down upon you and the rest of the motherfucking creatures on earth: the mice, the roaches, the ants, the amoebas. The system is the system. The list of things is the list of things—all working like electrodes from your toes to your brain, reminding you exactly *who* and *when* you are. When you are lost, the first thing is: *cry*. It's not written in stone, it's written in blood.

You are in a desert; you are alone. Perhaps there is a crowd in the distance as tall as the World Trade Center, yet you never get close enough to make out any faces. But suddenly one day: you see one. A face. And the crowd is nothing but a girl. Like you. Then there's a momentary flicker, then back to dark. The girl was pulled away and the gash replaced with a slab of sheetrock or muslin or cardboard. You are back to your individuality.

But I knew that a girl named Gwin was there. And she knew it of me as well.

Birds of a feather, people.

THE NIÑA AND THE PINTA

What was the passage of time? Did it move like pages in a book, blowing on the street after someone had let the novel drop, so that nothing, nothing, made any sense? I kept thinking: Well, at least the mother's second boyfriend isn't around to mess with me. The wind blowing through crevices, cracks, chipping plaster, and sheetrock. Cold comfort. The way the wind swung the line after I'd been cut down. I knew not to trust it.

There were also the patterings of miscellaneous feet. Most belonging to mice (soft) or to Boss Man (loud as cast-iron skillets). One time or maybe more, I heard the patterings of old lady toes, you could hear the age in the bunions. Tentative yet persistent. When nothing happened, I learned not to trust those either.

BLACKGUARDS

In the beginning. One time I saw Gwin and I tripped over my words. Blubbered, to be exact. Was it because she was upside down, and my job was to mop the mess below? I'm Fern in the flesh, I croaked. Remember me?

Gwin was blood. Yet and still: I saw a tiny smile crack underneath all that wallpaper paste. It seemed to say: *Where have you been all my life?*

IN MEDIAS RES

So it was me and Gwin for the longest amount of days and nights (or dim walls and darkened walls cause there was no window, no sun, no slink of the moon to guide us).

Me and Gwin. I learned that she dug music, but at first I couldn't get her to go beyond that. I thought of other topics. Which do you like better? I asked her. Whispered through concrete. Which do you like better—mothers or aunties?

Gwin answered back, I know neither.

I answered back, Me, too.

I do love me some Prince. Does he count more in the mother direction or the auntie direction?

I have no idea, I said. Does it matter?

Maybe it was a year (or a year and a half or two years or two years and a half) before we heard another voice. We had begun to think of ourselves as Adam and Eve, only we couldn't figure out who got the man part.

The new voice. It was not singsongy and it did not weep. The plaster walls of that haunted house that had (for so long) hidden Gwin from me and me from Gwin (now) suddenly opened up like Moses parting Jamaica Bay, and there she was. The new girl.

Eyes round as subway tokens. Mouth as dark as the Number 7 subway tunnel. We couldn't get her to speak for days or weeks or maybe even months—what was the passage of time? Silent as the grave. She just used her eyes for looking.

But that was okay. We were fine just to wait.

IN MEDIAS RES II

And then one day she—the new girl—began to open up like a flower, a brown-eyed Susan your dark-skinned Mystery Date wears in his lapel. Full of possibilities.

The new girl had perhaps stepped out of Andrew Lang's *Yellow Fairy Book* (Gwin's favorite volume, especially the story "How to Tell a True Princess"); Gwin said she looked like what a standard girl should look like. Me personally? I would have compared this new girl to Chaka Khan with the fur bikini and feathers, swear on my brother's life. I could tell her soul had seen delight and recuperation. I could tell people had once loved to look at her. Nothing customary about her at all.

From the mice we gathered her name was Jesenia. And from the beginning we worshipped her like God, Jesus, Moses, and the V. Mary all rolled into one.

She appeared on a day when both me and Gwin were duct-taped together in PIPES LOW & HIGH—who knew that stomachs could feel so jagged and smooth at the same time? You could say we were wearing duct-tape bikinis. You could say our ribs stuck out like a row of smiles.

Through hazy lazy floozy eyeballs, we saw her there—a girl dressed in white from head to toe, with an *actual* flower behind her ear, sporting a pair of real shoes. Sunday school shoes. White stockings and a white net over her head, attached to a white beret, real old lady. We nearly stopped breathing. The color white—we'd almost forgotten it!

Gwin and I forced ourselves to get clearheaded; we struggled to unstick at least some part of our conjoined bodies. For God's sake, Gwin shouted, We ain't fucking Chang and Eng!

We asked the new girl who she was (the mice could get things wrong at times). No answer. We told her our names. No answer. Don't let us scare you, I said. We aren't always like this. Yeah, Gwin added. We just got a new tee shirt just last week or just yesterday, sometime. We take turns. There's not too much blood.

No answer. She looked at us long and hard and eventually went away. Or was led away. Who knew—in the beginning, Gwin and I were used to mirages.

Are you sure you seen her?

Are you sure?

You?

Later, when our minds recovered from all that *duct-stickiness* and *rope-upside-downness*, Gwin and I tried to puzzle out a new approach to this delicate creature, whose skin, like her clothing, was the color of a coconut's insides, as seen in the September 1977 *Ladies' Home Journal*; we didn't want to scare her. For truth, we did look a mess. Had either of us seen a comb or toothbrush? Had soap touched our skins—ever? The answer would have been clear to a dead person. Suddenly we felt ashamed.

We saw her next in the LOWER-EMPLOYEE-WORK-DEPARTMENT—what was the passage of time?—Gwin and I preparing that day's lunch out of the pages of an old cookbook that supposedly belonged to Boss Man's mother, *Easy Mouth-Watering Buffets*. Jesenia still wore those white shoes, only now they were streaked with red and orange and blue and brown. Her dress was a man's tee with the collar bone scooped out. She wiped her eyes with her shoulder until her shoulder began to melt. The tears were invisible (we knew that kind well) and the sounds barely audible, like the choked paper of easy tuna fish creams and potted meat soufflé. Jesenia's mouth opened and closed quietly enough for a mouse to hear. Still, Gwin and I stretched our unified head lengthwise toward her shoulders—as long as we could since the silver chain tying our torsos to the butcher block table reached but so far. Our hands were free.

We asked her a question. *Do you know more than we do?*

We asked another question: *Are our names on outside lips?*

We asked a third question: *Do you know where we are?*

All this time Gwin and me had been thinking this was a house but now wondering if perhaps we were stuck in a really big apartment? Was this the South Jamaica Houses? It smelled a little like the South Jamaica Houses. People heard everything you did in the South Jamaica Houses, including sneeze, fart, kiss, scream, and die. The mother's second boyfriend claimed to have survived the South Jamaica Houses back in the day: Supreme Team looking to mow you down if you so much as said a word, he told me; sitting back satisfied, fake Cheshire cat grin, probably never held a crack pipe in his life, the sucka, why was he sealing his pretend lips with a pretend finger?

Do you know more than we do?

Jesenia's words came slowly. I remember her syllables forming. *Why you girls don't know where you are? Shit yeah, you in a house. We all be.*

Subject-verb agreement, Gwin whispered. No, I whispered back. Poor syntax.

We got no idea where we are. You like the Eyewitness News that comes on at six on Channel Seven. Tell us what you know.

She didn't smile. It seemed her words vaporized like Star Trek beams. We knew she was scared. (DUH, you might be saying. But it wasn't DUH for us, not then.)

Gwin said, Look, girl. Whatever you call yourself. We been locked up. Hanged on ropes. Had our memory-brains washed out with soap. We have no idea. Tell us what you know.

Ditto, I murmured. What's your name, you don't mind us asking?

Jesenia clapped her hand over her mouth. Were her fingernails painted white? Maybe more of a Maybelline opalescence? But her eyes—at us. Holy shit and then some. You mean you girls locked up here? Holy fuck. The minute I get out this joint I promise you my boyfriend's gonna come back and rescue you and shit.

Gwin persisted. What I mean to say is: Is it morning outside? Is it night? Do you know if any ladies that look like our mothers are standing in the street, looking for us?

I said, Did you maybe see a mixed lady wearing a nurse's uniform walking around calling my name? A mixed lady that maybe looked *sad or mad*?

Jesenia did not let her hand fall from her mouth. Now her neck was melting, her ears. Her eyes pure salt.

I said, What's your name? You want to know ours?

Somewhere in the distance, we heard the roar of Boss Man. Over vines and treetops and flat salt lakes reminiscent of Don Juan Pond over in Antarctica.

She sobbed. How long you girls been here? He told me it would just be for a few days. He told me I could go anytime.

Gwin asked, You have a cell phone? Our mothers used to keep one in the glove box in order to call 911. You have one?

Jesenia answered, Don't need nothing like that. He said I could go when I wanted anytime cause it was just to see how I liked him and he liked me.

Gwin said, Then why you wearing that silver chain? That don't look like anytime to me.

But he told me.

(If there'd been a way to laugh—but then again, we were not mean-spirited.)

Jesenia crumpled as far to the ground as her chain would allow, then held her mouth to her other shoulder, which also slowly began to sag.

We asked her if she had a mother. Jesenia started crying even more.

(Later—a day or a week or a month later—Gwin and I agreed that that had been an unnecessary question, given the fact that we could be separated at any moment and needed to use our words wisely.)

When we saw her next—unchained but as stretched out as a rubber band—we didn't ask anything. The new girl hissed, a long pliant sound: Don't go looking at me like that. I'm just visiting. Then my boyfriend is coming to get me, end of story. And I can tell you this. Play your cards right and I might tell my boyfriend to come back for you. He won't mind. Don't look at me with them eyes. He's good like that.

She sounded drunk. But Gwin and I knew that Boss Man didn't approve of drinking on the job.

And anyway, who were we to judge? Tape over our stomach, hands, and feet. Pasted together in the corner of PASS-THROUGH-CHASM (just like Chang and Eng, no matter what Gwin said). Jesenia had no chains and yet she was hanging, just like we'd been doing all this time. Rusted clothesline posture. Drooped like a prize doe. She turned her head toward us but then looked away. We had no choice but to stare. Had we been looking like prize deer all this time, too?

Gwin said, You never answered our question. Where are we? Is it morning or night?

I have no idea, Jesenia said. But I used to have an idea, all the time.

And then it was one week or two weeks or three before a light came on from some kind fairy-tale god somewhere; and we all lay together on a mattress, Gwin with her arm taped to her body because it was probably broken and Jesenia with her arms taped to her body because she'd tried running through the walls. All of us, naked, wilted. Where were the white shoes? Nothing nurse or cotillion, Sunday worst all day long. What shoes had I been wearing when Boss Man recruited me? Where were they now? Jesenia turned toward us, her face dark as an umbrella. I changed my mind, she whispered. We getting outta this shithole. Sooner than you know. Word to the mother.

What's that supposed to mean? I asked, honestly.

Word, Jesenia replied.

SURVIVAL TECHNIQUES

You'd have thought all was clear as day. Her resolve, ours. But then.

She whispered to us through walls. You know? He's not such a bad guy if you get to know him. Know him like I do. Your parents probably got so sick and tired of you, and it didn't help, your attitudes. Now here he is, giving us all a second chance. And I'm feeling nothing but ungratefulness coming out you. Girls, listen. I'm not going crazy. This is about growing up. It's about love.

Could she hear me and Gwin quivering? Laughing? Weeping? Could she sense us through the layers of plaster, plywood, and rot? There we were. Duct tape and ropes. Rust air. Chains and cardboard. Could she recognize?

I see I got my work cut out for me, Jesenia continued. We heard the rustle of the chain. We continued to dry up.

TYPICAL SCHEDULE

1 a.m. Rousing. Rusting. Rustling. Tussling. Bustling. Screaming. Mothers.

1:30 What is it, the monthlies? Shit, the monthlies. Take the rag/baby diaper/cardboard/egg carton/torn-up sheet. Wash it forever as there is no more where that came from.

1:45 Three grapes—old but who cares. Work: count the scrapes on the basement floor. Make sure washing machine is empty or full with one of you.

2 a.m. Tussling. Mothers. Father-types. Nightmares following around like lost dogs.

2:15 (Once a week. Shower from garden hose attached to washing machine sink attached to . . . ? Boss Man says hidden spring runs beneath us. Sunswick Creek. Believe. Remember that old horrible thing called *school,* which you now love more than your own soul. Screaming. Mothers.)

2:30 Cardboard eggs or real. Recipes for fruit velvet and steak Diane. Teeth inspection. Teeth extraction. Learn how to hide pliers but learn how to find them, too.

3 a.m. CHORES.

3:15 CHORES.

3:30 CHORES. MODEL EMPLOYEES.

3:45 Garden hose up the wazoo. Boss Man says this keeps the monthlies at bay. Hot water from the washing machine who you always thought was your friend.

4 a.m. Convos with all forms of rodentia, ghosts, children. Mothers. Brothers you might have treated better had you known. Had you known.

4:15 Attempted friendship. Tussling. Is it everyone else AND you or is it just YOU? Keeping feelings of jealousy/vengeance at bay. Sleep.

4:30 It's a reality. Get over it.

5 a.m. Sounds: a siren. A bird. A crash. That's nothing for you. A slap across your ever-loving face. Learn to be deaf.

5:15 CHORES.

5:20 Rousing. Fear of not being able to rouse.

5:30 Relief at the ever-powerful magic of rousing.

5:45 Breakfast: an egg. Shells and all—who knows when an egg will come along again? Beggars can't be choosers.

5:47 Dream of the past. (I told you heifers to stop that. Don't no one remember you! Isn't nobody coming for you, either! And it's no way you gonna make your stupid night dreams come true, so shut up!)

5:48 Clean out buckets. Nighttime slop. Daytime agony.

5:49 I WILL MAKE YOU SHUT UP.

6 a.m. It's your birthday. Pretend cake with Cool Whip frosting. No, not the day you were born to your mother. The day you were born here. Make believe you blow out the candles. One, two, three. Whitebait and syllabub.

6:45 Monthlies eventually go away. Are you too skinny? Are you no longer a female?

6:50 No, sadly. You are doomed to be a female for eternity. WORK. Shadows. Voices. WORK. Outlines. Rope. Chains. Light. WORK. More light.

BECAUSE ONCE UPON A TIME

There were all the things Boss Man did.

SORT OF EXACT DETAILS

Push me up, push me down, push himself inside us. Spread my legs, press my ribs, push himself inside us. Rip my hair right off my head, slip his tongue into my blood, scalp me, scalp us, smack us, whack us, tear our lids off one by one, push himself inside us. Rub his fingers, rub his hands, rub along my private dips, rub till I was *squeaky clean*, push himself inside us. Ram his dick a hundred times, now in this hand, now in that, "getting ready for bigger and better things," push himself inside us. Pull my teeth out one by one, spit the blood into my face, push himself inside us. Finger up and down my ass, one spoon or fork or knife at a time, push himself inside us.

Hold off just a tiny bit—in the beginning. He said he wanted no babies. No babies with any of us—then SHOVE HIS EXTREMITY TOWARD GENERATIONS OF KIDS. Push himself inside us.

Break our nose by two-by-fours, fingers, fists, foist the one stainless steel pot we owned in and out our brains, fracture our wrists, call our mothers motherfuckers, our fathers fucking freaks, our innocent young brothers bastards. Wake us up in case we fell asleep. Itch into our unconscious. Slide into our subconscious. Drive nails in our ears, serve screws and sawdust for meals, push himself inside us.

Tell us fairy tales, fall drunk asleep. Leave us alone for days and days, decomposing, decompressing, later claiming he was visiting family, later admonishing: How could I forget you? Tenderness in voice, was something happening? Good or bad? Was this what it meant to see your life flashing? Saying things, promises, promises. Tell me you miss me. Tell me you wanna work forever. Shut your mouth. No, open it so I can push myself inside you.

Telling us we were lucky to be alive, lucky to have him, such a gracious employer, a sweetheart, better than Jesus Christ or the Virgin Mary all rolled into one.

It's gonna be all right, just you wait and see. I don't hate you girls. I actually like you lots.

Tenderly removing a swath of hair from our over-cried mouths. Getting ready to again commit something for which we had no human name.

RETURN TO ME

Boss Man asleep somewhere. Meanwhile, Jesenia's voice floated to us on a cloud of sheetrock. We could not see her. We didn't have to.

Tell me the last thing you remember, girls, she called out.

A bed, Gwin answered.

Platform shoes, I said.

A turtle.

A tampon.

Ambulances.

A VHS tape. No, a DVD.

Egg and bacon on a kaiser roll *salt pepper ketchup*.

Muddy footprints on the carpet. Callaloo and scotch bonnets.

Laundry detergent in those little laundromat boxes.

My father's Afro pick.

Mine's, too.

Oh, I didn't know you had a daddy, Fern.

I used to make him up from time to time. We called him original but that's the name everyone gives to specters, I think.

Shame.

Were we normal?

Perfectly normal. Same goes for me and Mr. P. Only he died.

So sorry, Gwin.

Apology accepted, girl.

Take one last look at your Memory Lane, Jesenia called out again. Then turn yourself face forward. Because if you *chicas* keep on looking back, those things will disappear forever. You'll never retrieve them—ever. You got to face forward and take that shit with you in another way.

I remember breakfast cereal and Don Cornelius's face, I said.

Please don't get me started on Don Cornelius's face, Gwin said back.

BUT THE BEAT GOES ON

MODEL EMPLOYEES. In chains, and we worked for Boss Man, all three of us: addressing envelopes that went nowhere, scraping plaster that could also serve as soap, patching holes, shining pipes. We were way busy. We learned to embrace busy. Because busy meant less time to worry about where to go to the bathroom (drain or floor). Busy meant less time to worry whether you felt eating pictures of pot roast and pink divinity from the September 1977 *Ladies' Home Journal* was the same as eating real food (if you close your mind, you can pretend a lot of things, Boss Man had instructed us when we complained of empty stomachs). Busy was a lifesaver.

Busy took hold of your sores and sighs and dreams of BEHIND WORLD, shrinking that all into something as small as a wart on your thumb. You can turn yourself into a machine, even if you've never touched metal before (at least not voluntarily). You can become a stainless steel box with gears that shift from *go* to *gone*, you can become a *permanent contraption*. The hell with skin and veins and period blood. This is how you make life. You stay busy. You don't look back. This is how you are born again.

ATTRIBUTES

Our favorite hobby? Our only hobby? Being part of a Mutual Admiration Society (or *MÁS*, as Jesenia liked to call it). We made the time for that. We weren't savages, after all.

Jesenia could twist her tongue into a U and juggle four rocks in one hand and recite the preamble backward and forward; she knew all the words to her best friend Felicia's favorite book, *The Devil's Handbook for Girls* (it didn't matter that this was the girl everyone in her high school called *Fast Felicia*—Please don't use the word *fast* around me, Jesenia asked).

Jesenia taught us about time. REAL TIME. For example: that I was stolen first, then Jesenia, then Gwin. Gwin just seemed like she was second because Jesenia was still on her honeymoon phase (aka, she got to sleep in Boss Man's car, strapped to the steering wheel, the windows rolled up, until further notice).

Gwin said, Thanks for straightening that out for us, Jesenia. Sequences can be a girl's best friend.

Jesenia could recite every last Aesop fable, every single multiplication table, every Roach Motel warning ("Keep out of the hands of children"). Jesenia told us the true version of every story we could remember, even the ones the librarians handed us during Saturday morning reading clubs. Jesenia's details blew our minds—how had we been so blind? *Cinderella was a super sweet girl with a Napoleon complex, unfortunately.* We hung on her every word. *Jack was a stupid ass for bringing home those beans. If I'd a been his mother, he'd a been smacked three ways to Sunday. Sleeping Beauty's problem was that she went for the first kiss. No one was telling her to rush. She should a known: buyer beware!*

Jesenia's voice was loud as she spoke to us—many times from some location in the house neither I nor Gwin could establish. Boss Man rarely heard the talk, too drunk, druggily occupied. He once told me, after shoving me inside BROKEN-DOWN-WASHING-MACHINE, that he had done me the biggest favor of them all. He never told me what exactly that favor was.

Another time, when Gwin and I for no *new* reason broke into mad, mad tears, Jesenia began a fairy tale, her voice as loud as the Jamaica Station bell: *This is the story of Goldilocks and the Three Bears. If I tell you this, will you promise to dry your fairy-tale tears?*

(When had anyone ever talked about our tears so sweetly?)

She cleared her throat.

> *There was a dark place in the woods and gingerbread on the roof eaves and comfy beds and cold noses. A girl (not stupid but no brainiac either) got lost in these woods but started finding her way and then the sun came out and then she started meeting new friends so what did it matter, a cold draft or a few smacks on the face? Hay que vivir la vida, the end.*

This was how all Jesenia's stories closed. Simple and sweet. Gwin and I ate that stuff up.

Can you tell us another one?

Maybe later. Dry your eyes. Promise me you ain't gonna cry no more.

We promise.

Remember what I said.

We remember.

She was quiet. And we wondered about her whereabouts in Boss Man's territory. Was she suddenly licking the dead wasps pasted to the corner of the LOWER-EMPLOYEE-WORK-DEPARTMENT? Or was she being rolled out with a human rolling pin near PIPES LOW & HIGH?

It was one day—a month or five months or five years into our stay with Boss Man—me and Gwin hanging like icicles in PASS-THROUGH-CHASM, our skin shivering, ears sewn open—it was that day that Jesenia announced she had come up with a few new endings to the old fairy tales. We waited, licking our chops. We imagined *her* imagining *us*—we felt her heat, saw her picture-perfect lips talking about bears and girls and grandmothers and queens and princes. So this is what happens, girls.

> *Goldilocks finally meets up with her mother and they go shopping at Queens Center mall. Later that night, the littlest bear asks Goldilocks to prom at Flushing Meadows. And the next day Papa Bear and Mama Bear file for divorce but are still the best of friends.*

Thank you, Jesenia, we said. You saved us, like, literally.

Our imaginings grew as our stomachs shrank, as our lady parts evaporated. Do you know what it's like to be saved? *Thank you thank you thank you. We won't come back with stupid beans!*

Because that was our Jesenia. Maybe a mostly one-sided *MÁS* but who cared? She was fine with us and we were over the moon with her. Jesenia's gorgeous stories healed us faster than Jesus touching the lepers. Or Moses, God, and the V. Mary all rolled up into one.

COMPLICATIONS FROM A FAIRY TALE

She liked us to worship her. There was a lot to worship. But sometimes it was all these weak moments. Sometimes Jesenia forgot to tell us a story after Boss Man went away. Or she forgot where she was in the story, leaving us literally hanging on the edge (ha ha, get it? Hanging on the edge?)—her voice quivered and quisped and quaked. She made up terrible endings. Sometimes a big bad wolf came in and devoured the littlest bear. Sometimes Mama Bear's voice curdled into sour milk or else Papa Bear broke all the beds with his heavier-than-sheetrock ass. Gwin and I would look up, and the nonexistent glass in our cement-filled windows would shatter. We didn't like it when Jesenia got like this. The dead wasps in the upper corners readied to sting us. The mice took out their knives and forks and eyed us with delight. Something in our wrong world was off. How could we help? We stifled screams in our throat. Please don't be like this, Jesenia. Don't you remember? You're getting us out!

We waited.

For the real storm to come. Boss Man surprising us mid-story and trashing us with MODEL EMPLOYEE reprimands. Eyes, ears, cheeks, chins. Bruises like Africa or South America; cuts on our arms and legs like the Amazon. Jesenia would apologize for being such a bad MODEL EMPLOYEE. It was all her fault, not *theirs*. He'd thrash her and tell her to shut her trap once and for all. Didn't she know she giving us *ideas*?

Please don't blame them. It was all me, Boss Man. I love you. Don't lose it. And you, girls, don't you go losing it either!

Idiotic words. Boss Man pummeled her for bringing us all together in a sentence.

He left. No light, no night or morning. Don't you know that losing isn't always losing, I wanted to shout in the shell quiet of our space. PASS-THROUGH-CHASM. DUST-BUNNY-DRAIN. BROKEN-DOWN-WASHING-MACHINE. LOWER-EMPLOYEE-WORK-DEPARTMENT. *Don't you know that losing is sometimes having?*

(No answer. I'd heard that last line as a clue on a game show when I was twelve—*POETRY CASH FOR DOLLARS*, where the winner got the BIG BIG STANZA POT—but I couldn't think of the author's name to save my life.)

MISSING: CHICA TOO LAZY TO FOLD HER OWN
CLOTHES AND PICK UP HER OWN DIRTY SOCKS
BUT STILL ASKED FOR A PRINCESS PHONE AND
THINKING NOTHING OF PARTYING TILL THE WEE HOURS
AY DIO WITH THAT BRONX IDIOTA DURING
THE BREAKING OF HER MAMI'S HEART.

QUERIDA. THINGS CAN CHANGE. VEN A CASA, MI VIDA.

JESENIA

But we loved with a love that was more than love—

EDGAR ALLAN POE, "ANNABEL LEE"

ROMAN À CLEF

I wasn't always into Boss Man. Took a lifetime, in fact, for me to get there.

In the beginning there was Hector: *mi mundo entero*, my *day for night*, my *Yves Saint Laurent*, my *quid pro quo*, my *Spanish Lullaby*. We stood together from second grade to eighth—finger paints, coatroom, Goldfish, tongues. Third grade Hector drew me a picture of Old San Juan and made me memorize it—for the kids we would have in the future, when we went back to the Old Country. Fifth grade he tattooed my neck with a Bic ballpoint pen: PROPERTY OF HECTOR. I know what you thinking, but it wasn't really that way. Hector wasn't mean. He wasn't even Puerto Rican. Not really.

Perdóneme, Sor Juana!

We went to different high schools. Life passed. Notebooks, ladles, wooden spoons, rice. I got good grades now and then. Hector got smashed in the head by nuns. One day he took me to junior/senior prom at Townsend Harris in Flushing, the place where I was supposed to be bettering myself. We're on the dance floor: people looking at him and looking at me and thinking, *Whatever, we always knew Jesenia Diaz was street.* Thinking perhaps that Hector maybe belonged to those Catholic schools that went in between condemned and newly renovated every other year, problem schools, but why make that assumption? (Even when it actually was true? Even if Hector himself counted Queens nuns as part of the condemnation?)

Hector was always interested in bettering himself. He read books, he taped *Unsolved Mysteries.* He forever asked me about Townsend Harris, the school my mama sent me to because it was the best place to better yourself; he wanted to know about my classes, and when I told him, he further asked about the magical mystical Mexican nun who used her powers of poetry to bring innerly life to outerly death. I told him that the teacher who taught us Sor Juana had been fired: "poems deemed un-age-appropriate." Hector laughed. *Coño.* Who would go and lose a perfectly good job in a high school that serves food like yours?

But the poetry, I said to him. The poetry opened my eyes, *mi amor.*

Hector scowled. Poetry ain't never been a nun, he said. Tell me something better.

And so I told him about the new teacher who made us read Arthur Miller plays from then on because they were the only books the school could afford. *Death of My Sons. The Crucibull.* American books, that's what I like to hear, Hector said. More like it.

(But me. I got bored. I missed that Sor Juana teacher. Mr. Fanon, World Literature 9. I looked out the window at all that was happening, and then back at the school. Fuck Arthur Miller. Fuck outta there.)

Junior/senior prom before my escape was beautiful, though: garlands and punch bowls and waxed floors and white carnation corsages. A turntable on the dance floor playing *Rodolfo y Su Típica*—whoever heard of this old-fashioned salsa shit? I asked, laughing. Why we're not listening to Selena? Or dancing that goddamn Macarena? Let's get this party started!

Hector looks back at me in the flattest face possible. He knows I made my comments in the utmost of love yet because pride runs through his conquistador veins, he turns and gives me the first of many SWAMPS that night. I told you to be on my page, he whispers.

If that's not love, then I don't know what.

Turns out *Rodolfo y Su Típica* was his favorite music, a record Hector had brought along for the DJ to spin, a surprise for me. A vinyl his cumbia-loving mother used to listen to before she got put away, his mother who'd hailed from the *actual Spanish continent*. Women's Correctional was upstate somewhere. Not surprising that his mother listened to that old-time junk. What did she do to get busted? I asked Hector—the second SWAMP that evening and I'm starting to get the picture. 1. Listen. 2. Don't *not* listen. 3. Pay attention, but not necessarily to the finer details. Hector tells me listen to Rodolfo and get some real music through my thick head; meanwhile here is the DJ *wailing* on this old-school garbage, asking the prom crowd who the hell listens to this old-school trash but he promised someone named "Hector" to lay it on so here you go. Hector bows his head and smiles. Even a stranger got my back, he says to me. A stranger don't leave me hanging. You hear that, Jesenia?

Meanwhile the white girls on the dance floor are noticing Hector and acting like they love this shit, hips all over the place, pure lies. They dance but know better than to look my way.

He starts moving with them. Those white girls smile and bop alongside *mi vida* like they been doing this all along. Hector suddenly breaks out his famous disco split, and the white girls pause. The room goes proverb silent. But I am weak, too weak to avoid that fatal disco split, and so I snort out my Diet Coke and Dewar's through the nose. Maybe too much laughter. Maybe I was just having an innocent fit. From where I stood, I could see his butt cheeks emerging victorious from that disco split, the pant legs having gone their separate ways. What a fucking shame. Hector had rented this Designer Discount Tux from Señor Clancy Formalwear over near Monsignor McClancy High in East Elmhurst, and now look: right down the middle, everyone could see his amazing ass—and I wasn't being mean or anything—but that shit *was* funny. The white girls peel back, *guffawing*, and white boys come to their rescue. Hector gets up, holds his legs together, and gives me a SWAMP with a side order of Black Eye. Why you laughing at me, he shouts—no more whispers— and the white girls just grin behind the backs of their knights in white armor. Couldn't those bitches tell I was on my way to being innerly dead? *¡Ay Dio Sor Juana!* Let me at them white girls, and they will rue the day. Them junkyard dogs know what's good and what's not—you better not look my way, you fake Latina-quinceañera-wannabes! Passion coursing through my veins but then it is Hector saying sweetly, Stop crying; they can't tell. And me responding, *But they just saw what you did, they peeped that SWAMP in the flesh,* and Hector responding, No, I mean, they can't tell how really bad you was to me.

Later there is indeed some good old-fashioned compassion. I don't know how but he comes round to his senses. Forgive me, Jessie, he begs. Sometimes the left hand don't realize what the right hand is doing.

I forgive you.

Really?

How could I not? You are my day for night. (*¡Bendícenos, Sor Juana!*)

Kisses my eyelids like an after-prom breeze. We proceed to love the night away, but when he's asleep, I get up and trash Rodolfo big big time. Hay que vivir la vida.

After that: it's the last weeks of school, final exams, girls and boys wandering around kissing their college acceptance letters, barely any eyes on me, the has-been, the premature wannabe wife and mother and worshipper of ardor—it seems the world will never run out of girls, white or brown, to laugh behind their hands at the girl who loves love.

In the school parking lot, Mr. Fanon of World Literature 9 takes me aside and says, Jesenia, it's Summer Remedial for you, please try harder, I know you have it in you. I haven't forgotten.

But I walk straight on past. Why is this guy gonna talk to me like that? I actually thought Mr. Fanon had a working brain, no wonder he got fired. Summer Remedial is almost as hell-boring as Fall and Winter Remedial. So what if I was a girl from the wrong side of the tracks with potential to spare? The white girls at Townsend Harris won't have enough hands to laugh behind if I stay. Summer Remedial? I knew my mama would be all over that shit. Fuck outta there.

So. Me and Hector started thinking of living together because who needs a high school diploma to show that you've accomplished your highest life's goal of being TOTALLY IN LOVE (another SWAMP when I ask this redundant question, Hector demanding to know why was I so goddamn stupid, didn't I want to keep on bettering myself? Me being almost but not quite but in the vicinity somewhat of seventeen or so years of age). Being TOTALLY IN LOVE meant you might could marry your soul mate and live happily ever after even if your soul mate was not completely on that page. I WAS ON THAT PAGE. Hector up here thinking of leaving Queens and heading up to the South Bronx where his cousins stayed. Do you know it up there? he asks. Lots of stores where your dollar goes a long way. Bruckner Boulevard, Bedford Park Boulevard. Southern Boulevard. Spanish food as far as the eye can see. Hector says his "cousin" "Andrea" said we could come stay with her until we found our own place.

You and me, Jessie, he says. I see our names etched in that Bronx sky right over the Botanical Garden.

(Can you feel how my stomach tingles even today? Him envisioning us in the heavens, our names staring down at the thousands of daffodils and pitcher plants? Me and Hector! *¡Mi Dios!* Thinking about that Adonis makes me hot even now. SWAMP or no SWAMP.)

(Mr. Fanon's favorite line once being:

> *Some may be worthier than others,*
> *but low valley*
> *and exalted peak*
> *are the same distance from Heaven.)*

(My favorite line once being:

> *Punish me if you like—*
> *punishment from you would be a joy.)*

So you see: Boss Man was not the evolution of my world.

We packed our few things and headed up on the Number 2 train to Prospect Avenue, walked down to 514 Beck, Apt. 3G (like in the comic strip where the ladies' hearts are all aflutter)—I'm about to ask Hector to carry me over the threshold, but then there's good old "Andrea" at the door, telling us to "make ourselves at home." In the middle of the day. I'm up here wondering: Don't this chick got a job or something? "Make yourself at home," "Andrea" says again. The pillows on the couch smelled of weed and new dog. *"Make yourself at home."* And so we did.

And you'd a thought it would've been a fairy tale of epic proportions. Me with the man I love—but into every sun some rain must shine, and it came in the form of an ugly little Cinderella cooking our food and fluffing the sheets on our conjugal bed. "Andrea" was everywhere. I learned to focus on other things. The sun rising over Longwood Excellence Academy in the north, the abuelas with their fruit shopping carts under the Bruckner Expressway to the east. What more magical landscape could one imagine?

We stood together for exactly seven days. The holy trinity times two plus one. Cheeseburgers, mofongo, Chex Mix, wine. Guava, breadfruit, mango. Electrical outlets that spark for no reason, mattresses made of ticking roaches. I began to have visions of a real future on Beck Street. Walking around, I see some sick window valances for sale on Prospect Avenue, some dope plastic slipcovers in a store on Southern Boulevard. Everyone will want to be us. We'll have the best parties, we'll play Selena ALL DAY. A stroller full of CTown groceries and a carpet unrolled straight from the Home Depot warehouse over near the Whitestone Bridge. We'll be everyone's fucking dream.

Hector, too, had visions of a future. I had said, Fuck It, to Townsend High in the name of love, but then Hector said, Hey, Not So Fast. We can't remain dumb our entire lives. Why don't we both go to Longwood Excellence Academy? Why don't we both get our diplomas like man and wife? Why don't we both be head of the class with school rings on our fingers and framed GEDs propped up on the windowsill for all to admire? It is possible, Hector said. Plus, if his mother ever gets out of Women's Correctional, she'll be proud as hell. Her boy out here NOT selling drugs or looking to go to Spofford with the other bad behavior youth. Her Hector outshining the lights on Fordham Road. When she gets out, his mother might take one look at our rings, our diplomas—at me, her new darling daughter—and say, *Hay que vivir la vida.* You done it. You both done it. Let's throw you the biggest wedding ever at the iglesia pentecostal! It will be a celebration of the holiest of trinities: me, you, and mi Hector! *¡Dale!*

This was his dream. Sort of my dream, too, I have to admit.

Hector never mentioned my mother. Because my mami Cindy is as *Boricua* as they come: *Tu sabes.* Nothing is good enough, skinny enough, pretty enough, fat enough—and then it is all too much. Too much fat, too much pretty, so much good you might lose your fucking head. What do you do when your own mami thinks you are a spoiled brat? When she "disapproves" of your men, your lack of staying awake in school, your fresh mouth—disapproves of you not going to Immaculate Conception to hear the mass in Spanish, of you wearing trashy clothes, boasting "motherfucking crazy ideas," such as thinking you could get married in the English corridor at Townsend Harris instead of actually graduating? Thinking you could slide into motherhood without being a real mother? Men like Hector like it when you ignore your own brains, she told me the last time I saw her. They won't have your best interests at heart. What about your husband Manny, I asked? Manny don't count, she replied. Manny was born half angel. He always has everyone's best interests at heart.

I got ready to say something else, but then Cindy slapped me—out of the blue, told me it was Summer Remedial or bust. Why was I so damn pigheaded? *¡Testadura!*

I took one last look at her, at Townsend Harris. Fuck outta there.

¡Ay Dios! Thank God Hector's mama would never press for information about my life. I would be lost for words.

Hector cherishes this fantasy, grows it into an actual plan in a matter of hours. Thank God his mother only has twenty or thirty more years at Women's Correctional so her whole life will not be a waste. She will emerge victorious and kiss our heads a thousand times. She will kiss our rings and certificates. She will teach me to cook, clean, dance, sing. She will see to it that I would not be so deserving of so many SWAMPS.

Like how, I asked.

Spoiled brat, he said.

But what if? I wondered. What if his mami would not be that way at all? Maybe she'd look at our rings in the glass case on the sill and repeat (as his "cousin" "Andrea" did many times behind my back), *The Bible say the girl is always the problem. Why you trust her, baby?*

I also learned that from reading Arthur Miller back in the day. The girl is always the problem.

But then close your eyes because everything is preordained, just like in Spanish mass, and dreams can come true. We live together. And on the seventh day it goes down like this: I'm fixing him his favorite dinner. Peas, rice, cube steak, garlic. Nothing from a box. For dessert, fresh fruit: *melón de la Mancha.* Sweet bodega mangos. *Cerezas de la Montaña.* Clementines. At the bodega you have to know the right fruit to ask for so *they* can know whether you're authentic Spanish or just a runner-up. I'm cooking and singing to myself and not bothering to look out the Beck Street–facing window of Apt. 3G to see *Mi Vida Loca* stomping home with two fists.

You don't know what mad is until you see Hector's fists.

YOU, he cries, tearing the front door off its hinges! How could I have been so beguiled as to be blinded by you—*Puta!*—you are pure lie!

I turn down the stove. *Puta? Pure lie?* That was major. My mouth won't move because face it: you can't say the truth if you don't know what truth you think they're after.

SWAMP, SWAMP, SWAMP.

(Unconscious. A passage of time. Later, at Lincoln Hospital, my head in traction, the doctors do believe Hector when he says *it was from a fall*. The doctors tell him to make sure I'm more careful. When I come to, my first thought is to strangle the living daylights out of that ugly little Cinderella, may she rest in peace. But her story comes later.)

SWAMP, SWAMP, SWAMP.

(If it seems like I don't much like girls, you're sadly mistaken. I love everything female—I even tried to become a member of REAL GIRL JAMMIN™ when I first started Townsend Harris—I even asked, *Am I too street?* thinking that might be a reason to reject me, but then they just grinned and said, *We take everybody as they are*. Hector at first happy, says yes you may join, then changes his mind, no, you may absolutely not. You aren't like them, Jesenia, he explains. Stick to girls like you. Who are those? I asked. SWAMP SWAMP—*you making fun of me?* No, baby, no, I answer.)

His cousin "Andrea," for instance, she's nothing like me. Grade A snake in the grass. Little did I know but on the seventh day, that Friday, "Andrea" began to follow me. Me, minding my own damn business—the ugly Cinderella, peering around corners and subway stops and into plate glass doors—tailing me like white on Goya Canilla. Why so suspicious? Why so untrusting? Had she heard me on the phone the day before, confirming my appointment with *Mott Haven Women's Reproductive Decision Making*? Had she lost sleep over that call? Did she believe I was committing a sin? Had she finally gotten proof of MY OWN VOLITION AND DIABOLICAL-NESS? Likely "Andrea" was thinking I was not worthy of Hector, that I was not worthy of a shared destiny with him. That I was not woman enough to even kiss his shoes (these were her deathbed words a few days later, God rest that bitch's soul). *Ay Dio.*

"Andrea" sneaks up to the reception desk and eavesdrops the conversation that takes place between myself and Ms. Stonington. (*Thank you for being so responsible, Miss Jesenia. A baby is probably the last thing a girl like you needs.*)

And continues to watch my movements as, a few hours later, I make my way by gypsy cab back to Beck Street, 514 Apt 3G. She comes in after me. Pretends to watch *Dr. Phil* and *Judge Judy* with me. Gets tired of waiting, takes out her phone and texts. I start to cook. "Andrea" comes into the kitchen and asks if she can help. Hector busts in. The gorgeous valances shudder in his wind. *Puta! Pure lie!* And it is then that his "cousin" grabs a knife and points it at me—*You see this girl here, Hector? She nothing but a baby killer! ¡Demonio! ¡Delincuente!*

The end of our seven days of creation. His fists of fury whale upon me, his fingers around my neck press the flesh straight to my earth's inner core. I am leveled. "Andrea" shouts (as if it needs clarification), *What that bitch did was get rid of your baby!*

How could you? Hector asks. *How could you?* SWAMPING like no tomorrow. I have never lied to my man. I have told him the absolute truth when necessary. So help me Dios.

I look over at that harridan "Andrea." Cousin, my ass. I know that kind of love when I finally recognize it. I will kill her in her sleep.

(Turns out there was no need for that, in the end. Mid-fight, "Andrea" suddenly faints. I am dead but alive. Hector calls an ambulance to Lincoln Hospital for the both of us. The ambulance people tell me there is hope; I'm not actually dead; but when they look at "Andrea," they shake their heads. Next day "Andrea" is life-support toast. Brain tumor, undetected. The doctors tell me to be more careful, to not fall so much. I for one wanted to ask them: You sure there was a brain in that girl's skull? But I am all SWAMPED out. *Forgive me, Sor Juana!* Hector leads me out the place in a wheelchair, then back to 514 Beck. "Andrea" stays at Lincoln Hospital for another day or so; then like magic she's dust in the South Bronx wind. Karma being the biggest bitch of all.)

At home, the constant question was: What kind of woman does her man like that?

Hector crumpled. When we got home from the hospital, he didn't have the strength in him to SWAMP me anymore. He lay his head on the kitchen table, cradling it, ignoring the recipe for pasteles (from the Spanish *People* magazine, FYI) I'd taken out to try the next week.

Why, Jesenia? Why, Jesenia? Why?

(He was my *quid pro quo*, my morning, noon, and night. What could I answer?)

Because, I start to say. Because.

Some few weeks earlier in the bathroom at Townsend Harris—fear like lightning through my gut—I discovered ALMOST FOR CERTAIN DEFINITELY SURE that I had a little pop-tart in my oven. A new kind of afraid, the kind you get after buying three tests from Genovese Drugs and smuggling them in your backpack. Not the kind of afraid where you think your mami will hate you forever for being a *malcriada*, but you still want her to love you nonetheless. Not the kind of fear where you actually *wish* your mami would stay in your corner to hate you forever.

No, this fear was about *my hate*.

That this pop-tart would cramp my style. I didn't want no bundle of joy possibly stopping me from being the best me possible in this new South Bronx world where everything was possible. Prevent me from entering Longwood Excellence Academy with Hector where we would both be AT THE HEAD OF THE CLASS. I couldn't let no little oven bun prevent me from grasping that class ring floating over the Bronx Botanical Garden.

A "baby" would only mess that shit up.

Now, of course one might wonder: Why would Hector want me to have his "baby" since that would also mean that HIS SCHOOL DREAM would evaporate like so much stale cola champagne? Excellent question.

But for that I have no humanly answer. Other than: it was what it was.

Add these other assorted musings to the pot: What if we wanted to do different love positions? A "baby" would just kill that. What if the "baby" came out a little darker or lighter skinned than he expected?

Men don't *naturally* understand the vagaries of the female womb. I ain't never slept with anyone else but Hector. That and still—God was always playing jokes.

Hector lifts his head from his arms. He slides off the kitchen table. There are salt traces down his cheeks. He gathers his strength, the dear boy. His hand takes flight.

Half-hearted SWAMPS. And to tell the truth, they feel more like mosquito bites, weak. But on the other hand. *Where the hell are you, Sor Juana? I want these motherfucking SWAMPS to stop!*

My heart's best treasure, Hector growls. Bullshit. I'll never love you again.

I go over to the sill where our diplomas will stand, where one day we'll place our school rings in a glass case for all to admire. I open the window. I look down the airshaft, where the air is sweet from chimichurri and Diet Pepsi. I commence to fly. I commence to fly through that space, slow motion. The sky has opened up, clouds part in the place where our names might yet be etched. Hector might yet change his mind. But then the pillow of the pavement hits my head like an early naptime.

(You know how fragile people can sometimes be? How they can forget themselves? How they forget all that was good and remember only what is bad?)

Me once again up in Lincoln Hospital. The doctors say, This is different, Miss Diaz.

But then they don't really put their finger on why. I open my eyes—is it days later?—and suddenly Hector's other "cousin" "Jennifer" is standing next to my bed like the evil twin from *Days of Our Lives*, the one who slips the poison into the IV drip. She tells me about "Andrea." She murmurs, You don't deserve a man like my cousin.

No, I answer. Where did you come from?

You'll be sorry, "Jennifer" says to me. Eyeing the IV like so much possibility.

You'll have to leave now, I say. And the bitch does precisely that.

God gives me another chance. I get better. I take my vows in front of the doctors and nurses: never ever will I look at that airshaft again. A brand-new start. They may or may not believe me. They don't stay for me to find out. I return to our love nest on Beck Street.

Hector, my love of all loves, my perfect warrior prince—he answers the door in his bathrobe AND IS MAD ALL OVER AGAIN. It's like I was never gone. He says, You know, Jesenia, how you went to that PLACE and they VACUUMED you out clean? Well, that's what I'm fucking doing—vacuuming you clean out my life. Don't knock on this fucking door again.

He shuts his bathrobe and calls for someone named "Fernanda" to come out the bedroom. Come take out the trash, he says.

"Fernanda." No relation, just an "associate" from Kingsbridge. By way of Flushing. Now I am starting to fully get these females.

It's over, he says, walking away to the new color TV. "Fernanda" comes over and raises her fist without looking. You nothing here, understand? God is gonna punish you big time!

I start to weep. To this day I have no forgiveness for the thing in me that dragged my womb to *Mott Haven Reproductive Women's Decision Making*. All I ever wanted, all I ever needed, was in the person of Hector—that god-boy-man. Mortal made Immortal. As "Fernanda" is steady reorganizing my face, Hector is flipping through the channels in his Gap khakis and SOUTH BRONX FOREVER tee that make him look like he's ascending Mount Etna.

(Mr. Fanon taught us about Mount Etna. The monster licking his chops at the bottom of its belly.)

"Fernanda" eventually goes to watch the TV with Hector. Effing bitch, I murmur—by then, I'm not sure I have teeth. Hector glares at me. Don't you address the mother of my child like that, he says. I look at "Fernanda's" belly under her robe, flabby as a bialy. No way in hell is there a kid in there. "Fernanda" blows a ring of her Newport into my face. Retreats to the bedroom. She is wearing my faux-silk robe and panty set. The monstress.

I been speaking to my mami, Hector says. She's going to get out any year now. But she had some advice for me.

Please tell me the plan, mi amor.

His mother's sister, Tia Prudence, is school secretary at St. Rosemary of the Crown on Westchester Avenue. She can get him into twelfth grade there; he would just have to lie about his age. But he could finish school at St. Rose under the wise eyes of the nuns and fathers—he could make his first and second communions, he could be confirmed, he could become an altar boy. He could go to Bronx Community; he could transfer up to Mercy. I've never loved nuns, Hector says. But with them the future might finally take place.

The baby between me and Fernanda is due in about ten or twelve months, he adds. Maybe longer. Mami has always wanted to be an *abuela*. I will not take away her dreams, you get that?

Give me another chance, I say. You and me against the world.

I faint, just as if I was carrying a baby all along.

When I awaken, Hector and "Fernanda" order me to make myself useful. I drag myself up off the floor. They tell me to go and get them Chinese food from China Fun by the Number 6 train. I feel afraid they will try and leave while I'm away, but I agree to do it anyway. Hector gives me the smallest SWAMP ever, not a mosquito but a gnat, a flea; he searches my face with his eyes. When you get back, he tells me, I will kill you for good.

And then I am outside.

It's more than 1 in the morning but less than daylight.

There are plenty of quiet streets at this time of night. I make it to the corner of Longwood. I get ready to open the door to the bodega. I forget what I'm looking for.

And just then, I see him. The baby. The baby that was sucked up in the vacuum cleaner at *Mott Haven Women's Reproductive Decision Making*. Don't laugh, but it was his face, staring right at me, next to the lottery sign in the window (ALL YOU NEED IS A DOLLAR AND A DREAM). The night air forms a halo of Cheetos around his little head; he's like a fun-size candy bar. I just want to tell you, he says, that there's no hard feelings.

(*Forgive me, Sor Juana.* I'm so glad it was a boy.)

I tell him I knew from the start there was no fucking way he was coming to this earth.

That hurts, the baby says.

I want to say I'm sorry. But then I feel my insides begin to creep out. I fall on the sidewalk. I literally smell like shit warmed over. I'm waiting for the baby to say something. Forgiveness is a good spare part to have in times like these.

But nothing.

(My new favorite line of Sor Juana's being:

> *I counted, counted*
> *All the ways love hurt me.*
> *One life, I thought—a thousand deaths.*)

I lie on the sidewalk. The moon is a huge sanitary pad. I think I'm bleeding to death—or is it just pee? Or am I really just full of shit? The night air is cold and crinkly. There are no voices—even the baby is gone. The bodega goes dark; the streetlights dim to silverish nothing.

I remember a line I read in Mr. Fanon's World Literature 9 (when I was still living in my mami's house and didn't yet comprehend how the world and its champions looked at a girl *like me*): "Martyr to loyalties, a witness to the things of this world, a hero ready to die for the precious imperfections of ordinary life."

Hector. My man of steel. It wasn't too late for us. I'd have to go back and tell him that.

Just then I feel an arm lift me into the air. Into heaven.

Not a baby. Not a vacuum cleaner.

Just burl galore. The smell of iron, the engraving of a certain touch. A thick neck and a thicker waist and arms like the logs in an enchanted forest. It's true what they say, about your life flashing before your eyes. I know I stink to high heaven, but Something Out There won't let me die. The bright clouds above announce my name in cursive. *¿Quién en amor ha sido más dichoso?*

I smile at Sor Juana's empathy and then.

You just what the doctor ordered was the first thing ever Boss Man said to me.

DEAR MISS METROPOLITAN

She listened in silence . . . I begged of her to pity me, for my dead mother's sake. And she did pity me. She did not say, "I forgive you"; but she looked at me lovingly, with her eyes full of tears.
  —Harriet Ann Jacobs, *Incidents in the Life of a Slave Girl*

According to Miss Metropolitan, *"Watching the police lead that vicious rogue away was a sight never to be forgotten in the history of humankind."* What she didn't mention in the article, however, was the way her heart had raced as she watched them handcuff the man formerly known as Ernst, Ernest, or Ernesto; she didn't mention the way her throat collapsed as the police spotlight shone on the boarded windows of his house where he'd kept the girls; she also failed to note that after the last ambulance pulled away, she believed she might be experiencing another attack of heart arrhythmia, a condition about which she'd told no one in the office. Every day, Miss Metropolitan felt certain she would collapse in the street and none of her neighbors would notice.

Dying alone had always been something of a bad taste in her mouth.

None of the above was reported in the article Mathilda Marron submitted in person to the *Queens Metropolitan* on December 14, 2007. She'd wanted to stick to the facts—as they'd taught her in newspaper school, back in the day. But just the air alone—in the frenetic nighttime of the victim-girls—sparked within her the need to describe, to unmask, to fully comprehend. When she arrived at the newsroom the next morning, the editor took the pages from Miss Metropolitan's hands—typewritten, double-spaced, marked up and down with Wite-Out and red pen—and thanked her. Last night was indeed a bad night, the editor said. Mathilda Marron flopped into an office chair, placed a hand on her chest. Yes, it was a bad night, she said. It saved lives.

She drifted. Remembering that wool-dark sky laced with the fragrance of snow. She had just closed her bedroom window and positioned herself at her vanity with a ream of stationery and the old blue Lamy she used for formal letters. *Dear Myrtle, I know you are a thief. That Rosenthal did not just walk away on its own.*

(Miss Mattie, the editor said. Are you all right?)

She begins to write more, but suddenly there is a commotion out-side. Mathilda pushes the letter away, floats to the front door of her small brick ranch (once belonging to Daddy, who'd inherited it at poor Mommy's death)—and there it is. Sirens shrieking, ambulances sparking the street. She feels a shudder in the sidewalk trees. There are people gathering beyond her yard. Stepping onto the porch steps, Mathilda feels the cold go right through her bed jacket. One of her oldest neighbor friends, Freeda Bent, is dangling not twenty feet away at the chain-link fence. Freeda? In this cold? Wasn't it near ten o'clock? Didn't Freeda always sit in front of *Law & Order* about this time? Mathilda wants to ask her friend what's happening but doesn't: she is a newspaperwoman, for heaven's sake, and her job is to find out the answers on her own. The street is pure mayhem, flashing lights and crowds and voices; as she wraps her bed jacket tightly around her chest, it occurs to Mathilda that she must be at the scene of a crime.

Freeda Bent turns toward Mathilda and shouts, Can you believe this shit?

A few feet over, a policeman—puny as the day is short, Mathilda notes—swivels on his heel and glares at Freeda. How he can hear her above the din is unclear. Mathilda cries out, My friend doesn't mean nothing, Officer! Pay her no mind.

But the puny policeman says nothing. His eyes are back across the street. Everyone's eyes are across the street.

Mathilda crimps down the broken cement steps and toward the chain-link fence separating her property from the sidewalk, the street, and the house where all the turmoil is happening. A line of EMTs hover near the front door, talking amongst themselves. Police pace up and down and sideways. Mathilda's bed jacket has fallen from her shoulders, but she aches too much to bend down for it. In another time, a gentleman would have offered her his coat as an act of gallantry. Chivalry is dead, she thinks, or at least on a CPAP machine, wheezing out its last dogged breaths. Where are those days? she wonders, huffing toward the puny policeman. She feels old as the hills but has not forgotten her mission. Good evening, Officer. Might you be so kind as to tell me what is going on?

Stay back, both of you, the puny cop says brusquely. One of his hands goes to his gun, the other to his radio. Mathilda and Freeda look at each other; wouldn't it be nice, Mathilda wants to ask, if people just went the extra mile to be kind?

It doesn't take a lot to be kind. A smile is a frown turned upside down.

She knows Freeda does not share such thoughts. Why bother asking? This neighbor woman, a confidante of twenty years, can be crude in situations requiring tact and a watchful eye. In situations like these, a woman like Freeda Bent has no real purpose.

(Wake up, Miss Mattie. Don't you hear me? Charlie, call 911. *Call 911!*)

But still: Freeda grabs Mattie's hand and the two women move toward the crowd, a bulwark of nightgowned, pajama-bottomed, hair-curlered persons flapping their arms in the cold. The two women get no farther than the curb of the sidewalk. Rubberneckers, Mathilda notes. What are they doing on my turf? Gawkers, pure and simple. They must have come a long way to witness this spectacle. Jamaica Avenue, Farmers Boulevard, the Long Island Expressway.

All the number streets. They should've stayed in their own backyard. Goddamn oglers.

Lord have mercy on this shit, Freeda says.

Do you know what's happening? Mathilda asks.

Yes but not exactly, Freeda says.

Long neighborhood trees darken the already pitch sky. An army of police smash in the door at the house across the street. A battering ram? A log? The wood splinters into the air and sounds of high wailing can be heard, cries forming circles in the air, from soft to loud to loudest. Shards hang off the doorframe. It takes no more than a minute for three bodies to appear. Three girl bodies, maybe. Three who clearly have not seen the light of day since—forever, Mathilda notes: they are nothing but pale brown rust. The girls (if they can be called girls) stand there and sway slightly. It doesn't seem as if they have any limbs.

The crowd in the street agitates. Mathilda finds their movements unseemly. She tries to listen.

That man been had those girls in the house for years and years! And we didn't know!

We didn't look!

They nothing but skin and bones!

I can't look anymore. Tell me what you see.

I always thought that house looked strange.

They say them girls been missing since Hurricane Floyd!

I lost my everything in Hurricane Floyd!

We didn't know! Look at them.

Who can blame us? Look at them!

Look!

Mathilda feels her chest constrict, like the rolling tight of an oriental carpet—Daddy's favorite one lay in the dining room, right under the cabinet containing Mother's European linens—oh heavens, is this real or a dream? Why is the wood debris dangling so dangerously in that doorway? Are those girls actual living creatures? Mathida almost can't breathe. Almost. Where is my steno pad? My writing hand should be moving. This has been her neighborhood for over forty years. The home of all her friends and their families and their children. This is where she walks and feels every spring pebble in the sidewalk, predicts when every summer leaf will hit the ground. Doors were not supposed to bust down like that; those splinters might just about kill any survivors. But survivors of what? Mathilda shudders. Her chest repeatedly tries to go back to normal. We've known this world since forever, she thinks. The trees, windows, the streets, the doors. When did our knowing stop?

And for truth: this block is like one big family, despite everyone not remembering each other's names. All the houses on Amity Lane have had their ups and downs, their yellings and divorces and money schemes and sudden demises. These brick ranches have the same safe-dangerous feel about them, with their cracked patios and barred windows. Police are sometimes called and then sent back to the precinct—*We was just having a little bitty thing, Officer, no need for you to get involved*. Peace is restored as fast as it is lost, usually without sirens or fire trucks or hospital vans. Freeda grabs Mathilda's hand and leads her off the curb and into the street. The crowd swerves. Mathilda thinks, There has never been anything like tonight: the high beams, the hollering, the splinters, the dust, the sweat, the snowflakes falling from the sky like daggers. People are trampling over themselves to get a glimpse of the girls, who remain swaying in the doorway, naked as the day they were born. No one has thought to clothe them. Where are the gentlemen of old? Cover them damn girls! Look— their eyes are brackish! Their heads practically bald! Mathilda wishes she had the voice to yell. Instead, she must listen to Freeda, who, above the ruckus, shouts into her ear, *Them girls look like death warmed over!*

Mathilda feels like smacking Freeda's face. These girls are the exact opposite of death, she imagines herself saying.

Plus: who is Freeda to be throwing stones? Freeda has no business talking, her house being a hot mess itself. Didn't people say that Freeda Bent's grandniece, Fernanda, had run away with a pimp *just because she could*? Wasn't her nickname *Fast Fernanda*? Wasn't she a drug dealer, because weren't all people who dropped out of school drug dealers? So *who* was Freeda to gossip?

And don't even get me started on the others—my so-called closest friends. Fancyella Brown: a sometime shoplifter at Dollar Haven who blames things on old age and gets to keep her items. Evie Knight: her husband passed from AIDS—so why is she walking around telling people he got sick from his *sugar*? Too much sugar is more like it. Don't get me started. And Ag Wheeless: isn't it Ag's granddaughter Madison still going around burning trash in people's yards, nothing better to do, the worst troublemaker on the block? That brat came up to our pew one time and told us, *Y'all ain't as sanctified as you think!* What nerve! What unjustifiable balls! And Ag Wheeless—that so-called paragon of virtue—attempting to explain away her grand-daughter's fresh mouth, ignoring the PLAIN FACT that Madison isn't doing anything but hanging out with a gang of sex-crazed, dumb-as-dirt hussies at the Queens Center mall when she should be in school, getting book smart—*who was Ag to talk?* Young people are supposed to be our future. Fix what's in your own backyard before you . . .

Mathilda can't remember her train of thought. I love my friends, she says out loud. I love my friends, don't I, Freeda?

Freeda, who hasn't heard a thing, whose neck is craned toward the action across the street. Pure electricity. Electrocution. Mathilda takes her reading glasses from the top of her head. The girls swaying in the doorway do indeed look like death, she thinks, noticing the faint outline of hands.

So. The time is now. She lets go of Freeda's hand, crimp/runs back inside to grab her large black bag with her newspaper equipment (the steno pad, her favorite pencils), then crimp/runs back down the cement steps. She is ready for action. Mathilda spies Evie Knight talking to Fancyella Brown at the chain-link fence. Evie straightens her lips as a form of greeting. Why hello, Mattie. We up here think-ing it's a murder in there, what about you?

(Just like Evie to be playing it off so casual. What is *up* with these old biddies? Didn't they know a cataclysm of unmitigated proportions when they saw one?)

Mathilda takes out her pad.

PRELIMINARY NOTES:
Law enforcement
Cop cars swarm the Cape Cod across the street—
not like rabbits, but like wasps, hornets, or summer
yellow ~~jacks~~
jackets.
Didn't that house used to be a Victorian?
Didn't that house used to have eaves hanging
down like honeycombs?
When?
When did it get so homely???
Homey? Dangerous door. Shards. Who will see to that?
And why all this commotion? Maybe just some runaways now
having to face the music.
~~Daddy's favorite saying.~~ Do rescues always necessitate such
din? Wouldn't soothing quiet be so much
better for any liberatory actions to be carried out successfully?
Daddy's favorite adage:
Better safe than sorry.

The puny policeman is gone. But another one comes rushing toward
them—a real handsome cop, a replica of Billy Dee Williams from his
finer days (Mathilda wonders if anyone today would know who Billy
Dee is?)—now he's waving at her and Evie and Fancyella—a funny
sight, under other circumstances: it sort of looks like he is tipping his
hat at them, in a Charlie Chaplin/Billy Dee sort of way. Men don't
wear hats anymore, Mathilda thinks, though they really should. Men
today need to take a lesson from the past; they need to act more
like Billy Dee and less like Billy Don't. (Oh, I made a funny—not
good at a time like this.) Think. Write. Think. Yes. Billy Dee—as
fine a gentleman as you could imagine—even though he had Diana
Ross wrapped around his finger in that one flick, him pretending
to be all goody-two-shoes and she a hot mess. Typical man, typical

woman. Why are we, as the poet says, continually in the business of mystery?

Girl, stop mumbling, Evie says irritably. You want people to think you crazy?

(Miss Marron! Miss Marron! Clive from Accounts Receivable just called 911. Do you hear me? DO YOU REMEMBER CLIVE? Hang in there, Miss Marron, *hang in there*!)

Mathilda takes out a different pencil, the one with the orange grip. Evie moves away as the police multiply like rabbits. The world becomes small and large in this minute, the sirens droning. These girls. These girls. The real handsome cop is suddenly standing over her. Ma'am, he shouts. Is everything okay?

Miss Metropolitan opens her eyes.

Good evening, Officer, she answers, languidly; but it is too late; he is moving past her and away, looking like a crab doing a cakewalk, shoveling onlookers onto the curb and grass.

Let's just get ourselves back inside, Freeda says, resting her hands on Mathilda's shoulders. Mathilda takes note that Freeda's hands are like blocks of ice. Never trust anyone with cold hands, Daddy used to say. Feet upon the oriental carpet, eyes glancing at the shape of the Rosenthal in the cabinet.

Yes, let's go inside, says Evie, coming back toward them. This out here is no place for good women.

Ladies, I need to find out what's happening, Mathilda says, pulling the cold hands from her body. It's my job.

Freeda frowns. You know this ain't your job, girl. This shit is crazy. What if we get our own selves killed or worse? Let's go home. I'm tired. Plus, I'm missing my show!

Mattie straightens her back. I feel like I above everybody else should know what's going on here. I have to be on the job!

Girl PLEASE.

Mathilda dips her pencil tip on her tongue. A chance for reporting doesn't come along very often over here. Not since that rap star (God rest his soul) drove down this street two years ago and was shot in the face. The only light is the one coming off the one functioning streetlamp; without that illumination, the shadows will complicate her writing. Never mind. In the communications course she took at Queensborough Community College (herself at the time a "returning student"), the journalism professors instructed the students to be resilient, to expect the unexpected, to not be afraid of the dark, to always be on the lookout. They said that life always happened when you least expected.

Well, here is darkness. Here is life.

Tonight was supposed to have been a letter-writing night to her sister in Jackson Heights; Mathilda had wanted to know where Mother's Rosenthal had got to, seeing as how the East Elmhurst U-Haul had recently sent a notice stating that *nothing belonging to MARRON was left in their facility*—no such name appearing in their records, and certainly *no fancy China dishes the likes of Rosenberg or whatever*. Well, that letter would have to be written later. Now it was these girls. *These girls*. What was her gut telling her? The police officers in the street continue to shout like soldiers. There are more people than the grass and curbs can support. More of them tumble into the street, and the asphalt seems to sink. People begin to climb up sidewalk trees to get a look. Mathilda hears the crowd grow into excess rumor:

Them girls must a been orphans because what mama would let her girls go to waste like that?

Oh, you got that right!

He may or might not a been their father.

Uncle, more likely.

I had one of those. Not this bad, though.

Give me five minutes in the room with that sucker!

God, why you do us like this?

Isn't it you're innocent until proven guilty?

Just look at that mess! Ain't that proof that it's guilty till proven innocent, plain and simple?

> PRELIMINARY NOTES PART TWO:
> Shutters flapping, potholes
> resurfacing, the moon gaping down
> at the street like a retarded child. Woe
> unto us this horrible night. May
> God have mercy on their ~~soles~~ souls.

(At the paper the editors have told Mathilda not to use the words *retarded* or *imbecilic*, but she can't help herself. Besides, what do those greenhorns know? They do not understand what it is to catch a real, happening story. They have no idea. And anyway, everybody knows that language is always innocent.)

The three girls are finally filed down the steps of the boarded-up house—their feet are bare. Snow falls. The girls never look up. They consist of two medium humans—if you count mere skeletons as humans—and a babyish figure. A toddler, perhaps. Or maybe a midget. They are like stones, Mathilda writes. Stones in a river—unpolished, unmoving, algal. She runs her hand over the second sheet of steno paper. Thank you, God, for steering me here. Thank you, God, for saving those girls. This is a real chance for real reporting. Thank you, God, because life waits for no newspaperwoman.

She wanders closer to the crowd that has formed in the middle of the street. People are whispering, choking. They are making up new stories, new formulations by the minute. They are calling it the house of horrors. Chamber of terrors. Fucking Dracula's castle. The girls were drugged. They were starved. Maybe it was some rape going on in there, maybe not. They must have been in that house for *numerous of years*, just look at them.

Someone points out that these girls were the subjects of a huge nation-wide manhunt years ago, one that went cold. Or was it a small man-hunt? Does anyone recall? *Daily News* or *New York Post*? What about *Newsday Queens Edition*? Hell, does anybody read the paper anymore?

People are pointing fingers and holding hands and shivering shoulders and shaking heads and turning cheeks. Someone in a voice from Howard Beach says they look like they must be teen hookers. Another voice sounding more like Fresh Meadows says they are runaways, just look at the eyes, thank heavens there are no girls like that our way. A voice from Jamaica Station keeps going on about their measly arms. *This is no Third World country, goddamnit! We don't treat ours like that!*

Mathilda makes a note of everything.

The handsome cop returns to her line of vision: a whole-wheat sergeant with Crisco eyes. Please move back, ma'am. A situation like this could get dangerous.

Miss Metropolitan keeps writing.

Please, ma'am. It's not safe. You need to go back.

He has the look and sound, she thinks, of a man speaking to his grandmother.

And quite honestly, she wouldn't mind it, being called such a thing: an honorary grandma, so to speak, since she herself has never had any children of her own, not after she was declared barren by the lady doctors years ago. *You will have other joys in life,* were their exact words. *And in any case, you need a husband to have a child, which is another obstacle in your path, dear Miss Marron.* Back then she suffered from too much *mind* in her sleep: hallucinations, night terrors, dreams populated by lizard-eyed babies. There was never any mate, not even so much as a toady—Daddy had seen to that, no man ever being good enough for his favorite girl. No man ever being the kind who understood oriental rugs and fine German porcelain and the need for a linen napkin at every meal. Men in Queens were not half the man he was—*why don't you get that, Mattie?*

Daddy, I think I'll be fine to take a 50 percent man, if that's the case.

Hush up, now Mattie, you just have to wait. Wait and see. Life will not pass you by. It's not passed me by. But that's because I have waited and seen.

(The lady doctors recommended an increase in the dosage of her Valium; that would chase away visions of mongoloids, they promised. *Please stop dreaming, Miss Marron. Because dream children are not the same as real ones. You will have other joys.*)

Ma'am, do you hear me? This is a crime scene. I wouldn't want you to get hurt.

(911 is on the way! Please open your eyes! Wake up, Miss Metropolitan! Wake up!)

Mathilda Marron bows her head deeper into her steno pad. Let's see. There are, of course, the initial (boring but necessary) questions of *who what when where and why*; then I'll have to add a description of the setting (*Bleak Housey, run-down, semi-Victorian impostor with remnants of gingerbread eaves looking like Hansel and Gretel along the front*); I'll also provide a description of the characters being led down the steps (*one Spanishy, one Black, one possibly Spanishy-Black*). I'll have to say a brief word about the action (*"Police officers majestically storm the house and make what seems to be a daring rescue"*) and go on to add other, possibly relevant observations (*"The girls seem to be fully naked even as the first stirrings of winter can be felt"*).

First stirrings. Miss Metropolitan wonders if the editors would get mad about such license being taken?

Who cares? She is a journalist full of creative urges—poetic ambitions—even though no one in the *Queens Metropolitan* office has ever taken her seriously. She thinks they think of her as some

weird old Black lady who writes a musty column and smokes cigaril-
los under the No Smoking signs. That she is permanently locked in
the past, likely as a result of some tragic upbringing, a domineering
father, a rebellious sister (she likes to tell herself that if the editors were
smarter, they'd use the word *Dickensian* to describe her childhood).
The whole staff talks behind her back, she thinks. They laugh at her
droopy clothes, the smell of her *White Shoulders*, her remnants of a Pam
Grier Afro; she thinks they think she lacks vision. The mailroom boy
once told her, No one on earth says *newspaperwoman* anymore, ma'am.

Ma'am, the officer says. His hand is firm on her shoulder. *Ma'am.*

She looks up. I am on the job, Officer. I have to get to the bottom of
things. Can you give me the skinny? (She is, she proudly realizes, in
complete possession of the current lingo.) What's going on, Officer?
I'm ready for the lowdown!

No, he says, he can do no such thing, police policy. He gently steers
her into the yard next to Evie, Freeda, and Fancyella, who receive
Mathilda's arms while continuing their conversation toward the
crowd. *Isn't that the dude who does the Eyewitness News? Oh honey, I do love
me some him!* Mathilda tries again and again to peel away from the
neighbor women, to no avail. They don't understand her. They don't
understand the role she must play.

But finally—they release her arms and she floats to her house. She
waves from the vestibule of her small brick ranch, then kicks off her
slippers. Mathilda looks around for her bed jacket, then remem-
bers she's dropped it outdoors. Baby-blue polyester with cherry
piping—$17.50 at the old Alexander's in Valley Stream. A gift from
Daddy. She'd always wanted to look smart. So how was it that the
Queens Metropolitan had overlooked her every single day? Management
appointed an editor fresh out of college—where was the experience

in that? And the copy editor? Another babe in the woods. The whole newsroom definitely needed more marinating—what could they possibly know of the stew of life? When had any of them ever pounded the pavement in search of real truth? They were nothing but a bunch of teenyboppers! Standards lowered to practically the *National Enquirer.* The evening headlines often went like this:

RAP STAR GETS SHOT!!! IS EXPECTED TO SURVIVE
HIS INJURIES!!!

Now who in the Sam Hill would care about that? She'd been around in the days when real men got shot for good reasons—for things having nothing to do with unintelligible rhymes and cuss words up the wazoo. Rap my eye.

Mathilda can already picture what will happen at work come morning: right off the bat the editor teenybopper will say: "No funny business, Miss Mathilda. Just give us the facts." The assistant editor teenybopper will warn that the paper might fold any day now due to "today's economy" and that "layoffs are inevitable" and that they all have to be on their "A game." (What clichés!) No editorial shenanigans. The reporting staff teenyboppers will have her latest copy in hand and sigh. *For the love of Pete, Miss Metropolitan, will you please stay on track? You ain't writing a Victorian novel here!*

The copy editor teenybopper will be blunter: she will remind Miss Metropolitan that this is 2007, and that the *entire* world is looking shaky; she is damn lucky to have a place at the paper, seeing that most readers no longer want to know about engraved wedding announcements or china patterns or the necking and petting of teens. *Some might see you as slightly out of touch*, the editor teenybopper will add, discreetly. The mailroom teenybopper (an actual teenybopper) will ask why anyone would actually send in actual letters to a newspaper?

Even old people used computers for their problems nowadays, in his opinion.

How dull they all were. No imagination, no intuition. Even a person like Brenda Starr, Reporter (of those comic strips of yore, God rest her soul)—even she was more tenacious than they!

A newspaperwoman's work is never done!

Unlike Brenda Starr, the editor teenybopper is actually a chubby, dreadlocked Trinidad gal. In real life maybe thirty, forty. No figure to speak of—no one in their right mind would call her "pleasingly plump." No perfume, no *real* jewelry outside of a Kunta Kinte necklace and a pair of conch shell earrings. Clearly no usage of Ambi Fade Cream, as far as Miss Metropolitan could ascertain. And here she was, the editor. *A woman in charge.* No heels, no lace, no polish. Go figure.

You're only as old as you feel, the mailroom teenybopper would often add, in an effort to lift the mood.

To an extent, Miss Metropolitan has felt that the staff's words may carry a grain of truth: after years and years of writing second-rate, Ann Landers–wannabe mulch, she is fed up:

> Dear Miss Metropolitan: How many should be seated at the main wedding banquet table?
> Dear Miss Metropolitan: What would you say to a husband who refuses to at least *try* being a social drinker?
> Dear Miss Metropolitan: Why is it wrong to expect a man to hold the door open for a lady?
> Dear Miss Metropolitan: Where does a new bride go to find the least expensive Rosenthal five-piece place settings?

Eighty-some-odd years of age: What was her relevance? Even now, as she watches all manner of mayhem from the safety of her living room window—who is she, what is she saying, and why should anyone care?

(Are you getting a pulse, Clive? Don't let this old lady croak on us! Oh please, Clive, please!)

It was the handsome cop again, up on her front steps, knocking wildly. Was this her coat? He'd hate to have her lose it. Mathilda looks at the run-down bed jacket—Alexander's was where her father bought all his Van Heusen. He was too cheap for Blooming-dale's, to tell the truth. Thank you, Officer, Mathilda says, closing the door.

She waits a good ten minutes. Next thing, she's in the middle of the street, feeling an outdoor wind purring around her neck.

The trees bend with humans gawking the scene. Why are those girls still there, lollygagging in the ambulances? Why aren't they already at a hospital? Could there be more inside, perhaps? Sometimes it is easy to overlook girls.

Mathilda goes back inside, up to the guest room (once her sister's, the bed still springing from all the boys she'd snuck in there), and sits at the desk by the window, in front of her Smith Corona. She rolls a piece of white bond into the machine and turns it on. The staff at the *Queens Metropolitan* would eat their words after they got her report on tonight's events: (*There appear to be three young persons emerging of such deep misery, my heart literally breaks at the sight.*) She peels back her sister's former curtains and takes a look. A man—her neighbor—Ernst, Ernest, or Ernesto—is being wheeled out of the house on a gurney:

(*Let this reclusive soul be all right, God willing. Remember: innocent until proven guilty!*) And above, out the window: (*One often forgets to look up at the heavens at moments like these.*)

It is a moment of real living, Miss Metropolitan thinks. She pulls open the window, which had been painted shut years ago. She is a writer.

And this is what writers do. She sticks her head outside, stares *penetratingly* at the man strapped to the gurney, now being loaded into another ambulance, her neighbor: Ernst or Ernest or Ernesto, a sand-colored man, a loner. Perhaps an ascetic. Never much in the way of a conversationalist, most times not even a hello. A face as sallow as the undug flowerbeds surrounding his house. She once asked him if he'd wanted any of her rose trimmings, to no avail. She'd invited him over for a cup of Christmas tea. 2001? 2003? Last year? She honestly can't recall.

The man on the stretcher does not look up. In fact, Miss Metropolitan cannot tell if he's breathing. They strap a mask on his face and slam the ambulance door. Are those snowflakes she's feeling on her cheeks?

A whole new set of police and firemen and ambulance people arrive after the old ones leave. The handsome cop is gone. This is normally a good neighborhood, she wants to cry out.

She wants to cry out: Look to those horrid Pomonok Houses on Jewel Avenue! That's where things like this happen—the projects! Or look to the white people neighborhoods—Forest Hills, Kew Gardens— where rich white men do nothing but devise devilish plans all day long! Look there!

She wants to find that handsome cop and grab him by the shoulders and ask, Do you think you know me?

Because you don't! For one, I have looked out at *that* faux-gingerbread house for years and years and have occasionally imagined its inner workings as a watchmaker would imagine the life of a Longines. Never has it occurred to me that *something might be wrong*.

There was no way of me knowing anything about that house. How could I? You don't know me!

Miss Metropolitan closes the window. Borrows an old cardigan from her sister's closet, makes her way downstairs and back outside, where she leans on a telephone pole and feels its splinters tear at her back. A new policeman walks up to her. She places her hand on his uniformed chest with confidence.

Listen, Officer. I have *gently* positioned their giant Yellow Pages into a clear trash bag to keep it safe from rain. I have gone around the broken windows and tried to mend them with cellophane. Never a word of acknowledgment! How hard is it to say thanks? Never mind. I'm not the type to demand recognition. I was just wanting to be a good neighbor. I'm just a person with a big heart. What if anybody ever caught me possibly dying on the street from a fit of heart arrhythmia? I'd want them to have a big heart, too!

The new cop is actually the old, handsome cop—why hadn't she noticed? Billy Dee Williams is not someone you forget. He looks at her, embraces her shoulders. I had a feeling you wouldn't listen, he says softly. She is embarrassed. How did she get here? Where are her friends? What about the letter to Myrtle? She does not want Billy Dee calling the lady doctors. She does not want him calling anybody. The neighbor women who are supposedly her friends will gossip. They will tell her to visit her doctors at Jamaica Hospital for a checkup. Fifth floor, Jesus Christ. They will spread rumors, they won't understand. I'm okay, Officer. Just doing my job.

As he leads her back toward her door, Mathilda suddenly halts. Does he hear it, too? The voice at the bottom of her stomach, the voice everyone on this goddamn block can probably hear? *How could you not have known? HOW COULD YOU NOT HAVE KNOWN?*

I think I'll go inside and make myself a cup of tea and bedtime, she says. Thank you, Officer. You've been kind.

(Those girls! Their faces—like old bricks! Their tear-stained cheeks, their lack of clothes! How could she not have known? She is a newspaperwoman, for heaven's sake! It is her fucking job to know!)

And once inside, with the door closed, she slumps next to the coat-rack in the small vestibule; there is a hole in the ceiling she's meant to have fixed for the longest time. Hadn't she thought of asking Ernst, Ernest, or Ernesto over to take a look? Now a monster. A fucking monster. She tosses the steno pad and pencil onto the floor. Tomorrow, before she heads to the office, she'll call her friends, the women from the block, and apologize for being so absentminded. After that, she'll get on her knees and ask God for something. Anything.

Third, she'll cab it down to the *Queens Metropolitan* building on the Van Wyck Expressway. She'll have her story in hand. All she will have to do is sit back and wait for the editor teenybopper to stroll in to work, lazy as you please. She will hand her story over like the Hope Diamond.

They will not deny her this scoop. Those teenybopper heifers.

They'll certainly hate her lede: *"Watching the police lead that vicious rogue away was a sight never to be forgotten in the history of humankind."*

They'll likely make fun of the old lady whose head is still in the century of ringing telephones and clickity-clacking typewriters—they'll ask why she didn't just email the piece?

But then she'll say: Well, none of you are Miss Metropolitan, are you?

(Took you fucking long enough to get here, fucking 911! Yes, she's breathing! Please tell us she'll be all right! We love her like an auntie, really we do!)

She watches the last police van drive away. Then: not a soul to be seen, just miles of yellow tape and the vibration of a few idling cars. No sirens, no neighbor women, no knights in shining armor. What is the passage of time? When she finds herself outside her house for the last time that night, steno pad back in hand—she notices the way the snow takes its time coming from the heavens. Her father is talking to her, and she must listen. *Do what you gotta do, Matt. You hear me? Do what you gotta do. And always remember: Actions speak louder than words.*

Miss Metropolitan starts to put down that very line but hesitates. Of course, actions speak louder—but what sort of thing would that be for a seasoned journalist like herself to admit?

FERN

And, as always, in parting, we wish you LOVE,
PEACE, AND SOUL!

DON CORNELIUS

FUTURE SCENARIO

No, I'm not a space alien and neither is you, Gwinnie said. We were on the outside. Our hides chilled to the bone.

It was winter, that much of the weather I remembered. No Christmas trees but a forgotten smell of Pine-Sol all around us. We'd been led down the steps in nothing but our birthday suits and the near-invisible residue of Boss Man's underwear. I could've sworn our heads were shaven clean, but Gwinnie later told me they weren't. We had hair, she said. But it might could have been invisible, too.

I nodded. Thirteen plus ten years old now.

Shivering on the back edge of the ambulance, thin white blankets thrown over our shoulders. I looked oven-baked in this new light, a gingerbread girl/Spirit of Christmas Past.

Don't mention food, Gwinnie said sharply. We can't trust these people. They might make us eat their pictures, and I am so damn sick of pictures. Her voice was different. Her eyes were different. I felt like crying. Gwinnie, I said. There were people around us, recognizing us. Some took out cameras. Some broke out crying. *Are they for real? They are not for real.*

The girl next to me began to cry. Did you say that my name from now on is Gwinnie? she asked. Someone opened my mouth and closed it. Moments later I felt the effects of a pill swimming inside my forehead and closed my eyes.

But the ambulance drove fast, shaking what was left of our stomachs. Who could fade out? We threw up sand, sawdust, mold, and fake coffee from the drain. Faces wiped, bottles instead of pills. First stop: the police station, where people petted our heads and made the sign of the cross. Next stop: the Blood Hospital, where needles slid into the threads that were our veins. One day, two, one week, two? Our eyes swam like pills in our foreheads. Next stop, eventually: the Ward, where doctors and nurses and janitors and lab technicians and multipurpose bloodletters touched our heads and felt around our skin as if we'd been blessed by Jesus, God, and the Virgin Mary all rolled into one. They held lights up to our eyes and asked if we knew who we were. How many fingers, which of our areas were hurting, did we know what day it was, did we know what president it was, which hurt worse: above or below, what could we remember, were we *otherwise okay?* They handed us water bottles with pictures of mountains on them. At one point a whole bunch of brown women came into the Ward, took one look at us, and bawled like babies. (Social services, a nurse snarled under her breath. Don't let them take your candy bars, girls. Here, have some more, on us, on the Ward.) The brown women whipped out clipboards, scribbled, wiped their cheeks, scribbled some more. They stopped every few minutes to look at us. *What happened, babies? Didn't you know the World was looking for you all this time?* They didn't once notice our stash.

In general we had lots of visitors in the Ward: kind eyes, wet cheeks, warmed-over faces, shaky hands, brittle necks, clouded eyeglasses, dripping noses, stone smiles. Do you recognize any of them? I asked Gwinnie. Hell, was her answer. One time a tangerine lady came in. Her skin was literally the color of a tangerine. She's actually Black,

Gwinnie whispered. I can tell by the huge cross around her neck. The tangerine lady started patting Gwinnie on the head. Blew her nose into her sleeve, kept asking the nurses for a seat when all she had to do was open her fat eyes and see that every chair in the Ward *was empty.* She wouldn't sit down. *Dey no words in de world,* she said to Gwinnie, blowing her rickety nose again and again. Gwinnie finally opened her mouth, and the tangerine lady tore out of the room, upsetting gurneys, crashing into human beings. I wish I knew what she was planning to say. After all this mystery—couldn't things now just be black-and-white?

I wondered if that was her mother. Don't even think it, Gwinnie said, heading into the restroom, *our restroom,* a private place we both loved and feared.

The Ward, we learned, was actually a part of the Blood Hospital. Needles every way we turned. The needles reminded me of safety pins. Safety. I once thought about killing a man. Thank God I didn't.

We stayed in the Ward for three weeks—they gave us a calendar with Mickey Mouse on the cover and showed us how to cross out the days. We took a mountain of pills and cough syrups and special shots that did or didn't hurt; we slept in beds cushy as peas. What was the passage of time? We were afraid of doing the following: eat, sleep, bathe, turn off the lights, turn on the lights, look up, pray, feel our limbs, walk, run, lie down. We had trouble keeping our heads on our shoulders. Malnourished, said one voice. Possible brain damage, said another. As if we were not working right! Hey, I wanted to say, we were the best damn MODEL EMPLOYEES the world has ever seen. More pills added to the already-growing mountain. Tubes, sticky floors, special toilets. Toilets with locks on the doors. Toilets with little plastic jars where you peed and got more candy bars from the nurses. Screams everywhere, mostly ladies, mostly muffled. Gun shots, beeping, maybe babies being born.

A nurse gave me a yellow drink; afterward I thought I saw my brother Bud standing in the room with me. But it couldn't have been him, not with those muscles. I fell back into dreams—there was cotton candy growing on trees and cowboy costumes you could take out of the toy store without paying.

She's been sedated, said another voice.

The tangerine lady reappeared and kept trying to stay, but each time, she wound up knocking over wheelchairs and gurneys and doctors while trying to escape. Jesus, Gwinnie murmured. When will she get it through her head?

What, Gwinnie?

Never you mind.

When it was time to say goodbye to the Ward, everyone cried; the ambulances drove us to a new hospital, one full of Adirondack chairs and vitamin food. Brick on the outside, marble stairs and terraces on the inside, far as the eye would take you. Who knew you could build a balcony *on the inside*? We were in Manhattan now. I always got my geography right. Except for the ten years I didn't. Adirondack chairs in the balcony sun, a six-pack of Coca-Cola. I remembered the red can. Here we are.

At this point Gwinnie and I could walk almost upright, and the soles of our hands no longer burned. There were no nails or screws or pins on us anywhere. Whenever anyone told us to breathe, we did so, loud and clear. The doctors in the picnic-chair hospital didn't wear stethoscopes, and the nurses told us we could call them by their first names. Julie. Rebecca. Yvonne. Tynesha. Marion. Shoshanna. Rhondelle. Not a last name in sight, not a Miss or Mrs. in the whole bunch. Is this how girls show respect nowadays? Gwinnie asked. *Is this how we girls are supposed to do?* She and I laughed. We got fine with that. Some hospital staff (hereafter known as *the* Hospital Staff) preferred to keep their names private because of TV cameras and liabilities and thrill-seekers and whatnot. That was also fine by us.

People hovered like wasps and came to big decisions: we girls had to be cured. We girls could not stay who we had become or what we might've been becoming. (It didn't matter what we wanted to be.) A white man came in once and told us to forget any words Boss Man might have taught us. You are free, girls. Your words are your own.

When had they never been?

A skinny white lady appeared one day; she wore a suit and tie, just like a man. NOW is NOW, she said. NOW is a place for happiness and rescue and awareness. You do not have to chew magazine pictures anymore or sleep under the bed. NOW is NOW. You are cured; you are being cured.

Gwinnie added under her breath: We are cured, smoked, healed, pickled, and preserved.

The skinny white lady laughed. On her badge it said LCSW. It's funny how humor can reach in and save a life, she said. We shrugged our shoulders. This conversation was making us tired. But it was nice to know we could open and close our eyes as much as we wanted and not get in trouble.

SHE WOULDN'T STOP

No one will treat you like a piece of meat anymore, the Hospital Staff told us (they all were studying for their associate's and bachelor's and master's in health and human services communications public administration health advocacy—and so forth. They all used to be an English major at Hunter. But that didn't pay the bills.)

White men, brown men, white ladies, purple ladies, orange ladies, scarlet ladies, too many to color. Hospital workers. Hospital onlookers. Touching and asking and answering. Flipping over pages on clipboards. Speaking in English, Chinese, Spanish; done up in bright lipstick and soft shoulders, muscle shirts or herringbone patterns. Taking our temperature against endless beeps. One time some *opaque* folks showed up holding church pamphlets, asking if Gwinnie or me remembered that Jesus had always been in our corner? If not, they were here to remind us.

Everyone was trying to communicate. Doctors from other hospitals. Nurses with girls at home like us. Firemen who'd taken up a collection. An elementary school in Bayside that had written a bag of letters. A school in the Bronx, one in Alphabet City. More doctors. Police officers with girls at home like us. One or two retired schoolteachers. Pastors. Rabbis. General Rabble of God. But also people that didn't believe in God. People that blamed God. Everyone trying to impart something. A lesson, a hope, a regret, a condemnation. What are they saying, Gwinnie whispered, her eyes as wide as proverbial flying saucers. We'd been in the picnic-chair hospital for just over fourteen Mickey Mouse calendar days. Try listening, I said back. They're forming words. We can learn their language if we try.

The first sentence, repeated over and over: *What he did, girls, was wrong.*

Second sentence: *You are the real victims here, no matter what.*

Good Lord, Gwinnie said. I thought they were saying something new.

THE MOTHERS

Of course they came up as everybody's (and their grandmother's) favorite subject. The Hospital Staff tried to get us to see the bigger picture:

She couldn't have meant to lose you;
She looked in every corner for you;
She tried to kill herself at least once but then;
She enrolled herself voluntarily at Bellevue and asked for a cure and then;
She cried. She wept;
She beseeched God for forgiveness (and when that didn't work, she turned to Moses and the Virgin Mary);
She pounded her head;
She pulled out her hair;
She went on a hunger strike, refused to die for a week, a total drama queen;
She returned to Bellevue, where they never let her go.
She escaped just to find you;
She carved little crosses into her arms just like a horror movie;
She never meant to be anything other than who she was.
Don't you know how much she suffered?
That was never me, she always maintained.
Just remember, girls. A mother's love is the greatest thing.

ONE DOOR CLOSES BUT

Gwinnie and I asked the Hospital Staff about Katanya, if we could see her. The baby. Oh, her grandmother came and got her, they said. Her grandmother? We nearly threw up our food (farina with brown sugar)—*Who said anything about a grandmother?*

But she did exist and had come to the Blood Hospital and waited and whisked the baby off to Woodside, Queens. A grandmother and a step-grandfather. We kept trying to remember what—if anything—Jesenia had told us about her home; her stories were starting to unravel in our heads. Why can't *we* be with the baby, we demanded. She's just as much ours, we brought her to life! The Hospital Staff told us to calm down, handed us a drink that tasted of mud. It lulled our voices as well as our minds—our eyes began swimming down our necks. Maybe it was best the baby didn't see you anytime soon. Maybe it was best everyone got better on their own. Doesn't time heal all wounds?

The Hospital Staff said, We think it's about time we told you our names. Why? we asked. And they answered, Because we love you.

THE MOTHERS II

That didn't stop us from begging to see Katanya. We screamed and shouted and everything in between. One day the Hospital Staff said, How about we try this? Do either of you want to meet with *your* mothers?

Gwinnie snorted. I said, But what if we forgot our mothers? The Hospital Staff stared. Yes, I continued, it is humanly possible to forget who your mother is. You remember the scent of Jean Naté, but you have no clue about the lullaby. The Hospital Staff opened their mouths. You mean, they asked, *that you could forget what you'd been trying so long to recall?* Yes, I answered. That's what I mean. What we mean. What a pity, they said. But then: Forgive us. We haven't walked a mile in your shoes.

The next day someone somewhere called in TV's Dr. Ezra. Or maybe he came on his own.

He was large and skinny and chalky and had his own psychology game show where people confessed to being drunkards or hoarders or mail-order brides or wealthy princes in Africa. He spoke like the chickens in the Bugs Bunny cartoons. When we awoke, we saw him sitting at the nurses' station, waiting for the green light. Because we always got to say when it was the green light. This was not BEHIND

WORLD, after all. TV's Dr. Ezra waved and walked into our room and saw us in our pajamas—Girls, he shouted. Girls!

We're officially women, Gwinnie said, rolling her eyes.

He brought us breakfast from Wendy's, and as we were eating, gave us his suggestions. Such as: maybe we should let a bit more time pass before we did anything *rash*. Like meet with our mothers, God bless. Or reach out to the baby, God bless. He said me and Gwinnie were still in a state of shock and recovery. Healing is a process, he said, and you women didn't do anything wrong, but eventually you have to think of yourselves, about anything that might could further damage you, please do that for yourselves and for me; you *women* deserve all the time in the world. When Gwinnie and I were quiet, he said, Think of yourselves first for once! You have no reason to say sorry! You are invincible!

TV's Dr. Ezra removed another bag of egg-and-bacon thingamajigs from his coat pocket. It takes a village, women. We're all here to help. You didn't do anything wrong.

That's what I've been saying all along, Gwinnie snarked. Though when we five minutes later threw up the Wendy's, we nevertheless apologized.

FORWARD AND REVERSE PSYCHOLOGY

He had a few tricks up his sleeve, TV's Dr. Ezra. The Hospital Staff rumored he was "into us for the ratings." His show came on at 4 in the afternoon (right after Judge Judy yelling at fat white ladies and their skinny Black beaus) and played on all the flat-screens in the picnic-chair hospital. All he cares about is getting rich, the Hospital Staff told us. TV's Dr. Ezra countered: What's so bad about that?

TV's Dr. Ezra wanted to be our friend. We signed *x*'s on the contract that said we were okay with him being our friend. On TV. In front of millions of viewers. You'll be doing the world a favor, he explained. Everyone will see you and learn a deeper truth about humanity. Your mothers will see you and learn a deeper truth about love. I know you can't possibly imagine this yet, but you are changing the world.

We wondered why TV's Dr. Ezra didn't already know we were masters at imagining.

He was planning a series of episodes around us. Tell me about Jesenia, he said. She'll be Episode 2, after we do Heartbroken Mothers on Episode 1. (According to the Mickey Mouse calendar, we'd been in the picnic-chair hospital for six months. We took enough pills and liquids and oils to dress a Thanksgiving turkey.)

What would you like to know?

Where is Jesenia? Can you tell me that?

We don't have an answer. But if you're interested in who she is, and what magic she makes, please listen. This is what we can tell you.

MODEL EMPLOYEES' INVENTORY (AS TOLD TO TV'S DR. EZRA DURING THE TAPING OF EPISODE 2 OF *HEAL THYSELF WITH DR. EZRA!* WHEN HE ASKED ABOUT THE THIRD VICTIM-FEMALE WHO PEOPLE ASSUMED WAS DEAD BUT HE TOOK OUR WORD FOR IT THAT MOST LIKELY SHE WAS HIDING SOMEWHERE SAFE BECAUSE JESUS CHRIST WHAT ELSE COULD'VE HAPPENED?

1. Jesenia could make a beautiful doll baby out of soap scraps and leftover extension cord.

2. She could paint a watercolor picture with beet juice and cigarette ash.

3. She could type an imaginary typewriter faster than anyone we knew, faster than in real life, in high school, the last year she was in it, ninth grade, both fall and spring semester— ninety-two words a minute, a Townsend Harris record.

4. Jesenia was a master makeup artist—better than Michelle Phan on all those YouTube videos we never saw until we were in the picnic-chair hospital and already too old for them. Precious skin, night-on-the-town lips. Feathered hair like Jennifer Lopez or any white girl. Whatever you wanted, Jesenia could do: repair you or make you a beauty queen.

5. Jesenia could fix a broken leg with cotton balls and safety pins. Why in the world did people think she was dead?

6. She could lift a broken bed using only her bare hands.

7. She could jump an eternity of jumping jacks, making it all the way to one thousand. And not even break a sweat. The

rest of us only made it to two or three hundred. How could a dead woman do that?

8. Jesenia could make up an apt saying for anything. *In order to form a more perfect union, do establish I love you, girls.*

9. Jesenia could make you forget how to cry.

10. She could make the mice in the basement sing "The Star-Spangled Banner"—in tune.

11. Jesenia had a secret telephone to God. She would not always let us listen in.

12. Be Strong. You Know Who You Are. Those were her words.

13. Don't give up hope. You know who you are. Ditto her words.

14. Don't cry. (But we did, many, many times.)

15. Jesenia could turn a box of Steak-umms and a box of raisins into clams casino. Never mind if both had an expired expiration date.

16. She was a wise judge of character. Life was meant to be lived. Just tell us who's spreading the rumors that she's dead. No, we have no idea where she is. But we know in our bones she's out there.

17. She could make everything out of one ingredient: water. Lasagna, birthday cake, spring salad—all crafted out of nothing but H_2O.

18. Jesenia took the blame even when she didn't have to. You don't like the food I made, Boss Man, then *do me*. But don't punish them. They ain't done nothing. Punish me. Let them hang free.

19. Jesenia could tame the universe. One day we'll all be brave, she whispered in front of passed-out Boss Man.

20. She could trap dust mice in her nimble fingers and set them free into the wild blue yonder.

21. Remove—with the help of Comet and Clorox bleach—our toothaches better than any old dentist. Be honest: how in heaven could such a creature no longer exist?

EPISODE 3: PAST AND FUTURE RECOUNT

The day I was captured by Boss Man. The day I was ensnared by Boss Man. The day Boss Man trapped me—to tell you the truth I was already feeling kinda sorry for myself. I was walking down the street, wishing for something, and then this man pops up and said, I have a puppy I need to find a home for—are you a good girl for it? His hands were like sandpaper when he shook mine; and later, after the mystery of the puppy was solved and he gripped me into the future, I thought my skin would be rubbed off the page, like it happens in cartoons. After the mystery of the puppy was solved, firecrackers suddenly explode in my stomach, blowing my head through the roof. Then my head comes back down again and I'm okay. That sort of thing. Tom and Jerry, Bugs Bunny.

The day I was confiscated by Boss Man, I screamed, natural reflex. There was no dog. He never thought I was a good girl. *You got the wrong girl here. I'm a straight B student! Let me go!*

Nevertheless Boss Man laughed in my face. Girl, please. You have no fucking idea!

That is one of the seven words you can't say on TV or radio, TV's Dr. Ezra says. Plus, you don't have to cry, Fern. All that is behind you. Can we do it again?

I start to scream. This wasn't on the agenda, one of his assistants up and says. But ratings gold, another adds.

Like magic, Ms. Refuge barges into the taping area and sweeps me up. She actually waves her thick salami arms around like she's scattering mosquitoes—*Show's over!*—and clearly TV's Dr. Ezra doesn't appreciate this but he gets up from his couch and leaves without a fight. The assistants follow. Ms. Refuge shakes her head, kissing me down to earth. She says, That man's just out of his depth.

ANITA BAKER SINGING "ANGEL"

Oh, Ms. Refuge! What a perfect moniker for this lunchmeat-Italian-bread-pickled heap of woman! She has been around since the first ambulance, which in me and Gwinnie's case is *since forever*. We noticed her little by little, like a dream that you slowly remember. The first true mother we might have ever had. Or the person you used to call "cousin" even though you had no idea where they came from.

Ms. Refuge. She did not shade her eyes when questions were asked. She was not into *PERMANENT FLEETING EMPOWERMENT*™; she couldn't care less about being *THE YOU YOU USED TO BE ONLY BETTER*™—programs TV's Dr. Ezra encouraged us to join ("First year free!"). Ms. Refuge took notes but showed every last one of them to us. You are not experiments, she said. But he does have a point. Maybe through you, the world can gain a better understanding. The world can be a better place.

We pretended we knew wherefrom she was talking. Ms. Refuge ate off our plates before we were done. She kissed away our tears. Our germs were her germs. We knew she liked it that way.

THE EXPERT

Some of Ms. Refuge's psychology classes were in real life held at York College, some online. This meant that a computer taught you how to be smart. They had their own computer textbooks!

According to one of them, entitled *Varieties of Mind*, there was this theory: in everyone lived the *Old and New, Repressed and Suppressed*, the *Id and the Ego and the Superego*, and so on, we never got all Ms. Refuge's words in correct order but even still: a person who might be unhappy but wanted to be *happier than unhappy* might find it necessary to tap into as many of these Varieties of Mind as possible. Some people called that: living life to the fullest. Others checked to see which therapists were covered under their insurance. Read this any way you like or take it with a grain of salt, Ms. Refuge said. We listened. We could tell she was glad we were listening.

Forget BEHIND WORLD.

Say hello to Old Mind and New Mind.

Or so the computer textbook seemed to say. Beware of potential difficulties: it could so happen that Old Mind would *sneakily slither* into New Mind when New Mind wasn't paying attention, and BAM! New Mind would be bowled over by surprises, things too numerous and complicated to name. Persons might collide with places, bits of conversation might turn into ranting raves, and perhaps a niblet of memory would trigger the owner of the New Mind back into some forgotten brain mash of childhood. You might walk away from that memory feeling pleased or lifted up. Or you might want to cut lines into your arms. You might go around, after the *true* amalgamation of Old and New Minds, saying: Hey, dancing *really was* my escape. Or: Hey, Prince *really was* the father figure that I never had. Or: Hey, the reason I can't stop eating all this cotton candy is because the world chose to move on without me.

(It could also mean that you're nothing but a cotton-candy-eating pig, Gwinnie pointed out when we were alone. But it's not a bad thing for us to be a pig these days, isn't that right, Fern?)

The computer textbook—and Ms. Refuge—had lots of explanations. We never felt at a loss.

But then it so happened that one cold day, we were loaded up into Detective Amor's car. Detective Love. Circa Thanksgiving 2009. We had no idea what was coming.

Old Mind could be a wolf in sheep's clothing, Gwinnie whispered to me. We might see the place and die right on the spot. You are stronger than you think, Ms. Refuge, who overhead Gwinnie's loud voice, said. Relax, ladies. There'll be no dying on my watch.

BUD

*He had entered the rough world of men, where a man's
acts follow him wherever he goes in the form of story.*

<small>DAVID MALOUF, *RANSOM*</small>

A VOICE IN THE NIGHT

Was kicked out five years to the day Fern disappeared. Up to then it was just a blue rage of time, one step after the other, a domino effect of misery where I looked into every culvert in St. Albans Park, along any awning on Merrick Boulevard, under any pillow in the back bedroom—and still, my sister was gone. Don't mention THAT DAY, Mum would say, out of the blue rage, to me, to no one, to the rug under her feet, into which she chunked her heels over and over. *Fern, chunk, Fern, chunk.* Mum would say, If I ever hear you mention THAT DAY again . . . but then, nothing; she'd go back to the usual unnormal normal state, almost as if Fern had been born a ghost; but not quite because there were Mum's shoes chunking in the rug and all those colorful medications down her throat. I TRIED, BUD. I TRIED.

Mum had resumed double-double shifts at Jamaica Hospital and sometimes came home with beef patties for dinner and sometimes nothing. The pills jangled in her nurse's pocket like spare change or old-time subway tokens. It was not possible (for her) to forget Fern, but it was possible (for her) to forget not to forget Fern. Mum would plump down in the new massage recliner DICK (formerly known as the mother's unpronounceable second boyfriend) had bought rent-to-own from Aaron's furniture (*Baby, you know that you actually paying nine hundred dollars for fifty-dollar trash?*) and he'd shrug. Laugh it off, standing with open arms to receive her home, on his lap, in the bed, drinking the last of the apple juice or my stashed coquito, kissing her lobes into heaven.

The house had gone to pot. Mum taking it really hard but then less hard and then Fern all but forgotten. One time she whispered something in my ear, and I shouted, *If I have to hear the word "I TRIED SO HARD" one more time, I'll kill someone. I absolutely hate that word!!!* And she simply jangled her pockets and went to bed.

DICK closed the door behind her, standing around, giving me major side-eye. A boy like you shouldn't be drinking like this, he said, lifting the yellow coquito bottle from behind his back. What if I went and told Anna about you? he asked. What if I told her about her precious baby boy and his hidden booze that smells like rotten eggs and on top of that all his homo magazines that he thinks no one knows about? You not the only one with a closet, Bud. Ha ha.

She'd love me just the same, I countered. But I was feeling unsure, unsteady. DICK threw back his molars. Ha Ha. Okay, smart boy. What if I went and told Anna all the other stuff you do? There's only so much the poor woman can take.

Go ahead, I said. I ain't done nothing wrong.

We'll see about that, he says. But then days go by. I wait for all the other things I do wrong. Days and more days. Suddenly he is nice to me. DICK says I can keep all the *Soul Train* tapes if I'm still into that crap. He says he will go out with me and look for my sister—he creases his eyes and says the pain never goes away. WE TRIED SO HARD. WE FUCKING TRIED SO HARD. He asks me if I want Golden Krust beef patties instead of CTown brand, just as I consider raising my hidden knife to his throat.

Weeks go by, Mum had 90 percent pill blood; you could see it in her eyes. Prozac, Valium, Fiorinal, Christmas Trees, Blue Heaven, LOLs, YOLOs, etc. She held one tiny pill up to the kitchen light and called it Anna-Christina, laughing and crying. Why are you laughing at your own name? I asked. Because I should have been a character in a novel, was her ridiculous answer. Look at all the tragedy! IT'S SO SO HARD! AND WE TRIED, WE TRIED!

Next night she wandered into her double-double shift at Jamaica Hospital and never came back. DICK told me, They need to run some tests, and I asked, What tests? and he said, If she doesn't stick to the program, then her ass is in jail.

DICK after that being nicer than nice as all get-out. Whenever he raised his hand, I began to understand it would not come down on me. Still, I felt afraid; the soles of my feet hurt whenever he came near.

I got some friends I'd like you to meet, he whispered. They like boys like you. We can make some money.

Mum came home with eyes like truck tires. DICK rifled through her purse, called 911. Ambulances fired down upon us and left one more time with Mum, a shadow of herself; DICK said it was for her own good.

But me: I had a different plan: not to be there when Mum came back and jail was no longer an option and her blood was sadness-free. I knew that when she saw me, she would automatically fall into hurt. I didn't want to hurt Mum. I would never hurt Mum. And I did not want to get to know DICK's friends. I would never kill Mum.

Five years to the day Fern was taken (because contrary to popular belief, what else could have happened?), I left or was chased out the door or was pursued by something that was ABOVE AND NOT ALTOGETHER KIND. Running to my friend Rico's, I got the last bit of tears out. Told him my plans as he cradled me. Let's find Fern, I said. Let's move away. Let's laugh. Let's dance in the streets. Let's get married. Let's start a family that does not rely on a lullaby or fairy tale.

Man, you tripping, Rico said, swallowing the Anna-Christinas I gave him. Let's just enjoy ourselves, man, he said.

The sky held moonfuls of capsule crystals, all waiting to spill out, into culverts, along awnings, under pillows. Rico kept laughing. I for my part found nothing to enjoy. Two months later I was on the street.

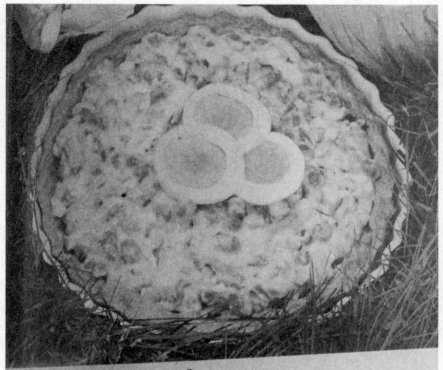

...frozen mixed vegetables for this tasty flan

...af to cool, beating from time ...me.

...t the cream until soft peaks ...formed. Fold into the pine-...le mixture. Beat the egg ...tes until stiff but not dry. Pour ...pineapple mixture over the ...tes and fold in lightly. Divide ...ween chilled soufflé dishes ...chill until set. Garnish with ...ted grapes, if desired.

PICNIC MENU *serves 8*

APPETIZER SOUP
RAISED BACON AND EGG PIE
PORK LOAF
ENDIVE SALAD
TOMATO COLESLAW
GREEN SALAD
BAPS
SUMMER PUDDING

warmed, wide-necke...
jug. Take the cheese ...
sprinkle on each ser...

RAISED BACON AND EGG PIE

For hot water crust:
1 pound (4 cups) a...
   flour
2½ teaspoons salt
½ cup shortening
⅞ cup milk or wa...
Beaten egg for gla...

FERN

*For years, I've dreamed of being more than just another
one of us.*

Mitchell S. Jackson, "High Pursuit"

EMPLOYMENT LANDSCAPES

It was Boss Man's belief that work would make us free. We couldn't just sit around on the couches and eat bonbons—even if those couches were made of planks and corrugated cardboard and nails and torn-up bath towels. Don't get too comfy! We were MODEL EMPLOYEES. Here were our stations:

<u>SHEETROCK-KITCHEN:</u> Here you had to shell canned peas that had already been shelled, peel canned peaches that had no skin on them whatsoever, scrub the green, gray, and black spores on the fading wallpaper that faded in and out of view, put peas and peaches into giant cardboard box near all manner of chains and do not eat for days or weeks or months.

<u>PIPES LOW & HIGH:</u> Here you had to peel the lead paint off and polish any pipes free of bumps and warts, knock against them if there was an emergency. Forget you knew the word *emergency*.

<u>DUST-BUNNY-DRAIN:</u> Jobs not entirely specified.

<u>BROKEN-DOWN-WASHING-MACHINE:</u> This is what you did here. Step inside, make yourself comfortable. Get used to the new coil of your body in that barrel, to the contemplative notes {B-flat} of the top slamming down on your head, and then to the hum of silence, *your* silence, in that washing machine; you had to understand

that it was all about the peace, the aloneness, the licking of wounds, the vowing of revenge. You had to wonder if Boss Man was actually doing a favor by stashing you in here. You kept quiet as a church mouse.

PASS-THROUGH-CHASM: Here you counted the threads in the sheets, unraveled them, loomed them back together. You greeted and killed water bugs. You didn't give them names. You pretended like it wasn't hard to see through blood.

LOWER-EMPLOYEE-WORK-DEPARTMENT: Here you polished the stones on the floor, the gravel. Here you scraped away the black stuff again, the green stuff, the orange moss that grew over everything when it rained. Here you realized you would not die from a common cold because a common cold could last centuries. Here you secretly dreamt—against Jesenia's advice—of a pair of pants, a pillow.

DOOR MIRAGES
(ONE FRIDAY IN 2002?)

They were everywhere, even with our eyes closed. When we first came into the house, we believed they would open and close like regular doors. We once belonged to the regular world, so why not? The chains and twine and ropes frightened us; we discovered that even when Boss Man opened them, the doors led to nowhere. He laughed at our mistakes. The doors were mirages. Even much later, when we *could* stand in front of them and bump them open with our paltry hips, the doors remained something out of a fairy-tale book.

It was our job to repair the doors—to fix their chains and ropes and twines as best we could, preparing the thresholds for his inspection, accepting any consequences if the doors were not up to code. My code's the only one that matters, bitch. Yeah, I saw you looking at me funny.

One day Boss Man was snoring off his hundredth Tom Collins. He'd told us to make sure the chain holsters were screwed tight in place. I know you devils be thinking about leaving the minute I turn my back, he said. Do what I say or you'll have hell to pay.

You're a poet and you don't know it, Gwin said. (Another tooth gone.)

She and I were chained at the feet and hands. This was still sort of in the beginning (Ms. Refuge would later tell us it was circa 1999–2002); Gwin mischievously whispered, How bout we make sure the chain holsters are loose—*just a touch*?

No, I said. But I was interested.

What about your safety pin? she asked.

It was stowed in my hair, which at the time was a wild mess of lice and leaves. I kept it there because Boss Man was scared to death of insects.

Let's use *my* safety pin, Gwin said.

No, I said. You'll get in trouble. You'll be all like George Washington's wooden teeth. Let's forget it. No, use mines.

Gwin swiped at my crown. It took a bunch of tries.

And sure enough. Boss Man heard us from the sleep of his booze; he wrassled himself partway up, fly down, pits awash, squinting his eyes as if trying to detect the *smallest change* in the landscape. My pin in Gwin's cheek. And it was as if Boss Man could see the lightbulb floating over her head; he put two and two together and smiled. From some far corner Jesenia snored—it was not unusual for her to eat pills and try to open the doors in her dreams, a thing Boss Man could not stop her from doing, try as he might. He kept his eye trained on us.

Two plus two. When he ¼ sobered himself up to the doorjamb and discovered the holster slightly loose, he laughed. Wondering how we'd had the balls to carry out such a thing?

And after he ½ way sobered up and delivered his Employee Reprimand, both she and I worked to keep our lips in a straight line. I think it took a month for Gwinnie's face to regroup. It took three weeks for my arms to go from primate to homo sapiens. *I'll say it was my idea*, were her last words before that Employee Reprimand. How I loved her for those words. In the scheme of things, though, her truth made absolutely no difference.

CASE STUDY OF FRIDAYS
(2003?)

Couches. Sometimes one would miraculously appear. Herringbone tweed with a few cushions missing, or a checkerboard flannel that reminded us of the lumberjacks on Bugs Bunny. Jesenia asked for and received a beanbag—Boss Man then *did her* on said beanbag and apologized afterward for busting a few of its seams. That time it was Gwin and me strewn on a bonded leather couch that stuck to our skin. Can't we go back to the sofa that smelled like a horse, she asked, politely. *Shut up, shut the hell up.* The next time it was the off-white loveseat that stank of somebody's insides. *Ask me again and see what happens, bitches.* Most often we had to deal with an invisible sofa. We didn't like that one the best.

Boss Man got us TVs. Sometimes it was a Zenith or Magnavox, ten inches or sixteen inches, white frame face with fake wood panel sides. We watched people dance and answer questions for money or parade around in nothing but their underwear.

The Quasar had a coat hanger antenna—*I'll be damned if I let those digitals make me go digital!*—as well as clouds of bumblebees battering the screen. I thought I made out my brother Bud's face in those bees. I thought I heard his voice. *It's not a question of if,* he was saying, *it's a matter of when.*

CASE STUDY OF FRIDAYS
(2006?)

Boss Man had us laying in an unidentified flying space. Our job was
to listen. He let our eyes be free; kept our hands and feet in chains,
the kind you would find on a bicycle. There was a carpet underneath
us and a blue recycling blanket on top. I could smell Jesenia next to
me: every now and then she had the fragrant properties of a real-life
girl. Boss Man said to us, I don't give a damn if you want a day off.
Your job today is TO LISTEN. TO ME. We did as we were told.
We suddenly felt afraid, like he had gone shopping for someone else.

Jesenia was all into it, moaning, Tell us, Boss Man. Tell us what you
want us to hear.

She was swaddled in tight white cloths, like a mummy; likely it was
her period time and Boss Man didn't want all that *excess fluidity*. Jesenia cleared her throat. She knew the real deal, she was magic. Jesenia
could charm snakes in a basket just by using her broken lips. Tell us
again about your mama, she said. I know you want to. Tell us that
story again, Boss Man.

Boss Man frowned. My mama was a cunt. She would tie me up.
Make me take tabasco in the eyes if I was naughty. Literally wash
my mouth out with carbolic. Laugh when the lightning in the yard
came *this close* to my head. Get mad as hell when the neighbor ladies

used to poke around. *Hey Miss, you sure your son's supposed to be out back strapped to that tree like that?*

My poor Boss Man!

Miss, those neighbor ladies used to say, *we don't like it how you be treating that darling boy.*

Heavens, Boss Man! You were a darling boy?

Miss, those old bags warned, *we gone call the cops on you. You should be loving that angel child. Don't you realize it's a gift?*

How could they not jump in? Jesenia cried. Poor little boy of mine. Thank you for the sweater you gave me last week, Boss Man, and by the way, how did you know unicorns was my favorite color?

One of them bitches had the nerve to say, *Miss, we are getting most fed up.* And there I was. The tree namely my best friend. My soul mate.

Why did it take so long for your mama to wake up, Jesenia sobbed. Oh Boss Man!

(Gwin and I stayed quiet. We listened. We'd received sweaters the week before, too, but they were old ones that didn't fit Jesenia any-more. Her stomach was taking on a life of its own, hint, hint. I could not remember the clothes I came here with, but wearing Jesenia's old sweater (pink with shadows around the neck and wrists) made me feel good, loved. Someone should have called the cops, Jesenia slobbered.

Boss Man was snoring. And then we three girls were simply staring up at the ceiling, away from those drunken knees: we stared at the buckling popcorn waves overhead where you could see the patterns of questions that had been floating around forever. Boss Man had accidentally left a copy of the *Daily News* on his lap, and as he slept, it drifted onto the edge of my thighs. With movements, Gwin was able to shove a page closer. I craned my neck. No dates, no weather. A man in a baseball cap and an advertisement for microwave clam chowder. That looks yummy, Gwin said when I described the page to her.

Jesenia was restless, though. Stop trying to read, Fern. I don't see the point in getting your hopes up. Why don't we all just accept that this is our home and that being MODEL EMPLOYEES is what we do best and pray that the universe outside don't care as much about us as Boss Man?

Was she right? I did not try to remove the newspaper from my thigh. I loved the feeling of the words there, near my core, my viscera, telegraphing messages in a language I enjoyed inventing.

WHAT THE NEWSPAPERS
COULD'VE ANSWERED

What is the actual day?

What does outside look like again?

What is the sound of the Long Island Rail Road at Jamaica Station? How does a blow dryer work?

What is the radio station that used to play all the hits?

Are there any neighbors?

What does this house look like from the outside?

What does a pizza look like?

Is it possible to forget what a pizza is but still remember the words to the preamble?

What is the actual day?

CASE STUDY OF FRIDAYS
(2001?)

We asked these things in our mind until Boss Man woke up, got mad, did his thing to our innards and outtards, left the house in darkness. We ached for a completely flat world. You wouldn't find our honorable mentions in any newspaper, anywhere.

CASE STUDY OF SUNDAYS (2002?)

Jesenia knew the position of the sun, even if there was not a trace of it to be found where we lived—she relied on the shadows and gusts of wind that blew into the house as we hung, lay, or kneeled. In time she taught us how to read what bit of sun there was. Twelve hours, twenty-four hours, summer, winter. We learned to hide these facts from Boss Man.

He came back from "visiting family out in Jersey" and lined us up on a cardboard pallet near PASS-THROUGH-CHASM, careful to link our chains together. I'm a tell you something, he said. Then he left. Days later (according to our sun) he came back, stared at us, burst into tears, left again. Meanwhile Jesenia had begun teaching us the heartbeats of the moon, the ways its tides set our bodies in motion. Gwinnie, you about ready to get your bleeding. I can see the Fourth Quarter in your face. You are ripe for anything, God bless.

Anything come outta me that ain't blood I'll bite its head off, Gwin sighed.

Jesenia angled her head toward me. We were a breath apart, normal flatness. Boss Man had tossed an open can of black beans at us, but so far, they only reached our toes. Sorry, Fern, Jesenia said. But your moons have passed once again. It's not a totally bad thing, Fern. You are young. You will find other ways to be a mama bear.

She was, of course, talking about my non-borns.

EXPLICATION

What is a non-born? Let me count the ways.

Each time one set in me—like that old junket pudding Bud used to make when we ran out of food—Boss Man'd get mad and kick me down some serious basement stairs. Or else throw me on the rope. Squeeze my neck in such a love-hold that the tissue-issue came trickling out the other end like a stream.

Six babies or maybe more. (Cold black beans are a great source of protein, did you know that? Jesenia again, that wizard of real information. They can help you have a baby that sticks. Have faith. We will summon those beans!)

My non-borns. Ballpark guesses, that's all. Boss Man said he did what he did because he couldn't abide the calm in my face. I want a MODEL EMPLOYEE who possesses passion and fire, he complained. You have neither. You don't laugh or cry or thank God I found you.

But what about Gwin? What about her?

What do you take me for? Gwin's nothing but a fresh-mouth skank. Shit for brains. In no way mother material.

So what makes you think you're the fathering kind, I asked, aware I might be bashed. But Boss Man suddenly became thoughtful.

Fern. Listen. You're not like other girls.

CASE STUDY OF SUNDAYS
(1999?)

There is a Ferris wheel and a cone topped with pink cotton candy and a pink squishy elephant slogging through a pink desert with pink Twinkies lining the sunset sky. There is me and my brother Bud and a mother and a father figure—the original father figure. There are long lines of cheerful people and the sounds of kids racing and crashing into hips and arms and legs. An organ plays a happy tune that is more silent movie than church. Girls lock arms with boys and boys lock arms with boys and girls rub shoulders with girls and smile with teeth that have been scrubbed clean into river stones. Food fragrances snake through the air, giving us all the shivers: authentic Pennsylvania funnel cakes, Chinese fried dumplings, Brooklyn chicken and waffles in Styrofoam containers. Did I mention the pink Twinkies up above? Nothing is holding us back—me and Bud and the mother figure and the original father figure. We feel sick to our stomachs but still ask for more, more, more.

BROKEN-DOWN-WASHING-MACHINE DREAMS

Let's not forget the mice.

There were the rumors that traveled down from those attic vermin to the basement, from PIPES LOW & HIGH to DUST-BUNNY-DRAIN. Rumors that Boss Man had a wife and daughter somewhere in Queens. Rumors that his son was a stillbirth named Harvey after Harvey Wallbanger. That Boss Man was an illegal from some country you had to escape from by raft or spiderweb or military boots or bloody cross (*Must a been Transylvania,* Gwin surmised). There was a rumor that the maternal punishments Boss Man endured had put him into the loony bin for months when he was a kid, and that he was expected to love his mother afterward, no questions asked. The rumor that he cut off her lips with a pair of grape scissors.

(Boss Man could very well have told the mice what to tell us. He had no pity whatsoever. And the mice didn't know when to stop.)

Supposedly he drove a school bus for years, for a Catholic school. Supposedly he touched the hems of the nuns there, even when they whacked him with their rosaries. They fired him for telling off-color jokes in the schoolyard. Supposedly he started a fight with a nun named Sister Ursula, a white lady; he told her he'd wanted to become one of them, a real man of the cloth, an altar boy at the foot of Christ the Redeemer, and she laughed. Supposedly he put his fist through her concrete, saying he wasn't used to taking no for an answer.

One time when I was in BROKEN-DOWN-WASHING-MACHINE, atoning for thinking that one of the windows was actually a window and trying to *see* out of it *with my eyes* and maybe talk to an old crone who couldn't mind her business *if you paid her*—I spotted a Polaroid picture flat on the floor. I was actually getting pummeled. But I barely noticed the fists, the slamming open and shut of the porthole door. All I saw were those white edges around the Polaroid, the curl of hardening paper against the soft, already faded colors of a mystery child.

Boss Man didn't notice throughout the pummeling that I was steady studying the Polaroid. He got up from his knees when he was done. Meanwhile I kept looking at that picture for days and days, finally discovering a way to tuck it inside the drum and preserve it there for safety. The child was a girl—Boss Man's daughter? I wondered. Could I have known her? The girl didn't so much as notice me back. She was annoyed, in fact—super annoyed. So much so that she started leaving the picture for hours at a time, stepping outside the white border and disappearing into the dust-mite air. She returned unexpectedly, quietly; she regained her footing within the shiny edges and leaned against the side of a house that looked like what I imagined this house once looked like. A rubber ball on the grass in front of her. Shingles sliding off the roof in slow motion. Stop staring at me like that, she yelled. I hate it when nobodies stare at nobodies!

I'm sorry, I said.

Insulted, she'd take off again.

SALVATION ARMY
FAST FORWARD

Fun fact: after we were liberated, I kept that Polaroid in the Salvation Army dresser Ms. Refuge found for us. The dresser propped open the door to the apartment bedroom Gwinnie and I came to share in the picnic-chair hospital. After Boss Man's death, I moved the Polaroid to a jewelry box sent to me courtesy of Cindy Diaz. *You girls are so strong, but you don't need to worry about the baby! She's well cared for!* (Years had gone by: was she still a baby?) We watched the Eyewitness News at 6: Boss Man had offed himself while awaiting his last court trial. A stray shoelace that doubled as a hangman's rope. Are you feeling what I'm thinking? Gwinnie asked, her face as set as soft marble.

Boss Man's death. Suddenly the girl in the Polaroid was talking all this gibberish. Why hadn't I tried harder to figure out who she was? Why hadn't I guessed her fate? When (a la Detective Amor and Ms. Refuge) I returned with Gwinnie to the house on Amity Lane, I saw no trace of the girl in the Polaroid. Things had been properly cleaned up.

And years later, when Gwinnie and I were celebrating Bud's newest kiddos with him and his husband in their Rockland County home—a split-level overlooking trails of sunburnt fishing people—the Polaroid girl surprised me in the kitchen. She looked around, took in our new surroundings. She ran her hand along a tin of flour. Is this where you're gonna live? she asked, not waiting for an answer—You know you don't deserve to, she added, disappearing out the sliding door to the deck. She took the actual photograph with her.

DAWN

Think of a place like the maternity ward at Jamaica Hospital. Think of a baby in that ward. Now imagine that baby gone, and think of the space where it has just been lying, that invisible patch where the air is changing shape. That is the true definition of a non-born.

The actual number of mine was likely circa eight. Circa nine. Circa ten. Or more.

I named them after a cowboy movie I remember the mother's second boyfriend watching while practicing his kung fu moves. He was downing her pills and offering me a few but I told him I could appreciate the fighting just like I was, and at that, he roared his molars off. I didn't like the sound of his laughter. It reminded me of his molars in the back bedroom.

The Magnificent Eight. Supposedly his favorite movie.

I had the names of all my non-borns scribbled in random ballpoint pen on a scrap of cookbook paper, stashed in the crook of PIPES LOW & HIGH.

In dreams they stood in a line on the plank we called the sill in SHEETROCK-KITCHEN. They smiled at me like a row of those dolls that jump out of each other's bellies—ruby lips and eggplant eyes and cranberry sauce dimples. Hi, I said to them. Hi, they said back.

I wasn't always made out of stone, Boss Man announced one morning, crack of dawn. We were hanging in sleeping bags that had been Swinglined to the sheetrock with heavy-duty staples. (This might could be fun, Gwin said at first.) Boss Man started crying some James Bond–smelling tears and then he unstapled us down. He let us walk chain-free. CHAIN-FREE. He presented us with a fleece blanket each. At night, back to the Swingline grind. But just in that moment where he wasn't made of stone—in that moment, the air was full of adventure.

CASE STUDY OF TUESDAYS
(2004?)

We used to wonder from time to time, what if there was just one open door? One he had perhaps forgotten. Just say if that were to happen.

We'd gotten better at reading the shadows of sun and moon in the house, the way morning darkness looked a certain way, the afternoon darkness another. Night started getting easier to figure out, you just made yourself lose sight of everything.

Say if there was an open door somewhere, though.

Like, say if a person were to open the door to our house—say, the old lady who lived outside somewhere but tried her best to come in, sort of like a water bug—let's say she was to sidle up to the side of the house and peer into some sort of actual window and find me conversating with the eight-plus progenies that Boss Man had made me kill. What would she do? WHAT WOULD SHE DO?

Just say it was her. Somehow. A little old lady with skin as brown as snow. A baby-blue sky right behind her shoulders. A west wind dipping down and sweeping those dusty non-borns off the sill and into the fresh air.

Perhaps that old bag would take one look at the sill to which I was chained and say: *My, my. You are a sight for sore eyes. What is your name and how can I be of service? You say you want the door opened? Let me try my best.*

I wanted her to succeed, even though I never told the others of her existence. I wanted her to open the door. How everyone would love me—how I would be like the next Jesenia Diaz.

Perhaps, I was thinking; perhaps she would be as strong as the planks on Noah's ark. Perhaps she wasn't just some old helpless bag. Perhaps this old biddy could effect change in the world. I kept staring at that actual, imaginary window. Say if the next thing was an open door. How our fists would fly in her face, useless hag. Yes, we were finally free. But now we will have to kill you.

(I shudder now to think how cynical I was then.)

CASE STUDY OF WEDNESDAYS (2005?)

What is the *real* passage of time? Does it move slowly or quickly or in the blink of God's eye? Seemed like we were gone for ages. 2000? 2003? 2004? Boss Man claimed there were no MISSING posters, no weeping relatives, nothing and no one. *Your mothers were actually glad to get you off their hands!* Alone, we cracked our knuckles to make sure they still worked. We lifted our heads as far back as possible just to hear the neck juice run down our skeletons. How can you be as light as featherbeds and as laden as flypaper? The walls had ears, the floors had eyes, the bulbs had hearts, the doorframes had kidneys. The chains over us had feelings, *emotions,* just like any human being. We were aware of all this. The rooms could tell on us, make the hurt stop and start up again like a game. *Monopoly, Chutes and Ladders. Stratego. Risk.* We were like a big huge large enormous empty blackboard. Aware that we were no longer schoolgirls solving math problems or scribbling secret messages on the top of detention desks. *Your mothers simply had enough.* The message was written on us, like that constant wind on our backs, the one that went absolutely nowhere.

CASE STUDY OF THURSDAYS
(2006?)

We ain't been thinking right, Gwin said one day.

What you mean? Jesenia asked. She was plainly big with child. Surprise, surprise.

Why we ain't been thinking *getaway*? Gwin asked.

No such a thing, Jesenia said. Besides, how can we think of a getaway when baby numero uno is arriving any day now. Sorry, Fern. I am respectful of your loss.

No need to apologize, but thanks for doing it anyway.

Jesenia said, I was thinking of the name Violent. Do you love that name, girls?

Do you mean Violet? we asked. Jesenia said she had to think.

Her stomach was as big as Santa's bag of toys. She scratched at it all the time, to make sure she would not be in possession of a non-born.

Boss Man was also on top of things. Fern, I want that baby alive. That is your job from now on. I can't trust that slut to take care of her own body. You have to make sure I'm a father of an alive child, you understand?

(Why would I want otherwise?)

If that baby dies, your ass is grass. I'm talking to you, Fern.

(Is not my ass always grass?)

Are you talking *to me*?

I wanted to laugh because I didn't realize I'd been thinking and talking at the same time. I wanted to laugh, but my jaw was still unaligned from the night before. He bound the rope tighter. My ribs became Jesenia's back and Gwin's legs, as if we were now just one person. As if the baby would come out of one giant baby hole made out of the three of us.

(What an imagination.)

The good thing about this position was that it usually meant he was tired. We didn't fear much prodding while twined together like an all-girl circus act. Plus, the rope felt like it was slipping. All due to his worn-out muscles. Poor thing.

This baby will make things right, Boss Man had said before leaving the house, slamming a nonexistent door. It was dark. We heard some birds and knew that it was dark afternoon. Soap opera birds, with all their drama. The rope got looser, loosest.

Once the baby came on the scene, it would be us four as MODEL EMPLOYEES.

Gwin managed to pull herself completely free. She stood up and watched Jesenia unravel herself as well. They both marched over to the horse sofa, like soldiers awaiting orders. I mean, Gwin said. Why're we being so stupid? We just a bunch of dumb heifers. We could take this rope and chains and Christmas wire and string him up instead. How would he like them apples?

Do you mean hang him?

No, not for real. Like a Christmas ornament, I mean. One we could take one last look at on the way to the FUCK OUTTA HERE.

Watch your mouth, said Jesenia. The walls listen even when he's gone.

There used to be BEFORE WORLD, Gwin said, stretching her head back across her shoulders. I want to go back to BEFORE WORLD. It really wasn't that bad, all things considered.

Girl, I don't care for any time travel, Jesenia added, breathing hard. I'm here in the present. I'm here and little Violent's about to be here, too. This is our home. This beginning has been happening for so long now—why change?

Because we all ain't stone-cold crazy, you lovely idiot.

My baby will have a mama and a papa even if from the outside it looks *somewhat askew.*

Gwin's eyes narrowed. I could tell she was tired of Jesenia's magical thinking. How many years had it been since we drew up that list of her incredible deeds? How long until we admitted it was all smoke and mirrors?

Gwin tried a different tack. Don't you want to be a good mama and teach little Violent things? Doesn't she need to see the world? Fern, what say you? Are you interested in seeing the light of the subway again? You want to take this baby girl around, don't you, like a good auntie?

I was losing my last bits of breath because no one had cut me apart and I'd neglected to remember certain retaining wires from the night before, all neatly crisscrossing under my tee shirt. Technically I probably could've unraveled myself. But it was all too much.

Jesenia moaned. Shit, this baby. She hurts. Shit. Girls, please don't upset me with thoughts of leaving. I don't ever want to leave. I know in time he'll change. He'll listen. Shit. He's probably got all sorts of goodness waiting to come out once he sees this little angel face. You know how people can change? She hurts. He might could be that kind of man.

Then she moaned again, and we knew what that moan meant. Little Violent's head was breaking through the tunnel. I freed my arms, my legs, stepped out of the rope, the retaining wire, the paper clips, and garbage bag twist ties. I reached for the toolbox Boss Man had left for this event. My job was to catch the little primate therein before she fell on the floor.

We were in PASS-THROUGH-CHASM. Blindfolds completely off our eyes and away from our necks, freed fingers cracking with thousands of liberatory air bubbles. We were standing a foot apart, breathing, knees not two inches away from the horse sofa. Technically we were free. It was the kind of thing, though, where you finally understand what those drunk military guys loitering outside the Jamaica Station VFW were saying: FREEDOM ISN'T FREE. We understood. We made ready for baby.

CASE STUDY OF BIRTHDAYS
(2005?)

Katanya.

It was the name Boss Man had picked out. A little bit of old world and new. He hated our suggestions (Gwin wanted Delilah. I thought Harriet was quite nice).

Jesenia brought up Violent. How do you love that name, Boss Man?

He laughed. Though Gwin and I hated to be on his side, we were laughing inside our heads as well.

You gonna be one hell of a father, Jesenia whispered. He smacked her head playfully. The baby still wasn't here, but he was pleased at seeing all the blood and pee that had trickled on the floor while he was out.

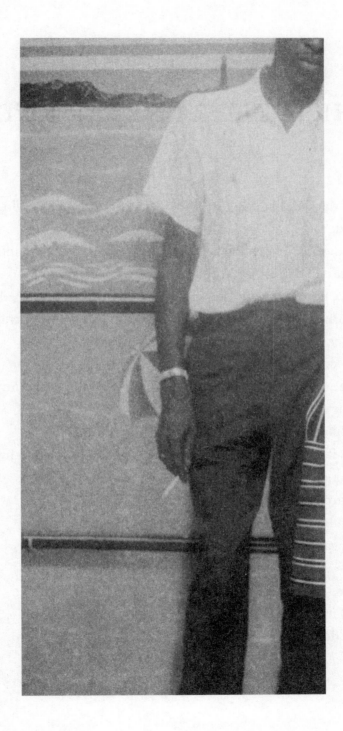

THE FATHER I NEVER KNEW

Tall dark and handsome. Built like a Mack truck. Blowing in the wind.

Always there for you when you need him. Bigger than life.

A man like no other. A rolling stone gathers no moss.

Work hard. Do your best in life and you will be rewarded. Don't sit around for handouts. Pull yourself up by your bootstraps.

Never say never. You can always go higher.

All your dreams, up in smoke.

One in a million. Takes one to know one. A rose by any other name.

Speak of the devil and he appears.

All's fair in love and war. As a crab walks, so walk his children.

Ask me no questions and I'll tell you no lies.

A hard head makes for a soft bottom.

Seen but not heard. One in a million.

His words, not mine. The devil's in the details.

I knew him like the back of my hand.

Tryna make a dollar out of fifteen cents.

Fool me once. Fool me again. Shame on me.

You don't choose your family.

Better the devil you don't know than the devil you do.

CASE STUDY OF BIRTHDAYS
(2006?)

Was it the next day? When I look back, I believe that that time might have been the longest time on record. Ask your local weatherman.

Oh. Oh. Are you ready to catch, Fern?

I don't see anything special, I said. Whispered, really, into Jesenia's ear. Her body smelled like a garbage can from the old days. She was right next to me, free.

That morning, Boss Man had augured something and taken off our chains. Cut our ropes. Unraveled our twine. I was next to Jesenia in PASS-THROUGH-CHASM, holding her tiny body, feeling her bones limp into mine. I looked down: her frame, which had run like water only a few moments ago, was now as parched as the window-sills. We traveled somehow to SHEETROCK-KITCHEN. We had no idea where Gwin was.

Oh, Oh.

Jesenia huffed and puffed and her legs went spastic and suddenly there was this *entire riverbed.* An ocean floor. *¡Dios! Don't look at the blood, I'm not looking at the blood! Oh!* Baby began to walk down the gang-plank, oh. Waving to us on shore. Oh, oh. Baby can't be arriving in a toolbox. Baby is not a wrench. Oh! Baby must find love awaiting her, softness. *Where are your arms, Fern? Catch her.* I always knew it was going to be a girl. *Catch her, Fern! Don't look at the blood!* No toolbox. No MODEL EMPLOYEE. No pictures of food. There is a way out, but what are we waiting for? *You know, Fern, yes you know. You know it in your bones.* Here she comes. Oh. Oh. Oh.

LATER EVENING

The baby did not flop into the toolbox. It floated into the pillows of my arms. They were scrawny, bloody, see-through as wax paper. But my arms were still capable of capturing a human being. The baby drifted on a dainty tidal wave of innards and outtards; the baby wore a long human braid round its neck, steaming into the room like so much anchor rope.

I was there to lift it away from the toolbox. Around us, a pool of muddy coffee water gathered, likely from PIPES LOW & HIGH. Shame on Boss Man, I thought. This here is a real living being.

It barely cried. You would not know this baby even had eyes, the face was so squinty. I hit it hard on the back. Nothing. I went and used Gwin's safety pin to sever the cord and then pin it shut. Still no cries. I placed the baby inside Jesenia's tee shirt and wound some tattered fabric around the mother so many times she looked like a kangaroo. Jesenia smiled, then fell back into a dream. Is there such a thing as automatic human warmth? The baby hollered and opened its tiny black eyes.

What do we got? Gwin asked from somewhere.

I forgot to check, I answered.

It's a girl, Jesenia moaned. I would never birth anything other. Take care of her before he puts you back on the chains.

Why do I think those days are over? I asked aloud. Stupid question. Of course we'd go back on the chains. Right as rain Boss Man reappeared at some point and reattached us. All except for the baby.

Had he been taken in by her majesty?

Because before all that happened: I'd cradled the baby's tennis ball head above the toolbox and thought about singing to it. But I couldn't think of any lullabies. But then I did remember a lullaby, a song in Dutch. What were the words? The mother coming home from a double-double shift and those sounds falling from her lips. A cat named Lasagna.

But it was gone. That can happen—the end of something once cemented in the form of bliss in your mind. Just like the memory of a pizza, which was still off-and-on fuzzy in mine. Go figure. There were things that you remembered forever, and there were things that just vanished. I thought briefly of my non-borns. All of whom had slipped out of me and evaporated into the floor before I had a chance to save them. This baby was more than the sum of all those puddles. She would be greater than any mice.

Eventually Jesenia's baby had eyes and a nose and a heart-shaped mouth that you could kiss and not just imagine. Her head smelled something similar to talcum powder, though it was just her skin and ours. Blood. Basement. Mud. Water. Attic. Rope. Skin.

There was this mystery softness. Strength. White Shoulders of memory. This territory was uncharted, but I was so happy to navigate it. *Slaap, kindje.*

BLUEPRINT

So he took the baby from us; nor did he search into its face for any gravel of love; and then it was a long, long space of peace—not even the screech of garbage gulls in the background. We were blindsided. Jesenia's milk ran and she used it to bathe herself. Boss Man returned to the house, then left the house again, our chains undone. We had the chamber pot, the rags for women's business (and now for post-baby cleanup). Water from a sink that had appeared out of who-knows-where? A bag of peeled carrots and three chocolate bars—not Snickers. He returned maybe a few days later, clanging and clumping, angry that dust was everywhere. Where were our **MODEL EMPLOYEE** cleaning skills? He didn't want to get mad. When we asked him where he had been—a question never dared until that moment—Boss Man showed his teeth. Said he went to get the baby shots—what the hell? All babies need shots. What—did we think he was some kind of monster?

I'm vaccinating her against *you*, he said, smiling, kicking us awake, reapplying chains. The chains suddenly had no locks. He tapped Jesenia particularly hard—she had slithered involuntarily against a couple of high and low pipes and was asleep. Boss Man pressed a bottle of sugar water into her hands, and then pressed some chocolate firmly into the inside of the baby's lips. Her name's Katanya, he said. And she don't need no titty milk. She's got special powers.

Jesenia put the bottle up to the baby's lips. Am I a Madonna? she asked. My mama would be so proud of me if she knew I was a Madonna.

Later he gathered us together, made us wash under a hose in SHEETROCK-KITCHEN (when did *a hose* get here? we wondered). You will love her, he commanded, spraying between our legs, the shit off our shins. Some remnants of her insides that had stuck to Jesenia's legs like embroidery. He handed the baby back to her, and Jesenia immediately lifted the child to her chest. I know there is something in there for you, she said. I been massaging them like you wouldn't believe. Like they were the two biggest coconuts on the island.

Nothing, though, not even a trickle. Plus, the baby barely moved. She was wearing a mauve blanket over a rainbow footie sleeper. When was the last time we'd thought of rainbows?

Gwin reached and took the baby from Jesenia's arms and placed a palm on her sternum. Too hot, Gwin said.

Then I will make my milk colder, Jesenia said, and began to blow and blow on her tits with her mouth. Her magician qualities never let up, because just like that: the trickle was cold. Sealtest ice milk from a human freezer.

The baby started screeching. Then it settled down. Took to suckling at Jesenia's chest. Boss Man went up the stairs, came back with the bottle. More sugar water, mixed with a little 2 percent. We were all technically free. Free—we could've left at any time. We could've taken that bottle and bashed his brains in. Free. No chains no ropes no twine. Was this freedom or wasn't it? No safety pins necessary. We hunched over Jesenia and Katanya, protecting them from invisible rays. I'm not running no three-ring circus here, Boss Man said,

as if reading my mind. PIPES LOW & HIGH. BROKEN-DOWN-
WASHING-MACHINE.

Mi vida, Jesenia sighed. Mott Haven Women's Reproductive can
kiss my ass.

Me, I felt so happy to smell the untarnished skin and baby vomit,
I drifted to sleep on my feet. Who knows what happened to Gwin.
She was quiet for more than a few days. When I awoke from my
own dreams, I was back in SHEETROCK-KITCHEN, feeling a
breeze from a new portable radiator. My chains back in place, slick
like newborn skin.

MUSTY WATERCOLOR MEMORIES

My dreams, while on my feet: a brown-skinned woman, round as a rain barrel, patting her lap, asking me and my brother Bud to come and find a place on the Salvation Army rocker. He has just learned to walk, and his head is all full of furniture welts. The woman's belly forms a shelf that juts out almost to her knees. The chair is barely there. Both Bud and I feel shy. We are baffled—how does one find a place on or next to a lap like that? The bit of knee and thigh we discern looks soft and comfy and inviting, but how is there enough space for either of us? Strange thoughts, because at the time (summer shimmery air, comfortable teeth) we are skinny as grass. Come on, babies, she says. Her face—steady as a unicorn's—is like nothing we've ever seen before. The room smells of Kool-Aid and sweet potatoes. The heavy curtains are drawn, and the radiators buzz; the heat practically rises off our skin. I won't bite, the lady says. I promise. Come sit here with me and let me tell you a story.

Of course we go. Of course we lose ourselves in all that flesh and fabric. Yam cologne. The delicate wrinkles of her voice. The Salvation Army rocker heaves with the weight of three humans, but we understand that that is what it was supposed to do in the first place.

POSSIBILITIES

We were plagued by dreams in which we saw them at the police station, jamming their fists up in some poor cop's face, threatening to kick ass. Taping fliers on telephone posts, sticking their nose into every store as far as Springfield Boulevard, asking if anyone had seen us anywhere? Some nights they were at home, watching the news while chewing their nails to rags. They would be hoping for information but also waiting for a new episode of *Law & Order* to start.

Myths can come true, we told ourselves.

Here was one: my mother telling her friends on the night shift (no more double-doubles) that life was no longer worth living without me. Here was another: Jesenia's mom crashing through our doors with a voodoo doll made in Puerto Rico guaranteed to work wonders—*Querida Altagracia de Dios! I will search heaven and hell for my daughter, my reason for living!* Here's the third myth: Gwin's mama leading the masses to Kingdom Hall, where she'd force the choir to sing, "I Would Die 4 U"; and afterward repenting everything she'd done, from killing off Mr. P to taking the Lord's real name in vain (when she thought no one was listening) to (long, long ago) forcing Gwin into an all-girls reform school in Astoria called Tunnelvision. Lord, yuh put us on de Earth to be wake, Gwin's mama would be praying, her long skirt hiding her street-swollen ankles. Tell me where me angel lurking.

Sometimes we saw their faces as incomplete as gibbous moons, their silken hands ready to caress or strangle us. We longed to be strangled by them again. We remembered that in real life they asked us things, begged for chores to be done like their lives depended on it. Why don't you wash those dishes, lazy? Do I have to see that dirty laundry one more time? In special moments, they would blame us for everything that had gone wrong in their lives. I was a child bride. I was a teen that didn't know no better. I was an old maid. We wanted all that to come back again.

I often heard soft feet padding the floors at the picnic-chair hospital apartment, but other than that, it was silence. Ms. Refuge said more time had to pass before I could see my mother. I had to heal—until then, *she* would be my mother. At night, when I closed my eyes, however, I saw the woman who raised me: hair-blown face, a dress made from Alkmaar linen. A crown atop her head woven from slices of Edam and Gouda. *Test Success for RNs Third Edition* clutched firmly in the hand.

And then I didn't see her. Much later I learned the truth. She isn't worth it, Bud said, making himself comfortable on an Adirondack chair, eating the last of my vanilla pudding. I am your mother now, too.

REFRAIN

Mothers. They have been known to say the same thing over and over. They show but do not tell; they give but take back immediately, all with the same hand. They will nag: Why can't you listen? Why do you make my life so hard?

They will inform: You're only young once. Don't waste it being a smart-ass.

They will console: He says he can't help himself so we should try to help him instead.

They will conclude: Stop feeling sorry for yourself.

They will promise: One day you'll be like me.

They will mythify: You're a good girl.

They will mystify: You forever have my heart.

HAROLD AMOR

Thy Children here today, galore,
Old St. John's! Our dear St. John's!
And true will they be ever more,
Old St. John's! Our dear St. John's!
Thy colors bright, the Red and White,
We'll wave aloft from morn till night,
Victorious, we'll show our might,
Old St. John's! Our dear St. John's!

THE ALMA MATER, ST. JOHN'S UNIVERSITY

Late late fall 2009. We had to wait this long. A few more minutes won't hurt. I can tell the gals want me to drive faster. They want me to get this over with. But I'm no Vin Diesel. I'm no Fast or Furious. On the contrary. My squad car is coasting down the street like molasses. Call comes in, robbery in progress on Bell Boulevard in Bayside, two armed men inside Mr. Pollo #1, perhaps a hostage; it's all units. I mumble something cause I can see it in the gals' eyes in the rearview mirror—they don't want me to go there. Not just there, *there*. The radio signifies something they feel they know all too well—and who am I to judge? One Black male, one white or Hispanic male, both considered armed and dangerous. How dangerous can you be if your idea of moving on up in the criminal world is to take down Mr. Pollo!? I chuckle. But I feel for these gals. I lower the radio.

Foxy Miss Tarnisha's right up next to me, acting like it's no big thing, like she's been in a cop car dozens of times. She's got the most wondrous eyes. Talking all sorts of female plans. I have an aim to put on my flashings, but then I look at the gals and their eyes have not budged an inch. Remember Troll dolls from back in the day? These gals remind me of them. I had a whole collection. Auntie threw it out on account of boys will be boys and whatnot. When I turned eighteen, she said sorry and surprised me with a whole entire eBay of replacement Troll dolls. Harry baby, can you ever forgive me? My left hand didn't know what my right hand was thinking. Auntie kept that collection for me till I graduated St. John's. It's over at the U-Haul in Elmhurst should I ever want to see those limpid pools again.

10-30. Robbery in progress. I ignore the call. The car keeps moving, NYPD #3459, wheels grinding as slow as an evening slug on your auntie's front step. Tarnisha catches on to the bug eyes in the back seat. *You sure we have to do this, Harry?* She's not talking about the call, she's talking about today's destination. I look back at her and mouth the words: *No regrets.* It will be just this one time back to the old neighborhood, and then these blessed creatures will never have to look over their shoulders anymore.

Blessed creatures? Tarnisha smiles. We've only known each other a relatively short time. But I've got the ring in my pocket. Two months' salary, Queens Boulevard, Kay Jewelers.

I trust you, she says. Old Mind and Young Mind are in your hands, Harry.

I smile. I love the way this lady thinks. Old and Young heads. It's these classes she's still taking over at York College—when she finishes her studies, she wants to open an office with a couch or some Adirondack chairs and let streams of hurt gals and boys come there to be healed. The class she takes—online for now, in the fall it will be with living beings—it's sociology or psychology or biology or maybe a mix of all three. It's got lots of term papers and curious observations. When we first met and talked about the gals, I said that time heals all wounds—to which Tarnisha replied maybe I should see a therapist myself, what with the strains of my job. Not saying you crazy, Harry. It's just. It's just. Things do go deeper, Harry. I smiled at my lovely Tarnisha when she said that. No offense taken, baby. That's soon-to-be-Dr. Tarnisha to you, she replied, winking. Now she's fiddling with the gals, reaching her arm over the seat to tuck something in or other. I look in the rearview—them gals are completely Cabbage Patch.

Good things come to those who wait. Tarnisha finally agreed with me and the department—*finally!!!*—to drive the girls back to Amity Lane. There's a case that needs closing. Maybe their googly eyes will take something in and have it click. Maybe not, but we have to try at least. It took Tarnisha long enough to agree to this—but who am I to judge? My hope? They will discover what's already in their heads. They will look at a piece of ground—dirt, a rosebush, a piece of fallen fiberglass awning—and remember a bit more of Jesenia Diaz. They will get healed perhaps. They might even grow up to write a book. Tarnisha nods slowly and says, Harold, I'm praying that this trip will be a productive way for them to encounter what they lived through, and what the world did to them.

We're on the same page. I love that woman's brains.

Me, I can't say as I ever took a psychology course I liked. Auntie insisted I go—along with my brothers—to St. John's—her basketball aspirations being somewhat incontrovertible. Remember Epictetus on God? *I move not without thy knowledge!* Well, times that by ten and you have Auntie on our hoop futures. Naturally she was thinking of her brother, my daddy. He was a star at St. John's before there was such a thing as stars. Great Black boys went to great learning places like Morehouse or Howard. They did not stay on Long Island; they did not darken the doorstep (no pun intended) of a Catholic university on Utopia Parkway (no pun intended). Auntie thought it was time for a change. She didn't want to see us go south. Brave woman. She paid for everything, even for my brother Moses, the high schooler that never escalated beyond class clown. Think of your daddy, she warned us, a wooden spoon over the peanut stew and then in the vicinity of our nervous Black butts. I want you to grow up and be like him. Understand?

We did as we were told. I went in for forensic science, and Auntie thought that was fine seeing as I would likely only play pro ball for a *short* time given my unfortunate height disadvantage (no pun intended). I signed up for a psychology class—it was scary as all get-out. Did you know that a set of keys is a symbol of power—and that people who walk around with big key chains want to be in control? Did you know that sometimes when we say what is really on our mind instead of what we're supposed to say—that we are guilty of what's called a Freudian slip? It was scaring me, all these mind things. I dropped the class midway; besides, basketball was kicking my ass. Pardon.

The Queens around us as we drive is made up of trout-mouthed boulevards that swallow us bit by bit. Tarnisha is going on and on. Not about her online classes but about her imaginary dream wedding— she was hoping this would take the gals' minds off the true destination of their lives today. I have always dreamed of an eggshell gown, Tarnisha says. What do you think, Gwinnie? Wasn't it you that said pure white is always a joke?

The one dark-skinned gal is quiet as the grave. Oft Tarnisha has told me of her spirited spirit. That the girl has a pure devotion for Prince but hates any mention of church. I look in the rearview mirror. Today that girl is quiet, an egg frying on the autumn asphalt of Kissena Boulevard.

I think you guys should get married in pure white and tuxedo, just like the Mystery Date game. This comes from the auburn gal, the one whose random thoughts multiply like an Easter bunny on crack. Pardon. This is no time for bad jokes. Being on the force can sometimes shove my humor, and I hate that. I don't believe I need therapy.

I like how you think, Tarnisha says back to her. Anybody hungry?

Can he go faster? the auburn one asks. I frown. I turn on the sirens instead, and she somewhat smiles.

Tarnisha is back on the topic of wedding plans. Could she know about the ring? Is she the kind that snoops through a man's phone, feels his pockets for loose change and adultery? Should it be a sweetheart neckline? she asks the girls. Yes, the dark-skinned one finally says. (Tarnisha's décolleté is one of her strongest features. Next to her brains, natch.) A long train or short? Reception at Daisy's 24 on Long Island or at the old Terrace on the Park? All-you-can-eat buffet or a set meal, a determined plate?

I love that skeleton of the world, auburn gal says. I glance back, tell her I love that World's Fair skeleton, too. Flushing Meadows Park: I remember trying to climb that bony globe with my brothers just after Auntie died, all of us feeling as if our exertions might bring her back.

My daddy worked his butt off for Brooklyn Ash Removal—by the time he retired, he was nothing more than a long cylinder himself, breaking off into the air with each step he took. There was no mom, and we never asked. There were family legends—not about a mom but about our kin, some dating back to colonies in Africa where the slaves returned after they tired of American shit. But these were just tales. We lost interest fast. Auntie worked for the MTA—now and then she brought home some of the exterminator's KILL that they used in the subways. And not once did we ever see a roach in our home at 59-32 Hollis Court Boulevard. Auntie passed away afterward, without telling us anything concrete about anyone's history. We just ate her peanut stew and watched our hindquarters.

My daddy would've loved for me or Marcus or Marion or Matthew or Millburn or Moses or Mitchell to go pro. He admired Julius Erving, Bill Russell, and all of the Harlem Globetrotters—my brothers and I could learn to be as great as they, he believed. Dreams. My father died a day before Matthew was signed to that traveling team in China; Matthew felt the fool afterward. Millburn and Marion told Daddy on his deathbed that they were about to be signed with the Knicks, and the old man fell back blissfully onto his pillow, and we never had to make him the wiser. Pardon, Daddy.

Now that those days are behind us, my brothers and I can admit: we all hated basketball. Forgive us, Daddy.

I want to ask the gals about Jesenia Diaz. I promise myself that I'll bring it up slowly, so as not to alarm or brutalize them. Tarnisha understands that I am a detective, after all. I have a job to do.

Jesenia Diaz. Her case is a fairy tale for the City. Is she dead or alive? Does she roam the streets of Queens at night (perhaps in Corona but I would include Cambria Heights in there as well, the latter being the kind of place prone to spectral nuisances) or is she buried where the new church is being built, across the street from where these girls were confined? The latter is probably the most logical explanation, though even after a lengthy excavation back in the day, we never found anything. Boxes of Polaroid pictures, some frill dresses. Never a body, and we did dig deep.

After the gals were extracted, we quarried the living neighborhood as well, shovels in backyards, knocking door to door, inspecting car trunks. *How is it none of y'all seen a goddamn thing?* This was my partner, Lucinda Sutherland, never any filter. *Y'all folks ought to be ashamed. These girls out here for ten years and ain't one of you ever thought anything looked amiss? I know y'all be sharing everybody business in church, rain or shine. So how was it godly possible to overlook these heavenly creatures?*

That Lucy. She had a mouth. Plenty of theories, too. Was afraid to actually touch the gals with her hand. I'll look through the glass, she said when we first followed them to the hospital. My heart will hurt me too bad if I look anywhere but through the glass.

I went to bed after the first week of looking and hollowing and burying back the nothing that we'd dug up. My wife at the time, Denise, she was always on my case about overtime. Talking about, *We're fine, we don't need the money. Why you don't spend half as much time with me?* and so on. Is it a surprise our love didn't last? I ran into her about three months after the divorce, and she told me she still had those victim-girls' eyes under her lids. What magic had I worked on her? *I thought I was a free woman, finally*, was Denise's parting shot.

Sluggishness is underrated. I study the gals behind me in the rear-view mirror—there is too much world going on for them. What were the last things they likely saw before they were stolen? Cell phones were different. Boomboxes, headphones, transistor radios? What about the singers? Music—well, in my opinion that will always be a miss unless you're talking Diana Ross. One classy lady who knew how to belt your heart. Can we get ice cream? the dark-skinned one asks.

Her name is Gwinnie, Tarnisha says, placing a hand on my shoulder.

Sure, but first we have to do what Ms. Tarnisha wants you gals to do.

Is that go back to the scene of the crime? the auburn one asks.

In a manner of speaking, I answer.

Watch where you driving, Tarnisha says. Hand back in her lap. If I could afford it, I'd swish her tomorrow off to Terrace on the Park and make her mine. The half carat I bought is burning a hole in my pocket. Daddy would've been proud; Tarnisha would've been right up his alley. He always loved round females with good heads on their shoulders. Hence, Auntie: we discovered just three years ago (thank you, DNA DREAMS COME TRUE™) that she was not really our aunt, but rather, the woman our father had left our mother for. She was the one who ensured he never once looked back.

Marion suggested looking for the real mother. *Our real mother*—do people still believe in that sort of fairy tale? Family is who you make it. Family is place, face, bed, and bowl. I know I should be mad at Auntie, but not a bone in my body agrees. Plus, I feel too much of Daddy's eyes on the back of my neck. I never even came close to loving a basketball at St. John's. But other things have been made to count. And I know he still would've loved me.

Two minutes later we stop at a Baskin-Robbins, where Tarnisha takes the gals inside; they reemerge with rainbow cones, including one for me: Rocky Road with sprinkles. How did you know? I ask. Tarnisha smiles. You aren't the only one who's got detective blood, she answers.

Not ten minutes later: Amity Lane. Streetlamps on, despite it being high noon. Engine slows but does not stop. If I was alone, I would've tossed the ice cream napkins out the window—this is that kind of block now—but I can't. I am on duty. I am a role model.

I look at the gals. They shiver and I can't tell if it's good or bad. They look back at me in the rearview mirror. These are not Troll doll eyes. These are Godzilla eyes. These are World Trade Center eyes. These eyes tell me: there's never been a question as to what happened to Jesenia Diaz. King Kong eyes. I feel my heart attack gear up slowly. They know. I know they know. They've always known. My heart flaps like a dodo's wings as I sink back into my seat. I stop the car. Why are we grown folks too blind to see? Even when we look—we are blind as bats. If only we'd learned to use the other senses God gave us.

Who wants to go first? Tarnisha asks, like this is a game. But the doors stay shut, and the ice cream paper from my cone eventually folds into my skin.

FERN

To wait . . . I wait in momentary expectation, feeling as though my breasts are being crushed, for the sound in the corridor of the footsteps of happiness.

OSAMU DAZAI, *THE SETTING SUN*

BYE BYE

So Boss Man was taking the baby and Jesenia with him to church. We never knew him to be a believer, but apparently—*somewhere*—there was a St. Anthony or a St. Margaret of Cortona or a St. Francis of Assisi that would abide his hog breath and pickled feet for an hour or two. Gwin and I were allowed to say bye at the door, which had miraculously grown out of a wall in SHEETROCK-KITCHEN. Jesenia wore white. We expected it to be the old dress, the one she'd arrived in, conserved in bleach and Brillo, the zippers torn to make room for the invisible fat she'd grown; but it was a new dress, an actual dress, one that someone in some sweatshop factory had worked themselves into a hunchback for; was it possible to feel grateful for our experience? Jesenia's eyes were never roomier. We could hear her heart beating. Thank you for telling me all about Prince, she said, kissing Gwin on the head. Thanks for taking my mind to a different place. You are an angel. Never forget.

(Would now be a good time to say we were all standing together, as if we'd met in CTown on a Sunday morning? No silver, no rust, no bruises, no blackened teeth. Boss Man could have been the store manager and we his customers.)

Gwin said calmly—and in total non-care of getting her butt beat—where you letting him take you, Jessie? Are you out your mind?

Listen, bitch, Boss Man began—though he did not raise his hand. He didn't even continue his thought. He could have been rethinking the price of collard greens. He could have been squeezing tomatoes for freshness.

Jesenia said, Listen, Gwin. I'm blessed. I'm letting the father of our child lead me to bigger and better things. See? A leopard can change its spots. Be happy for me. Be happy for us.

We're getting this brat baptized today, as it so happens, Boss Man said.

Jesenia's voice quavered. Do you mean that, Boss Man? Do you really mean that? We're gonna make this baby a true baby of God? You're gonna make an honest woman out of Katanya?

Shut up and let's get going.

He wobbled Jesenia and the baby out the magical new door *with his hands*. The door swelled back into sheetrock and looked as it always had: a magnet for dead wasps, a place to be chained, a board behind which hundreds of mice called our names.

Gwin looked at me. You know we *can* if we want to.

No, we can't, I said, shaking.

Jessie might never come back, Fern.

We can't leave because we have to wait and see, because if she does, I don't want things to change. (I didn't comprehend myself. Thank God, Gwin did, however.)

Oh, Fern.

Oh, Gwin. What have we done?

No chains, no ropes, no safety pins. We moved ourselves to the new beanbag chair Boss Man had dragged home shortly after the baby was born, thinking it might make a nice crib—how he flipped when he saw that that would not be the case. Maybe one of the last of my teeth to go. He settled on the Easter basket. But Gwin and I had experimented and discovered that the beanbag, red vinyl with peace signs all over—was like sleeping on a cloud in heaven. Its tag said, DO NOT REMOVE UNDER PENALTY OF LAW.

Wanna see me break the law, Gwin asked. Our hands were supposed to be tied but they weren't. We could if we wanted to. That door might rematerialize. Boss Man might get hit by a school bus. All these wonderful scenarios.

We had to make sure Jesenia and Katanya could always find their way back. But us, no. We couldn't, not even if God reached down and offered us a million dollars and a dream. We had to stay.

A NAGGING FEELING

What was also different this alleged Sunday was the way night eventually came down. A smell of midnight trees under the floorboards, one I hadn't thought of in ages. Do you remember eating those little tree helicopters when you were a kid? I asked. Both Gwin and me tucked into each other. *We could have gone but we didn't.* I loved those helicopters, Gwin replied. Taste the same as peanuts only like maple. I miss the circus, now that you mention it, I said.

Eventually we heard Boss Man rematerialize the door. Baby Katanya howling in his arms though there was no full moon anywhere. No sign or sound of Jesenia.

Gwin near my shoulder in BROKEN-DOWN-WASHING-MACHINE, slowly realizing something, slowly crying. We did tempt fate after all, she said. Why was I so stupid? Why didn't I keep my stupid ideas to myself?

There's no way Boss Man could've known, I pointed out. The steel drum tightening around me.

Boss Man finds out everything, Fern. He knows every crack and line in our head. He knows what we were plotting.

I wasn't plotting a damn thing, I said. Thinking: We could've opened the door. We could've done that. And then.

Well, Gwin said, nothing to do now but freeze. All our bad thinking may have cost that girl her days.

Are you getting religious on me, Gwin?

Hell no. It's just. What did I start? Let's freeze, Fern. Let's just freeze.

Yet tears still ran down Gwin's face.

Let's freeze harder, I suggested.

So we froze.

We froze.

Slowly the baby's crying died down. We did glean the sucking of a bottle, the most awful belches. That slob, Gwin snarled, her chains clinking. Don't you think so, Fern? That motherfucking slob.

But I was still frozen. It would take another couple of realizations for me to thaw out. Jesenia appeared back in LEWD two days later, with eyes swollen as gumdrops. No questions, no answers. After that, Gwin and I were practically water.

A LOVING MEMORY OF A LONG AGO BRA-WL (GET IT? LOL)

It was all about a brassiere.

Where were they? No idea. When was this? Long ago but maybe last week? I couldn't see Jesenia, but I could tell from her voice that she was hanging from the poles. Maybe in LEWD. The baby was on its way. Boss Man believed it would come out faster if gravity was involved. He fed us all Goya black beans, turning us into individual sticks of dynamite. He told us to mind the chamber pots.

Even *he* sensed there was a clever wind in the house. The peeling wallpaper, the buckets containing our unmentionables—mouse poop, girl pee, wannabe-mother vomit. The clever wind made it so that these normal smells hit our noses like a fortress. The clever wind caressed us like an old friend. The floorboards stretched broken in all these little places. The moldings ran at the base of the wallpaper, a fleeting philodendron pattern that once must have made someone moderately happy. We were growing stronger every day. Who in their right mind would call this a house of horrors? We knew every nick and seam intimately; you might even call that *care*.

In the days before Katanya joined us, there was talk of a fourth bed (the Easter basket not yet a clear thought in anyone's mind). There was talk of a fourth place in the MODEL EMPLOYEE lineup. Everyone would have to pull their weight, Boss Man instructed. When we looked again, the point of where the baby would sleep was moot. Her having a job amongst us was no longer a nightmare—she'd already been saved from the house like an old supper of Goya kidney beans. Time worked a miracle that time.

But this was the fight: someone—Gwin—had used Jesenia's last pre-baby bra without telling her. Jesenia learned this when she saw Gwin snoring in BROKEN-DOWN-WASHING-MACHINE wearing a pair of eye coverings—supposedly to keep out the light.

It's practically the last thing I had from the Time Before Now, Jesenia said, crying, likely lifting the bra from Gwin's face. Wrap it around the washer door handle when you're done, please, Gwin said, half asleep. It needs more stretching out. (A 34A cup, flowered, slightly padded, gray elastic fray along the straps.)

Once she became fully cognizant, Gwin explained, My eyes need protection at night.

You can't tell it's a bra anymore, Jesenia cried. My last thing. It used to have pink carnations.

Gwin laughed. You get me thinking. Remember Carnation Instant Breakfast? I used to love me that powder tasting like a white fairy dust. Remember Sealtest Vanilla Ice Milk? My mama chowing it down like it was good for the figure and for premium gospel concentration. Kingdom Hall songs were the work of white devils. Remember Charleston Chews, Goober Grape spread? Now, Jessie. Don't worry, you can still wear this as a bra if you want. You know nothing is forever around here.

That bra was my last gift from Hector.

I'm so sorry but I needed to sleep.

Fern, Jesenia said, through the walls. I was back up in the attic, swinging in a hammock I'd fashioned out of dinner napkins (on sale at CTown, an early "birthday gift" to me from Boss Man, who'd said, Don't take this to mean I'm an all-heart sucker). Fern, listen. This bitch thinks she can just *up and take* my bra and use it as a lampshade over that crater-face of hers. All the beauty sleep in the world can't make a difference. Boss Man even says so.

Gwin crawled out of BROKEN-DOWN-WASHING-MACHINE. I imagined she bore no trace of a chain. She said, I'm a take this bra and stuff it down your malnourished maladjusted malcontented motherfucking mouth. (Gwin's "birthday gift"? Her very own *Word Power for Tenth Grade*.) Stupid goddamned girl. How you like them apples?

Are you taking my name in vain? Jesenia asked. No chain, no rope, no bottoms. I imagined she went and lay herself on the rotten cardboard slices next to DUST-BUNNY-DRAIN. She didn't have to be there. None of us did. We all could've left. We could have.

Just please leave me be, Gwin pleaded. And heavens don't call me a bitch.

Jesenia was silent. Then: Heavens only know why I did such a terrible thing. I'm sorry, Gwinnie. I don't ever take anyone's name in vain. I have *Mott Haven Women's Reproductive Decision Making* to thank for that.

I heard Gwin kick the washing machine, saying, I don't know why the hell I'm fighting you. I love you, Jesenia Diaz.

I was mistaken. I was wrong and you were right. I still remember the difference, mija.

I got to think of our ticket outta here, Gwin said. Ain't no way we raising that baby to be his next bitch.

We can change him.

(Silence.)

So are we soul sisters again?

Gwin laughed. When was we never?

SILENT BURSTS IN BETWEEN

Katanya turned out to be some kind of miracle—who would've thought that about *babies*? She learned to sit at five weeks! By six months she could walk; by eight months she could talk! She wanted to call someone Mommy, but Jesenia was already gone by then, and we wouldn't let her call us anything that dangerous. Better to nip those myths right in the bud!

Boss Man, though. He'd kiss her head, rub her tummy. He dressed her in actual clothes; we never saw her naked again. She had real Pampers, at first from Dollar Haven and after that from a place called Babies R Us. I admired the colorful spelling on the shopping bag—*Hey, Boss Man, do you think I could keep this Babies R Us bag as a souvenir?* I don't give a shit, he said.

Transformations! Miracles!

Boss Man changed her from one fancy dress into another, *just because*, and he did not yell when I modeled the shopping bag later that afternoon. How do I look, Gwin? I asked. The baby said, Mama. Gwin said, I have a feeling that I've seen you in another life. Boss Man did not yell, but he did forget to throw us a can of Goya pink beans until the next day. I know, because the midnight trees smelling up the floorboards let me know.

Another time the baby reached for me and I took her and she said, MAMA.

Don't give her any fucking ideas. This from Boss Man. He reached her away from me with his hands.

Then later, another marvel. Boss Man looked me in the face *without anything*. You ain't got no real reason to cry, Fern. It doesn't take a mental doctor to see what you're about. Face facts: Your litter weren't nothing but smoke and mirrors.

Shock. And horror. I thought for sure he was going to belt me one. Boss Man had in all this time never warmed up to any semblance of tears, especially on us.

I pressed my luck. Where's Jesenia? I asked. It'd been a while. Where's she at?

Back to the old Boss Man. *Jesenia who?*

And later: You know, Fern. Maybe it would do you good to let the baby call you something like Auntie. Just maybe.

The baby said MAMA.

But I still had my limits, miracles or no miracles.

MYSTERY DATE

A letter is shoved through a crack. A letter, the thing we learned to do in third grade: where on the envelope to write your address and where to write the address of the person who's about to get the good news, with the date up top and the word *SINCERELY* down below and all the spaces in between, where polite and good news would take up about two whole lines. This letter is shoved inside quickly, and we don't understand how this happens. The crack belongs to something that can't rightly be called a door. It is a sizable slab of corrugated cardboard, multiple fingerprints, and teeth marks. This letter, however, looks brand new.

Dear Sir, it begins. No spaces. Then the date: 12/24/06. The handwriting is also something out of the third grade, script as smooth and slanted as a nautical whale—penmanship, they used to call it.

I know you are alone and I wouldn't presume to impose . . . history being often unforgiving to those who deserve it most. Won't you be so kind as to share a Gingerbread Cake with an Old Woman who has no one left in the world? Forgive me my boldness. It so happens that my Dear Father has been gone these many years, and I am alone, fretting even more, ever since the Big Terror in the City. I know I could use a cup of Christmas cheer in the company of someone other than the neighborhood nags who visit me—gossips, the bunch of them.

What say you? If you are equally in want of some company during this sentence of yuletide gaiety, please do ring the bell at 124-22 Amity. I'm right across the street, you can see my every window. Seems none of our hearts are yet recovered from those falling towers though it has already been a good five years now. Happy Holidays.

What you got there, Boss Man screamed. He dashed it out of our hands but did not lock us up.

Back to work, bitches! Don't make me tell you again!

Where is Jesenia, Boss Man?

Jesenia who?

It's almost the end of '06? asked Gwin. She was looking into a shard of mirror, feeling her face slowly straighten itself out. What falling towers?

Never you mind!

What is the date, Boss Man? You ain't got nothing to lose!

Time is in the eye of the beholder, he said, grabbing me by my bones though I'd said nothing. Shut up. Go get the baby dressed. I got to take her to church! She's not gonna turn heathen like you!

But there was Gwin, BOLD, grabbing Boss Man by the shoulders. What falling towers?

BLUEPRINT II

Later on, in the courtroom—May 2008—Boss Man claimed to the world that he *did* try to make things as good as possible for his MODEL EMPLOYEES. No, he didn't run no house of horrors. No, he was not that kind of man. Swear on his mother's grave.

With a pair of monster-movie black eyeglasses roped to his face, he read words off a wrinkled piece of paper.

Boss Man described our *home* to the judge and all the people lining the walls, eager to get an imaginary glimpse of the Queens House of Horrors. Boss Man swept away pretend tears and now and then looked in our direction. *All I wanted to do was love these angels. Honest. When is a house not a home?* Gwinnie stood up from the plaintiff side in her new navy suit (thank you, Ms. Refuge, for catching that petite ladies' sale at J. C. Penney) and shouted, THAT WAS NO MOTHERFUCKING HOME, YOU DEVIL!

I stood up in my red velvet dress with the new-girl bow around the neck and shushed her back into her seat. All eyes landed on us like kamikaze jets. The judge blew his nose. I kissed Gwinnie on the head—she, too, had a new-girl bow. She was right, no doubt. But the physical reality of the situation was: there'd been no other word than *home* for the ten years we were there.

When it was my turn, I stood in the little sidecar next to the judge (a whitened man) and the jury (all whitened people) and took a deep breath. Yes, I hereby swear I am Fern Daisy Delores, so help me God as my witness. There was a swaying motion. *You've got the wrong girl here; I'm a straight B student!* The judge offered me a chair, but I couldn't take it on account of my promise to myself in that first ambulance that I'd never allow wood to voluntarily touch my skin again.

I told the whitened people what I could: that to be inside the house was hard at first but then it got to be routine, close to (but not completely) a quasi-breeze: it wasn't *all savagery*, mind you, chamber pots being emptied at least once every three days; that was a real job. That was someone's *real job*. Did neighbors complain of the stench? We had no idea. What is a stench? All we saw were the chamber pots, solid proof we'd existed that day and the day before.

It was easy to take care of those chamber pots. Owing to the fact that our diarrhea didn't come often. Pictures of food didn't make our stomach turn the way real food did—contrary to expert witnesses from the Blood Hospital (here I nodded at a doctor I recognized who immediately blushed and turned her head). Plus, none of us could ever make that much shit if we wanted. Cramps, yes, retching. Periods, yes. Babies, most definitely. But diarrhea was not a thing. None of us actually swallowed enough pictures of food for that. Not even Jesenia, who had the most pictures and real food combined of us all. Plus, she was the only one allowed to be late on her period, the only one who got to have the baby for keeps. When Katanya came to us (thank God for missing that toolbox) you could say life shifted. It took a while to see. The chains fell off. But we hung ourselves back up because *no one told us not to.* We looked for those chains. There they were, right next to the chamber pots where we left them. It took a long time to get that through our head.

(I was not the babying kind, Gwinnie'd replied earlier, when asked about any maternity issues. The judge left it at that.)

The judge said, Tell us about your children, Miss Fern Daisy Delores. We want to hear about that.

You mean, *them*?

I'm terribly sorry. Please accept my apology.

Amity Lane, I continued. With a name like that, you would think the house had a garden full of flowers. A swing set and monkey bars. Happy people, chicken soup. When I found out the name of the street, I thought someone was playing a trick. God? How could you live on a street like that and not know the truth? I still haven't figured out if God does or does not exist.

(Some people laughed. Some cleared their throats. Do you have your pills, Ms. Refuge mouthed at me when I turned in her direction.)

You said you gave birth there, Miss Fern Daisy Delores? Can you say something about that? Take your time. Nothing can happen to you now.

I looked around first, I could definitely hear the air going out everybody's heart in the courtroom. Four old ladies chewed on handkerchiefs. Gwinnie's Mrs. Kiluk sat a few rows over, shaking her head, thinking: *I always knew this girl was a survivor. My math was never wrong.*

There was Bud, third row on the right. Silent as the back bedroom. His eyes brought back the rust-colored sunrise.

I turned to Ms. Refuge. Courage. A true phoenix from the ash.

My kids, I said. They were just the non-borns. I up and down swore I'd always be there for them, and I thought they felt the same way. But maybe let me tell you about the first time.

The first time you were raped? The first time you miscarried? Be specific, Miss Fern.

No, I said. Let me tell you about the first baby.

Please proceed.

I cleared my throat. Boss Man brought me to the front step, started fussing with his keys. A night bird's silhouette sang into the air. Be patient, Boss Man whispered. I was looking forward to the puppy he said was right behind the door. My heart was opening its mouth. There was no grabbing or heartbreak, he just couldn't get the door open. He told me it was a German Shepherd mix and that he already named her Molly because he knew that was a name most good girls liked—was I a good girl? I was, wasn't I? He could tell.

(Miss Fern, please calm yourself.)

The streetlights were on. I knew better than to talk to anyone when the streetlights went on. He was right in that I WAS a good girl.

(Miss Fern, we can resume later. Should we take a break? Please calm yourself. *Bailiff!*)

Because I never forgot that first time. Fall-winter rain pretending to be snow, salt and sweet on my tongue. A tiny wind. Hadn't I learned anything? Don't talk to strangers during a tiny wind! My foot was on the threshold. I was a good girl, I'd heard the mother say so. There it was again, the night bird singing on a branch nearby; and there it went, off to another tree, and then to another, to a house, another street. This was no night for birds. Boss Man was fumbling his keys; my face was new. Brand spanking new. Was he cursing? I couldn't tell—not when there was a sweet little puppy named Molly waiting for me right behind that door. This was no night for me. But I didn't pay attention; all I heard was the puppy yelping for joy, seeing myself putting a purple leash around her neck and walking back to the mother and saying: LOOK.

(Ms. Refuge rising from her seat and saying, I think we WILL take that break, Your Honor! Fern, come back down!)

A girl like you deserves a love like this, Boss Man told me, creaking open the door. I stepped my one foot over the threshold, and it's true I didn't cry at first. No dog no cake no bird. I felt every smash as he lunked my head up the stairs Was this the attic? A secret dungeon? I cried and I cried. Was this a garret? My tears were a prevention— they prevented me from correctly identifying the place I knew I would remain in—for more than a day. A prison. How was I able to discern that so soon? I cried and cried. And I didn't stop until maybe this morning, coming to this court.

(One last question before you go. Why were you crying, exactly? What was he doing to you, exactly? We have to have this on record, Miss Fern.)

I cried because I wished I'd turned around and looked at that night bird for real.

LICENSE FOR A SEASONED JOURNALIST

(*Night-bird,* Miss Metropolitan scribbles on her steno pad, from the farthest corner of the courtroom, adding a hyphen. *How can anyone think that poetry won't win in the end?*)

FROM: Clifford Teatown, *A Reporter's Journey: My Life with a Laptop, a Cold Pint, and a Mystery* (Factual Press: An Imprint of the New York Times, 2027).

[. . .] I'd been asked by former staff intern at the *Queens Metropolitan*, Amina Whitehead-Mensah, to follow up on a tip about a "mysterious figure" who happened to frequent the Turtle Bay Diner II, right off the FDR. Would I be willing to come out of retirement? The tip could very well be nothing. This was late 2018. Amina had recently graduated from the distinctive journalism program at the CUNY Graduate Center and finally gotten a *real job*—albeit in the mailroom—of the *Times*. I remembered Amina fondly from before, when she'd worked for a hot minute as a grunt at the *Metropolitan*— not a bad gig at all, considering—and then moved on to bigger and better things at *Newsday*—a totally legitimate rag. For as long as I'd known Amina, she'd wanted to work at *Newsday,* and who could blame her? We considered the *Metropolitan* little more than a fish wrapper, the kind of weekly you found gratis on the windowsills of local delicatessens. But in the end, even *Newsday* was just not hot enough for Amina. Hence the Gray Lady—my suggestion, as I'd done a spot of time there and figured it was *always* a good thing to have *more of us, anywhere*—but please don't get me started. I love the Gray Lady. As did Amina. So what if she was answering emails, even making coffee (did women still do that in the 21st century???) on a CUNY Grad Center degree? That's another story altogether . . .

[. . .] Amina called me three days in a row. I was living in Cambria Heights then, my beloved Patricia having departed this earth some time before. Buried in the Old Springfield Cemetery on Springfield Boulevard, God rest her lovely soul. Amina laid out the facts, asked me would I help. Perhaps this time she had the right lead . . . who knew what would follow? She wanted to shine and she wanted to take me with her, old as I already was. Would I be willing to find out as much as possible on this mystery woman, the one she believed—in her heart of hearts—was Jesenia Diaz? (Yes, yes, Amina said, laughing, there is such a thing as Journalism Heart!!!) All kidding aside, though. Amina's mother was recovering from cervical cancer, and allegedly it was her wish to see her girl settled, "in a real newspaper," like the *Accra-Queens Connection*. Hold back your laughter. Amina said that though her mom was rather sickly, she was, at her core, *pure drama*—and the *filia* needed to do this, to prove to the honorable Ghanaian *mater* that writing was indeed a solid career. Perhaps one day, Barnes & Noble would carry Amina Whitehead-Mensah books on their shelves! On Nooks and Kindles and what have you!

[. . .] On my end, I believe Amina was perhaps seeing me as some sort of father figure, and for that reason wanted to stay in closer touch. We hadn't spoken in a while, but who was to say?

[. . .] What to make of this mysterious figure? Back then, so much had been conjured of the victim-females that it was literally making all of New York City sick to its stomach—*wasn't there anything else to report on?* Even 9/11 cooled down as a news topic after a while!

People did not want to follow the victim-females story anymore; they were tired of their own helplessness and shame. They wanted the papers to go back to Trump/Giuliani bribery cases or undocumented high school valedictorians who'd gotten college scholarships. Yet Amina Whitehead-Mensah wouldn't budge. She called me on the day her mother passed. "Would you mind stopping by?" she asked. I could tell over the phone that this first-rate reporter was doubling over from the weight of her own tears. Still, a good story, like time, waits for no one. "I want you to meet with her, Cliff. Will you do it?" Amina gave me a time and place to be. I never knew how hard-boiled she actually was. "Please do it in the name of truth, Cliff." Tall order, you might think, but all jokes aside.

[. . .] Small, darkish-light, and homey—qualities in a woman that made me feel at once comfortable. The hospital café was unusually warm, the windows fogged. We spoke as if we'd been friends forever. The café hot chocolate was not bad, by NYC standards—I wanted to be sure to note that in my observations. Sadly, I forgot to write down the preciseness of that female's features. She had a gentle voice, one that lulled me like a spell. She spoke of herself in the third person. I mentioned the GoFundMe donations that had been set up in her honor, as well as the throng of social service professionals waiting to reach out to her, after all these years. She giggled in such a girlish way, I deemed her much younger than she actually was. How many hot chocolates did we have that day? Three, four? When I returned from the men's room, she was gone. It took me forever to recover from my haze. I am still kicking myself to this day.

[. . .] Amina stared me down hard—searched my soul, you might call it. "Did you talk to her, Cliff? Did you find out what happened, Cliff? Where's she been all this time, Cliff?" Rapid-fire questions, a journalist worth her weight in gold. We were sitting in the lobby of Bellevue Hospital, and we were alone, not counting the nighttime employees. I had to tell the truth about all those hot chocolates and the little boys' room—what a rookie mistake! "Did she at least give her real name, Cliff? Did she say why she's been missing all this time?"

Amina's face was lit by a million imaginary candles. My shame got the better of me. I told her I would do all I could, never called the poor girl back . . .

[. . .] Does anyone remember the newspaper years of yore? When the evening edition of your favorite paper would be handed out by a young urchin on the corner? Where were those innocent days? I wished I could have been Amina's dad. The privilege to protect her, to keep her flame alive. Chivalry is not dead!

After that whole disappointment, I thought I could just go back to life as I knew it.

But you see, Amina had pulled me into the journey, for better or worse. I could not let go. There was no way to resist.

From: MAGNET interviews with CUNY Graduate Center students, CUNY *Adjunct Faculty Bulletin*, December 2010.

Q: What makes you most proud to be a MAGNET Scholar?

A: I always do my homework; that's what being a part of this program has taught me: don't slack. Never let the trail go cold. I do believe I will have found the rest of the clues as to Jesenia Diaz's disappearance by the end of my written exams. I do believe I will be able to start my cold-case book shortly thereafter.

Q: What impact do you imagine your work will have on future generations?

A: I do worry about the state of women in the world, specifically in the United States, especially in New York City, the melting pot of so many females. Historically, we've believed that our simultaneous waves of liberation would carry us through to a new day. Instead, racial discrimination, violence against women, human trafficking, forced marriage, date rape, and all manner of misogyny have tamed those waves. What will our daughters have to look forward to? If we can't protect them now—what future hot water will we be in?

Amina Whitehead-Mensah, PhD candidate, Departments of Journalism, English, and Urban Planning

WHAT YOU KNOW

Sometimes I think if no one knows you,
then you are no one.

DAN CHAON, "BIG ME"

Periodic Assessment and Interview REVALUATION™ PART {D}
Cuyahoga Department of Child and Adult Social Services

Funded in part by

Silver Dust Films, LLC
110 Fretwell Street, Suite 76A
Cleveland, OH

And in association with

Cuyahoga County Bureau of Elusive Cold Case Files

Cleveland Division, Cleveland, OH

Subject: PLU-0905-7754-KL: Katanya Diaz-Mann aka Rosario Louisa Diamante

aka Allison Diaz
aka Dolores Diaz-Brown
aka Marsha Brady Diaz
aka Katanya Diaz
aka Katanya Mann
aka Jane Doe 1-A

**Tertiary Post-Suicide Attempt Follow-Up and Exit Interview
Allen Mandelbaum Hospital, Cleveland, OH**

April 28, 2039

A-1 I realize you already have my background information, from ten years ago, and ten years before that. The movie people are new this time around: one year ago they contacted us saying they wanted to make a blockbuster out of my life. Cindy said Fuck You and hung up the phone. Just a few days ago they sent their sympathy on the "suicide attempt" but also reiterated I was "box-office gold." The movie people said that ill-used kitchen appliances make for optimal flick fodder. I'm awards ka-ching, they said. Oscars, Golden Globes, Trump Spectacle Awards, etc. And finally, yesterday: they sent a letter—certified, I didn't know such things were still done—asking Cindy if they could interview me for ONE day, no more. A voice-over, maybe, if I didn't feel like showing my face on-screen. During the actual filming, they'd use a stunt double, of course, and all meals would be comped. Cindy said, These suckers phone me one more time I'll eat *them* alive. The look in her eyes, though, said so much more. More than it said ten years ago, and ten years before that.

A-2 I hate to disappoint. Far as I'm concerned, I've said everything there is to say. There are no pockets of hidden information, no tiny tidbits of subconscious story lurking inside me. Why do they want to do a movie now? Everyone knows everything, and they have known everything since my time on earth began. The house of horrors baby, the missing mother, the partially insane grandmother, etcetera. Clearly me sticking my head in an open oven was some-thing new. But that was me simply being a drama queen. Meant absolutely nothing. Would not enhance or decrease potential movie value whatsoever. Why can't I make those fools see? Cindy always said I'd never get out of the spotlight, and for once she was right.

A-3 Whatever, here goes.

A-4 Other than the oven episode, I am a healthy, clean, well-adjusted young woman. Sound mind and body. Same as the last time I had to answer these questions (2029), and the time before that (2019). Before today, you have mostly been interested in my real mother, Jesenia Diaz.[1] And to that end, I have been fully com-pliant in terms of reporting anything I might have "discovered" about her. I certainly would've told you if she and I had met. But 1) for new information to surface, then 2) something *new* (and relevant, btw) would have to have occurred. Cause and effect, you see? And yet: NOTHING NEW OR RELEVANT HAS OCCURRED. In answer to Parts {A} {B} and {C} of the standard REVALU-ATION™, I had this to say: I will never, ever try to off myself again. Suicide is a deal breaker. The open oven was a humongous mistake.

A-5 I love facts. Facts can't hurt us, not really. And there is no rea-son to keep things to myself. If my real mother suddenly appeared in my dorm room, that would be a fact. But to recap: she's still on the lam. Perhaps she's no longer walking the earth.[2] The most accurate (and verifiable) description of Jesenia Diaz would be that she is and was a fantasy, the product of so many imaginations.

---

1. Clearly the mental health of a daughter left behind was not top of your list of priorities but whatever. As a famous chanteuse said so many decades ago: I will survive.

2. A possibility I hate contemplating, I must add. Possibilities are not facts.

A-6 2007: Tested negative for HIV. Tested negative for hepatitis. Tested positive for whooping cough. 2009: Tested negative for tapeworms, crabs, positive for lice, ringworm. Why get tested for crabs, you might wonder? I was just a babe. The hospital said it was a formality, nothing to worry about. (She's no hooker, Cindy said *right in their faces.*) 2019: Tested (in spite of Cindy's protests) with a pregnancy stick. (She's just a kid, Cindy cried. Don't you perverts have anything better to do? What the hell kind of *good guys* give a baby a *baby test?*)[3] 2029: Tested for manic depression, paranoid schizophrenia, hives, bipolar disorder. 2039: Tested for Covid-19, Covid-20, Covid-21. False memory syndrome, lead poisoning, hysteria. A BIG NEGATIVE on all that.

A-7 I am currently six feet two inches, brown hair, hazel eyes, slightly more athletic in build than previously. The movie people said I am shaped perfectly for a crime drama, but then one of the costume designers said I looked better suited for an extra's role, given that I was made up of mostly "masculine lines."[4] She even called me *handsome.* At my last interview[5] ten years ago, I considered myself "pleasingly plump"—though in the interview ten years before that, when I was a mean-hearted twelve-year-old, I may have denoted myself a *chubster.*[6]

A-8 I have indeed maintained a relationship with my adoptive mother aka birth grandmother aka Miss Cindy Diaz—as well as my adoptive stepfather aka step-grandad aka Manny Romano Diaz. When I first got to Oberlin, I maintained contact by regularly

---

3. Tested for *baby-itis,* anyway, and of course, result came up barren.

4. Asshole. Had the nerve to write this in an exploratory report. I will fuck her up especially, Cindy added.

5. With you, the alleged "Family Services" . . . Whatever.

6. My emphasis.

attending to the *pulmonate post*[7] that appeared in my student mailbox. I used to go through Cindy's and Manny's letters once,[8] then answer them *in my head,* long missives that read: LEAVE ME IN PEACE. I AM NO LONGER YOURS. I'M STILL ON THIS EARTH, AREN'T I? LEAVE ME BE.[9]

A-9 I used to receive packages from Cindy containing old-fashioned *pasteles* and jars of *sofrito.* Once in a while, groundnut stew. Those tastes sure could take you back. The Oberlin postmaster Earl asked me, "Your mother single?"

A-10 I was a student at Oberlin University until recently. But you should already know this. Creative writing major with minors in both calculus and architectural studies.

B-1 I was a student there until two weeks ago.

B-2 Yes and no. What happened two weeks ago was this. A man I believed to be a representative of the aforementioned movie people (going by the name of "Clifford Teatown")[10] came busting into my room at the Home Away From Home motel in Orlando. To find me, he must have done some superb detective work. I was barely conscious. Clifford saw me there, got on the horn RIGHT AWAY, summoned an ambulance. Where'd this weirdo come from? I wondered as I slowly came to (a bit oven-buzzed, truth be told). Clifford switched off the gas and pressed down my sternum with his hands and then (after what seemed an eternity) lifted me onto the ambulance gurney. My eyes had been opening and closing like a sale at

---

7. Snail mail, FYI.

8. You can tell it's Cindy's letter by the olive oil stains. You can tell it's Manny's letter by the whiff of Old Spice.

9. Knowing full well that the correct locution is: *am I not?*

10. Really? He couldn't come up with a better alias than that???

Blinds To Go. *What's happening? Can somebody please tell me what's happening?* Clifford Teatown meanwhile repeating, "I'm here, I'm here, you're going to be all right," and believe me when I say he looked like all the fathers in the world. The ambulance people did their thing, ignored me when I said *I wasn't planning on going through with it* because likely they've heard that sort of excuse a thousand times. Likely they've seen men like Clifford Teatown a thousand times. He would not let go. To me, Clifford Teatown felt like Drs. Strangelove and Zhivago all rolled into one.

B-3 Just because a girl thinks of offing herself doesn't mean she's lost her mind. On the contrary. There *is* such a thing as the heat of the moment. It *can* happen that undue amounts of reflection can weigh unduly on the brain, making normal thinking unfeasible.

C-1 No one has any proof of my birth mother's existence. This is what I tell Clifford in the ambulance on the way to Fun World Medical Center. In case she is who he's after. He says he has nothing to do with the movie people and begs me not to get angry. He fesses up: "You see, my work friend, Amina Whitehead-Mensah, well, she and I . . . well, we think your mama's *out there*. And it is our duty as seasoned journalists . . . blah blah blah . . . Wouldn't you want to know for sure, Miss Katanya?" Clifford Teatown looks guilty as sin, and I nearly smack him in the mouth. But I'm too weak, and maybe I was dreaming. Nevertheless. I tell him that my real mother is no fucking Roswell alien waiting to be uncovered, and then I pass out for good. Check the ambulance records if you think I'm lying.

C-2 Manny and Cindy, if you insist. They were determined to go on believing falsehoods. Circa four years ago, they wrote me that someone in the *Missouri Prairie Borer*[11] claimed to have spotted my real

---

11. And with an overly healthy interest in my case—*the* case, I should add . . .

mother under the arch in St. Louis, supposedly carrying a protest sign. BELIEVE WOMEN, it supposedly read. Three years ago, it was someone in Wyoming[12] alleging to have spotted my real mother in the vicinity of Jackson Hole, begging for food, beer, and skis. Cindy and Manny grant an audience to every one of these lies. They say things like *You never know* or *Let's at least hear them out.* They've fallen prey to the most outlandish hoaxes. The buck stops here, however. I am against all those charlatans who make claims about my real mother, or who attempt, through supernatural or natural means, to discover her actual whereabouts. I am against those fraudsters who say they have my best interests at heart while actually attempting to unearth salacious secrets. I have nothing to offer. I'm about as blank as a page of onionskin.[13] And though I'm currently studying to be a novelist, the blood flowing through my veins is FACT. My fiction ideas are informed by the truth—whose aren't? I don't rely on hunches or gut feelings. I am built of nothing but dead-as-doornail veracity. I don't want people to be left with questions. It's a terrible fate.

C-3 I don't care. But Cindy and Manny, they want me to care. What girl forgets the woman who birthed her into existence?

Those maniacs. They've prayed that some new evidence will appear. They desire a sign, a symbol, an augury. *Jesenia Diaz, where are you* (please add italics here to your transcription)? Being of "fierce determination" but little patience, they want their questions answered lickety-split. Cindy in particular—she claims to have trouble sleeping because of all the racket my real mother is making, walking in supernatural snow boots in the attic over her bedroom.

D-1 There is nothing new to uncover here. If you persist, however, I'd ask that you please check through the files, as I've established the

---

12. Writing in the *Desert Pickyoone*.

13. This is what I told Clifford when he said he wanted to get to know me better. I didn't care that he burst into tears.

facts YET AGAIN during this morning's PRE-PRELIMINARY ORAL REVALUATION™. There have been no new sightings, no noteworthy events, no new premonitions, no out-of-the-ordinary dreams. No wandering chip-on-shoulder specter, no bent-on-revenge apparition, no slapdash spirit with an ax to grind. There's just been me. And the stuff that's been under your noses all this time[14] and what was under your noses when you interviewed me ten years ago and ten years before that.

D-2 Hell no. Hauntings have never bothered me. Before we moved out west, there were a number of ghostly events occurring in our home in Woodside, Queens—all yawnworthy.[15] White sheets draped around clattering chains, doorknobs rattling, ropes swaying in non-existent wind. A hand that went in and out of my dreams like a snow shovel. Cindy and Manny called in a soothsayer to predict my future, but she wound up eating all their frozen fruit pops. I was never moved. Of course, such details titillated the movie people[16] (whose titles, as you well know, include the 1999 sleeper hit *Bloodbath for Barbara,* 2016's classic *Attack of the Orange Toupee,* and 2021's *MAKE AMERICA GRUESOME AGAIN!*). They told me they already had a name for "my" flick: *Once Upon a Time in Queens.* As if that name would scare anyone!

D-3 When I first came to live with them, Cindy and Manny strove to keep me safe. But they suffered at the hands of pranksters and thrill-seekers who couldn't seem to leave my story alone. Mischief-makers egged the house, rang the doorbell, masqueraded as priests

---

14. "The strange mystery of the haunted house" starring Yours Truly.

15. Woodside was where Cindy and Manny took me after the Rescue. They labored under the mistaken belief that our lives could go on like normal in Queens. Fools.

16. Their actual representative, Mr. Big McLarge Huge (I kid you not), introduced himself secretly when I was in the hospital. I could not stop laughing.

wanting to exorcise the place of all bad juju. They held séances right on the front lawn; they spoke in various, weird-sounding tongues. Time passed, me watching from the sidelines, hating and loving Cindy—of course, I blamed her for everything.

D-4   Then just two years ago, as I was beginning my sophomore year at Oberlin University, I saw something on campus. I'd been conducting a tour for prospective students and their parents as part of my work-study job. As we walked down every beautiful path, I was careful to put on my "studious" face.[17] Indeed—a parent mistook me for another parent and naturally we all laughed. No one ever expects to see an old, big, large, huge college coed.

We were on the path to Conservatory Pond. A hunchback approached from the opposite direction, stopping twenty feet or so in front of us, then proceeding to squat in some of Oberlin's famed elderberry bushes. Not a dirty squat. But an inappropriate one nonetheless. It looked as if she were trying to yank something from between her legs—none of the high school senior boys found that in the least appealing, even though I could tell they all had sex on the brain.[18] These were my observations:

a. Her skin was like lines waving in the heated air.
b. She was more silhouette than sheet.
c. She had facial features but no real expression.
d. After some tense moments of pulling, she gave up, shrugged her shoulders, and blew us kisses.
e. She hopped behind a magnificent elm, one of the campus's oldest—and vanished, as they used to say, into thin air, leaving a trail of diaper-smelling smoke in her wake.

---

17. Bright teeth and cherry cheeks. People want to see this even on a Black person.
18. They're teens, for Chrissakes.

D-4 I led the group toward Ward Art as the strains of Kurt Weill on untuned pianos followed behind us in the air. I suggested the group check out the new Faith Ringgold retrospective as well as attend a lecture being given by Professor Karina Benjamin on the intersectionality of the American Civil War and metal rock—in other words, I composed myself (no pun intended). Brought calm to the surface. Rescued the tour, left the parents happy, the kids somewhat less mortified. Returned immediately to Conservatory Pond, but, of course, by then she was gone.

E-1 When I think of my real mother, I have to take stock of her many manifestations in my life: in Woodside, she was animal to me; in Cleveland Heights, vegetable; and now, at Oberlin: mineral. A little bit of silver dust that occasionally flies through my dorm room window at night. What's an old undergraduate girl to do? In earlier, less-technological communications,[19] Cindy and Manny told me to keep my eyes more open and my wits about me. They knew how ghosts could demand something from you without seeming greedy. The message? *Don't never ever trust them, no matter what.*[20]

My first writing professor at Oberlin University was the venerable Dan Chaon,[21] who suggested I start keeping my dorm room window closed after sunset—unless I actually believed there was more to gain by keeping it open. All fine and good: I've never backed away from a writerly challenge. I told him I would keep myself open for a story should one happen to present itself logically. A philosophical phantom. He smiled and gave me an A.

F-1 On the contrary. I'm barely religious at all. In Queens there was no end to the TV preachers—Creflo Dollar, Tiffany Trump

---

19. Aka phone calls.
20. I'm a writer at heart and, for better or worse, hate the hell out of superstition.
21. Before I took his fiction workshop, I was nothing, no pun intended.

Jr., Jimmy Swaggart VII—to whom Cindy sent oodles of cash for answers. In Cleveland, Cindy felt that a living breathing preacher would work better. Dragged me to True Christian Discovery Center, where Pastor Junius Korman presided, King of the Bad Breath Clergy.[22] Where she found this cat I have no idea, but she believed he might have THE ANSWER—making me sit through countless Sundays in a blazing pew, where I learned to supplicate and ask forgiveness and thank God for little mercies and scold Jesus for being such a lazy-ass.[23] Pastor Junius lectured us on how to have a Godful heart—how to be the bigger person, forgive those that trespass against you and whatnot. When he said things like that, Cindy's eyes lit up like a Christmas tree, her favorite word of all time being: *forgive*. When he learned of my "status,"[24] Pastor Junius advised me to forgive seventy-seven times, because that was the True Christian Discovery way. The *only* solution to getting past the sins of others—as well as my own, unwitting transgressions—would be to forgive the sinner (whoever that might be, my birth father, my birth mother?) seventy-fucking-seven times. Pastor Junius suggested I meet with him to discuss my "compromised/uncompromised" state of innocence. Cindy said, "Don't even think about saying no." I was set to go, to lie my head off and watch him luxuriate in those lies. And then: divine intervention: Pastor Junius suffered a massive heart attack. You could feel the collective sighs of relief in the pews. "Don't speak ill of the dead," Cindy warned. Though I could tell she had secretly gotten fed up with his ass as well.

We stopped going to True Christian Discovery for a while. Cindy got restless, guilty. By the time she forced me to return, they had hired Pastor Monica, a former junior pastoress from the

---

22. As previously noted ten years ago and ten years before that.

23. Who the hell came up with that line, "Jesus saves"? What a load of crap, Cindy used to say in private.

24. As "innocent female-tragic" of the so-called Queens House of Horror.

Church of Christ Immemorial on Sandusky Avenue, Cleveland sticks. Pastor Monica walked in smiles, a head full of self-defense and care. My first impression? I opened my mouth along with the others, thinking, *The Lord Is My Shepherd. I Shall Always Want Pastor Monica.*

G-1 You already know this. Pastor Monica was not full of mercy talk.

G-2 She spoke to me—to us—like we had brains. She did not go in for the shock value of the Bible but instead dove into what was directly in front of her: Do good be good return good. She never crowded me with platitudes of pardon or clichés of condonement. Pastor Monica's *least* favorite saying was: *Forgive and forget.* Because who says you have to forgive to move forward? You sure as hell aren't forgetting. The Lord works in pretty factual ways, she said. On Super Bowl Sunday she preached, *Let's hope those Cowboys fumble and break their hateful necks!* to everyone's dismay and pleasure.

Cindy claimed she wasn't a fan of Pastor Monica. Though that didn't stop her from attending True Christian Discovery and tithing the hell out of the collection plate.

As far as the east is from the west, so has he removed our transgression from us. A lovely line from Pastor Monica, more to Cindy and Manny's taste.[25]

Or this: *Who is a God like you, who pardons sin and forgives the transgression of the remnant of his inheritance? You will hurl all our iniquities into the depths of the sea. You will forgive us.*

She was about wisdom; she was about growth; she HATED when someone turned the other cheek. I hear you want to be a writer, she

---

25. Though I loved hearing her voice, I decided to stop going to services at True Christian Discovery. I knew I would miss her. But our allegiances—mine to fact, hers approaching yarns—would forever be a barrier.

said to me one day. We were fixing Homeless Buffet in the basement.
I hear you like books.

My heart raced. I'm going to be a student at Oberlin one day, Pastor
Monica. I want to study creative writing. I want to solve a mystery.

Pastor Monica took my hands in hers. Listen, Miss Allison. Rein-
venting oneself is highly overrated. You can change your name a
thousand times. But remember that you are perfect just as you are.
Your dreams are perfect; your reality is a garden of delights. Let us
think of those glorious words in Proverbs: *She is clothed in strength and
dignity, and she laughs without fear of the future.* It is never too early or too
late. That is you, my dear. Over and over.

In my heart, all I could answer was: *Yes, I'm saying yes forever yes.*

H-1 It's never too early or too late. Hence my status as college student at the ripe young age of thirty-two. Took me long enough to get
here. Everyone thinks I'm twenty-two. The Jamaican cafeteria workers think I'm seventeen. Time is not just slippery; it's Niagara Falls.[26]

H-2 I realize you are operating at the instructions of Cindy Diaz,
whom I had (until now) successfully avoided confronting much of
these past two years. I believe Fun World Medical of Orlando, Florida, contacted her (at the behest of Clifford)[27] to suggest she bring me
back to Ohio for "recuperation." Legally, the hospital couldn't tell
Cindy everything that had happened; they didn't want a lawsuit if
I turned around and did it again and claimed it was because they'd
blabbed my secrets. In any case, Cindy made some sort of arrange-
ments. Manny came and got me. End of story. Until now.

H-3 I close my eyes and open my mouth. The post-Pleistocene
winds tickle my tongue as we head north on Highway 1. Capistrano,

---

26. Or, more appropriately for Ohio, Hayden Falls. I have not stepped foot in New York
since Woodside.

27. He liked to call himself my guardian angel.

Hermosa, Point Conception. Another convertible passes us with a golden lab hanging its tongue in the same position. My compadre, I think to myself. Cliff is going over the speed limit.

H-4 On the plus side, the time wasted in Fun World Medical (how many Rorschach blots can a girl decipher, goddammit?) made me realize that the world needs me more alive than dead. Clifford was there to watch Manny take me away, back to Ohio; he then sent me a clandestine email (bless his heart for still having *that* technology in this day and age!) hoping I was recovering nicely. He asked me to forgive him, and in my mind, I was wondering: What for?

At home, Cindy came to my bedside and watched the silver dust flow through open curtains, shaking her head in disgust. Who is this man Clifford Teapot? she asked. Why he sending you all these letters? It does not feel right, *chica*. Who is this man?

H-5 Six letters in all on delicate onionskin, from apologies to exhortations to questions about the color of Jesenia Diaz's hair to the confirmation number of the rental car he'd secretly booked. *We* were going to find my mother. Cliff and me. We'd wait things out a short while and then zip away. Nothing romantic, mind you. Cliff was already old as the hills. It was just business and facts, 100 percent. If Jesenia was out there, we'd be the first to find out. "In the interests of true journalistic integrity, I cannot leave you hanging, not after Fun World Medical," he wrote, and of course, that made me smile. *Please do not tell anyone, Katanya.* I laughed out loud. California, here we come!

H-6 Why California? Isn't that where everyone goes for reinvention and hair?

H-7 Cliff driving the raspberry Porsche so fast it becomes a blur; my hair whipping the shit out of bad memories. Hold on, he cries, gunning the engine up and down the coastline. We are in pursuit of clues. We speed past the languid ocean on our left, which has no choice but to continue on without us.

I-1 You know this anecdote. Cindy is part Santeria, part Altagracia, part Pastor Junius Korman, part Walter Mercado, part Anansi tale-teller. When I was ten, I demanded to know where I came from. Cindy looked me in the eyes. I found you long ago, she said, in a pile of ashes near a park on Kissena Boulevard. You weren't clay, you were ash. A dusty little mouse waiting for my hands to breathe you into life. Now go wash the dishes and make your bed.[28]

I-2 As is indicated in this file (and the one from ten years ago and ten years before that), the police really couldn't be accused of goofing off. Far from it. Responding to Cindy's hunches in the past, they've steadily made certain discoveries—albeit the wrong ones. They discovered a grave in Woodside (good) but containing the wrong torso (bad); in Kew Gardens, they found a girl's head with hair swirling down her back (positive) but with the wrong teeth in that head (negative); the police came upon fingerprints in Jamaica that could have been the right ones (hopeful) but turned out to belong to a dead girl in a completely different basement (total letdown). The police found lots of stuff, courtesy of me. I never felt proud, though Cindy told me I should. She told me never give up hope. Because each time could be the time they uncover a birthmark, a bruise, the nearly invisible line going from stomach to lady parts. Marks of my birth mother. Mystery solved. No such luck, however. Take MaryAnn Doe. #37889-12. Bashed in head with scars along breasts, found at Alley Pond. Alive, this MaryAnn would have had no idea how to make lasagna out of beef jerky and raisins. Take Sue Doe. #409-904. Throat slit, fingertips burnt, found near JFK swamp. Alive, this Sue wouldn't have understood the logic of combining Steak-umms with

---

28. Cindy has always lived by her fairy tales. It was and still is exasperating.

cardboard cutouts. Take Jane Doe. #264039-5. Drowned in Dutch Kills, face bloated beyond recognition. Alive, this girl was probably already mistaken for dead. How could that be Jesenia Diaz?

J-1 You already know this but here goes. Ten years ago, a lady shows up in our driveway in Ohio and steps out of a white limousine. A "surprise friend"; she introduces herself at the front door as "Miss F."[29] She hands me a heart-shaped box from Neuhaus in New York City and asks if I remember her. No, I don't. She asks if I like pizza; I tell her I can take it or leave it. She is made to stand in the doorway because Cindy has a policy against Jehovah's Witnesses. I want to invite her in, though. It would rankle Cindy to no end. You know this. She and I had been in the middle of this knock-down-drag-out, and I wanted to rankle her. On the other side, I wasn't feeling particularly charitable to strangers in that moment. Miss F. asks if I love nougats cause that's what she had me pegged for, a "chewy chocolate kind of girl." I force a smile. Miss F. says there's no need to ask her in—even though by now she's inched her way into the living room—but if now's not good, can she come back another time? Sure, why not? And so she did just that—as you already know, per your reports—she came back *the following day*. Brought me a silk scarf from Macy's. Asked me how I liked Ohio weather—FYI, the weather in New York is spectacular, she said. Try Suffolk County. Or try farther north, that's where I was just on vacation, Rockland County. It has the most amazing trees.

Trees?

One day, we plan to live there with my brother.

We?

(Was she giving me clues? I started to miss the certainty of Cindy's knock-down-drag-out.)

---

29. This has all been duly noted in the last report, if you cared to actually look at what you've already asked. Sigh.

Miss F. had a lot of acne on her face. Long eyes, spaced-out teeth as sharp as can lids. Not really what you'd expect of a surprise friend but whatever. She asked if I recalled her in any tiny way. Her voice, her hands. No detail was too small. It would mean the world to her if I did.

I told her I didn't, but that wasn't a deterrent. Miss F. came back to the house, always around the same time of year. Same little stories about her brother. Same disappointment when I told her that no, my memory hadn't gotten better since her previous visit. She once wanted to know if I would kiss her cheek, but I declined.

The last time Miss F. visited us, Cindy waited a respectable distance and then ripped the nougat truffles from her hands, crying, Who in their right mind would stir up this pot?[30]

I mean no harm, Miss F. said. It's just.

This is a baby girl who's got her life together and shame on you for wanting to take her back.

It's just.

Get out! You show your face around here any more I will personally stuff YOU inside a toolbox![31]

Recently Miss F. has taken to sending me gifts at my P.O. box at Oberlin. Nougats. Chocolate-covered cherries. A ghost orchid, a bedspread woven with crystals. Diaries with heart-shaped locks wrapped in pink cellophane. A stainless steel necklace with my first initial. A stuffed animal that when you press its tummy says: *I wuv you.*

(I didn't think there were any clues in those gifts but who knows.)

I started seeing Miss F. all over—at night, during the day. These sightings should not be noted as fact because I was under duress and could have easily been hallucinating. I saw her behind bushes, in the corner of my closet. When I am asleep, she has put her hand on my shoulder and sent electrical waves straight to my gut. She has giggled on my neck; she has grasped my hand in a crowd. In my heart of

---

30. Ironic, yes, since the whole time I was Cindy's ward that's all she did: stir the pot.
31. Cindy could be so EXTRA!

hearts I don't believe that these sightings should be taken seriously at all. And yet.

Mostly I have felt like I wanted nothing more to do with Miss F. But I also know that if I never saw her again in real life, I might die.

J-2 Jesenia Diaz. Sometimes with a *J*, sometimes with a *Y*.

K-1 This tidbit may intrigue you. Three years ago, I got a postcard that said, Hi Baby. Nothing more. No date, no *Love, Your Long-lost Mom*. I was skeptical. I'd gotten things like this in the mail before—things Cindy Diaz had tried to sweep out of eyeshot, tossing letters and postcards in the trash and erasing suspect phone messages on our antiquated answering machine. Hi Baby. I still to this day have no idea why those two words have stuck. The postmark was Florida. Maybe it was the simplicity.

K-2 To get more specific: the front of that postcard featured a run-down bar (made to look that way, I imagine; what is genuine these days?): *The Lady's Grille. Two locations: In Orlando on the Turnpike and in Cocoa Beach on Trumpville Esplanade! Lady's Happy Hour From 4–10, Every Day!*

K-3 Flash forward: Manny and me in my dorm room. We had been saying our goodbyes—me to finish out my freshman term at Oberlin after Christmas break, him to return to Cindy back in the Heights. Suddenly he notices the postcard on my desk. Looks at it, breathes in deep. Asks me if I wanted him to "destroy this bad boy."

K-4 Important to note: this is the essence of Manny Romano Diaz. He is the builder of childhood bookshelves, combatant of closet monsters. Spongy-soft side of Cindy, for those of us who fear her direct impact. He used to send me a CARE package each month—as you are well aware—not with food but with extra notebooks, pencils, and bags of cotton candy; one time he even sent me an old-fashioned laptop computer, all to help me "better myself."

K-5 I want him to know I can handle the past on my own. The post-card is meaningless—haven't I received dozens of cards and letters from quacks and pranksters and thrill-seekers who just want a tiny piece of me, of my history of origins? I'm no fool. I feel like saying to Manny: I am a writer, for Christ sake. I wasn't born yesterday. I think I would know it if it was my mother trying to contact me. A fact in my bones.

I wind up saying to Manny: No, I got this. Thanks, anyway.

K-6 I don't know what became of that postcard.

K-7 Yes, it was Clifford Teatown's theory that Cindy Diaz broke onto campus, entered my dorm room while I was in fiction workshop, and nabbed that sucker. We lay/sat in the ambulance heading to Fun World Medical, and he was holding my hand. It was possible— given all he knew about Cindy—that she had burned the postcard among a stack of Dominican "Come to Me" candles outside the Oberlin *Rathskeller*—had she ever fully let loose of her secret *botanica* ways? he politely wondered.[32] But another contention was that Cindy had taken the postcard back to Cleveland Heights and set it on a pyre in the backyard along with three strands of my hair, an old newspaper clipping from our days in Queens, some cocoa beans, and a spray of Glade air freshener. Don't forget the prayer to Altagracia. No spell would be complete without that, Clifford added. When we get out to California, let's start at the very start: the place where the swallows return. No candles necessary. We'll head your mama off at the pass! ·

---

32. A rat in the *Rat*—how apt!

Clifford Teatown laughed. I laughed, too. I remember that.

L-1 In terms of new things that have ABSOLUTELY NO MEAN-ING: there *was* that dream from three months ago. The dream of the hand.

I've seen it before. Woodside, Manhattan, Cleveland Heights, Oberlin. Even during my secret trip to Florida two weeks ago. There was the hand. All I had to do was close my eyes and let it lead me—which it did—to a fence covered in supermarket fliers. Down a sidewalk plastered with faint gray footprints of snow. No real grasp of that hand[33] other than that it was huge, brownish beige, perhaps a bit hairy. The tiniest of pimples along the back ridge, like the bumps of a dinosaur. It is dark of night and I can't read the supermarket fliers trapped in the fence, but I think they may be from CTown. Sale this week on hamburger meat and elbow macaroni and Goya black beans. There is no wind in the dream and yet the fliers chase me along the fence, fluttering like all get-out. I feel like I'm riding on a giant's shoulders, the hand still intact.

L-2 You already know this but what the hell. In the days after we came to Cleveland Heights some twenty-three-four-five-odd years ago, my name was Katanya. School begins? I change it to Allison, in honor of the girl who goes underground and is miraculously happy in the end. But one day I started to feel that was bullshit. So I turned myself into Mira, after Mira Diamante, the 2019 winner on Tiffany Trump Jr.'s Teen Star Kitty Kat Talent Showcase in Atlantic City. Mira Diamante became a spokesperson for (in her words) "girls that think they equal to boys but aren't." Hell no, some serious reflection, automatic name change. I experimented. In the ninth grade, we read a book called *This Bridge Called My Back*, and that's where I fell for the name Rosario. Cindy felt it sounded too old-school and why did it matter what the real-life Rosario had done? That was her

---

33. No pun intended.

baggage, her Bengay back. The lesson? Don't carry someone else's baggage. Change your name to something nice, chica.

L-3

> "We are new.
> They gave us life, kept us going,
> brought us to where we are.
> Born at a crossroads.
> Come, lay that dishcloth down . . ."[34]

M-1 This is among my earliest memories.

We left Queens in a hurry. Cindy had always fantasized about Ohio being a place of white picket fences and "middle America"—bad things didn't usually happen to the white people here so why would they happen to us?[35] We took the car along I-84, didn't even stop for a McDonald's. We got to Ohio, parked at the first town that didn't look (according to Cindy) like a concentration camp. We bought a house, moved twice after that, to the water, to sandstone country, where my kindergarten teacher was stunned at my lack of knowledge, that I didn't even know how to spell C-A-T. Why you talk to my child as if she's an animal, Cindy screamed, flying me out of that classroom. We packed our bags yet again.

M-2 Shit's like the Underground Railroad, was Manny's assessment, as we drove through the cities and neighborhoods and eventually got to the house that was to become our final resting place.

N-1 In my first bed in our house in Euclid,[36] I closed my eyes and saw a pair of tight jeans, a missing mouth, silver necklace that rustled

---

34. Rosario and Aurora Morales, "I Am What I Am." From *This Bridge Called My Back*.

35. We weren't white but whatever.

36. A pink canopy with pictures of Disney's *Jungle Book* stamped over the sheets and bedspread.

with the wind. I saw a face like my own. I opened the door to the closet in my little girl's bedroom. Nothing. But later on, there was the sound of monster-style scraping in the farthest farthest back.

N-2 Manny once said to me, I only want you to be happy. I don't want you to be right.

O-1 Elementary school: regular ups and downs. Middle school: I was just rolling along fine but then some Idiot Boy discovered *the dirt*. The dirt that followed me everywhere.[37] Idiot Boy walked in (to social studies, where Mr. B. was giving us the *hardest test ever*) and announced he'd "found out some answers."

Answers to what? Mr. B. and others wanted to know.

"To *things*."[38]

Mr. B. told Idiot Boy to sit the hell down and get back to the test at hand,[39] but Idiot Boy wouldn't shut up. Do you know we have a famous person here? Do you know we have a famous girl without a real mother? he asked. Eyes widened; the usual mayhem ensued.[40]

Don't get me wrong. I was BORN used to this dirt.

Everyone started looking at me funny, the lunch lady, the janitor, the hall monitor. Even Mr. B. *How do you feel? Are your dreams normal? Do you hate men? Are you a feminist? Was there a school set up in your dungeon? Did you contract diseases? Do you still hate men? How old are you really?*

All I wanted to do was disappear into the normal wasteland of eighth gradeness. But once *the dirt* was dug, there was No. Turning. Back.

---

37. Headlines included but were not limited to: *"Girl rescued from House of Horrors!"* (*New York Daily News*); *"Mute Girl, unused to light of day, delivered from den of evil!"* (*Christian Daily Spoon*); *"Modern Day Helen Keller(s) taken from veritable lunatic asylum!"* (*National Enquirer*).

38. "Your name doesn't happen to be Katanya Diaz, does it?" And so forth.

39. A) What was slavery? B) Who was Harriet Tubman? C) Where was she buried? D) Name one moment from her life. Ten points out of ten.

40. Parents calling Cindy on the telephone to offer condolences or to ask questions or to say their kids were having a sleepover and sorry we can't invite Katanya due to potential nightmares but maybe next year. Teachers staring at the blackboard with immobile chalk. Reporters calling the house during a slow news day, because I was always a breaking story.

O-2 Cindy—she was livid. She raged when phone calls came in from TV stations looking for an "update."[41] Before we moved to Ohio, Cindy blew a fuse when the poet laureate of Queens published a haiku about me in the *Queens Metropolitan*.[42] After we moved to Ohio, she raged when *Plain Dealer* reporters came to our house with their notepads and cameras and assorted technologies to see "how the youngest victim was doing."[43] Cindy walked outside with a Little League bat. Manny threatened he would talk to lawyers. Cindy said no need for that; she would use her fists as attorneys.

P-1 Name change always seemed the best option. Who cared if the eighth graders still saw the same person before them? A new name would erase the *me* everybody fantasized about. I asked the middle school principal Mr. C. and he said it would be okay and then he told folks that if they called me anything but my new name (whichever it was that week), they would get detention. Case closed.

P-2 The only bit of hard evidence I currently own (which you already know about) is that scrappy scrap of denim fabric that was pinned to my baby bonnet in the ash pit and which Cindy has recently stolen, along with the postcard from the Lady's Grille.

Q-1 The Hand. As I've mentioned before. The Hand.

Q-2 For God's sake! The Hand took me places; the Hand was kindly. You already know this. It carried me to a screaming church where ladies danced up and down the aisles in tongues. The Hand led me to two men sitting outside a deli asking me if I was a daddy's girl.

---

41. *Cleveland Good Morn*, Episode 112: "Upstanding Beautiful Girl rises from the ashes—is this for real?"

42. "Madman's frenzy oh/Living well the best revenge/can be hard and beautiful alone." Signed 2009 Queens Poet Laureate Talia Shalev-Jenkins.

43. *Cleveland Plain Dealer*, November 21, 2020: "Meet the Mermaid from Hell."

Laughter. But the Hand did not do laughter. The Hand sped past an old woman standing at a chain-link fence who asked if Santa had brought me anything nice in my stocking. The Hand gently shoved me into dark stairwells with pots and pans built into the wood. The old woman at the fence once said to the Hand, "I can't stand the price of oil nowadays. People like you and me could freeze and nobody would notice because the way the oil prices keep going up." The Hand nodded. The Hand led me to a bag filled with lollipops with chocolate centers. To a pink pony pillow called a Pillow Pet. To a window that had been boarded and unboarded and reboarded and covered in sheetrock and much later on, red gift wrap paper. The old woman appeared and reappeared, like Rumpelstiltskin waiting under a bridge; stretching her own hand out to me, offering a hard lemon candy. "You two remind me of my daddy when he would hold my hand wherever we went," she said. "But that was so long ago. Little girl, won't you ask your granddad if the two of you could come over for a cup of eggnog?" The Hand snapped shut and disappeared with me in it.

R-1 School was great once it went over to college. Everyone is unto themselves, and that is how it should be. Plus, college is a great place for lies. Cindy begged for Cuyahoga Community, but I said no way Jose. She said I would be on the honor roll there. I told her I needed distance and that my destiny was Oberlin. Cindy pretended to cry for days. I did not relent. Best. Decision. Ever.

R-2 The small denim scrap about which you questioned me ten years ago and ten years before that bears the letters

GRE

embroidered in faded white thread. It is a scrap; I took it from our place in Queens and kept it safe in a pillowcase. No one knew about this scrap; no one saw me rub it against my face. No one saw me kiss it. No one saw me talk to it—and certainly no one saw or heard it talk right back.

S-1 We were in a diner in Columbus, having spent the day touring the shale stone cliffs. Manny told Cindy: Let the girl order whatever she wants. Then he took the menu from my hands and told the waitress that I would have the omelet with cherry peppers, anchovies, and spinach.

Brain food, he said, winking.

Cindy frowned, saying that we should've gone to that Dominican place she peeped on College Road.

Looked over at me. I'm tired of your questions, chica. Don't make me mention that asshole again. He called you a name I don't remember. Then he switched it to the name of that character on *One Life to Live*, the pretty one. He thought you would grow up to look like her. Or like your mother.

(He. We never mentioned his name. He was just he.)

Did he love her? Do I look like her? Did he think of her as his wife?

Cindy took out her cigarettes. The moment was over. What do I care what that shit stain thought? *¡Culo!*

She was crying. I could bleach your hair, she said, stretching her meat-waggly arm[44] across the table, taking my chin in her hand. I could bleach your eyebrows, she said. Make you really memorable. Then the world would forget.

Y'all be wanting anything else? the waitress asked.

I want us to run far away, Cindy cried. She slid her body over the booth table, upsetting the maple syrup. Why do *we* have to face *your* demons, *mami*? Why do *you* have to come from *anywhere specific*? Why do you have to have a history? Manny and me are your history, baby. You began with us. Period. Let's run away.

---

44. Made so by years of homemade carne guisada and rice.

S-2 Before we leave the diner, when Cindy and Manny are in the bathroom, the waitress grabs my hand. Young lady, are you being kidnapped? Want me to call the police?

Later, Manny will say, Thank God people have their eyes open nowadays.

Cindy replies, Fuck that bitch to hell.

S-3 Cindy's favorite saying of all time: Expect nothing and you never go away empty-handed.

In the twelfth grade I did some searching in the virtual card catalog and discovered a book all about vintage fashion, specifically about weird clothing brands; one existed between 1999 and 2010 called: GREATGIRL JEANS. Pretty unoriginal. Of course, when I asked Cindy, she said she'd never heard of it. Forget the jeans, she warned me. You were born of ash, *mija*, not some ragged piece of cloth.

S-4 I learned to be a newsman from reading up on my two great-great aunties, Clifford told me as we sat on a cliff at Mussel Shoals. Julia and Charity Teatown. Both ardent followers of Ida B. Wells, both fellow crusaders in the anti-lynching movement. Bet you know nothing about that. They faced the worst terrors on our soil and yet they did not stop looking forward. I read everything the public library offered, which wasn't much. But they nevertheless made me. They were what you might call *fact women*. And we, standing on their shoulders, have got to bear their burden. Bet you didn't know that.

S-5 California here we come. We're already here, matter of fact.

T-1 Several months ago I received the following:

Hey girl thought I'd drop a line see how U BE doing ☺ in the
event U have stopped having thoughts about a such
person :) as I who did all she could outside of having

priests and pastors take the devil out :(Lord. I miss U. I want
U to take me serious. Try FUN WORLD, right next to
Disneyland off the Turnpike, you can't miss it. It's the Fun World.
I will be there. Serious. I have wanted U more than you
No.

U-1 There was that author[45] Dan Chaon made us read in fiction
workshop who once said:

"We write what we don't know we know." Risk—supposedly that's
the name of the game. Stroll that pencil through the streets of the
brain, unlock the mansions, each one roomier than the next.

U-2 Dan Chaon. In the old days he was a believer in pencil and legal
pad. And where would I be if he hadn't read my first pages in that fiction workshop three years ago and praised me to the heavens? Smoked
too much and made fun of lazy-ass students wanting to be rock stars.

U-3 Here's a quote of his. "The feeling of being an outsider, and the
identity theme, is hardwired into me. I always feel that way."
      I never knew the exact date Cindy discovered me. She said I fell
from heaven and landed in a pit of ashes and thank God she was
there to find me or else who knows? I might have suffocated under
all those cinders had it not been for her. But I have no memory of
a pit.

V-1 When I was about four or so,[46] I saw this quicksand pond in Episode #137 of *Courageous Cat*: "The Frog pushes Courageous into dangerous Quick Sand Lake." And I saw it again in Episode #564: "Minute
Mouse cries for help after mistaking Quick Sand Lake for Fun Lake."

---

45. As previously mentioned, Grace Paley, last of Sarah Lawrence College in New
York.
46. My age on the adoption certificate was five, but I never believed that to be the truth.

Turn that damn noise off, Cindy shouted. She didn't like it that I watched cartoons; she felt they took away from true learning.[47] She said *Courageous Cat* would get me nowhere but wait till I got my hands on *Anne of Green Gables* or *Sor Juana Inés de la Cruz*. Stories with happy endings, poems of inspiration. Those would make me smart, totally original. Manny on the other hand understood the need for a child to interact with visual hilarity and exaggerated conflict[48]—that's what all those cartoons were about in those days. Maybe they are still the same. I wouldn't know. I haven't really studied a TV in years.

W-1 At Oberlin, I raised my hand. We all raised our hands. We disdained clichés. We searched for innovation. We talked about the fresh white heat of a first draft and the agony of looking back over our words the next day and finding nothing but cinders. We averted our gazes; we plunged face-first into the sun. Cleveland everyday presenting itself as a blank slate, a movie screen waiting for our ideas, characters, conflicts, resolutions. When can an ugly city be beautiful? Ask a writer.

W-2 One time Manny put aside the *Reader's Digest* and instead took out his *Daily Bread*:

> Woe unto them that join house to house, *that* lay field to field,
> till *there be* no place, that they may be placed alone
> in the midst of the earth.

X-1 Though I have seen the questions on this form ten years ago and ten years before that, I continue to be perplexed. RACE AND/OR ETHNICITY: what am I?

The answer: I am a product of a hand, a belt, a chain, a pit. What would you call that race?

---

47. Whatever that was.

48. "So let the girl watch her *Courageous Cat*! She don't have nothing to lose!"

X-2 Okay, all jokes aside.

Manny comes from the border between Haiti, Black North Carolina, Black Nebraska, and the DR.

Cindy is Hispanic or mestizo or runaway maroon or creole; she says she is "universal."[49] She refuses to say even one single sentence in normal Spanish "because that is no longer the language of the God I grew up with." Yeah, right.

I, on the other hand, feel about as specific as they come though I still have no idea what to put on the RACE AND/OR ETHNICITY line. Rumor was I had a biological daddy somewhere in the five boroughs. Rumor was my mother died at his hands and traveled to heaven in a state of pre-manufactured bliss.

Rumor was—and is—that my mother is alive somewhere. Just because I laid my head on the door of an oven oozing brilliant gas doesn't mean I don't want that rumor to be true.

Y-1 Once upon a time in Queens, I went through Cindy's bottom dresser drawer and found the following:

An envelope marked *Quinceañera Future Maybe*;
a pair of banana earrings;
three unsmoked cigarettes;
a marriage license, unsigned;
newspaper clippings from a Queens newspaper;
a blank cassette tape;
Cindy's social security card;
Manny's social security card;
an application for food stamps;
an old copy of *TV Guide*;
Mardi Gras beads;

---

49. Manny once asked her if *universal* meant she was the same thing as clear. God, how I loved his sense of humor!

three thimbles;

wire cutters;

a baby pacifier and a pair of baby socks;

three small posters, folded ten times over, of missing animals;

tweezers;

an Afro pick;

white patent leather Sunday shoes;

a photograph of the back of someone's head.

Y-2 Once upon a time in Queens, Cindy stood between me and Courageous Cat with her hands on her hips. You would've perished if it wasn't for me, girl.

Z-1 "It's like going into a dark room . . . you stumble around until you find the walls and then inch your way to the light switch." A quote from the old days in my writing workshop,[50] one now giving me strength to face my demons. Demons being, of course, an absolutely real thing.

Z-2 Two weeks ago I ran away to Florida. Florida's Turnpike. I booked a kitchenette at the Home Away From Home motel and waited. I told no one I was going.

Z-3 I chickened out at first. Took a walk around the tourist shops, contemplated buying some Navajo turquoise or a pair of alligator sandals or a decal that read, WE ARE NOT YOUR TIRED OLD AVERAGE DISNEY CHARACTERS—WE ARE FUN WORLD! I walked past the men lining the alleys behind the restaurants. Egg-colored, waffle-faced, piss-visaged, ice-cubed, gray-fanged—they smiled and asked me if I was lonely. I said back: *Yes, but not for you.* And they laughed but I could tell they'd expected a different answer.

---

50. Dan Chaon, natch.

Z-4 I kept walking. McLaughlin's Pub. Feeny's Irish Eyes. Whispers: An Adult Lounge. Pure Unadulterated Funk Bar and Grill. Sammy's. Highway to Hell. Ginny's. Wino's Eatery. Juggler's Canteen. Soft Spot Lounge and Bar. Miami Heat One. Miami Heat Two. Wild Rosie's. Confessions.

No such place as Lady's Grille, no matter where I asked.

Z-5 The first time I saw Pastor Monica take the pulpit of True Christian Discovery, she waited for the crowd to die down, looked in my direction, and said, "A glad heart makes a cheerful face."

Z-6 Eventually I went back to the Home Away From Home motel and locked the door. I flipped on the light, flipped through the refrigerator: nothing but ketchup packets and a half-pint carton of expired half and half. My thoughts lingered. I found a beer under the small sink, opened it, then went straight to the oven and powered it up. I have no recollection of that beer.

Z-7 I have no recollection of that refrigerator door. I have no recollection of that light switch. The credit card I gave the front desk (courtesy of Cindy Diaz's "college emergency") was maxed out. I have no idea how Home Away From Home thought they'd be paid.

Z-8 I have no idea if I left the water in the bathroom sink running. I have no idea if I pulled up a chair to the stove or simply kneeled, church-style.

Z-9 I felt myself carried into an ambulance and then Clifford's hand and shortly afterward a bed. Later I learned I was a new resident of Fun World Medical Center. Clifford Teatown hovering like a mama bird: I was worried, he said. But I hope you enjoyed your little venture to Fun Lake. You were talking it up like nobody's business!

Z-10 If ever I was to want a pretend place to come alive, it would have to be Fun Lake. I've written about it in my diaries. Of course, you know that. I think I even wrote an essay that was published in the school newspaper. "Dreams Can Come True" by Allison Diaz. Cindy read it over and asked, *Are you kidding?*

Z-11 Five years ago I was awarded a citation from the City of Cleveland—but what the fuck did Cleveland have to do with anything? The citation read: FOR YOUR BRAVERY IN THE FACE OF NEAR DISASTER, etc. etc. Meaningless words. What did I have to do with disaster? Cindy and Manny had moved us here for safety, to stay out of sight. To avoid kooks, teens, priests, movie people. Yet here I was, holding my hands out for a large glass trophy with my name engraved in handsome cursive.

Z-12 If anyone should apologize, it should be the shortsighted borough of Queens, New York.

Z-13 The movie people should consider this. How does *Long Long Ago* sound as a title?[51] I'll have to ask Big McLarge Huge to get back to me.

Z-14 Long, long ago

I was discovered in a heap of embers. A kind but misguided woman saw me and fished me out with a wooden spoon. She wore an apron spun of golden threads and placed me in her pocket. I was no bigger than a thumb. The sun shining brightly. The birds chirping. The woman took me home to her sort-of husband, who burst into tears, saying, She looks just like her mother, God forgive us.

As I grew and grew. Dried my tears. Went out into the world. Stopped asking for directions.

Returned home. Back to the bedroom I'd known forever. The

---

51. Bitching, I'd say.

motel did not press charges. All is good; I open my window and allow the silver dust wafting out there to come in and coat me whole.

Go west, young woman, this silver dust says, every time. Ten years ago and ten years before that. Why have I always been looking in the wrong place?

Z-15 Clifford meets me on the curb outside Manny and Cindy's house. Even though the top is down, the convertible smells of cigarettes and future California. We gonna find that woman, he says, smiling. I can tell his heart has been realigned in some way. He's not even thinking of his newspaper story. He wants California for me alone. He wants us to escape the movie people. Every girl should have her mother. You only get one, isn't that right? Roll down your window baby. California, here we come.

Z-16 Wake up, my darling. Yes, this is Cindy talking. You were doing that thing again. No, there is no such a person as that. Have some water. Have some Social Teas. Wake up now, Katanya. From here on in you'll go nowhere farther than my arms. Let me hold you. Those movie people are still on our ass. Who needs a movie after a life like yours, huh? I'll keep them away. You are the life that's meant to be lived, don't you know? Always have been. Wake up, the sun is shining. Coffee or tea?

Z-17 I sat up in bed and looked out my bedroom window, searching for Clifford's car. A glass of lemon seltzer bubbled on my nightstand. The sun moved in slow circles around the sidewalk trees. How un-writerly, I'm saying to myself: The twist ending: where you wake up and realize it was all a dream. What a hack move! Thinking I'm on my way out west when in reality . . . Dan Chaon would be horrified.[52] I fall back into my pillows and reaffirm—crying, crying—my absolute need for fact.

Z-18 But that doesn't mean Fun Lake can't exist somewhere.

---

52. Clifford is nowhere to be seen. Did he even exist? PURE HACK!

FERN

And when we win, the trains will move back on their
tracks, through the forests, through the mountains. If we
win, the ghetto will have never been, and there will never
have been a knock on the door.

AFFINITY KONAR, *MISCHLING*

HER TRUE-TRUE NAME

This was so long ago. *Mi nombre,* Jesenia sighed. Chained up in the LOWER-EMPLOYEE-WORK-DEPARTMENT, one of the last fights I can recall. She said, My name is a thing I can't remember no more.

The problem being: had it been spelled with a *Y* on her birth certificate, or a *J*, like the Boss Man said it was?

He was adamant. There's nothing to worry about, bitch. You are Jesenia with a *J*. Plain and simple.

I don't believe you, she ventured.

Don't feel bad, Gwin and I assured her from the wall boards to which we were fastened. The smell of fig, raisin, and coconut floated in the air. I said, We love your name; we're in love with it. Jesenia with a *J* is so much better than ours. Don't you think it sounds as nice as Jessica? Like Jessica from *One Life to Live*? You know how pretty she is?

I guess.

Jesenia with a *J*. Like Jessica on the boob tube. All that gorgeous blond hair. Don't you wish sometimes you could have all that gorgeous blond hair, Jesenia?

Okay. I get it already.

"J" like in J.Lo. Jenny from the Block. Jennifer Bennifer. This was Gwin, who'd been sneaking out of her chains to watch the Magnavox. She'd seen new things. Never an exact date, though. Not one she could remember. The world was going on without us. She'd tell me things, sneak back into her chains with Boss Man none the wiser.

The next day Jesenia called out to us: I think I had a Tía Magdalena who spelled my name with a *Y.*

Oh, we whispered back.

Sí, sí. She was an aunt who lived half the time in the DR, the other half in Haiti. She was like Dr. Jekyll and Mr. Frankenstein.

Oh, we whispered again, louder.

So if it's with a *Y,* it would mean the first part of my name is a true positive.

Oh, we whispered. Thinking.

When I see Boss Man tomorrow, I'm a tell him he is wrong, Jesenia added.

We'll be right behind you.

What if he gets mad? My darling Boss Man can get mad when you least expect it.

We'll be right behind.

Oh, girls! Where would I be without you?

Let's not even go there, please.

THE DEVIL'S HANDBOOK FOR GIRLS

By Clorinda Renay Keely-Dawkins, PhD

Woman's Destiny Books, Burlington, VT, 1979. All Patents Pending.

Number 34 in the series

EVERYTHING IS POSSIBLE©

INCANTATION #1
(To be read aloud in an afterschool bathtub with three apple-
scented candles in anticipation of a full moon)
Dark Noble
Of All Things Funkadelic
Hear Me
Make me
Shapely in Mind and Body.
Let me fear not Your
Sanguineaceousness
But deliver me
Into my own Whirlwindnaceousness!
Dispel all images of horny principals,
Chunk-ass cheerleaders,
And bitchy biology teachers
Teach me instead to remember every goddamn day that
I
Am
A
Strong
Independent
FEMALE!
May Love Have Mercy!

The four neighbor women had come to the house that afternoon
hoping that a little bit of bleach, some Castile soap (cheap at Dollar
Haven), and a few fragrant honeysuckle boughs (free from the church
across the street) would brighten the place. It was June and the house

was raggedy. They wanted to make the exterior shine so that when their dear friend Mattie Marron returned from Jamaica Hospital's loony bin, she would feel blessed. Restored. Better than she was in the first place (because wasn't it true Mattie could sometimes annoy the mess out of you?). How awesome would it be for Mattie to come back to a home scrubbed free of ghosts and strict fathers and other mental disorders! And how wonderful for them to once again see Mattie leaning over the chain-link fence, talking with them in blissful Black lady conversation, just as she'd done these many years! The four neighbor women put on their gloves—rubber, not church—and filled buckets with hose water and bleach. They didn't know when to expect the Jamaica Hospital van, but they did know cleanliness was next to godliness. No one deserved the fate of eternal lunatic. Wouldn't Mattie be tickled? They would make the place happy; they would make it nice, because friends like them didn't grow on trees.

In between scrubbing and scraping, one of the four neighbor women would lift her face to the sun, glazing it in the rays like a Christmas ham. Remember how we used to keep our own places spic and span? Lord God, how I miss those good old days.

This was Evie Knight, prone to memory lane. Freeda Bent rolled her eyes. She avoided memory lane to the best of her ability. Fancyella Brown pointed to the fiberglass awnings over the windows they'd been unable to reach and shook her head. Endless bird shit. We doing the best we can, Ag Wheeless said, settling in one of the folding chairs on the porch. Don't lose hope, ladies. Their hands trembled from the work; and yet, the more they scrubbed, the grayer everything seemed to appear: the rusted rails, the crumbling cement steps. The shabby lawn furniture. But what did people expect? They weren't superwomen. No one else on the block had even bothered to collect poor Mattie's mail or rip the CTown fliers and plastic bags from her chain-link fence. No one else had thought to organize a neighborhood watch (which turned out to be just the four of them) in order to catch the vagrant who'd been hanging out in Mattie's yard at night, setting fires in the ash cans. The four neighbor women believed themselves to be churchgoing, upright, astute in the ways of the children of men, and utterly charitable. They did not deny, however, that ever since those victim-females were rescued, the world seemed to be going to hell in a handbasket.

They worried about their dear friend: How would Mattie fare this time? With her being frail as a weed? Probably the loss of vital brain matter?

We reap just what we sow, said Fancyella, prone to neat endings.

Ag shook her head. After those victim-females were discovered in the house across the street, Mattie began to lose it. But why? None of it had been her fault. Three girls locked up for over ten years, tormented by some sexual madman in long johns and paper food! Where were their mothers? Could someone please tell them: WHERE WERE THEIR MOTHERS?

I worry about our dear Mattie, Ag said.

They themselves were also blameless. None of the four neighbor women had suspected a thing. How could they have? They did not own crystal balls, they couldn't have walked up to the so-called Queens House of Horrors and asked to see the madman living there, now could they? Mattie, too, had said she'd known nothing—and yet. The day the so-called Queens House of Horrors was bulldozed (the four neighbor women absolutely hated that name; why malign Queens, why throw the baby out with the bathwater?) Mattie went outside in her nightgown to throw rocks at the backhoes and scream at the construction workers. Didn't matter. The City went ahead and began erecting a church that fall that would take the place of the so-called Queens House of Horrors—and by then, Mattie seemed to have slipped completely off the lap of sanity; she cornered Pastor Edgell and the Queens poet laureate as they got ready to cut the ribbon on the door of Amity Wisdom of the Word Unitarian. *How many damn churches do we need in Queens? This land is hallowed ground! It does not deserve the fate of Christian people!*

(Yep, it's nothing short of a disgrace to those victim-females, Freeda Bent had said to Mattie that day, leading her back to her steps. Though she herself had been the first to sign the neighborhood petition demanding the house be razed.)

Ag was the one who'd gotten the call about Mattie's return—but how Jamaica Hospital had known to contact her was unclear. *We're sending a van with her in it. Be ready.* They phoned Ag some days after she'd sat down with a white man store detective to sign some papers at her kitchen table, including the promissory note for all the merchandise her granddaughter Madison had stolen from Spencer Gifts at the Queens Center mall; if she agreed to pay in full, the store would not press full charges. Of course, it would mean a lifelong ban and community service (and not at any of the fun punishment places like BLACK GIRLS JAMMIN!™ or RESPECT BLACK GIRLS OR ELSE!™); she'd be doing something like cleaning trash off the Long Island Expressway, or handing out afterschool lunches at Light at the End of the Tunnel. *Thank you for reporting these items stolen from Spencer Gifts, Mrs. Wheeless. We want to avoid the police at all costs and therefore look forward to the young perpetrator learning her lesson through hard work and repentance. Spencer Gifts has always had its customers' and perpetrators' best interests at heart. Please sign in all the right places, Mrs. Wheeless. We understand your granddaughter (aka Madison Wheeless, the perpetrator of said theft) is missing, but she still must be held accountable. One makeup set. One book. Three novelty gags. Three black candles, "Sexytime" incense and incense holder. Sign her name*

at the X, Mrs. Wheeless. We only get one life to live. You've done the right thing.
Jamaica Hospital had told Ag to expect the van after one in the afternoon; a more precise time could not be given. Is she okay? Ag asked.
Jamaica Hospital told her that the doctors would not want Mathilda Marron discharged if they thought otherwise. Ag waited, then said, I heard my friend drunk a whole bottle of Pine-Sol. To which Jamaica Hospital said they weren't allowed to say.

BRING BACK LUCK SPELL #1
(To be chanted in any principal's office while awaiting detention or suspension)
Oh Dark Noble,
I am but a vessel of readiness
Awaiting your touch!
While in Detention or In-School Suspension,
Conjuring, Practicing
In the girls' bathroom or the handball court or at
The desk of Industrial Arts, Home Economics, and/or
AP History,
I speak and listen and act:
Waiting to be free forevermore,
In your CARE,
And fuck all them that think
A girl ain't nothing but a thing.
MAY LOVE HAVE MERCY!

Jamaica Hospital's fifth floor was supposedly where they kept the loonies, though none of the neighbor women had actually been there to visit. The first, second, and third times (2008, 2009, 2009) Mattie had been taken away in the Jamaica Hospital van, the house was left to rot on its own. The four neighbor women stopped at the chain-link fence and talked NIMBY. But what of Mattie's ruins? Their families had advised them not to get involved. In fact, Ag's daughter

Damitra specifically said she would call the cops if she saw her mother anywhere near Mattie's home; it was for her own good. The fourth time Mattie was taken away (2010), the four neighbor women found Pastor Edgell (newly of Amity Wisdom of the Word Unitarian) standing in her yard, raking the late-fall leaves with a house broom. I am my sister's keeper, he said, smiling. No outward religiosity-fangs about him, but with pastors you never knew. (Once they get you in their grips, they won't let go, Fancyella Brown liked to say.) The four neighbor women hurried along. The fifth time Mattie Marron was institutionalized (2011), they lamented how mugwort and garlic mustard were already ravaging Mattie's garden, the birds slinking in the gutters and along the fiberglass awnings like common criminals. The four neighbor women chatted about the unusual cold of spring, and how now that bin Laden was dead maybe the food prices would go back down; they laughed at memories of Mattie's poor hand at redecorating the place after her father passed years ago, poor thing still didn't know if she was coming or going; eventually closing their eyes and going about their business, willing the house to fade into the background like so much brocade and fussy wallpaper. But then they retraced their steps and looked again and realized: it was their duty. Mattie was their duty, their responsibility. Forget Damitra. Forget Pastor Edgell. Forget that late-night trash-burning vagrant-hooligan who'd been tormenting their streets, ringing bells, ordering phantom pizzas, sugar in gas tanks, dog shit on front steps, in general making everyone's life so miserable—forget that devilish lowlife. They would overcome. The four neighbor women would take it upon themselves to get Mattie's place in order. They would overcome. This ain't nobody's ghetto, Fancyella Brown later told the *Queens Metropolitan* reporters.

The four neighbor women made plans to revolutionize Mattie's garden, but then Mattie returned before they could put those plans fully in motion. They waited a few days, then approached her doorstep with bundles of butter-and-egg flowers in their arms. *Welcome Home, girl! We missed you so much! We only want to help. We understand how hard it must be!* Mattie stood in the threshold, hands on hips. So what you saying, my place looks a mess? People that live in glass houses, don't forget that, ladies. No need to sweep my anything. And please will you get them weeds out my face?

No one had noticed this sixth time when Mattie was taken away in the Jamaica Hospital van. Little over a year after the last time. It had been an otherwise routine day: family fights and arguments over molded food in the fridges and pilfered beers and the wrong TV shows at the wrong times. Wasps scoured the house fronts; an ice cream truck parked its wheels up on the sidewalk, waiting reluctantly for children and retirees. The Jamaica Hospital attendants rolled out the van like boiled eggs. They climbed the front steps and banged on the door; Mattie could be heard bolting chains. The attendants managed to get the door open; the four neighbor women—having been magically summoned to the chain-link fence—felt their hearts drop into their knees. Other families came out and stood on their small porches, voices rising over the faraway rush of the Van Wyck—*Just cause she's old don't mean you should do her like that!*

PRELIMINARY FRANK QUESTIONS #2
E) Precisely how long have you been lost with your life?
F) When was the last time you felt REAL?
    a. Has any raggedy-ass boy ever called you a "tease" when in reality your heart is calling you
    b. "womanish"?
    c. or "super-womanish"?
G) When were you last truly aligned with HAPPINESS?
H) When was the last time you spoke honestly to the Dark Noble?
I) When was the last time your mind was truly blown?

Freeda Bent glanced up the jagged holes in the fiberglass awnings. The world had been changing for the worse—starting from the day of those victim-females. The *Queens Metropolitan* reported that a baby had been born in the house. What if the victim-females living there had been bad in the first place? Fast? Slutty? What if they'd run away from home after being asked nice to wash the dishes or fold the laundry? Lazy? Ungrateful? Freeda had taken a secret interest in the case, traveling by bus to the Queens Public Library, South Jamaica branch, to look up the microfiche. The kidnapper and the baby: a dead match. The lifeless faces of those living girls as they were lifted by the EMTs down the steps of the ramshackle house. The crowds in the street: was that the corner of her own winter coat in the frame? Freeda wondered what had happened to that one baby, if it had grown up, lived its life, and suddenly ventured back to the block without any of them knowing it? Had the baby been looking into random windows, trying to figure out who to get even with? Had the grown baby been the one setting delinquent fires in Mattie's yard and placing dog shit on Ag Wheeless's front steps? Dumping sugar in Fancyella's gas tank? Why in heaven's name would that grown baby be angry? None of them had done anything wrong. They were blameless. The face on the microfiche showed the outline of skinny chubby cheeks and disparate eyes. The four neighbor women had simply lived their lives and ignored the ramshackle house and felt their very bones rattle once the EMTs made their way down the steps with those living-dead females in their grasp. Children. Children. Was she going apeshit crazy? Freeda wondered. Help me back to the bus stop, she asked a schoolgirl one time, not noticing the look of revulsion in the girl's eyes as she gripped the sleeve of the cryworn woman in faint-pee pants. Thank you, young lady. You sure do know how to take care of your own. I can tell you've been raised right.

SPELL AGAINST WILY FEMALES #3

(To be said while imbibing your grandma's dandelion wine
or your mama's Olde English 800 hidden in the back of the
fridge in those foolproof plastic containers)
Dark Noble, Your breath
Doth take me away
Better than any Calgon known to womankind.
I am aching
Full of longing
Hear me, Dark Noble.
Respond.
Let me know:
Did I at least make Pep Rally Squad?

Evie Knight had brought along two large thermoses of Long Island
iced tea and a cylinder of red Solo cups. Fancyella Brown had prepared a massive banana pudding that she now pulled from a shopping bag and placed in the center of the card table. She realized she'd
forgotten the bowls and spoons. It was nearing four o'clock. I worked
myself to the bone making that banana pudding, ladies. Shame to let
it go to waste. What we gonna do?

The idea of drinking their banana pudding out the same cups as their
booze was alarming. No way Jose. They still had their pride, for God's
sake.

Why don't you run back home and get the bowls? Evie suggested. Or
run down the block to CTown for paper ones?

Fancyella frowned. Have you looked at my corns since I got here?

How could I have missed them corns? I see them every Tuesday
Elder Services.

Don't go making fun, Evie Knight.

Wasn't my meaning, Fancy. Didn't mean you any harm. Really, I didn't.

I know.

The grass had burned into hay at their feet. Though it was only June, they'd been having the worst heatwave on record, according to the *Queens Metropolitan*. I know Mattie has that grand old Steuben, Evie Knight said, patting the sides of her wig close to her face. Isn't there a way to gently break in one of these windows and get us some of those *delightful* cordial glasses?

Ain't gonna be a delight when your behind winds up in jail for breaking and entering, Fancyella said. She folded her arms across her chest; Ag and Freeda nodded. They all were deathly afraid of trouble. Had they gone back to any of their homes for the spoons or bowls, someone might have noticed them in the door and yelled. Or maybe not—these four neighbor women belonged to that variety of crone who is more annoying leitmotiv than engaging family member. Their men were generally of little help. Their grandchildren barely looked up from their devices. *Hey Auntie, you standing in my light. Did you buy me the Doritos like I asked you to?* The mothers and fathers of those children—usually playing Scratch-Off tickets or also on their devices—would in most cases glance up when they saw one of the crones, then start in with the usual harangues: Had she taken her pills? Had she cleaned up after herself in the bathroom? What about her Social Security check? Had she cashed it, and was she even *thinking* about her share of the household expenses?

Or: the families might not notice if the neighbor women came home. They might continue biting their nails, scratching their eczema, flipping through channels, getting ready for work. Or: they might get mad. *Don't you know you can't be butting in everybody's business? Leave the old girl alone!*

Ag knew better than to call her daughter Damitra, whose only child, Madison, had recently run away. Damitra blamed Ag for the disappearance. *Why you had to tell on her, Mama? And for what? A gag book on witch's spells? A party favor? What was you thinking? She's your granddaughter!* Before Madison disappeared, Ag had told the girl she was going to call the authorities in order to teach her right from wrong. Go ahead, Madison said. *You don't know me!* Had that been their last conversation?

Two months earlier. Ag had no idea what had drawn her to Madison's dresser drawer in the first place. She was bored, she was nosy, she opened it: there were the girl's cigarettes—not the e-kind, the real ones—and the diary she kept locked up under miles of duct tape, an often lively read. Why did Ag persevere? She rifled through the panties, the brassieres, the fliers for BLACK GIRLS RESISTANCE!™ and LONG LIVE THE GIRLS OF NUBIA!™, the shredded bag of weed nibs, the secretive pills and Black Israelite pamphlets. It wasn't until she spied the spine of *The Devil's Handbook for Girls* that Ag felt a pang in her heart, a thud that cleared out all the other organs, a shockwave down through her toes. Ag reached into the back of the drawer and pulled the bag containing the book into the light. No receipt. Everything a devil worshipper might need, well, I'll be damned. Where in the world is my grandbaby headed?

Ag pretended to put the book away. She thought long and hard. She waited. Madison came home one morning and smelled like a den of iniquity. Ag confronted her about the book; Madison told her to mind her own fucking business. Why couldn't she have anything of her own without some grown-folk eyes spying on her every move? They had more words, looks. Then Madison up and disappeared. Damitra called the police when the girl didn't return home; she scowled at Ag even while on the phone: So what if her baby smelled of alcohol? So what if she occasionally *borrowed* from Spencer Gifts? Why did that matter to Ag now—and not when Damitra herself was a child?

Two days before her granddaughter disappeared, Ag did indeed call the store. Are you perhaps missing a copy of *The Devil's Handbook for Girls*? I hate telling on my grandbaby, but I just want her to go down the right path. We all make mistakes. I want her to learn right from wrong. Tough love's what they call it, right?

When the white man store detective arrived at her home, Ag claimed the book had mysteriously disappeared. She told him her granddaughter had vanished. She prayed the man would not look under her bed. She signed the papers and let him out with a smile.

That night, she flipped through the pages of the *Devil's Handbook for Girls* and felt the thud again, her entire chest constricting into embroideries of blood. She felt her hips expand, her bones crumble. Am I dying? she wondered. She placed the book under her arm and went to lower the stove where she'd begun a midnight snack of pork chops. Later, in bed, she dreamt of one of her former husbands and woke up cold as an air conditioner. He'd offered her a ride to their own wedding in a pumpkin coach. Room for just one lady, he'd said, and then she was drenched.

Ag carried the book to the others during Tuesday Evening Elder Services at the church across the street. She slipped it from her knitting bag and slid it into the lap next to hers, saying, Ladies, it's time for action.

Your Madison ain't home yet? Evie Knight whispered. Or are we talking about Mattie?

Pastor Edgell was walking behind everyone's folding chair in the basement, reading aloud. *And after that they had mocked him, they took the robe off from him and put his own raiment on him, and led him away to crucify him.*

Evie said, Your granddaughter has her own mother wit about her. She'll come back, don't you worry.

I can't stop worrying. This book might could hold the answer.

Fancyella suppressed a smile, passing the book down to Freeda's lap. Damitra will never forgive me if that girl don't come home, Ag whispered. She so mad she might put me out on the street. And all because of something so small. I was trying to do the right thing. I love my grandbaby. Isn't that plain to see? I was trying to do it.

Do what? Freeda asked.

Are we supposed to use this for Mattie or Madison? Evie Knight asked again. I'm confused. I'm tired and I'm confused, and I barely have enough love left for yours truly.

Dry your tears, Fancyella said to Ag. I've been around your Madison. Girl has enough mother wit for the entire city of Queens.

THE DEVIL'S HANDBOOK FOR GIRLS
FOREWORD by Clorinda Renay Keely-Dawkins

Young women of tomorrow and today,
You needn't wait, as others have in the past,
To be free of unnecessary constraints,
sob-story mothers, hash-tagged aunties,
idiotic cousins, harpy-fathers,

misunderstanding uncles,

fair-weather frenemies,

Insta-ignoramuses all.

You are your own salvation!

Please find here a treasure trove

of delights, necessities, and urgencies

That will hopefully guide you to happiness,

To the Dark Noble

And his Hot Hot Self.

May we never look

Elsewhere for comfort but to him

and to our own spell-casting souls,

amen.

Please to enjoy!

The frontispiece featured a sexy brown lady in black negligee and poofy mules, a sister straddling a backward chair with open eyes and clothes ruffled up along the splats. Sexier than Pam Grier, sexier than Madame C. J. Walker or even Beyoncé Giselle—hadn't the four neighbor women all looked like that once, in happier, hippier days? The four neighbor women could, if prodded, remember a time when they'd possessed a degree of appeal. When they made men fall in love with them, when they'd enjoyed urges that had nothing to do with church or preparing food. They marched, they organized block parties, they collected signatures over the proposed landfill near Sunswick Creek. But then it was children. Houses, bought and paid for over thirty years. Yards, garbage, garden hoses. Church, nonstop, in neighborhoods one more ramshackle than the next. Extrawide shoes and thieving grandkids. Obsolescence. Ag thought of her granddaughter Madison (who screamed to high heaven when she came home after a night out doing God knows what and discovered her grandmother reading her diary)—Madison, who could easily have been one of those victim-females—Madison, brash, disrespectful, mule-headed. Plus, what kind of name was that to give a Black girl? Oh, well. God helps those that help themselves. *Nothing's sacred around here! You nor my mama don't give a shit about me and please don't tell me otherwise!*

Madison had come to the dinner table and told her mother she'd be staying after school for a homework project. Maybe spend the night at Fernanda's house. Be careful out there, Ag said, to which Madison winced. She opened the door and left. That was the last time they saw her. *Mama, why did you have to mess with my girl? How long you gonna ruin our lives?*

SPELL AGAINST WILY FEMALES #16
(To be said in a closet which you are trying to get out of because you already promised your mother you wouldn't sneak out again, ever)
Dark Noble,
Beseech Thee Thou Thy
Lowliest subject
And Makest Thou Thee
Her into a
STRONG
INDEPENDENT
FEMALE
who can pick a damn lock.

Late late afternoon and the Jamaica Hospital van was still not there. Ag pulled *The Devil's Handbook for Girls* out her brassiere like a magician's scarf and laid it flat on the table on the porch. Fancyella got ready to laugh. She took a thermos in her hands and gulped from its edge. Tell us what you want us to do, already, Ag. Let's get this over with. Count me out, Evie Knight said, standing and reaching for her Solo cup. Absolutely no witchcraft over my dead body! You know we aren't that kind of woman, Ag.

PRELIMINARY FRANK QUESTIONS #27

Dark Noble,
Would I look better with braids
or a fade?

There were no children out, no men, homeless or regular, no boys pushing lawnmowers on the small patches of dirt that passed for yards in this part of Queens, no enticing women, no retirees working on cars. Why had Mattie been gone so long? What was different this time? The banana pudding was on its way to soup if they didn't get spoons and bowls. They knew better than to pray for someone to walk down this deserted afternoon street and come to their rescue. But.

It was as if God Himself had heard them.

A boy jogged along the sidewalk, no mirage. Fancyella shouted him over to the chain-link fence and asked him to go to her house for bowls and spoons. Someone would let him in. All he needed to say was that the bowls and spoons were for Mrs. Harkey Brown. Second kitchen cabinet to the left. Avoid Harkey at all costs. Do not touch anything you may pass by such as the bric-a-brac closet or the new flat-screen. She would give him one dollar now and one when he returned. Make it two when he comes back, Evie said. Both Freeda and Ag nodded. That boy does look worthy of three dollars, they said.

SPELL TOWARD GOOD GRADES #44

Take 4 Archway cookies, any variety
Four strands of your mail carrier's hair,
Four grains of Canilla,
Four eyelashes from your former best friend.

Burn and recite:

Dark Noble,

See this pyre

And make it so my mind is crazy absorbent.

I need to pass Regents math!

May Love Have Mercy!

Ag hadn't told Damitra that she'd kept the book. Now with Madison gone, what difference did it make? She carried it with her everywhere, fanning the pages occasionally to get the scent of her granddaughter in her nose. She pressed it so hard between her hands it left a mark. She stowed it in her brassiere and came to love its hardness. God, she'd muttered. God.

Ag, God responded. You one bad bad woman.

<u>LOVE POTION #5</u>

Use the leftovers from the leftovers from yesterday. Add cinnamon. Attend all varsity games

And don't complain about the cold.

Near 6 and the boy had not yet returned. The second thermos had been opened and closed and opened again. The first one was empty. Where were the bowls and spoons? The banana pudding was being sipped as well—each took a swig from Fancyella's giant dessert Tupperware. The four neighbor women closed their eyes. What manner of things had been done to those victim-females? The newspapers were never specific enough. How was anyone supposed to do something when no one knew enough?

It wasn't until half an hour later that they saw the boy again. He hunched over the chain-link fence, dangling a package of Dixie cups. I see you couldn't wait, he grinned. That ain't what we asked for,

Evie Knight called out. The boy laughed. Whose boy are you? Ag called out. You've seen me around, he replied.

You Jacob and Miranda Cozzens grandson? Fancyella asked. You Belinda Snell boy? Belinda that works at the Dollar Haven?

Y'all got my money? the boy asked.

Just give him the one dollar, Evie Knight said. He should know the right way to talk to his elders.

The boy came closer and threw the cups at the women. Freeda took two dollars from her waistband and smoothed them in her hand. She asked, Tell us whose boy you really are?

SPELL AGAINST GUILT #2
(To be howled after the first waning moon of Black Friday at Macy's)
Oh Dark Noble, You see through it all
And have no desire to punish me
For living my life as I see fit
And rewarding me with your lovely
Loving hands, loving breath, loving body
Oh Dark Noble!
Let my mother not notice when I take her Macy's card!

I got something interesting y'all might want to see, the boy said. He then whirled around and pointed to Ag. And I got a message to you from Maddie, special delivery.

You best tell me what that is! Ag shouted, rising from her chair. The boy laughed. The fatness of the alcohol in the afternoon had set in so much, she could barely make out his outline. Where is my grand-daughter? Tell me now.

Or what? the boy asked. You gonna call the white man store detective on me like you did Maddie? Try it and see what happens.

SPELL AGAINST FEAR #3
Oh Dark Lord,
Why is math even a requirement?

As the boy talked, Ag suddenly remembered the freaks: the crack-pots who'd come in droves just after the liberation of the victim-females. Visionaries, scholars, clergy, snake oil salesmen. They came from every cracked corner of the world, them and their bullshit: priests looking to perform exorcisms on the house where the victim-females had "survived"; real estate agents driving by to show off the place where "the Queens Horror had occurred" (*new property values!*); walking tours led by no-goodniks who dragged whole groups of Manhattan tourists down Amity Lane in order to "imagine the unimaginable." Hell in a handbasket, no doubt. And then there was that vagrant messing around Mattie's yard hell-bent on destruction. Flour in gas tanks, twenty pizzas sent to Evie Knight who had been a self-declared lactose intolerant her entire life. Delinquents. Definitely one. Maybe more.

SPELL AGAINST FEAR #4
Oh Dark Lord,
Is it wrong to throw dictionaries
out the school library windows?
I shiver.
Make me not shiver.
Cleanse my mind of dictionaries

Especially the one where
MICHAEL ROBINSON LOVES AMY BARNETT
Is written on the front cover
Instead of what should rightfully
BE THERE.
Give the vice principal lumbago,
No thought of detention,
No call home,
And let me continue on my path
to whirlwindnaceousness!
LOVE HAVE MERCY!

The ne'er-do-wells. All full of pranks and mischief and disrespect and need. Young voices, loud voices. Throwing eggs at the new church across from Mattie's house. Toilet papering it as well. Screeching, loving, laughing. Where was the respect? Ag wondered. Where was the sanctity? Those victim-females certainly deserved better than this. Even if they might've been bad in a previous life. Only a few weeks before she disappeared, Madison had told Ag, If I have to thank God *one more time* it wasn't me in that house, I will literally go fucking crazy!

STRIVER'S SOLUTION TO LIFE #1
Eat three red M&M's, one cup Grape Nuts,
one packet of Cherry Unsweetened Kool-Aid and two Valium
pills
(should be available in your mama's medicine cabinet).
Flush a toilet three times. Jiggle the handle vigorously.
FIND YOUR LOVED ONE'S PICTURE AND PLACE IT
UNDER YOUR PILLOW.

Follow me, the boy called out. The women slowly rose and grabbed the railing. Make sure you bring that second thermos, Fancyella whispered. Who knows if we might get thirsty along the way? The boy wore high-top sneakers, shorts, and a hooded sweatshirt, which, when the four neighbor women squinted, seemed to blend in with the trees. The women cobbled behind him in the street. When I think of my grandbaby, Ag said, whimpering the last of her sentence inaudibly, grabbing her pant legs and lifting them as though crossing a river.

JINX REMOVAL SPELL #30
Dear Dark Noble:
I am ripe, supple, engaging.
I have nowhere else to turn but you.
Did I get into the HBCU? Or am I eternally community-college-bound?

(For his part, the boy could feel wings spreading out from outside his collar bones. I love you, Madison Wheeless, he whispered in his head. I will get you to ride in my Benz, and you will like it much more than the Beamer Troy Wilkins drives.)

WISHFUL THINKING #5
Record your dreams for seven nights in a row.
Reject the advances of any man or boy for one month.
Chew hard butterscotch candies right before showering.
Steal five dollars from the high school office and place it under your pillow.
See if things don't change immediately!
Money-back guarantee.

Stand behind these trees, the boy instructed them, and they did as they were told. Wait, the boy said. The air was warm. Despite that, Ag wrapped her shawl around her shoulders and squinted toward the horizon, past the sun and rooftops and chimneys that made up their part of town, past the factories and apartment buildings she knew lay beyond that. How was it possible to vanish into thin air on a street where everyone knew your business? Vanishing was the province of lonely parks, factory streets, and rooftops. Vanishing happened to the white sorority girls over at St. John's that partied too damn much. On Amity Lane, good people were always claimed, never discarded like garbage or old clothes. Ag took a deep breath and watched a plane purr softly downward toward LaGuardia. Are we so bad? Ag wondered. We just want to do the right thing. Always.

"EVERYTHING IS POSSIBLE!™"

She'd left the book back on the porch where someone might go up and take it. She hoped someone would. Be quiet, the boy said, leading them around to the back of the church across the street.

<u>LOVE SPELL #36</u>
(To be cast moments before you see your ex get it on with his ex, the bastard)
Take three hairs from your beloved's Afro pick;
Burn in a teaspoon of sugar in your mother's kitchen;
Three times under a gibbous moon, recite:
Boy, take notice of me, and name me your one and only,
In the yearbook or other publications similar in nature.

How did it get to be 9 at night? The second thermos never seemed to run out. The four neighbor women didn't want to appear drunk when the Jamaica Hospital van showed. But that thermos was everlasting. Where's my granddaughter? Ag asked. They were standing in the churchyard. Shut it, the boy answered. We have to wait till the coast is clear. So shut it.

And the four neighbor women would've remained like that, under the elms and willow, waiting as they'd done all their lives; but suddenly here was Damitra, stomping into the yard, full of her usual steam. Ag felt that thud in her body once more, embroideries of blood, evaporated kidneys; she dropped her shawl. Please, girl. Don't make a scene. We just wanted bowls for banana pudding.

You just wanted bowls? Mama, what're you going on about?

We've been waiting for Mattie. Cleaned her place, had a bit to quench our thirst.

Damitra boomed. *A bit?* You all get piss-ass drunk before your quote unquote friend comes home? What would Miss Mattie say seeing you out here—for all the world to see? I could smell you four houses down. And what, pray tell, are you doing standing in this yard? It's nighttime, Mama!

Damitra was on a roll. Ag knew there was no escape.

We just want to make things right, Ag murmured.

What the hell does that mean?

Damitra turned to the others, who shielded their faces with their hands.

Mama, I have told you time and time again to stay out of other people's business. You know where that will end you? Why you ain't listening? Out here drunk as a skunk.

Leave us, Damitra, Ag said. We ain't bothering no one.

You are an embarrassment to me and to the block, Damitra blurted—
then covered her face, burst into tears. Last week a doctor at Elmhurst
Hospital told her there was a black spot on her X-ray. She'd told no
one. Stop your yelling, baby, Ag said. We only want what's for the best.

I have no goddamn idea what you're talking about, Mama!

SPELL AGAINST UNNECESSARY REMORSE #21
MAKE MY FAMILY SEE ME IN A DIFFERENT LIGHT.
IF THEY DO NOT, DARK NOBLE,
STRIKE THEM DOWN AND GIVE ME THE KEY.

Damitra left. Ag went over to the leftover forsythia bushes where the
boy'd been hiding and grabbed him by the scruff of his neck, as if
he were a puppy or kitten. Look, if you know where my Madison is,
you best tell me now.

There was no moon and no stars. You might scare the girl off, the
boy said. Have patience. Ag let go, and the other women listened.

HISTORICAL PRAYER #1 BY A ONE MISS ANNIE
BRADSTREET
Nay Masculines, you have thus taxt us long,
But she, though dead, will vindicate our wrong,
Let such as say our Sex is void of Reason,
Know tis a Slander now, but once was Treason.

Before it had been recently defaced (for the sixth time), the plaque
at the church across the street stated the following:

In honor of the four young women
Out of malevolence arises
NOBILITY

Donated by the Queens Police Benevolent Society
Jamaica Hospital Relief Fund
Kingdom Hall of Greater Queens
Townsend Harris High School Alumnae
Amity Wisdom of the Word
October 2010

He tapped against windowpanes of the church, pulling new vines from the glass. He found the sloped basement door and wrestled with the handle, eventually throwing it open. Come, he ordered. The answers you looking for are down here.

Is it my Madison? Ag asked.

The boy smiled. Go down and talk to her, he said. She doesn't want anyone to know where she is—no one but her dear old granny.

Why should we believe you? Evie asked.

The hell you want from me? he asked. I don't give a fuck if you go or stay. I'm just the messenger.

UNCONDITIONAL LOVE HEX #1
(To be said behind the backs of rival cheerleaders, school nurses,
lunch ladies, or any other annoyances of the feminine persuasion)
OH BEAUTIFUL DARK NOBLE
HELP MY FEMALE COMPATRIOTS
UNDERSTAND THAT WE ARE
ALL IN THIS TOGETHER.
SISTERS UNDER THE SKIN.

They shook their heads at his language, then followed each other into further darkness, clumping down the cement steps, breathing loudly.

This was likely a sub-basement, far down from the basement kitchen where Charity Breakfast or Tuesday Evening Elder Services were held. Ag wondered, Why in heaven's name is there a *sub-basement*? A spanking new Maytag washing machine sat under an eyebrow window as well as a mile-high stack of vintage *Ebony* magazines that shone in the moonlight. Ag felt around for a light switch but couldn't find one. Maddie, she called out. Maddie, are you here? Grandma's come to help, baby. Just let me hear your voice.

They all heard the outside door slam shut, the boy laughing.

His face lined up with the glass; they could tell he was on his belly. Madison told me tell you she's done with you but if you ever want to see her again, bring some money and a new car to the first parking lot at the Queens Center mall.

I don't tolerate no one talking to me like that, Ag called out; but the boy was already gone, in hysterics.

WE EDITORS AT WOMAN'S DESTINY BOOKS WOULD LIKE TO INVITE YOU ON THIS MOST GREGARIOUS OCCASION TO VIEW OUR OTHER TITLES, SUCH AS *RAP LYRICS FOR HOUSEWIVES* AND *THESE ARE A FEW OF MY FAVORITE NEFARIOUS THINGS*. PLEASE ACCEPT THIS FINAL PRAYER AS A TOKEN OF OUR THANKS FOR YOUR PATRONAGE.

Crying and screaming didn't seem to do anything. The four neighbor women surrendered themselves to being locked in after twenty minutes of raspy pleas had gone by. None dared break the eyebrow window. Though Ag could feel tiles under her hands, the sub-basement floor felt like actual dirt. She kneeled onto a musty beanbag that had been slopped into a corner. Evie and Freeda sat on the bottom basement step. Fancyella slumped against the pile of magazines. Where had the second thermos got to? After an hour of noise, they closed their eyes and dozed in and out of dreams, getting up every now and then to use a mop bucket they'd found in the corner of the sub-basement as a toilet.

If the hospital van's out there waiting, too bad, Fancyella said.

We've never been superwomen, Ag said. Her voice on the verge of tears.

From someone's backyard, a rooster crowed in the darkness. Evie began crying. I just hate thinking I have to spend my life locked away here. I'm actually blessed with an outstanding conscience. I believe in God and I've never been anything other than pure as the driven snow. I was against that devil book from the get-go. Why should I be condemned like this?

Who says we locked here forever? Fancyella asked.

We're being punished, Freeda said.

What in Hades you mean, girl? We ain't done nothing!

But we should have done something, Fancy. Any little thing.

What are you talking about? We already knew Madison Wheeless was a ho! Let me get my hands on that heifer, she won't sit down for a week!

Ag shifted her bottom from one side of the beanbag chair to the next. So this is what it came to? Her granddaughter Madison—nothing but a ho. Why hadn't the girl listened to a single thing she'd said in all these years? The advice was always sound: Stay safe; don't talk to strangers; thank God every day that it wasn't you. Thank Jesus it wasn't you. There but for the grace of God go you. *Remember, Madison: Those girls might could've turned out to be damaged goods. Be glad you a good girl.*

The faint moon shone into the dirty window. The others soon snored. Madison was known for her wildness but never anything like this, Ag thought, before drifting.

Night. Mice, brush, vines, sprinklings of rain. Upstanding faces on magazine covers. Silence. At dawn, nothing had changed.

Ag awoke to a gray morning. The slow hum of Queens electricity running in the ground. One siren. Then another. The crashing of garbage trucks. Help us, Ag thought. We'll do better. Then it was the sound of footsteps, the clanging of metal. We did the best that we could, she whispered. I realize it wasn't enough. But we will do better. The rooster crowed again. Then the smallest bit of laughter from outside. The others awoke and began scrambling, shouting for help. Come shout with us, Evie said to Ag. Don't just sit there! Someone has to hear our commotion.

But why bother? Ag wondered. She closed her eyes.

Mattie was not coming back. God would not be on their side. There was no hospital van; it was all a ruse, a prank phone call, perhaps. No one would miss them. They'd die here, interred with household cleaners and blood and rodents and not a soul to mourn them. God would laugh. He would cry. *How could they not have known?* God would be waiting for an answer, and He had all the time in the world.

Ag pursed her lips. Why would anyone in their right mind come looking for them? It was just deserts, plain and simple. Oh God in

Heaven. Fucking hell. How come she didn't realize sooner rather than later that it was *always* a bad idea to ask the devil for help?

Ag rocked back and forth; this is what happened when you played with fire—she rocked and rocked, the same way Madison sometimes did and her mother, Damitra, before her. Screaming was impossible; all the words were gone; all that was left was the rocking. Ag believed this, even as the basement door cracked itself open and sunlight set the washing machine and beanbag and *Ebony* magazines ablaze. God had washed His hands of them, Ag thought, rocking. Pitiful creatures. He was through, *finito*—even as Fancyella and Freeda and Evie grabbed at the policemen's legs climbing down the stairs. God wasn't having none of this. He was fed up—with the old ladies, with the vagrant, with the devil, and even with Pastor Edgell, who (while walking behind the men) kept asking if someone would *please* tell him what *in the world* was going on?

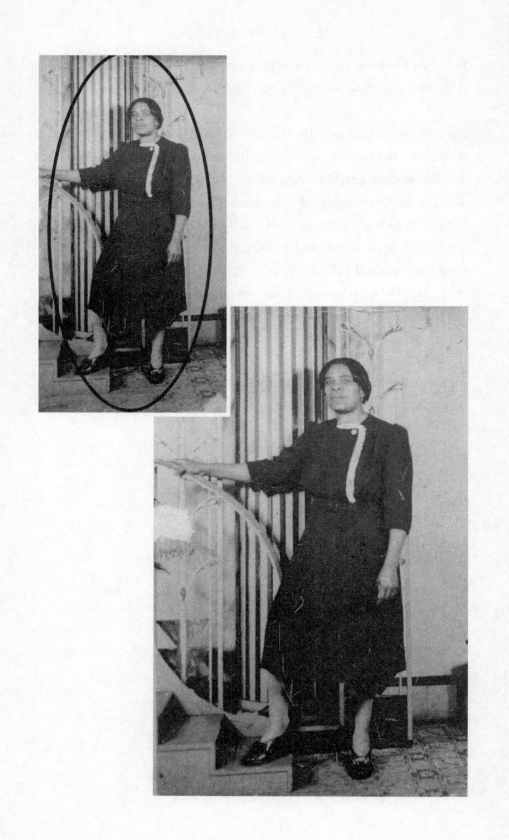

SYMPATHETIC INVENTORY

Attn: Mrs. Myrtle Marron-Campbell
45 Sinclair Lewis Boulevard
Jackson Heights, New York

U-HAUL OF ELMHURST
SELF-STORAGE UNIT #133/JK

Dear Miss Myrtle, Please to accept our sincerest apologies for having mis-placed your items. The following is the inventory of MARRON #133–135 SELF-STORAGE LOCKERS which have been readied at your earliest convenience. When you come, please be advised of cobwebs and other such vermin as they may appear unannounced. We have no idea where this inventory has got to in all these years, please understand that we are sorry. Due to the fact that it is Many Homeless in the area (in particular to the Sunswick Creek Bridge) it can be likely that some of MARRON possessions have been made off with BY THEM. We have no idea of knowing the full extent. Please be advised that the inventory will remain in the main dock until tomorrow at which time it will be disposed of therewith. U-HAUL of ELMHURST would be amenable to a cash-only auction. We are sorry for your loss. Have a blessed day.

133

Box 1—Marked: "Mother's Rosenthal/MARIA CONTINENTAL"— ten dinner plates, ten salad plates, one soup tureen, one sugar bowl, one creamer, four demitasse saucers, thirteen bouillon cups, thirteen bouillon saucers, nine soup bowls, one large coffeepot, one medium teapot, three tea tiles. Condition: good with some wear.

Box 2—Marked: "Father's Books/The World Bibliophile Series"— *Père Goriot*/Balzac; *Emile*/Rousseau; *Essays*/Montaigne; *Anna Karenina*/Tolstoy; *Crime and Punishment*/Dostoyevsky; *The Sorrows of Young Werther*/*Elective Affinities*/Goethe; *Don Quixote*/Cervantes; *Alice's Adventures in Wonderland*/Carroll; *History of the Fall and Decline of the Roman Empire*/Gibbon; *Complete Greek Tragedies*/Lattimore. Recommendation: Salvation Army.

Box 3—Marked: "Father's Music"—Beethoven: *The Complete Symphonies*; Mozart: *The Magic Flute*; *Opera Gems* featuring Leontyne Price and others; *A Night at the Opera* with Leontyne Price and others; Bach: *The Well-Tempered Klavier*; Marian Anderson: *Prima Voce*; Lester Young: *Lester Swings Again*. Recommendation: best offer.

134

Box 1—Unmarked: Articles of male clothing (box torn at edges, some items may be missing): three pair shoes (Florsheim), seven pair Haband trousers. Four Alexander's dress shirts; one cummerbund. Coins. Assorted cigar bands.

Box 2—Marked: "Church and Cotillion Sundry"—Articles of female clothing (box torn at edges, some items may be missing): seventeen feather hats; thirty pair high-heeled shoes; five leather belts. Several opened lipsticks. A broken cameo.

Box 3—Unmarked: Photograph Albums (please be advised that most pictures here have endured rain and such natural disasters as to be highly unreadable at the present). Photos look to contain folks such as grandmothers, aunts, cousins and neighbors and sisters, most of the female persuasion. Some settings may be in the country. Mold, insect damage. Recommendation for all three boxes: toss.

135

Box 1—Marked: Contents of { . . . } Amity Lane: ALL GLASS/FRAGILE/ CAREFUL!!! Three vases marked Waterford; seventeen cordial glasses marked Steuben; one large bowl and two candlesticks marked Orrefors.

Box 2—Marked: Contents of { . . . } Amity Lane: collection of Miss Elaine bathrobes. Box torn at edges but contents appear intact. Recommendation: toss.

Box 3—Marked: Contents of { . . . } Amity Lane: Box torn at edges, split in half. Old newspapers and clippings pertaining to case of "sex-slave girls" in "House of Horrors." Mold and water damage. Recommendation: toss.

Box 4—Marked: Contents of { . . . } Amity Lane: collection of candles, pillar and taper, some fruit shaped. Five flashlights, in working order. Brown bag of plastic silverware including ladles and serving utensils. One pasta spoon. Recommendation: Donation to Light at the End of the Tunnel, Queens, New York. Do not forget tax receipt. Toss only if they refuse.

ONCE UPON A TIME IN QUEENS

Love opened a mortal wound.
In agony, I worked the blade to make it deeper.

Sor Juana Inés de la Cruz,
"Con el dolor de la mortal herida"

THE DAMN FAIRY TALE ENDS, FINALLY

At dawn's early light, Goldilocks detects the sounds of big bear feet. She's in the bedroom, the closet of Baby Bear. Instinctively she bedecks herself with pine needles and tar: somewhere, in some boring class at school, she'd read that bears hated the smell of girls mixed with sap. Baby Bear might mistake her for a piece of tree detritus, a blip of waste he forgot to scrape out from under his claws. Certainly he would not harm her.

The Bears come home. They talk; they play Monopoly; they look out the windows at the mulberry trees and the fruit stains below; they observe the strategic placement of the sun: not ideal for any real foraging. So they go to bed, a midday nap after countless bowls of honey. Goldilocks follows them with her ears. Truth is, she can't move. She is cramped within this closet, frozen stiff, like a flea trying to hide on a hairless dog. The pine needles pinch; the tar stinks. There's no real clothes to admire, and this stupid Baby Bear has got nothing in the way of dolls or teen magazines. She clicks her ears open and determines that the Mama and the Papa Bears are asleep. Snoring as loud as a backed-up toilet. Goldilocks inches her way up and out, dribbling the needles across the plank floor. Baby Bear languidly casts his eyes on the yellow head over his bed. He smells juniper and forest floor dirt, then realizes what he is smelling is the ugly girl's breath. But he is too slow. She stabs him in the eye with a handful of needles.

I got you, she whispers, her other hand going for his ursine scruff.

BECAUSE ONCE UPON A TIME

There was the bear house, and then there was ours. A rickety contraption made of boards and screams lined in mice fur and girl teeth. All available to the eye if you care to look. Totally up to you.

MIRACLES

After our liberation, TV was something out of this world. Forget Quasar, Magnavox. Forget hanger antennae. Flat-screens were the name of the game. We watched *Sesame Street* and laughed at how boring it *still* was. But then we saw a TV commercial featuring a light-skinned Black man, wanting to call himself president of the world. Oh shit, said Gwinnie. How the hell he think he's gonna do that?

He's already up and done it, Ms. Refuge said. She sat in the oval chair in the corner of our picnic-chair hospital apartment. That man is already your president.

No way, shouted Gwinnie. But I could tell her happiness.

The president of the world did not look crazy or lunatic like a runaway slave, but what did we know? He had great shoulders; in fact, we noticed that he did not look once over them. Was he watching the same new TV we were? Had he seen the cities on fire, we wondered, or the snow mountains melting, or the people collapsing in the streets, chocked by various hatreds? All things we ourselves had seen on TV since our liberation, but perhaps those were our own figments.

We were intrigued by this man who claimed to be president of the world.

Not the world, Ms. Refuge corrected. Just the United States.

He looks it, I volunteered.

Gwinnie asked, Is it possible he's run away from a loony bin where he's been holed up for so many years he don't know up from down? Bad from good? God from the devil?

Ms. Refuge got a long laugh at that.

He's good, she said to us. This is a whole new start, ladies. It's not sink or swim anymore. It's just swim. It will be swim from here on out. That is our hope.

LE CREUSET: AN INTERRUPTION

Cold weather, 2039. Dig if you will a picture, coming at you straight from the pages of *Architectural Digest* or *Garden & Gun* or *The Advocate*:

Bud, my brother. Ruffle-headed and sleek, surrounded by the trees of Rockland County, drenched in the sunshine of life, his mess of kids milling about with nothing but documents of passion love in their eyes—Bud, a man composed of what some schoolteachers used to call "fierce determination," who cracks eggs into the cast-iron skillet and asks his eldest daughter, Calliope, to chop fine some parsley and bay laurel. He is expecting me and Gwinnie today. A day so far into the future that the rusted memories of our home in Queens—the roads, stores, awnings, souls, and skies—have shriveled away like apple cores. We will spend the night and possibly the rest of our lives with him and his husband. Bud's in the kitchen stirring the eggs with abandon—if the kids want them every single day, then why not? In his head he's playing "Girls Just Want to Have Fun" even though the song feels a tad sacrilegious. When Bud goes to make the pancakes, he starts humming something entirely different—something techno, without words, only beats. DUN DUN DUN DUN. Breakfast is ready, he calls sweetly, wondering if the other kids will notice he's cut the strawberries into rosettes or that the linen napkins bearing everyone's name have been starched and pressed? Don't you be late because I am ready, he adds.

Bud and Dwayne have carefully orchestrated the day. Arrival of the aunties, ten minutes of hugs, a 12 noon lunch, 12:45 walk around the property, his and Dwayne's ten acres overlooking Demarest Kill with its wide, willowy canopy of trees. Forest hugs, kisses. Afterward lots of kiddie questions, tag with the girls and boys back up to the house, the unwrapping of a thousand gifts; and then all of us sprawled on the couch on the upper floor of their split-level, where photo albums—mostly of the nine kids, a few of me and Gwinnie, several of Dwayne's overweight Newark fam—are laid upon laps and parsed through with fiery fingers. *Can we have dessert now?* What else to do but sit back and luxuriate?

Gwinnie's hands quiver; on the way up to Rockland County, she became quite out of the blue. Started asking strange questions, like did I ever think of my mother and why did I insist on calling her *the mother* and why didn't Bud do more in all that time to save me, save us, who cares if he was just a kid, weren't we were just kids ourselves? This is not Gwinnie. This is SO not Gwinnie. Yet she preserves this fire in her chest, an occasional intensity that can only be extinguished by the tree air and relief of Rockland County. We still have a ways to go. She fidgets so much that Ms. Refuge suggests we turn around. Maybe this is not the right time for a trip, it being so close to the winter days, and you know how you both can get when winter cold is upon us . . .

Her voice tapers off and sets Gwinnie into full-out inferno. No one did what they were supposed to, she cries. We were nothing and how do we know that's changed? How do we know we're not nothing now?

We've hit Sleepy Hollow. Ms. Refuge pulls over and gets in the back of her old Mercury and wraps her arms around the two of us. Gwinnie looks at me. I think this time it will be different, she says. I think this time Bud and Dwayne will want more. What do you mean? I ask. You know what I mean, Gwinnie says, pulling out of the hug, igniting again. Your brother and his fine-ass husband keep dancing around the BIG THINGS like when will we come live with them? And you know how long it takes for us to unravel the BIG THINGS, don't you, Fern?

He's your brother, too, I say. Both of them are.

Gwinnie lifts her eyes. Is it because they think we're so desperate for babies that we'll babysit for free? Is that what they want, free labor? We've had enough of that. Please, Ms. Refuge! Open the window!

I pull away. This is and is not Gwinnie. Ms. Refuge reaches up front for her purse with our pills. I think of Bud as he is now—the most generous of hearts—and how I imagined him over those lost years—he won't really talk about them, except to give me a hint or two. Getting high and trying to join the sailors in the desert but being discovered too young and thus merely falling asleep on sidewalks and dreaming of Harvey's Bristol Cream and clove cigarettes in fifteen-year-old lungs and sleeping with dream men on more sidewalks until the pavement ran clean out. In another part of the world, us all alone. Me and Gwinnie and Jesenia and Boss Man—all alone. Katanya, all alone. I don't realize that I'm speaking out loud. Gwin swallows her whole Poland Spring bottle and shouts, And now Bud's up here looking for a pair of fat old live-in servants?

Gwinnie, I have no clue what you're talking about.

You can see it in their eyes, she screeches. Though I have no idea when she has ever looked that closely.

Ms. Refuge gives Gwinnie some sparkling pills, and she's quiet for the rest of the ride. We roll down all the windows as we leave Sleepy

Hollow, and there is a feeling of unlimited patience in the air. I have no idea why. Anything can happen. When we get to the house, Ms. Refuge sends us in; she'll wait in the driveway until the visit is through. I hook arms with Gwinnie and lead her to the doorbell. She might stay still and smile politely; or, when Bud answers, she might look my brother up and down with something like disbelief, carefully nibbling the famous chocolate chip cookies he's brought to the door; she cocks her head and casually asks about the salon, her eyes gleaming fire—but before Bud can answer, she will crackle, *Isn't that a cliché? The gay hairdressers? Couldn't you two think of any other job?* Dwayne might be there, as well. And we'll enter the house and she will laugh and Dwayne and the kids will sort of laugh, too; Bud will just look at me and I will look back. Forgive me, his eyes will say. Fern. I never stopped looking for you. Or maybe those eyes will ask: Why didn't I look harder? You have every right to hate me, Fern . . .

Nothing about my brothers is cliché, I will say, breaking the tension in the room. We still have our coats on. Gwinnie is a runaway roller coaster. I say, Bud and Dwayne are as original as . . .

But then everyone has forgotten the outburst and is already looking at pictures in photo albums and talking in new directions. My mind settles back into unprovoked patience, certain that Gwinnie will behave.

(I am seven years old, walking through the Herald Square Macy's. Mother's treat. She is pushing a stroller full of coats and hats and Bud toward the lap of Santa Claus. The mother says, Ask him for anything you want. He will make it come true. Bud suffocates under the tweed and faux-fur. When I get to the lap, I announce that I would like an Easy-Bake Oven.

Santa laughs. First you have to tell me, young lady: Have you been good?

She's been perfect, the mother says. She makes me powdered eggs.

On the subway ride home, the mother pulls out an early gift from Santa—a doll named Alice From Wonderful Wonderland. She has pearl-blue eyes that blink when you hold her upside down. She's not what I want. There were a million of her in the store, but she's not what I want. I throw the doll on the subway floor, and the mother simply replaces it on my lap. Time after time after time. People stare. The mother is a steady simmer. I look and it is the first time I see her eyes. They don't blink; they just stay where they are. Bud begins to cry—I can tell he's trying to take her mind off me, the two-year-old genius. But the mother is already full boil. People stare. Why would you cry over an oven, girl? A doll is much nicer! Didn't Santa tell you to be good? You have to listen, Fern. A girl has to listen!)

(During previous visits to Rockland County, whenever I wanted to know more about this particular scenario, Bud would shake his head. Enough with the fairy tales, he'd usually laugh.)

Pure gaiety. Photo albums and more photo albums. Everyone in the house is happy and maybe everyone will have forgotten what Gwinnie said earlier. Or maybe they will still feel secretly insulted. Maybe the mess of kids will cry themselves to sleep. Or maybe Dwayne will put a hand on Gwinnie's shoulder and suggest we take a trip over to Raging Beauty later on. I'd love to do you up real fine, Sister, he murmurs.

Gwinnie bursts into tears in front of everyone. She can't stop crying. I get ready to call Ms. Refuge on my cell phone and tell her we will be needing that ride back to the picnic-chair hospital ASAP.

But then everyone is back to the albums, all flames spiraling downward—how many of these albums do Bud and Dwayne actually have? I wonder, laughing. The kids lean in and talk about what *truly matters*: the carousel at the new Palisades Amusement Park; the Monster-ator at Great Adventure in New Jersey and all the ensuing throw-up; the July 4th pie-eating contest in downtown New City and the throw-up there, too; a dog in the pet store on Third named Zingers that needed a home; angel, the best flavor of birthday cake. *Look, here was when I had five killer mosquito bites. Hey, this was the day DaddyBud and DaddyDwayne won the Scratch-Off and took us to dinner AND LET US ALL ORDER STEAK AND SPAGHETTI.*

Auntie Gwinnie, the older ones say, Remember this picture, when you made a puppet with both those Thanksgiving legs? Remember all that grease on your face? Gwinnie picks up another photo, the one where everyone is piled onto her bed, waiting to fold in for the night like a sardine can. Do you know how much I love you, she'll probably say, tearing up again, but no need this time for any further restoration. All fires have been put out completely.

The photo albums then go back on the shelves, and the beds are untucked. A supper of cheese and jam and whole wheat bread, polite words all round. Lights left on in the hallways, in case there is some spooky memory left over from the Monster-ator. Shut eyes all sleep.

Or maybe, instead, this will happen: we'll take two cars over to Main Street, to Raging Beauty, where all the hairdressers look as old as their grandmothers. Wonderful things will happen. Gwinnie and I are admiring our heads in the mirrors. Is it real? we ask. Gwinnie gets a new color, sunshine purple, subdued in its over-the-topness. I decide I want just a little off the sides—there's not much there to begin with—and I say to the hairdressers it's time I grow gray gracefully; no more color, please. We look at each other and continue giggling. *Are we really real?* Gwinnie will fall into Dwayne's arms and say, Sometimes Old Mind comes back with a vengeance. I have no idea why, forgive me, please, Brother; and Dwayne'll just respond, Old Mind never leaves none of us, and why don't you know by now that I can never be angry at you, not for the least fraction of an hour?

Tears and laughing and tall tales on the ride back home. We're actually traveling in two taxi cabs, because the two minivans owned by Bud and Dwayne are in the shop. Or maybe it is that one of the boys has them and is out for the afternoon and evening. Who knows? Who is in possession of a crystal ball, the kind that can look backward and forward and explain all things like it was common sense?

We land back at the house and we eat again: Dwayne has secretly prepared a goose stuffed with apples and his one uncle's famous hoppin' John. First servings, seconds, even thirds. Dwayne waits until the plates are clean, then sticks his apple cobbler in the oven. The kids whine but he shushes them: Good things come to those who wait. Patience, kids, patience. I reach for his hand, though I feel my senses tingling. Is it that we're all just impatient for that cobbler? Is it that our hearts are singing with happiness? The kids start to beg for a quicker, easier dessert, like some of that strawberry Häagen Dazs in the downstairs freezer or some of those butterscotch candies hidden in DaddyBud's coat pockets. Dwayne folds his arms across his chest. Listen, kids. *Good things come to those who wait.*

We can't wait a minute longer, we'll burst! the kids holler.

Oh yes, you can, Gwinnie laughs. Just look at us! Don't you know that *waiting* is mine's and Auntie Fern's middle name?

She's at it again. I'm not mad but I'm tired of being understanding. Thinking: we're here as visitors, Gwinnie: BEHAVE! But on the other hand thinking: why shouldn't you say every damn thing that has been held up in your belly for the past umpteen years?

Gwinnie, can't you act right for a couple of hours? Look at me! I'm doing it, so why can't you?

The kids don't laugh. They have all heard things about us, but I daresay Bud has spared them specific horrors; they look to their fathers, and I can literally see their tiny hearts beat in jagged patterns across their little chests, even the boys, who are older. But then the two daddies click their eyes and suddenly break into song, like a family in the mountains, corny as hell: *Edelweiss, edelweiss, you look happy to meet me*. It's ridiculous. It's ridiculous to the point of being scary how much Bud and Dwayne are complete and utter schmaltz. Just why are they doing a musical number? Just why are they inviting MORE INSULTS from Gwinnie? I close my eyes; my head throbs. Gwinnie is not Gwinnie, I want to tell them. I want to get up and drag her back to the picnic-chair hospital and forget this whole night. The kids start to sing along. Gwinnie claps her hands, like a tot at the circus. Sometimes I get so mad at her. But then, how could I? Gwinnie says, Guys, how did you know I love *The Sound of Music*? It's something Nurse Happiness turned me on to—what, you got yourself a crystal ball or something?

(And later, in the guest room facing the road, on the twin bed facing mine, she will cry in truly fresh-rescued fashion. Ambulances, sirens, fire trucks, police. I slide into her bed to comfort her. She says, Why can't I get it through my thick head that it's *you and me* that's been those butterscotch candies inside your brother's pocket this whole time?)

But now. Kisses, lights, action. Dessert eaten, the urge to look at MORE photo albums swiftly stomped out by the adults. The outside sky has become royal-purple night; all songs are done; quiet floats back underneath our skin. Time for bed, Dwayne shouts, lifting two girls over his shoulders like sacks of potatoes. They all go wild, begging for their turn, even the two boys who are near as tall as their fathers. When has there ever been this much laughter on earth?

Bud touches my hand. Have you decided whether you both will come live with us? he asks. I touch his face, don't say a thing. Because I'm determined to live in this one picture forever, regardless, forever.

THE ID, THE EGO,
AND THE SUPEREGO

After the liberation, the mother came for me. Who knew the passage of time? She'd done up her hair nice, smoothed behind her ears, just like her wigs; when she reached for me, I smelled the Herbal Essence of long, long ago. *Slaap, kindje.* Her nails were bitten off. There was a small green gift-wrapped box she kept slipping in and out of her pocketbook. We were sitting in a McDonald's just around the corner from the picnic-chair hospital, and we were trying to look happy. The gift paper looked like lizard-skin Christmas. The mother smiled long and hard at me; she looked so much better than ten years of dreams.

My baby, she said, stretching her arms toward me, across the table. Tiny blue fibers flew from her sweater.

There were lots of pills I had to swallow with my McDonald's. I was expecting the little green box, but instead she took out a brochure for the Grand Canyon—had she already told me that the *new* new boyfriend finally proposed! Hadn't she told me about him already? You'd love him, the mother told me. He was what got her through the trauma of losing her children; without him, she surely would've died. Freddy. That's a name that's easy to say, isn't it? she asked.

French fry air made it hard to breathe. The mother asked me if I would like to come along with them to the Grand Canyon. Her pocketbook kept opening and closing and spilling out new things: perfume, lipstick, a bottle of Excedrin. But no little green box. She told me it would be her heart's dream if I would come with them on their honeymoon. I asked her if I could think about it, and she said she wouldn't have it any other way. We finished our food, walked back to the hospital. She wrapped her arms around me. I never saw her again.

SEE

Long after the liberation, a policeman came for a visit. 2009. He'd actually come many times before this, but now was different. Ms. Refuge stood before him in the door, hands on hips. These girls have no need to go back to the scene of the crime, Harry. Harry, I'm telling you the truth. The policeman mumbled a few things and left. Then Ms. Refuge melted her big body into one of the plastic armchairs and shielded her eyes. We could tell she was crying even though she told us she was just doing some heavy lifting with her mind.

Two days later, the policeman—a detective, we learned—showed up again. The air around us smelled like holiday stuffing and gingerbread (not from a magazine picture) though we couldn't spot a single stocking anywhere. Ms. Refuge walked beside him in the unit, like an old-fashioned Currier and Ives couple about to skate. Ms. Refuge was a firm believer in the theory that there was always another layer to things. Her face had changed in those two days; it was smoother now, a paved roadway without potholes. She came toward us with outstretched arms. The place that once hurt you—it will only continue to do so if we let Old Mind have its way, she said. Girls, I think maybe it might be a good idea after all to return. I want New Mind to tell Old Mind: Everything must change.

The old place. Our home. Our first home as the family we are now. Gwinnie and I didn't talk of that place hardly ever.

Detective Amor walked us to our beds, then moved back to the door. He rubbed his temples and tried to smile—his teeth had the same sort of brown ours had. There was a long list of questions he had for us. When he was finished, Detective Amor lifted himself from the threshold and said, See you soon.

I just love the way that man's brain works, Gwinnie said, swooning herself right into the pillows. I love the way he said *see*.

The questions of Detective Amor flew out of our minds as soon as they were asked. Main thing, Ms. Refuge was by his side, nodding and shaking patiently. It was evident she'd made a decision. It was evident she would be there to protect us, wherever those questions led us.

More frustrating and hard to swallow, though, were the questions of TV's Dr. Ezra. They were boring, trying to make us look, as he said, "into the mirror of our past." We sometimes told him what we thought he wanted to hear.

And sure enough. Just before our voyage to the scene of the crime, TV's Dr. Ezra paid us a visit. He wore a microphone attached to his ear like a giant silver cockroach. The crew planted themselves close by and flashed fingers and nods between them. TV's Dr. Ezra said, It's been a while, girls. Or should I say young ladies? Let's get down to the nitty-gritty. Have either of you heard from your best friend Jesenia?

No.

Don't you wonder about her? I mean, do you ever wonder about her?

She left before we did. We used to worship her like crazy.

But where? Where did she go?

We couldn't say.

Would you girls consider going back to the house with me? Would that feel okay—with me?

Why would we do that?

It might be cleansing in a different way. It might be helpful. You might have sweet dreams at night from now on. I don't know that a cop could do all that.

Are you saying we're dirty? Gwin asked.

Ms. Refuge stepped closer. Okay, Doc. That's it. Close up shop now or I'll take these cameras and trash them.

(Ms. Refuge! We so loved it when she got tough!)

I only want what's best for these two survivors, ma'am. A psycholog-ical perspective would be beneficial to all parties. Plus, the girl could still be alive. A visit to the house—

Ms. Refuge pushed him and the camera crew out the room and toward the elevator. She thanked TV's Dr. Ezra and shook his hand for what seemed like a million hours.

(After that Ms. Refuge hardly ever left our side. But she had to have, right? She had to have gone home to shower, to eat? Maybe she had a mother there who wanted to know her comings and goings? Maybe Detective Amor called and took her out for pizza? How in the world could we *ever* have forgotten what pizza looked and tasted like? A picture is never worth a thousand words.)

From the elevator, Dr. Ezra called out, Girls! You have my utmost respect! Remember: Be kind to yourselves and the whole world will follow!

The elevator door snapped shut, and then we went back to normal. I don't know why we don't miss Jessie more, I said.

Maybe we do. Maybe we don't know we do, Gwinnie answered.

Are we bad?

Never in a million years. Jessie would agree on that a million percent.

NIGHTMARES

Ms. Refuge framed my face with her hands. I don't want you to rush into anything, dear Fern.

I was nervous. I was wanting to say something along the lines of: Why would anyone want to leave a clean hospital bed that was not under a sink or fastened to a rusted silver chain? Why would anyone want to move away from the mountains of Macy's sweaters and Lego helicopters and porcelain tea party sets and Urban Outfitter winter socks and Hello Kitty Halloween masks and Las Vegas Monopoly games? Not to mention all the other gifts—including the trove bought at Dollar Haven by Nurse Happiness (did she count now as a new friend?): pink foam hair curlers, pencils, yo-yos, and plastic egg timers? We felt like pashas. There were so many brands of sanitary pads and tampons around us, piled into pyramids, obelisks—the choices of feminine care being just like the thirty-one flavors of ice cream.

Ms. Refuge saw my face. Are you still afraid of Amity Lane?

No, I said. Easiest answer. The truth was, I *still* lived at Amity Lane. I didn't want to tell anyone that. I didn't want them to make me go back there and get disappointed when they realized I *still* lived there, my brain not working hard enough, and everyone thinking all their extraordinary efforts were for nothing. *What are we wasting our time for? You'll always be damaged goods.*

Fern, you don't have to go to the house. You don't have to do anything you don't want.

But what if Old Mind is making himself too comfortable in my head?

Ms. Refuge smiled. I like the way you think. But maybe I was too harsh on Old Mind. Maybe we should leave Old Mind be. Old Mind might be there for a reason. At least, for a little while. We need to respect Old Mind as much as we do New Mind. We need to recognize a place in the body's house for all minds. We must be ready.

I didn't understand. But what I thought she was saying was: Go back. Don't be afraid. You never lived there, not really.

I'm ready, I said. But why was I crying so hard? Ms. Refuge pulled me close, no more for today.

FURTHER INVESTIGATION
INTO DETECTIVE AMOR

And there he was, expected and yet—all of a sudden.

Dark skin, bottle nose, teeth like cinnamon chewing gum. He carried a grown-up bouquet of roses and asked us our names (for the thousandth time?) and got right to business after we said fine, fine. *Are you ready to take this little trip, gals? These flowers are for you.*

(A trip back to the scene of the crime. It would only take a bit. Only if we felt like it. No rush. But duty does call. We have to be okay with this. Miss Tarnisha will come along. But only if we felt up to it. But duty does call.)

But why go? As previously mentioned: Gwinnie and me were totally happy in the picnic-chair hospital apartment. We didn't want to leave. Beyond the air conditioners, our windows let in the lights of the beautiful parking lot. Shooting stars and traffic signals. Plus, everyone and everything came to us there: doctors, shrinks, social workers, fans. Bouquets of flowers with secret cards tucked in: *You Girls Are Survivors! You Girls Question the System! You Girls Are the Reason I Believe in a Higher Power. You Girls Make Me Want to Dance!* More toys arrived each day and more clothes and more clothes and more toys. Mountains literally. Laundry carts full. The Hospital Staff tried to pinch a few for their kids at home but Gwinnie's and Ms. Refuge's eyes were like hawks. Little girls in pigtails showed up who wanted to be our friend until Ms. Refuge revealed to us that they weren't actually girls but grown women dressed like girls, and it wasn't anything to be ashamed of, falling for their sick ruse. Lonely souls, Ms. Refuge explained. I suppose they see something in you two that acts like a trigger. That pesky Old Mind . . .

More priests, more nuns. Quacks.

God, I hate the word *trigger*, Gwinnie once said.

Why is that?

It reminds me of something I always wished I had but couldn't really build out of my thumb and index finger.

Detective Amor started the car engine, tried to light a cigarette. Ms. Refuge, in the front seat next to him, snatched it from his fingers.

She then turned to us. Are you sure, girls? Are you sure? Your well-being comes first. Your well-being. It's my only job. You can stay or you can go. My job is to listen and to protect. I'm here to make sure you see the sun rise and set each and every day. I wouldn't want to cause you any harm. This is not your job. But do you think it might be possible? It might do you some good. Are you sure, girls? Are you sure?

Why wouldn't we be, Gwinnie answered, her eyes in a haze, arms crossed over her chest. Both of us in the back seat. Both of us transformed.

RELIEF

The old digs. PIPES LOW & HIGH. DUST-BUNNY-DRAIN.
PASS-THROUGH-CHASM. Would it give us too many nightmares to go back? Or not enough of them?

ANOTHER JOURNEY

The detective car is smelly—traveling in some long direction down the long Long Island Expressway. We are heading backward and forward, up and over: ultimate goal: the so-called Queens House of Horrors. For some reason I feel like I'm going to disintegrate with happiness.

There are streetlamps and wildflowers on the dividers, and pollution waves glistening the sky, and the sun—the sun, which never seems to stop shrinking everything in its path—it is a huge powder puff of goodness. Ms. Refuge holds a rectangle cell telephone in her hand—it is nothing but a gigantic picture. Where are the buttons?

Cars on the street remind us of ladybugs and dragons. The concrete medians fly past us like huge molars.

Ms. Refuge is chatting about the weather and the blasted traffic and why do they always have to be doing construction just when *she* gets on the road? Somewhere along the way she mentions something about a wedding dress, and the detective glances over and grins. She starts telling small jokes. Wedding jokes. He grins at everything, saying things like, *So you think you want a Kay Jewelers wedding, Tarnisha? Well, as Dr. King once said, it's always good to have a dream!* We pass *rockets* that are called gas tanks. Houses lining the highway, separated by *moats*. Gwinnie absently wonders out loud whatever became of the policemen who saved us? The ones who carried us down the stairs out of Boss Man's house and lifted us onto the gurneys and who applied to our lips the first drops of water from a bottle with trees on it. Where'd they go? We never saw them after that night. They never once said anything about us being inappropriately clothed, Gwinnie says, closing her eyes.

I think some are still with the force. Should I try and look them up? Ms. Refuge asks.

Gwinnie turns to face the window. I myself am too invisible to answer.

STILL IN THE POLICE CAR BUT WITH PAINS OF RECOGNITION

As we drive past LOVE JONES DELI AND BODEGA, our collective mind thinks of Jesenia—why, if we loved her so much (as to *still* make lists of her accomplishments *in our collective mind*)—why hadn't we tried more to find her? No clue. We pass QUEEN RASHIDA'S HAIR and ENVIOS DE DINERO!!! and our collective mind goes back to the little red digital clock that kept flashing time on the VCR as Bud and I watched those *Soul Train* tapes. GUARANTEED PUPPIES AND KITTENS on Kissena Boulevard makes us remember Mr. P and his secret smile whenever a Prince mixtape was popped into the car stereo. A sign for GRAND CENTRAL PARKWAY. A sign for UTOPIA PARKWAY. NORTHERN BOULEVARD—we see in our mind's eye the old clock at the Jamaica LIRR station that chimed out the hours my mother would stay on the night-nurse shift. YIELD. DO NOT CROSS MEDIAN. LITTER FINE $1000.00. Gwinnie's mother falling asleep at the kitchen table, a stack of record albums as her pillow.

We drive in the police car and wonder how is it possible to move on and stay put at the same time. We are getting closer, we realize. How should we continue to navigate?

TO UNDERSTAND

New Mind: To understand why we have to go back—way, way back, back to the time of brown water and bruises and safety pins and paper food.

Old Mind: A miraculous open door. We shivered, naked except for skin and maybe a pair of Boss Man's underpants. Or maybe fully naked. We were taken away. Hands touched us; washcloths cleansed us. Blood was removed with the flick of a hand. I don't want my head to explode, Gwinnie said to me in the ambulance on the night we were liberated. She said, I'm thinking we made a mistake, Fern. Should we go back to LEWD? I'm afraid. We can crawl back if we need to. I'm afraid of this air, this rubbery wheely smell. I'm afraid. Maybe we should go back and hide, Fern. We can crawl.

I don't think I can trace my footsteps anymore, Gwinnie. I mean, my crawl-steps.

I love how you just called me Gwinnie. Is it really my name now?

Let's just hold on to each other. Let's just see. Maybe we'll float back.

What about the baby?

She is floating back with us. I'm sure of it. We'll catch her later.

I think we should go back. What if we get in trouble? I don't have any bones left to get in trouble with, Fern. Boss Man will surely mean my end if we don't go back.

But neither of us even turns our heads as the ambulance pulls away. The house fades from view just like every other house on the block.

(We see a street sign and can't believe our collective eyes. Amity Lane! Damn, I say under my breath. How I wished I'd had that name to think of all this time.)

Old Mind: We look out the tiny window of the back: people moving like snails on the sidewalks, streets. We thought Boss Man had made her his wife like she'd asked him to. Maybe there was a new house, one without chains and boards and elbow macaroni. Maybe they were truly happy, not as MODEL EMPLOYEE and Boss Man, but as Jesenia and Nestor.

Old Mind: The night we are liberated, we begin our secret hearts: silently agreeing to go ahead with our lives as if we are already used to routines. The ambulance will end up somewhere, and we will get out and follow; morning will follow this night, and breakfast will follow the sun. Already police ladies are calling us *Sugar* and *Sweetie* and testing our cold arms and calling for more blankets. We get to the Blood Hospital and the Ward and the picnic-chair hospital and, somewhere along the line, meet Ms. Refuge for the first time; she holds out her arms for us as if she's been waiting in that position for ten years. She checks over the clipboard in her hand, flipping through papers but then stopping in her tracks to look at us again. Maybe she thinks we're a figment of her imagination, because when we first meet her, Gwinnie and I are as see-through as wax paper. We have no idea where the baby has got to, but in our secret hearts we trust she is fine. Ms. Refuge sniffles. Her arms wind back around us, and we can't break free and we realize how stupid freedom is, when you get down to it. I myself have no memories of Jean Naté or 4711, but I suddenly realize that a nose is probably the best-kept treasure in the world. When was the last time a lady smelled like Ms. Refuge? Like lilacs and hairspray and jelly beans—and not elbow macaroni sauced in blood? All noses rejoice.

New Mind: In the police car heading toward our old home. Ms. Refuge sits up front, talking quietly to Detective Amor, removing her knitting from her pocketbook. Gwinnie squeezes my hand. I don't know if I'm squeezing back.

FIRST CONTACT

With Detective Amor and Ms. Refuge, weaving in and out of cars, people, places, skies. A slow weave. In fact, we are driving so slow the sidewalk ants overtake the car. Where should I park? Detective Amor asks, pulling up to the vacant lot.

Amity Lane.

The police car pulls in front of the place where we used to live.

We step out—mud everywhere, even on the curb, where it's supposed to be clean and white. There's no house here anymore, but we can still see its outline shimmering in the air. Our legs have healed; to prove it, we put one foot in front of the other (a miracle!) and walk as if we'd been doing it *here on this street* since eternity. Stone steps leading to nowhere, a patch of onion grass here and there, stubby stumps of trees. Scaffolding, a wheelbarrow. A sign boasting of the new building—a church—coming our way; on the diagram, it resembles a shoebox. Ms. Refuge is chock-full of helpful facts, which she thinks will be a comfort to us. The church will contain a youth and senior center in its basement, one run by a community-based organization called Light at the End of the Tunnel. Daily meetings.

Gwinnie starts blowing her nose something awful; in the Blood Hospital a nurse told me that people can develop allergies to the smallest, most minuscule, invisible thing, and perhaps that is Gwinnie's problem now. Ms. Refuge doesn't notice because she is reading a poster nailed into a two-by-four and continues to be *Miss Information*: There will be a plaque in your honor, she says, to celebrate the life of the "*victim-females.*" A plaque etched in bronze for eternity. *Hey girls! You're heroes!*

Heroes.

For the first time since we met her, Ms. Refuge's mouth is beginning to bore me. She goes on about how a donation fund has been set up by the Queens City Council; and how a special dedication will take place in the future, complete with a special poem delivered by the Queens poet laureate, all about our special fortitude; perhaps a parade will be marched in our honor throughout Flushing Meadows Park, complete with high school bands and cheerleaders.

Isn't that great, girls?

Ms. Refuge is getting misty again. This is your new history, girls. How does that make you feel?

Then she frowns. Never mind, girls. Let's get back in the car, it's just too much. Harry, I told you it would be too much!

We are quiet. I feel as if all my sweat will actually wash me away. Both Gwin and I look at the ground, all that's left of the original. We were brought here to try and jog our memories about Jesenia. Maybe we do actually know where she is. Maybe we will remember some little detail. *Any detail counts; remember that, gals!* I look at Gwinnie and her braided head. She looks at mine, blow-dried into bark. Why were we actually here? It was life-threatening.

Gwinnie frowns. We know what we don't know we know, she says. The hell with Old Mind and New Mind. We don't want to end up like.

Yes, I shake my head.

NOT A DREAM

Gwinnie and I are standing in front of the place where one day a plaque will bear our names.

(Boss Man has us all in a car. We aren't idiots; we're wide awake and driving miles away. The question of opening the car door and flinging ourselves out isn't even a question. We stay put. The baby was left back asleep on the beanbag. Jesenia next to us, unmoving. Gwin and I have our theories. Say nothing.)

WHAT WE KNEW BUT
IT TOOK A WHOLE DAMN
VILLAGE TO ADMIT

We pulled in front of a bridge. Boss Man got out. He came round the side. Pulled Jesenia into his arms. She moaned—her first sounds. Gwin and I screamed. Boss Man told us to shut our heads. Which we proceeded to do. Were there trees? Were there numbers?

When he came back, he said, It's all done. You three ruined it all for me.

What you talking about, Boss Man?

Why does life have to be such a bitch, Boss Man asked, climbing into the driver seat. We heaved, sighed, released. No locked doors, no ropes. No private parts, no non-borns, no pushings. He drove Gwin and me back, where we both stood for hours afterward, pretending to be chained, looking through a boarded-up kitchen window as if through panes of fresh glass.

REAL AND FAKE CHAINS

There was the sound of roller skates whizzing, and a siren; two sirens. Sadness did not become Boss Man. Why should we feel sorry for him? Yes, life was a bitch. Who didn't know that?

We were free. It was messing with our heads, Gwin and me.

Boss Man left the house. And then more than one miracle took place.

THE DOOR

Will it open? Gwinnie asked me.

I don't know, I answered. I'm afraid.

Try it.

MORE PICTURES FROM THE COLLAPSING OF OLD MIND INTO NEW

A breeze of real air on our skin.

We were standing at a window or a door made up of slats, doing our chores as MODEL EMPLOYEES (counting the lines in the wood and writing the sum total on a piece of paper using a crayon stub)—and we noticed that the slats had been moved far apart from each other, as if a giant wooden spoon from heaven had reached down and separated them. For the first time we could see the Outside.

A branch, a fence, a stoop. A bird hopping on the ground from one spot to the other. It was just Gwinnie and me, resting our palms on the slats. To any normal mind, the Outside meant Freedom. Forget your rags, just get the hell out!

But it goes without saying that we were not normal minds. How many people on earth had to tell us that for it to finally ring true?

We were standing at the window or door butt naked. Maybe a pair of his panties, maybe not.

We were naked. We let the slatted rays of moon hit our bellies and titties and toes. We were a collective mind, thinking only one thing: *The outside is warm.* A branch, a fence, a stoop. A bird. Our eyes could not go any farther.

But we could tell things.

The Outside was not like a basement. Not like a splintered wooden floor. Not like a peeling linoleum kitchen where mice are your confidantes. The Outside was tiny rays of goodness—dust, dirt, the smell of dog shit, fresh asphalt. The Outside truly hit us where the sun didn't shine. *I like this,* is what was rolling about in our collective mind. Our hands rested on the slats while we hyperventilated. We forgot to finish the jobs we'd been given.

It grew from smells to sounds: a boy and another boy. Children. Candy wrappers with candy in them. Double Dutch feet in someone's driveway. Crows hopping in the middle of the street.

It grew to tastes: hot dog spores from some corner stand, flying up and catching in our mouths. Remember hot dogs?

In 2039 at fifty-five years old, Gwin sat next to me on the bench in Central Park and asked, Do you recall that evening, Fern? Our imaginations ran wild!

How could I forget?

Didn't it suddenly want to make you grow?

(Or maybe she said *go?*)

The Outside was a magician, casting a spell on me that emptied my head of all things except the mother's boyfriend, and that one time he said to me: *It's not like anybody would believe you, girl.*

Me up there pressing my body next to Gwin's: brown skin, browner skin. Our feet planted at the opening, all four of them, God bless.

GWINNIE'S IMPOSSIBLE DREAM COME TRUE

The first, easy days in the Blood Hospital. Mr. P actually made it past the fat guards and head-scratching doctors and eye-rolling nurses and baggy newspaper reporters. No security tag, no pat-down, no nothing other than a fat winter coat hiding six sacks of White Castle. There was no miniature green Bible. But from the side pockets of his coat, Mr. P pulled out two giant bottles of orange soda. Maybe you was told I passed, he said. Maybe you was told I was staying over in the Pomonok Houses. You always did know the difference between the truth and a lie, Gwindolyn. I know you kept your questions. I know you kept your heart from turning waterless. What you may not know is that once I got sober, I never stopped looking for you, not one single day.

Mr. P held his stepdaughter for more than five minutes—not a dry eye in that Blood Hospital. When they peeled away for tissues and smiles and height assessments and more head-to-chin kisses, Mr. P sat on one of the hard plastic chairs and began to cry. He told Gwinnie that recently her mama had tried to throw herself in front of an oncoming train at the St. Albans LIRR station. Luckily she was saved by a track worker. *You still feel for her, don'tcha, Gwindolyn?* She was taken to Long Island Jewish. She was STILL at Long Island Jewish. She's like a kind of vampire, he continued. No mirrors allowed anywhere near her. No food, no voices. She wants to know what you went through, Gwindolyn.

Should I forgive? Gwinnie said.

I'm not asking.

Thank God for that track worker. Gwinnie looked out the window at a flock of East River seagulls, aimed with her index finger and thumb.

LAST LOOKS

Did Jesenia splash? Did she sink? Did she hold her head tight in an effort to prevent it from tearing off her shoulders? Did Jesenia yell? Did she call our names? Was it really night? Was the tide in? Was it out? Had she been there long? Did Jesenia splash?

(There must be a reasonable explanation, given the water we kept seeing creep up on us, dripping from our foreheads onto our armpits, bellies, ankles, soles. A totally reasonable explanation. For now, let's move on.)

LETTER FOUND IN BOTTLE AT BOTTOM OF SUNSWICK CREEK

I don't want you to grow up like me. I don't want you to scrimp and shovel and save and beg and cry and get nothing in return. I worked like a dog from the time I could open my eyes, and it wasn't none of those jobs kids are supposed to have, like babysitting or *helping out in dad's office*. Hell no. The jobs I had included collecting cans from neighbors and cashing them in at the grocery store, my arms dog-tired from all that carrying, and then what do I get? Maybe a quarter or two in profit if I'm lucky. No, I don't want that for you. The can job was just my miserable start. Hurts my arms now just thinking about that shit. I want you to go to college one day. Whole hog, not this community crap—a college complete with dorm rooms and backpacks and hash brownies and hall parties. I want you to meet a good guy. I want you to meet a good girl. I want you to wear that fucking class ring *on your finger*. I want you to graduate. I want you to trade that backpack in for a briefcase, I want people to mistake you for Manhattan. I want you to buy a house, preferably not in New York or the entire East Coast. I'd like you to be able to watch sunsets in all their glory. Pismo Beach. Laguna Beach. Tijuana. I want you to have spare time. I want you to enjoy a glass of wine by the fireside, and not always in the company of someone else. I want you to rule the stars by learning how to use your words. Thank heavens for baby girls, as they say. Girls were never meant to be the death of us.

WHAT'S GOING TO HAPPEN

Detective Lucy comes to see us. Winter 2039, just after the start of the Thanksgiving season, the artificial tree hoisted up to the renamed Rockefeller Center: SENECA SQUARE. The whole city has gone car-less. Abortions are given away for free in the form of pill packets distributed in subway stations and schools. Populations are luckily diminishing in size despite the fact that diseases are also on the downswing. We can't stop marveling at this world. Old and new, in one fell swoop. Just what we always wanted. Gwinnie and I had been doing some exploring and voilà—there was Central Park in Manhattan, right under our noses, a wonder. We started going there. Lunch, doctor's appointments, more lunch, a warm bench (I'd since forgiven the sins of wooden surfaces). Before thoughts of Rockland County, Gwinnie and I were feeling like Central Park in Manhattan might become a new home away from home, a picnic-chair hospital in disguise. Who knows, it might still be?

Detective Lucy's face was lined with grim. Last we saw her, she came to tell us of Harold Amor's car accident. Years ago—did we still even remember his face? I hate to be the bearer of bad news, she said now. But some new bones have been found. They might belong to your friend.

Gwinnie looks at me, and I at her. How long must this dance continue?

Gwinnie excuses herself to go to the bathroom in the diner on Fifty-Ninth Street, the one where Ms. Refuge is standing at the counter, ordering our sandwiches. From my vantage point I see Gwinnie and Ms. Refuge talk. Gwinnie falls to her knees (which at this point in time are made, like mine, of plastic and screws). She gets up. I see her put her hand to her face and look across Central Park South to me, on the bench. Over the years I've seen all sorts of waterfalls from Gwinnie. Ms. Refuge leads her back outside, to dry off.

I'm so sorry to put you through this again, Detective Lucy says. But it just might be her. Just warning you girls. Be prepared. Just saying.

THE TRUTH

This bears repeating. The actual name of the organization that was starting to help Gwin "get her life on track" so that she could "better her life" for the good of "all Queens and beyond" was not called Tunnelvision. It was called Light at the End of the Tunnel, a kind of funky Salvation Army and Fresh Air Fund all rolled into one. The women wore turbans and made pronouncements on the purpose of the soul— every soul, even the bad ones. They allowed dance music to be on at all times. They talked to the kids and looked them straight in the eyes. The men stayed in the kitchen and then brought out the most amazing plates of spaghetti and meatballs. They asked the kids who wandered in (as if from a storm): *Where do you see yourself in a week? A year? Five years?*

Gwinnie said they gave you this delectable free food and didn't mind if you took third helpings. They would pronounce a few more things—not exactly prayers but not *not* prayers—and send you on your way. Unfortunately, there was not enough space to have kids spend the night. Though they would turn a blind eye if you slept on their front steps. They might even leave the rest of the lasagna or baked ziti out there in a pot and claim it was raccoons that ransacked the place the next morning.

They would not judge a too-short skirt or bra that showed through any shirt. Gwinnie said that they helped girls like her not only survive but *flourish*.

TO THOSE WHO WAIT

She wasn't expecting anything. Neither was I.

Her mama showed up. I know it one step at a time, she said. Yuh nuh ready, are you?

Gwin perked up. Is that present for me?

The woman held a large doll baby that looked as if it could contain a hundred smaller doll babies. Yuh might too old for dis, Mrs. Gwin said. But maybe it a step in da right direction.

Gwinnie took the toy and nestled it under her chin. The warm lights above our heads in the picnic-chair hospital apartment glowed with satisfaction. The woman burst into tears. The cross she usually wore at her neck was gone.

Forgive me crying, baby. It one step at a time. Yuh nuh ready, are you?

OLD SOULS

(Katanya rose from the bed in her grandmother's house. She'd heard screaming downstairs. Up until now there had not been a reason to leave the house. It had been months, and Clifford Teatown had not called once. Clifford—he'd left her high and dry. If he returned, she would not forgive him. But she wanted him to ask for her forgiveness, anyway. But who was it downstairs? The movie people? Katanya had never heard voices like these before. Yelling as if their lungs towered above the earth. Who was it? A woman? A man? She set her feet on the cold wooden floor. What if, what if? How did that song go again? *Fairy tales can come true, it can happen to you*—what if? Katanya smiled. The yelling ceased. She got back into bed and closed her eyes. Cindy's frying pan aromas refilled the air. The authors were probably waiting on her, Katanya told herself as she began counting backward. Mother. Father. They were forever waiting at the doorbell of her dreams, the correct answers crumpled in their hands. No one, she realized as she fell completely backward, would ever let them in. Yet and still—fairy tales can come true.)

FUTURISM

Another time in Central Park, our feet tired from admiring the Christmas windows at the newly revived Lord & Taylor, our tongues tasting firsthand fresh snowflakes. There's too much sun for this weather. Gwinnie talks with a cigarette falling over her lips—in all this time, why haven't they done away with these cancer sticks? It's 2039, and so far into the future, I want to laugh. Gwinnie says, You know, Fern. Life doesn't start or stop because of a door. Life goes on, door or no door. You know that, Fern?

Yes, I say. I do.

(Jesenia. We ourselves did not want to die. Even now, when we are feeling like we should've wanted to die—we're glad we are alive.)

Ladies, it's time for lunch, Ms. Refuge says, approaching us with a sack from Subway. Two sandwiches, one for each of us. She used to point out that she was just short of retirement, she would one day be saying her goodbyes, but then she never retired. Maybe she has crossed and uncrossed that bridge many times. Maybe she can't allow herself to enjoy what others call the joys of old age. Maybe we won't let her.

Take this sandwich, Fern. We need to keep putting meat on those bones.

A salami with lettuce, tomato, and peppers on a submarine roll. Gwinnie's eyes are heaven: liverwurst and onions and peppers. Do you think anything is possible? she asks.

Anything is possible, I answer. Gwinnie smiles.

Ms. Refuge turns to me. Fern, it's a cold wind out here. How about we all walk to the diner on Columbus Circle and get you some hot soup? Gwindolyn? Let me take your sandwiches back for a second, dears. You know how they can get when you bring in outside food, right? We'll order the soup and take out the sandwiches when they aren't looking. Don't let the waitresses see.

I hadn't been eating for so long. That was a remnant. Bud vowed to fatten me up if it was the last thing he'd do. His husband, Dwayne, took classes up in Hyde Park and became, in Bud's words, a world-class chef. We'll have you back to who you used to be in no time, Bud said. We're waiting, Fern. Our house is always here. You just let us know.

Yes, we will let them know. But first: here is Ms. Refuge, jamming our two foot-longs into her clutch pocketbook and sliding that inside her coat, doing the penguin henceforth. *Follow me, ladies; you know I don't like to decieve but I just bought these sandwiches and money shouldn't ever be wasted*—and then leading us to the crosswalk, looking both ways. She's wearing gloves; not winter, but the kind you'd find on a debutante. Ladies, she says. The new doctors want to meet with us in about an hour. But right now, I want to get you into that diner. Soup and skin and bones!

The snow stops; the sky emerges through its clouds and turns a color I used to think I'd never see again in this life. Ms. Refuge reads my mind. She grins ear to ear. *God, this is so lovely, look, look, in the middle of things.*

(How on earth could a person forget the gentle upturn of lips?)

A strong wind blows my hat clean off my head. Gwinnie hobbles into the street to get it—a gray woolen cap knitted by hand and sent anonymously by parcel post. She leaps through the oncoming cars to the other sidewalk. She shades her eyes against the sunlight and holds it up—victory! Gwinnie waves.

(So many years, and we still have so much more to say to each other. We have to stay awake for those who might still be calling. We'll know them if we hear them. *Sleep, children.*)

I shade my eyes, too, against the winter sun and grin and point to Ms. Refuge, who is steady pressing the WALK button, as if it might decide to say something else.

AUTHOR'S NOTE

When I began this book, I only thought about words. Words to describe the indescribable violence and trauma that made up the world of Fern, Gwin, and Jesenia. Over time, though, images came to me, and their purpose felt integral to the words, and to my ambitions for *Dear Miss Metropolitan*.

My own photographs began to appear within the text like dreams—fragments that extended beyond the expected reach of the story. Grace Paley did indeed once say, "You write what you don't know you know," and this is how I've come to view both dreams and images. They are what we don't know we know. Bygone pictures such as the Unisphere and "Alligator Bait" resonated with ideas of official and unofficial histories. And it's hard for me to remember anyone in my corner of Long Island who didn't worship at the altar of *Soul Train*; dance, dance moves, dance clothes, dance hair—*Soul Train* was about notions of authenticity, of who really was (and was not) Black. Who was cool. Who belonged. Those complications also formed *Dear Miss Metropolitan*.

At first my own photos danced around the edges of the more famous ones, but slowly they started up a conversation with them. The more I wrote, the more I sensed other dimensions to the project: those of motion, of distance, of historical pain and healing, remembering and forgetting and remembering again. In my eyes, the images high-lighted the fragmentary nature of the girls' world; they spoke to the power of their imaginations as Fern, Gwin, and Jesenia sought to survive and even dream of freedom.

The following works either appeared in *Dear Miss Metropolitan* as actual text, or served as inspiration for my own creations. I am grate-ful to include them here:

Tracy K. Smith's poem "An Old Story" appears in her collection *Wade in the Water* (Graywolf Press, 2018).

The NCLEX RN Prep Plus Guides (Saunders, 8th Edition) inspired the nursing exam questions in *Test Success for R.Ns Third Edition*.

MST3K provided the name Big McLarge Huge in its hilarious send-up of the movie *Space Mutiny*.

Excerpts from William Wordsworth's sonnet "Surprised by Joy" are taken from the *Norton Anthology of Poetry* (W. W. Norton, 1975).

Jesenia quotes from James M. Redfield's book *Nature and Culture in the Iliad: The Tragedy of Hector*, expanded edition (Duke University Press, 1994).

Katanya quotes the poem "I Am What I Am," by Rosario and Aurora Morales, which appears in the anthology *This Bridge Called My Back: Writings by Radical Women of Color*, edited by Cherríe Moraga and Gloria Anzalduá (Persephone Press, 1981).

The quotes attributed to Dan Chaon can be found in an interview he gave to Tom Barbash in June 2004 for *The Believer*, and in an inter-view he gave to Molly Antopol in September 2009 for *The Rumpus*.

The lines from Anne Bradstreet's poem "In Honour of that High and Mighty Princess, Queen Elizabeth" were taken from *The Works of Anne Bradstreet*, edited by Jeannine Hensley (Belknap Press, 1981).

Jesenia quotes two poems of Sor Juana Inéz de la Cruz ("My Divine Lysi" and "Love Opened a Mortal Wound") which are taken from *Sor Juana's Love Poems*, translated by Joan Larkin and Jaime Manrique. Reprinted by permission of the University of Wisconsin Press. © 2003 by the Board of Regents of the University of Wisconsin System. All rights reserved.

Excerpts from the following songs from Prince are quoted throughout the book: "When Doves Cry," "Diamonds and Pearls," "Raspberry Beret," "Baby, I'm a Star," "1999," "Little Red Corvette," "Let's Pretend We're Married," "Crazy You," and "Mary Don't You Weep."

I also reference lyrics from *The Man of La Mancha*, from Diana Ross's "I'm Coming Out," and from Billy Ocean's "Caribbean Queen."

PHOTOGRAPHS AND ILLUSTRATIONS

Page 45: "Missing: One Thankless Daughter," courtesy of the author.

Page 56: "Unisphere (under construction)," New York Public Library Digital Collections.

Page 92: "Missing: One Pretty-Nuff Girl," courtesy of the author.

Page 126: "Missing: Chica Too Lazy," courtesy of the author.

Page 128: "Queens Street Sign," courtesy of the author.

Page 148: "For Your Darling," courtesy of the author.

Page 174: "Merchant's Gate, Columbus Circle," courtesy of the author.

Page 184: "Work in Progress," courtesy of the author.

Page 191: "Picnic Menu," from *Cooking for Today*, edited by Hyla O'Connor (Octopus Books, 1976).

Page 225: "Coney Island," courtesy of the author.

Page 238: "Alligator Bait," courtesy of CardCow.

Page 270: "Assemble Church of God," courtesy of the author.

Page 312: "Botanical Garden," courtesy of the author.

Page 318: "The Devil's Handbook for Girls," images courtesy of Martha Colburn.

Page 348: "At the Stairs," courtesy of the author.

Page 352: "Soul Train TV Show," Michael Ochs Archives/Getty Images.

Page 369: "Woman of the Sea," courtesy of Lianna Oestricher.

Page 397: "Porch Furniture," courtesy of the author.

endpapers: House of Mrs. W. K. Vanderbilt, New York; Mott B. Schmidt, architect

ACKNOWLEDGMENTS

My profoundest thanks to the following people who made this book happen:

My husband, Linwood Lewis, without whose cherished love this book wouldn't have been written;

My children, Ben and Karina, who have made this journey worthwhile;

My agent, Lisa Bankoff, whose championing of my work has been an incomparable gift;

Retha Powers, lifelong friend, editor extraordinaire, who attended a First Person Plural reading in Harlem and changed my life forever;

Amy Einhorn and the staff at Henry Holt, for bringing this book into the world, including Sarah Crichton, Maggie Richards, Patricia Eisemann, Sarah Fitts, Marian Brown, Yona Deshommes, Christopher Sergio, Caitlin O'Shaughnessy, Hannah Campbell, Janel Brown, Jason Liebman, Steven Seighman, Allison Carney, and Kenn Russell. To Allison Warner, who created an incredibly beautiful cover. A special thank-you to Natalia Ruiz, whose assistance was vital.

My mother, Elke Schmidt Bluth, for everything.

My in-laws, Clarissa Lewis and the late Linwood Lewis, Sr., for the gifts of time, encouragement, and love;

Debra Spark, for her advice and generosity;

Martha Upton, for being the most angelic reader;

Denise Wheeless, Pamela Oestricher, Maureen Pilkington, Lucy Rosenthal, Linsey Abrams, Stacy Parker Le Melle, Melanie Lynn Danza, Cassandra Medley, and Mary Dillard for their cherished friendship and support;

Robyn Bage, for lasting friendship and an early place to write;

Christine Perez for additional help with the Spanish; Maila Corts for help with the Dutch;

Nancy Eisenman, who has helped me in ways I can't enumerate;

To my 2017–18 First Year Studies writing workshop at Sarah Lawrence College, who gave heartfelt advice on a chapter in this novel: Hazel Frew, Malik Torres, Vidhi Dujodwala, Madison Burke, India Manigault, Kyla Shinder, Hunter Aarniokoski, Ben Willems, Aden Schamess, Kim Doan, Olivia Hoefling, Jamilyn Taylor, and Adrienne Samuels;

And for the completion of this novel, I owe a tremendous debt of gratitude to Sarah Lawrence College, the National Endowment for the Arts, the Bronx Council on the Arts, and the Corporation of Yaddo.

My stepfather, Larry Bluth, passed away as I was editing *Dear Miss Metropolitan*. Next to my mom and my husband, Linwood, Larry was my most tireless cheerleader, reading and rereading my work, recommending it to his piano students, his friends, family, and fellow jazz musicians. Larry looked for connections between our art forms—his as a jazz musician and mine as a fiction writer—and his deep engagement with craft has guided me these forty years. It is impossible to express how much I learned from him; his intelligence and wit were benchmarks for me, right until the end, when he announced the title of his "new book" on our post-Obama reality: *Withering Heights*. Larry loved the world that books opened to him, and his desire to continually grow as a compassionate human being left a tremendous mark on me. *Dear Miss Metropolitan* is dedicated to his memory.

ABOUT THE AUTHOR

Carolyn Ferrell is the author of the short-story collection *Don't Erase Me,* which was awarded the 1997 Art Seidenbaum Award for First Fiction of the Los Angeles Times Book Prizes, the John C. Zacharis First Book Award given by *Ploughshares,* and the Quality Paperback Book Prize for First Fiction. Her stories and essays have been anthologized in *The Best American Short Stories 2018*, edited by Roxane Gay; *The Best American Short Stories of the Century,* edited by John Updike; *Black Silk: A Collection of African American Erotica,* edited by Retha Powers; *Children of the Night: The Best Short Stories by Black Writers, 1967 to the Present,* edited by Gloria Naylor; *This Is My Best: Great Writers Share Their Favorite Work,* edited by Kathy Kiernan and Retha Powers; *Giant Steps: The New Generation of African American Writers,* edited by Kevin Young; *Apple, Tree: Writers on Their Parents,* edited by Lise Funderburg; and other places. Her story "Something Street" was reprinted in *The Best American Short Stories 2020,* edited by Curtis Sittenfeld. She is the recipient of grants and awards from the Fulbright Association, the German Academic Exchange Service (DAAD), the Bronx Council on the Arts, the National Endowment for the Arts, and Sarah Lawrence College. Since 1996, she has been a faculty member in both the undergraduate and MFA programs at Sarah Lawrence College. She lives in New York with her husband and children.

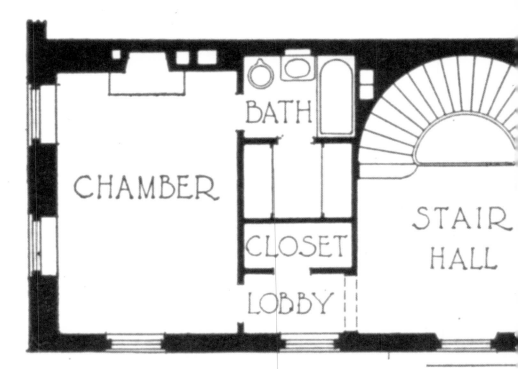

SECOND FLOOR PLAN

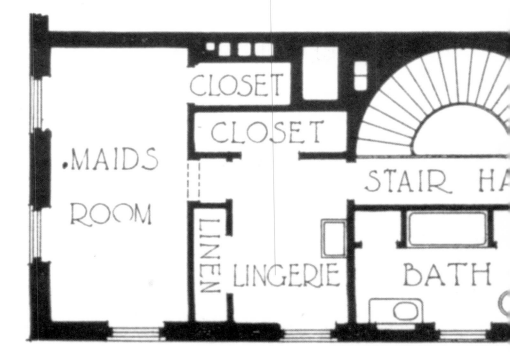

THIRD FLOOR PLAN